SPECIAL

Their skills honed to a razor's edge, their discipline unmatched by any fighting force in the world, the U.S. Special Forces are prepared to strike at any target, anywhere.

OSAN AFB, SOUTH KOREA

The men of Sgt. Dave Riley's Special Forces team get the go-ahead for an astounding mission—aimed at the heart of mainland China.

OPERATION DRAGON-SIM

Bleeding real blood and using real firepower, Riley and his men are caught up in a deception that reaches from Beijing to Washington. With good men down on the ground, and an entire army hunting them, the Special Forces warriors have their backs against the wall—and only one way out . . .

"Special Forces veteran Mayer knows his business . . . Fascinating . . . Imaginative . . . Nerve-wracking."
—*Kirkus*

"Produces enough suspense and action to satisfy the most jaded of thriller fans . . . The author of *Eyes of the Hammer* delivers another rousing tale."
—*Library Journal*

St. Martin's Paperbacks Titles
by Bob Mayer

EYES OF THE HAMMER
OPERATION DRAGON-SIM

OPERATION DRAGON SIM

(published in hardcover as
Dragon Sim-13)

BOB MAYER

ST. MARTIN'S PAPERBACKS

Chapter opening quotes from *The Art of War* by Sun Tzu, translated by Samuel B. Griffith. Copyright © 1963 by Oxford University Press, Inc. Reprinted by permission.

Operation Dragon-Sim was published in hardcover under the title *Dragon Sim-13*.

Published by arrangement with Presidio Press

OPERATION DRAGON-SIM

Copyright © 1992 by Bob Mayer.

Cover illustration by Jerry Pfeiffer.

Library of Congress Catalog Card Number: 91-46502

ISBN: 0-312-95233-3

Printed in the United States of America

Presidio Press hardcover edition published 1992
St. Martin's Paperbacks edition/February 1994

St. Martin's Paperbacks are published by St. Martin's Press, 175 Fifth Avenue, New York, N.Y. 10010.

10 9 8 7 6 5 4 3 2 1

To the members of ODA 055, B Company, 2d Battalion, 10th Special Forces Group (Airborne), 1984-1985:

M. Sgt. Dave Boltz
Sfc. CW2c. Jim O'Callaghan
CW1c. Rodney Grow
Sfc. Craig Truskey
Sgt. Jaroslav Lupinek
S. Sgt. Bob Rooney
Cpl. John Jones
Sgt. Mike Johnston
Cpl. Emory Slifka
Sgt. Frank Metayer
S. Sgt. Tim Dedie
Sgt. Bob Allinson
S. Sgt. Renee Garza
S. Sgt. Brian Shipley

GLOSSARY

AAP Alternate assembly point.

AK-47 Standard Soviet automatic rifle. 7.62mm caliber.

AO Area of operations.

A team Basic operating unit of Special Forces.

AWACS Airborne early warning and command system.

Blackhawk Newest army transport helicopter. Dual engined.

Briefback Briefing given at the end of isolation period by the A team to show the commander the plan and that the team is ready to execute the mission.

Chem light Chemical light that when cracked will emit a low-level light for several hours.

Claymore Crescent-shaped antipersonnel mine that shoots out hundreds of ball-bearing projectiles in an arc when fored.

C-130 Hercules four-engine turboprop plane; can hold up to sixty-four parachutists. May be jumped from either two rear doors or off the ramp.

Combat Talon Modified C-130 used by air special operations to infiltrate denied airspace at low altitude under almost all weather and light conditions to conduct air-drop, air-land, or surface-to-air recovery methods.

Detcord Detonator cord—a line of explosive that burns almost instantaneously.

DET-K Special Forces Detachment, Korea.

DMDG Ditigal message data group device.

DZ Drop zone.

E & E Escape and evasion.

1st SOW 1st Special Operations Wing. Air Force's special operations aircraft (AC-130, MC-130, HH-53) are all in this unit.

550 cord Nylon cord used for parachute suspension line.

G-1 Administrative section of a headquarters responsible for personnel actions.

G-2 Intelligence section of a headquarters.

G-3 Operations section of a headquarters.

HH-53 See Pave Low.

IAP Initial assembly point.

IR Infrared. Anything IR (chem light, strobe light) cannot be seen with the naked eye but is like a regular light when seen through NVGs.

Isolation The time period prior to a mission when an A team is isolated to do mission preparation. Ends when briefback is accepted by the commander and the team departs for the mission.

J-7 Chinese made jet fighter. Armed with two missiles and a 30mm cannon in the leading edge of each wing root.

Klick Kilometer.

LZ Landing zone.

M60 Medium machine gun. 7.62mm caliber. Belt fed.

M79 40mm grenade launcher.

M203 M16 rifle with a 40mm grenade launcher built in under the rifle barrel.

MC-130 See Combat Talon.

MP5 9mm submachine gun.

MTT Mobile training team.

NSA National Security Agency.

NVG Night-vision goggles.

ODA Operations detachment Alpha. See A Team.

OP Observation point; position from which surveillance is conducted.

Pave Low (HH-53) two-engine, single rotor, heavy-lift helicopter designed to operate in special operations missions at low altitudes under nearly any weather or light condition.

PVS-5 See NVG.

PZ Pickup zone.

Q course Qualification course conducted at Fort Bragg for all soldiers who want to be in Special Forces.

RFI Request for information.

RPG Rocket-propelled grenade, Soviet made. Consists of a launcher and separate rounds for firing, like a bazooka.

SAS Special Air Service.

SAW Squad automatic weapon. Light machine gun, 5.56mm caliber.

SF Special Forces.

SOCOM Army Special Operations Command based at Fort Bragg, North Carolina. Headquarters for U.S. Army Special Forces, U.S. Army Rangers, and Civil Affairs and psyops units.

SOP Standard Operating Procedure.

SVD Soviet sniper rifle.

Type 56 Chinese version of the Russian AK-47 automatic rifle. Fires 7.62 by 39 cartridges.

UH-60 See Blackhawk.

US-SOCOM Joint Sevices Headquarters for all U.S. special operations forces at MacDill Air Force Base, Tampa, Florida.

Z-9 Also called Haitun by Chinese. Designated the SA-365N Dolphin by its manufacturer, Aerospatiale, which sold fifty of these to China. They can hold up to eight passengers, and by adding machine gun or rocket pods to the sides can be used as a gunship.

PROLOGUE

*"He who knows when he can fight and
when he cannot will be victorious."*
Sun Tzu: *The Art of War*

**University of Beijing, People's Republic of China
Summer 1966**

The breath of the Dragon was consuming its own brain. Tears rolled down the man's face as he watched his books and computer tapes fed into the roaring bonfire. Eighteen years of work. The man averted his eyes and turned to the officer who had led the Red Guards onto the grounds of the university and initiated the fire. He asked only one question. "Why?"

Prefacing his reply the officer spit at the man. "Stinking Ninth Category. You and your counterrevolutionary friends will no longer work against the Great Revolution." In conclusion the soldier swung an ax handle, the end impacting on the front of the man's head. He staggered and blinked, trying to remain conscious as blood cascaded down his face.

The man did not understand the reasons. He didn't think the soldiers feeding the fire truly knew either. But the bleeding man did understand that his life's work here was over. The Old Men in power had decided that this was to be the new way. The man didn't resist as the Red Guards dragged him away along with his fellow scientists.

They were taken to Tiananmen Square and lined up. The man recognized many fellow educators and scientists from the university in the ranks that faced a makeshift platform. A political commissar, screaming out his words from the platform, confirmed the man's fears. "You have sinned against your fellow workers. You have been more concerned with having expertise in your intellectual fields than following party doctrine. You have failed to follow Chairman Mao's Socialist Education Movement. You must learn from the Peo-

ple's Liberation Army. You must learn from your fellow
workers. We believe you can be saved."

The commissar nodded toward the row of army trucks that
lined the far side of the square. "You will be reeducated. You
must accept the need for manual labor. It is the essence of our
life. You must have a greater regard for the goals of the party
than for your trivial, specialized academic pursuits."

The officer gestured and his comrades rushed forward, bul-
lying the prisoners in the square toward the trucks. The man
allowed himself to be swept along. There was nothing he
could do. As the trucks roared out of the square, his thoughts
lingered on his wife and four-year-old son. He knew now that
not only was his life's work over, but he would never again
see his family.

The Cultural Revolution was in full flower.

Guandong Province, Fall 1966

The man swung the rusty hoe into the hardscrabble ground.
The scar on his forehead itched where the ax handle had
hit. The wound had not healed well at the People's Community Farm. He shook the sweat out of his eyes as another
worker came near. The man recognized the scientist from the
university's staff. In better days they had argued together over
many intellectual matters. Now the scientist had more important information he wished to impart. "I am leaving tonight."

The man was astonished. Leaving? There was no place in
China where the party would not find him. "Where are you
going?"

"Hong Kong. And then America."

The man shook his head. "They will never let you into
Hong Kong. They will send you back and then things will be
worse for you. You will be considered not capable of being
rehabilitated."

The scientist looked up briefly and met the man's eyes.
"There is a rumor that for people with expertise in certain
fields of knowledge, the door to Hong Kong will open. It is
said the Americans and the British are taking in some of
these people. It is said they believe that the enemy of their
enemy is now their friend."

The man thought about that. It would not be hard to leave

the farm. The few guards did not believe that there was any-place for their prisoners to go. The scientist's last sentence especially caught the man's attention. He absently rubbed the twisted scar on his forehead while he thought about what had gone up in the flames at the university and the bleak future here. He considered the possibility that he might be able to get his family out some day.

"I will go with you."

1

"War is a matter of vital importance to the
state; the province of life or death; the road
to survival or ruin. It is mandatory that
it be thoroughly studied."
Sun Tzu: *The Art of War*

Fort Meade, Maryland
Wednesday, 31 May 1989, 2020 Zulu
Wednesday, 31 May 1989, 3:20 P.M. Local

The small flashing light on the wall screen crept across the
overlay of the eastern edge of China, heading with agonizing
slowness toward the safety of the ocean. The men in the
room watched the light's progress with mixed feelings. From
the back of the room, Doctor Meng could tell that the air
force general, Hixon, was the most anxious. With two good
reasons, Meng knew. That light represented Hixon's prized
toy, the B-2 Stealth bomber, and, more importantly, Hixon
was in charge of the mission.

The aircraft was displayed on a screen measuring almost
forty feet wide by twenty feet high, which dominated one end
of the Tunnel. Facing the screen, in ascending rows, were
banks of terminals where the various officers responsible for
the mission worked. In the rear of the room, on a slightly
raised dais, sat Meng, who oversaw the whole operation
through a terminal that linked him to the master computer.

Meng glanced down at the computer screen as new input
scrolled up. In a low voice, consistent with his small stature,
he read the results. "There is sixty-five percent probability of
target destruction."

Hixon didn't like that. "Hell, they went in right on top of
the son of a bitch. There's no way they could have missed."
The air force general signaled for one of his officers to type

out a message over the SATCOM link. "Tell them to repeat transmission of strike data."

The general's words were transcribed into the keyboard. The letters went through a scrambler onto a tape, which transmitted the message to the National Security Agency (NSA) headquarters next door. There, a large dish antenna beamed the message to orbiting satellites, which then directed the beam down to the B-2's radio receiver, where the message was unscrambled.

The general turned his attention to the clear lower right corner of the forward electronic screen, where the answer would be displayed. In less than five seconds the reply appeared.

THIS IS PHOENIX ONE/ ROGER/ RETRANSMIT-
TING STRIKE DATA/ END/

Meng's boss, General Sutton, sought to comfort Hixon. "Sixty-five percent is rather high for a mission like this. Within acceptable parameters."

Hixon ignored the information and concentrated on the dot on the screen. Another 120 kilometers and the aircraft would make it out of Chinese airspace.

Meng watched as the data appeared on his computer terminal. As he expected, the retransmitted data from the aircrew spelled out the same results as the original. The aircraft had indeed made it to target and had delivered its bombs. The only question was whether the ordnance had done the job it was supposed to do.

A new message appeared on the screen.

THIS IS PHOENIX ONE/ PICKING UP SOME
TURBULENCE/ TERRAIN IS GROWING MORE
BROKEN/ REQUEST PERMISSION TO GO TO
1,000 FEET AGL/ END/

Hixon scanned the telemetry he was receiving from the SATCOM channel regarding the aircraft. The general didn't want to take any chances. He typed in the reply himself.

THIS IS HELM BASE/ REQUEST DENIED/ END/

Another message pulsed onto the screen.

PHOENIX ONE/ REQUEST PERMISSION TO USE
FLIR/ END/

Hixon immediately denied the request to use forward-
looking infrared radar.

HELM BASE/ DENIED/ END/

Meng raised an eyebrow at Sutton. "I thought the reasoning behind using the B-2 on this mission was that it wouldn't
get picked up on radar and wouldn't have to fly so low, sir."

Hixon looked at the civilian scientist with irritation. He
didn't like some civilian egghead telling him how to do his
job. "Yeah, that's true but—"

He was interrupted by the disappearance of the dot. General Hixon slammed his desktop. His telemetry link went
blank. "Goddamnit, we've lost the link! How the hell did that
happen?" He typed into his keyboard furiously.

PHOENIX ONE THIS IS HELM BASE/ STATUS
REPORT/ END/

The only answer was a blank screen.

PHOENIX ONE THIS IS HELM BASE/ STATUS
REPORT/ END/

Meng looked up from his computer. "Aircraft satellite
transponder is off. We have to assume that Phoenix One has
gone down."

Hixon turned on the frail old man clad in a white lab coat.
"Bullshit! There's no way those bastards could have spotted
her. It would take a miracle for them to have run across it
randomly."

Meng spread his hands in a conciliatory gesture. "There
are many possibilities, General. Their most modern military

jets, which by the way we sold them, do have look-down radar and may have overflown the flight path. The data is unclear as to the B-2's stealth capability against such a system. A lucky visual missile shot, perhaps from a ground site? You knew that the flight out would be much more difficult than the flight in due to the destruction of the target, alerting the Chinese to the presence of the aircraft."

Hixon wasn't buying it. "Your goddamn computer is wrong. That plane is still flying."

Meng did not like being cursed at, nor did he enjoy being told that his computer was wrong. His computer was the heart of this entire system—a system that had taken Meng two years to design and the Department of Defense two years and more than a billion dollars to build. Meng glanced over at General Sutton, who, knowing how Meng felt, quickly intervened.

"If you'll be patient, General Hixon, in a few minutes we'll have a readout on what happened to Phoenix One."

Meng's fingers caressed the keyboard and accessed the aircraft file. He dumped in the data, sifted through the flight record, then looked back at the air force general. "You are most correct, General Hixon. The Chinese did not find your aircraft or shoot it down."

"What the hell happened then?"

"The pilot made an error. In the dark, he flew his aircraft into the side of a mountain."

"What!" Hixon was livid. "No way. Where are you coming up with this bullshit?"

Meng transfixed the general with his black eyes. "This 'bullshit' as you call it, General, is coming from the flight simulator that your men were piloting at Edwards Air Force Base. If you'd like, you can pick up the phone and call them yourself. The data link to the crew will no longer work, since the computer cut it off as soon as it determined that the plane had crashed." Meng stood up. "Dragon Sim-12 is over. You may pick up a copy of the analysis prior to the outbrief tomorrow, sir."

Hixon was shaken but not defeated. "There's a big difference between flying a simulator and the real thing. And there's a big difference between our running the real thing and this computer game you've set up here."

Meng addressed the general in a calm voice. "General, my system works fine. Perhaps you ought to ask yourself why you think using a billion-dollar-plus aircraft to attack a dam of limited economic and strategic value is a valid plan. Did not your own staff suggest using a B-52 with cruise missile firing from standoff? Did not your own operations officer suggest leaving flight plan and en route decisions up to the airship pilot—a suggestion that the printout of the communications between here and the aircraft will clearly show you blatantly ignored a few minutes ago? I believe that the after-action report may well find that it was your refusal to allow the aircraft commander to increase his altitude or use his radar that led to the crash."

Sutton tried intervening. "Perhaps we'd best wait—"

But Meng wasn't done. "The purpose of these simulations, General, is not just to test the validity of various war plan and strategic retaliatory strike missions. More importantly, it is also to test the effectiveness of the command and control structure of these missions. Your people in this Tunnel are the primary ones being tested, not the aircrew at Edwards."

With that last comment, Meng turned and strode out of the room. He was waved through by the various security guards manning every corridor of the underground complex. Built next to the sprawling new headquarters for the National Security Agency at Fort Meade, Maryland, the "Tunnel," as it was referred to by those who worked there, was actually a series of three major tunnels approximately 180 meters long by 60 meters wide. The main tunnels were connected by two cross tunnels at either end, which were basically corridors. Tunnel 3, the one Meng was just leaving, was the most secure and housed the mainframe computer that was Meng's brainchild. It was also the room where the strategic mission simulations, commonly called Strams, were conducted.

Tunnel 2, where Meng was heading, held the offices of the computer experts whom Meng controlled. Meng's own office, at the north end, was blocked off from the rest of the Tunnel by a thick cinderblock wall. Tunnel 1, to the east, was the outer tunnel, the workplace of the military staff officers who helped translate the various operations plans for the Strams.

Meng slammed the door behind him and sat down at his desk. The office was dominated by a series of large flat tables, arranged in a circle about his desk. It was on these tables that Meng laid out the flowcharts for every Strams exercise. He normally labored over the specific programming of every mission for at least two days.

Strams had a history that spanned almost a decade. Until Meng came along, it existed only as a concept in the mind of an idealistic army chief of staff in the Pentagon during the early 1980s. This chief of staff had watched what his own service was doing at Fort Irwin, California, and wondered if the same thing couldn't be done at the strategic level, particularly to test command and control structures.

At Fort Irwin, the army had developed a massive simulation of armored combat against a Soviet foe. The complex, called the National Training Center (NTC), was designed to approximate the conditions of mobile, armored combat as closely as possible, short of actual war. Every single soldier, vehicle, and aircraft at the NTC was equipped with a system of laser emitters and detectors that simulated the action and effect of the various weapon systems. Two battalions of American soldiers were stationed at Fort Irwin full-time to act the roles of the Soviet forces. These units used Soviet tactics, had vehicles that looked like Soviet vehicles, and in general acted like the enemy. The army NTC system, in fact, had been copied from the air force Red Flag program, in which a flight detachment simulated Russian aircraft and engaged in mock combat with American pilots.

Even more importantly, at the NTC every vehicle and major weapon system was tracked by a computer, which then correlated the results so that in the aftermath of a confused desert battle, the participating commanders could sit down with observer-controllers and analyze the battle step by step with computer printouts and videos. The NTC program had proven invaluable for training armored and mechanized infantry task forces up to brigade level—so invaluable that a similar setup for light infantry units had been subsequently located at Fort Chaffee, Arkansas, and designated the Joint Readiness Training Center (JRTC).

The chairman had designated a task force made up of a few officers and directed them to set up a strategic training center. Part of the impetus for this task force had also been the after-action reports on the Desert One failure and on the less-than-perfect invasion of Grenada. There was a glaring need to test the U.S. military's ability to conduct strategic missions requiring high-level command and control. The truth of the matter was that the ability to test the plans and the capability of the commanders and staff diminished rapidly the higher the chairman looked on the U.S. military strategic ladder. The ability and reactions of a tank crew commander or a jet pilot in simulated combat could be tested relatively well, but there were no means to test the abilities and reactions of high-level commanders and staff.

The early Strategic Simulation Task Force pondered the situation for more than a year. Doctor Meng had been invited to participate when it became increasingly obvious that such a strategic training center was going to have to rely heavily on computer simulations. Meng had a long history of consulting with the Department of Defense (DOD). He had been teaching computer programming at the Massachusetts Institute of Technology (MIT) for almost eighteen years and was internationally recognized as one of the three top computer simulation programmers in the world. Initially Meng had been told that he would be needed only for six months to get the program started. Those first six months had dragged on to two years as Meng had wrestled with the myriad variables required to be programmed into such a system.

Working out of two offices, with only one assistant and a secretary to help him, Meng had attacked the problem from several angles. He'd looked at the NTC system and extracted those parts he deemed useful. Meng also looked at another army program called ARTBASS, a tactical-level computer simulation program designed to test commanders and staffs below division level. It consisted of a building where the various unit commanders and their staff were placed in separate simulated field headquarters and communicated with each other by radio. They were allowed to see only the part of an electronic battlefield that their actual immediate units would occupy. The computer simulated the effects of various engagements between the American units and a computer-generated Russian enemy. Meng realized that he was being asked to construct a strategic-level ARTBASS. The difficulty in doing so lay in the fact that at the strategic level the number of variables affecting outcomes increased geometrically to an almost unmanageable number.

The factor Meng had discovered from studying both the NTC and ARTBASS simulations was that communications would be the cornerstone to any scenario. At the strategic level the commanders and staff never saw the face of battle. They worked entirely with electronic inputs and outputs connecting them with the forces that would execute the mission. Meng believed that he could simulate those inputs and outputs.

Meng visualized a building where the commander and staff to be tested would be isolated. All messages and data traffic would be run in and out through the computer, allowing Meng's program to control the action. After outlining this idea to the chairman, Meng was invited to tour the Pentagon's Emergency Operations Center (EOC), the nerve center for any strategic operation conducted by U.S. military forces. Meng was not surprised to find that the EOC was a data and communications hub very much like what he had proposed.

After two years of struggle, Meng had completed an outline of Strams. By that time the army chief of staff who had authorized the project in the first place had retired, and Meng was faced with all of his work languishing. Meng would not have minded except that he had been drawn into a security quagmire. He could get out of Strams but his work could not. The entire project had been conducted under such a high level of security that every computer program and piece of paper was highly classified. Meng would never be able to use his work in the civilian computer world. Additionally, Meng had found himself increasingly drawn into the challenge of making his simulations more and more realistic. War is perhaps the most chaotic of man's ventures, and trying to simulate it was the greatest programming challenge.

Faced with the prospect of the project being disbanded and

having his work lost, Meng had seized an opportunity to breathe life into his creation. During the Libyan crisis, Meng was tasked to war-game the retaliatory missions proposed by the various services. Using borrowed computer time, he ran through the various strike missions and sent his results to the chairman of the Joint Chiefs of Staff. The resulting bombing raid on Tripoli so clósely matched what Meng had predicted that interest in Strams was revived. With the blessing of the secretary of defense, work on the facility had begun. The Tunnel, built to approximate the Pentagon's EOC as closely as possible, was placed at Fort Meade to have access to both the vast intelligence system at the National Security Agency and the communications facilities controlled by that organization.

The initial series of Strams exercises in the Tunnel was conducted in 1987. Dubbed Bear Sim-1 through Bear Sim-23, the exercises had focused entirely on military actions against the Soviet Union, ranging from selective nuclear strikes to military, economic, and political sabotage of the Soviet infrastructure by surgical strike missions. Meng continually refined the simulation as he learned what worked and what did not. After ten missions, the entire setup had become so realistic that the secretary of defense had designated the Tunnel as the alternate EOC in case the Pentagon center went off line.

Meng had been forced to run the Strams in sequence using the same target country because of the difficulty designing the opposing forces (OPFOR), or enemy, program of capabilities and possible responses. That overall country program was called the scenario program. The one for the Soviet Union Meng had labeled as Bear. The various U.S. military scenarios based on contingency oplans, or operations plans, were the numbered Sim programs.

When the Bear Sim programs had run their course, Meng was ordered to turn his attention elsewhere. He had then run four scenarios in the Middle East—Lion Sim-1 through Lion Sim-4. At that point, in the fall of 1988, he had been directed to scenario-program a new target country: China.

Meng labored for more than two months to develop the Dragon scenario program. The first Dragon Sim took place in

January 1989. Since then the Dragon series, and the whole Strams program, had been receiving less and less attention as peace prevailed around the world. To revive the project, Meng wanted to switch its emphasis to terrorism or to the drug war, and indeed after the two Dragon Sims remaining on the long-range planning calendar, the focus would shift to international terrorism.

Meng was finding scenario programming for the new Medusa series to be most challenging. Since it took more than two months to program a new scenario, he had requested that the last two Dragon missions be scrubbed to allow them to concentrate on the Medusa program, but General Sutton had overruled his civilian counterpart. The units participating had already prepared their operations plans and scheduled the operation. Meng had learned early in this job that the military was not very flexible in its operations.

Meng looked at his calendar. Dragon Sim-13 was starting in two days. The oplan sat in his in box. He hated the thought of flowcharting this exercise, since he wanted to get a jump on the Medusa program. He was finding the new program most interesting, considering the number of terrorist organizations in the world and the almost innumerable ways they might act. It was his greatest challenge yet.

Meng grabbed the oplan for Dragon Sim-13 and glanced through it. An army Special Forces mission, he noted—at least it would not be boring. He'd enjoyed the one Bear Sim mission with the Special Forces people. They had shown quite a bit of imagination in their planning and flexibility in their responses to the challenges presented by the computer, unlike many of the other organizations that had been run through Tunnel 3.

Meng began separating the pages of the oplan, preparing to lay them out on his tables and begin the program flowcharting. He would let his primary assistant, Ron Wilson, do the after-action report for Dragon Sim-12. Meng didn't want to have to deal with that obnoxious air force general anymore. Besides, the sooner he got 13 and 14 out of the way, the sooner he could work on his Medusa program.

Meng glanced at his watch—nearly 4 P.M. He pulled the remote control out of his desk drawer, flicked on the color TV mounted on the far wall of his office, and flipped through the channels until he got to CNN. As the CNN logo rolled across the screen, Meng put aside his work and walked over to stand right in front of the TV. The lead story, as he had hoped, was on the one subject that concerned him more than his work. The screen was filled with the image of the Goddess of Democracy overlooking the hordes of students filling Tiananmen Square in Beijing.

Meng felt his heart catch as he viewed the spectacle. It was a sight he had never expected to see in his lifetime. Moving even closer to the screen as the camera panned the ranks of the students, he tried to examine every face as the camera swept along the sea of protesters. With foreboding Meng listened carefully to the announcer. "There have been unconfirmed reports that elements of the 38th Army have moved into positions around the city of Beijing. Whether these reports are true is not known, nor is it known whether the government will use these troops in an attempt to abort this movement that has been going on for more than seven weeks now."

Meng was aware that someone else had come into his office. He didn't let the new presence distract him as the report continued. "So far, things have been calm. The troops that have been stationed around the square have reacted in a peaceful, almost friendly manner to the crowds."

Meng turned his attention away as the story shifted to some self-proclaimed American expert discussing the situation. Meng didn't need an expert to tell him what was going on. He looked over as Ron Wilson spoke out. "Sort of makes you feel hopeful, doesn't it?"

Meng shook his head. "It fills me with fear more than hope."

Wilson looked at his colleague in surprise. That was the most emotional statement he had ever heard the normally stoic Meng utter. "You don't think this will get resolved peacefully?"

Meng shrugged. "I cannot foresee the future. But I do know that those Old Men in charge will not bow to the desires of a group of students."

"But isn't the entire country behind the students?"

Meng tended toward a more cynical attitude of human nature. He knew that the students and the others with them in the square were good people. He knew that very well. But they were a tiny handful compared to the entire population of China. "The majority of people in the world, not just the Chinese, are concerned only with putting food on the table and having a roof over their head. Concepts such as democracy are a long way from that. The only thing those Old Men in charge understand is power, and they are the ones who wield it in China."

Wilson pointed at the paperwork piled along the circle of tables. "I guess the possibility that things could get nasty over there is why we have these plans. Options for the president to use if he wants to apply varying degrees of military pressure to the government over there, short of all-out war. It's our job to test those options for him."

Meng sighed. He doubted very much that any of these plans would ever be used. The American Eagle seemed much too afraid of the Sleeping Dragon.

2

"Generally in battle, use the normal force to engage; use the extraordinary to win."
Sun Tzu: *The Art of War*

Chonjinam Drop Zone, Republic of South Korea
Thursday, 1 June, 1300 Zulu
Thursday, 1 June, 10:00 P.M. Local

The two rear, side doors of the air force C-130 were open to the chill night air. Sergeant First Class Dave Riley took a firm grip on either side of the left-hand door and leaned out of the aircraft into the 135-mile-an-hour wind, searching for the drop zone (DZ). As the aircraft made minor adjustments in direction, the lights of a small town sparkled and danced below in the clear night sky. Off to the left, the flicker from houses on the mountains could be seen even with the aircraft at eight hundred feet.

As the plane crossed Highway 4, Riley pulled himself back into the aircraft. "One minute," he yelled, holding his index finger aloft to the nine jumpers already hooked to the cable running the length of the aircraft. The dim red glow of night lights in the cargo bay made the interior only slightly brighter than the sky. Riley could make out the glint from the wide-open eyes of the first jumper as the man shuffled a little closer. The lead jumper was now poised within three feet of the open door.

Riley leaned back out of the door, locking his elbows and blinking in the wind. He could see the lights on the drop zone. The small lights, arranged in an inverted L pattern, indicated that the jump was a go. The base of the inverted L designated the point where he would release the first jumper. This drop zone was small—only ten seconds long. Riley had one second per man to get his entire team out. A few seconds late or early would put some of the jumpers in the trees or rice paddies that surrounded an open field. As jumpmaster, Riley's primary concern was the safety of his jumpers.

Riley took a deep breath and watched the release lights grow closer. Even though he had been on airborne status his entire twelve years in the army, he disliked jumping. No matter how many jumps a man had, or how accomplished a parachutist he was, there was always that element of chance involved—especially at night. The ground couldn't be seen clearly during descent. You could easily land in a soft sand pit or in a hole that could snap your leg like a twig. A safe landing was determined by the winds, the pilot, and the jumpmaster, as well as the jumper. That was one of the reasons why Riley always preferred jumpmastering—so he could control two of the four variables.

At least the drop zone was marked on this particular mission. Riley hated blind drops, where the jumpers had to trust the navigation of the air force to locate the drop zone, then exit the aircraft simply on the green light, with no spotting by a jumpmaster. Riley had a lot more trust in his jumpmastering abilities than in an air force navigator's skills.

Loaded down with a parachute on his back and a rucksack hanging in front under his reserve, Dave Riley appeared dwarfed by his equipment. At only five feet seven inches tall, and weighing barely 145 pounds, Riley was by far the smallest man on the team. His dark skin and black eyes were inherited from his Puerto Rican mother; it was hard to say what physical characteristics had been imparted by his long-forgotten Irish father. His angular face reminded people more of a native American's than a freckle-faced Irishman's. Riley's body was that of a middleweight prizefighter—lean, ropy muscles with no apparent fat. He needed that strength to hold himself in the doorway of the aircraft wearing equipment that more than doubled his weight.

When he estimated the drop zone lights to be at a forty-five-degree angle from the plane, Riley leaned out and did one final 360-degree check for any other aircraft or hazards that might be in the area. The safety was controlling Riley's static line, keeping it from becoming entangled as the wind blew it about. These last seconds seemed to take forever. Slowly, the drop zone edged beneath the aircraft. Satisfied,

Riley pulled himself back into the plane, turned to the lead jumper, and pointed at the exit. "Stand in the door!"

Riley grabbed the static line as the first jumper took his position in the door. He peered over the man's left shoulder, watching the lights pass under the aircraft. The green light lit up on the side of the door. Half a second later, Riley screamed "GO!" and smacked the lead jumper on his rear. The man was gone.

The rest of the jumpers swiftly shuffled forward and out—sucked into the dark night sky. As they flashed by, Riley grabbed each man's static line with his right hand and passed it smoothly to his left, pinning it against the trailing edge of the door. Riley was right behind the ninth man. He slapped both palms on the outside of the aircraft and threw himself forward and out, tucking his body into a tight position. "One thousand," he counted as the turboprop blast tore at him and he could see the tail of the aircraft between his feet. "Two thousand" as the aircraft roared away. "Three thousand" as he felt the beginning of the opening shock.

Before Riley made it to four thousand, the deploying chute jerked him upright. In the space of four seconds he had gone from a forward, free-fall speed of 135 miles an hour to practically zero. His first action was to check the canopy to make sure it had deployed properly. As he scanned the nylon umbrella over his head, he reached up and gained control of the toggles that steered the MC1-1 parachute. He waited a few seconds, until the chute automatically settled in line with the drift of the wind, then he pulled the left toggle, turning into the night's slight breeze to counteract the eight-mile-an-hour forward speed of the parachute.

Jumping at eight hundred feet left little time for sight-seeing, but Riley took a quick glance about and in the moonlight counted the nine other chutes stretched along the trail of the aircraft. At least everyone looks like they're over the drop zone, he thought. Chonjinam drop zone was so short that sometimes an entire team didn't make it out on a pass, in which case the aircraft had to circle around and do another. That was okay in training, but on a combat jump one pass was all the air force would give them. Riley's standing team policy was that if one man went out the door, everyone on the team went in the same pass. That made for some fierce arguments with aircrews, since the last members of Riley's team would occasionally jump on the red light—the navigator's signal that they'd reached the end of the drop zone. Riley had implemented this policy for two reasons: to instill a solid sense of teamwork, and to train exactly as if the mission were real.

One hundred and fifty feet above the ground, Riley reached down and pulled the two quick releases that dropped his rucksack to the end of its fifteen-foot lowering line, where it dangled below him. Landing with the bulky rucksack still tight against the front of the jumper's legs made him a candidate for a broken leg. Lowering it too soon, above two hundred feet, induced oscillations that swung the jumper back and forth, leading to a much harder impact. The dark ground rushed up as Riley kept his eyes focused forward on the horizon. Pulling his knees tight together, Riley pointed his toes down and prepared to land. He grunted with the shock of hitting the ground, and rolled onto his right side.

Riley stood up and began unbuckling himself from the harness. As he did so, he scanned the area to see if he could spot other team members. Another jump done. Now the ground mission began. Once out of the harness, the first thing he did was unsling his M16A2 from his shoulder and prepare it for action. Although he was carrying only blanks and knew that there would be no "enemy" on the drop zone, old habits were good to keep.

Riley grabbed the apex of his canopy, s-rolled the parachute, and shoved it into its kit bag. Then he shouldered his rucksack and threw the kit bag on top. His slim frame was bent almost double with the combined weight of forty-eight pounds of parachute and a hundred pounds of rucksack. Staggering toward the tree line on the northern end of the drop zone, he made his way to the assembly point. Riley figured that a troop of cub scouts armed with butter knives could wipe out his team right now, separated as they were and laden down with rucks and chutes. Infiltration was the most vulnerable part of any Special Forces operation.

It took Riley twenty minutes to make the eleven hundred meters to the assembly point. He was sweating in the early summer night air. Along the way, he linked up with two other team members. Pete Devito was the team's senior medic; he easily carried his gear atop his bodybuilder's six-foot-two, 220-pound frame. Riley considered Devito a good man. They'd been together in the 1st Battalion, 1st Special Forces Group, on Okinawa during a previous assignment, and Devito had shown himself to be a conscientious soldier and medic.

The other man, Smith, was the team's junior engineer and one of the first-termers on the team. For a while, desperate for bodies, Special Forces had allowed soldiers to enlist in the army, go through basic and advanced training, and airborne school, and then straight to Special Forces school. The traditional way was to accept only seasoned noncommissioned officers (NCOs) into Special Forces training. Older NCOs complained about the young kids, but Riley liked them. Sure, they could do foolish things at times and were occasionally immature, but overall they were smart, most of them having spent some time in college, and they added a youthful enthusiasm to things. The process of allowing first-termers into Special Forces had been discontinued a few years ago; Smith was one of the last of the breed.

Behind his innocent-looking face, Smith had a devious mind. Combining him with Hoffman, the team's senior engineer, made for an extremely effective demolitions team. Both were young and inexperienced, but extremely intelligent. Hoffman, with his mop of red hair and thick glasses, had been dubbed Little Einstein by the team. Give him a problem, and in a few minutes it was solved.

As the three men passed into the tree line, a voice called out to them in the dark: "Running."

"Cloudy," Riley replied, followed by Devito and Smitty, calling out their mission code names as running passwords. They entered the small assembly area nestled among the trees. Five other members were already there—three providing security and two digging. They'd have to dig a mighty big hole for ten parachutes and helmets, Riley knew. For a moment he allowed himself the luxury of being angry at his new team leader. During mission planning, Captain Peterson had insisted on caching the parachutes, despite Riley's arguments to the contrary. That's the way the young captain had been taught in the Special Forces Qualification Course at Fort Bragg and, by God, that's the way they were going to do it. By the book. Riley felt that a man who didn't let common sense overrule the book was a dangerous fellow. He had seen enough of this type in his twelve years in the army.

Riley took a quick count in the dark. Eight of ten present. He was missing the new team leader—that figured—and Comsky, the team's junior medic. On first impression Riley had wondered how Comsky had made it through the extremely rigorous Special Forces medical school. He just didn't seem to be clicking on all cylinders at times. He even looked slow and dumb. Only five and a half feet tall and barrel chested, Comsky had thick, bushy eyebrows and a body covered with hair. He'd been dubbed the Ape by the other team members when he had first walked into the team room, and the nickname had stuck. He played the ape role sometimes to amuse the rest of the team, scratching his arms and swaggering around the team room. However, given a medical emergency, he seemed to come alive and worked as well as any Special Forces medic Riley had seen—in fact, better than most. Comsky was also one of the strongest men, pound for pound, Riley had ever met.

After fifteen minutes, the last two members straggled in, beating their way along the tree line. Riley checked his watch. Fifty minutes to assemble. Piss poor, he thought. On a real mission, if they'd been spotted jumping in, the drop zone would have been crawling with enemy forces by now. And the team leader wanted to sit here just off the DZ for a couple of hours while they dug a big hole to dispose of their parachutes. Not only that, but there was no way they could properly camouflage the hole in the dark. Anybody coming by, unless they were blind and stupid, would instantly recognize that something was buried here. They might as well put up a sign: "Parachutes Buried Here!" But Riley would play the game. He'd give Captain Peterson a little more rope to hang himself. That was the only way the man was going to learn.

The training mission tonight was to move about six kilometers from the drop zone to a power line and simulate destroying it with dummy demolitions that the team carried.

The mission had to be completed by 0400 the next morning; at this rate, Riley knew they'd never make it. It was already 2315, and he estimated another two to three hours to finish the burial cache. Riley settled down for the wait as the team members rotated between burial detail and security. Digging in ground laced with roots and rocks, while trying to be as quiet as possible, made for slow progress.

At 0100 Captain Peterson started getting nervous. Riley figured that Peterson had finally gotten it through his head that they weren't going to make it to the target on time. Peterson came over and whispered to him.

"Sergeant Riley. I don't think we're going to make the target at this rate. The men don't seem to be digging fast enough. Here's what I want to do. Leave four men here to finish the cache and the rest of us go up and hit the target. We'll link up at the exfiltration point. You pick the men to stay. In fact, I want you to be in charge here. I'll take the other element up to the target."

Lord give me patience, thought Riley. Sounds like he memorized that little spiel. There's nothing worse than changing a plan in midoperation, especially if contingencies haven't been planned for. The captain's intimation that the team wasn't digging fast enough pushed Riley past his limit. He had had enough of this nonsense. Time for the captain's Special Forces schooling to really begin, Riley thought.

"With all due respect, sir, would you care for my opinion?" Without waiting for a reply, Riley drove on, speaking in a quiet, biting, forceful tone that the captain had not heard in the week he'd been with the team. The captain stood silent as he watched Riley's dark face in the moonlight.

"First off, sir, I told you that we'd never get these chutes buried in time. Secondly, we don't even need to cache the damn things because once we blow the power line, under the enemy scenario in this exercise, any so-called enemy with half a brain is going to figure out what happened. If we don't make exfiltration by 0700 it isn't going to matter if we made the parachutes disappear by magic into the fourth dimension, because we're going to be running so fast and hard, we're going to have a lot more important things on our mind. Like staying alive. So forget the parachutes. We leave them here as

they are. I'm signed for them. If they get ripped off it's my
ass. We hit the target like we planned with all ten team members and we go now!"

Riley turned from the stunned team leader. With hand signals he let everyone know to put on their rucksacks and move
out quickly, then watched with satisfaction as the many hours
of drilling paid off. Within a minute they were moving, the
team leader sullenly falling into place in the formation.

The lead man, weapons specialist Sfc. Tom Chong, wore
nightvision goggles, as did Riley and the last man. The bulky
goggles were a pain to use sometimes, but on night missions
like this they were worth their weight in gold. Through the
goggles the moon- and starlight was computer enhanced, and
everything appeared almost as it would in daylight. The only
drawbacks were that all images were in a shade of green, and
the viewer lost his sense of depth perception to a large extent.
The advantage of being able to see in the dark more than
made up for these disadvantages.

Chong could see like a cat in the dark, even without the aid
of the goggles. The point man also had an uncanny sense of
location and direction. Riley depended on him extensively
during night moves. On many previous exercises in rough terrain, even when Riley himself had been confused, Chong had
found the way. Riley had worked with some excellent track-
ers, but he had never seen anyone able to move like Chong.
The other team members referred to Chong jokingly as their
resident native. Chong had been born in Korea and spoke the
language fluently. He had also attended the Defense Language Institute at Monterey, California, to learn Mandarin
Chinese. Chong had helped the team out numerous times with
his ability to speak the local language as they roamed the Korean countryside. He also got them better deals when they
shopped in the native markets.

The slim, dark-skinned man in the lead had the azimuth
and distance to the target memorized, as did Riley. Using his
pace count, Riley figured that they were within a kilometer of
the target when the team leader signaled a halt. Riley moved
back to the captain to find out what was up. He found the detachment commander crawling under his poncho and making
a map check with a red-lens flashlight. In doing so, he was

making enough noise to attract the attention of anyone within five hundred meters. Riley figured that Peterson had learned this little trick in Ranger school. He waited until the team leader was done.

"We're about two kilometers from the target, Sergeant Riley. I think we need to head more to the west."

"Sir, we're less than a klick away and right on track. Chong is the best navigator I've ever seen at night and he knows this land. I've been checking his azimuth and pace count and we're dead on. Trust me, sir. Unless of course your pace count is much different." Riley waited. He figured that the new team leader had not been keeping a pace count since leaving the cache site. The lack of an answer confirmed this.

Riley gave the move-out signal. In twenty minutes the team was on target. Following a quick halt to drop rucksacks, the team broke down into its various tactical elements.

Riley settled back in his overwatch position and observed the team run through the maneuver they had practiced. Four team members split into two groups and moved out along the service road of the power line to provide security. Each two-man team had one of the new squad automatic weapons (SAW) and a pair of light antitank weapons (LAWs). Two other team members were fifty meters back in the tree line, where the team had dropped all ten rucksacks, and would link up once the charges were set and blown. Riley and Captain Peterson observed from the tree line as the two team engineers ran up and placed the charges on the tower holding the power lines.

From leaving the tree line to completing wiring their charges, Smitty and senior engineer Sgt. Dan Hoffman took two minutes and thirty seconds. They double-primed the plastic explosive for a nonelectrical detonation as they'd been taught to do by Riley. Before he made rank and became team sergeant, Riley had been a Special Forces engineer also, so he rode his engineers hard and set high, exacting standards.

Hoffman did a last check and then moved back toward the tree line, unreeling his detonating wire. Once the engineer reached the overwatch position, Riley flashed a red-lens flashlight at both flank security teams and they rushed back. After accounting for all personnel, Riley signaled Hoffman to blow the charge. Hoffman pulled the igniter and yelled "Boom!" Riley jumped.

"Sorry, Top. Just thought I'd do it for effect," Hoffman admitted sheepishly as they moved back to pick up their rucks.

Riley was happy with the actions on target. Less than five minutes from leaving the rucks to picking them up. The team could do better, but that wasn't bad. They threw on their rucks and moved out. The dummy demo was left in place to be evaluated and removed the next day.

The team made it to the pickup zone (PZ) thirty minutes early. It was just getting light enough to see out into the dry streambed where the helicopter was supposed to land. At exactly 0658, Riley stepped out onto the rocks under the watchful guns of his team and turned on his strobe light. Light flickering, he waited. The appointed time came and went. At 0702 Riley shut off his light and came back to the team.

Exfiltration was supposed to be a highly coordinated and exactly timed event. A window of two minutes prior and two minutes after the designated time was all that was allowed for security reasons. In this case, however, Riley mused, the highly coordinated part seemed lacking.

Another blown exfiltration because the helicopter didn't come. Since he'd been on Team 3, Special Forces Detachment-Korea (DET-K), Riley had not been exfiltrated on time on more than half his training missions, due to helicopters not showing up on time or at all. It worried him. He'd been told by other, more experienced Special Forces NCOs about helicopter pilots in Vietnam who had flown through all sorts of obstacles, both natural and man-made, to pick them up. But in this peacetime army, it seemed that the birds wouldn't fly if there was a cloud in the sky.

Riley heard the muttered curses of the team members as they realized that they had a fifteen-kilometer walk back to the truck pickup point. God help us if we ever have to do this for real and those birds don't show, Riley thought. We'd be walking a hell of a lot farther than fifteen kilometers.

Fort Meade, Maryland
Thursday, 1 June, 1800 Zulu
Thursday, 1 June, 1:00 P.M. Local

Meng pointed at a stack of papers on one of his desks. "Those are your copies of the oplans for the units involved, along with my initial mission assessments."

Ron Wilson looked at the bulging stack with little enthusiasm. After just having finished the debrief on Dragon Sim-12, he wasn't thrilled about jumping right into the next mission. In his opinion, Doctor Meng was pushing the whole project too quickly. Wilson knew that Meng wanted to get onto the Medusa scenario, but this pace was too much. "What's the time line, Doctor?"

Meng didn't even bother turning. "Top sheet."

Wilson looked at the schedule with dismay. "Inbrief tomorrow?"

Meng looked up from where he was still flowcharting the mission. "The operation starts here tomorrow morning. I'll inbrief the strategic mission commander and his staff then. You can relax for a little while. I want you to look over the Medusa scenario for me anyway. You'll pick up your shift day after tomorrow on Sim-13."

Wilson sighed as he started sorting through the pile of papers, all stamped top secret. He was getting very tired of all this work. His responsibility in the Strams exercises was to back up Meng. The two of them usually split the time for the exercises, each spending twelve hours on duty.

As he started reading the first oplan, Wilson saw that this next mission was going to involve special operations aircraft and troops. That meant the majority of the actions on their end would be to monitor the message traffic between the strategic mission commander at Fort Meade and the forward operating base (FOB) that would launch the actual mission, at least until it became time for the part on the ground to begin. Then the computer would kick in, generating the simulated message traffic. For the people back at Fort Meade, the whole operation looked realistic and continuous from start to finish.

Wilson looked up. "Are we going to offset the aircraft and the team involved?" An offset meant sending aircraft and troops on a mission similar to the one in the oplan but in a local training area rather than the target country.

Meng looked up briefly from his work. "No. Once the team gives its briefback, we go to the computer exclusively. The offset didn't work well in the Bear Sim with Special Forces. The computer can do a much better job than the offset. Besides, we're not testing the team. We're testing the people in Tunnel 3." Meng turned back to his work.

The setup was complicated and Wilson didn't appreciate having inadequate time to get everything going. He glanced at Meng hunched over his tables. Wilson considered Meng a weird genius. There was no doubting the man's ability at programming. He could accurately portray a mission from start to finish to the strategic mission commander and staff in the Tunnel, using the oplans, simulated mission, and feedback from the employed element. But the man had the personality of a rock. He wasn't friendly with anyone on the staff and usually ran the actual Strams exercise by himself once it started, sleeping in his office in the Tunnel for the duration of the mission. It irritated Wilson to have Meng hanging around looking over his shoulder during his shift. Meng slept less than four hours out of every twenty-four, which meant that he was constantly around. Wilson wasn't sure whether it was because Meng didn't trust anyone or simply because he had nothing else to do. An aging photo of a young Chinese woman and a small boy sat on Meng's desk, but Wilson had never heard him make any reference to a family. He wished that the old man had someone waiting at home.

Wilson gathered up the mass of papers and stuffed them into his carrying case to lock in the safe. He didn't have any more time to ponder the idiosyncrasies of Doctor Meng. He wanted to go home and relax for a little while before having to start split shift again.

Yongsan, Seoul, Republic of Korea
Thursday, 1 June, 2230 Zulu
Friday, 2 June, 7:30 A.M. Local
Captain Mitchell slammed down the phone. "Goddamn support pukes."

Sergeant Major Hooker looked up from his desk. "What's the matter, sir?"

Mitchell pointed at the phone. "I hate those damn things. All I ever get is bad news over them. First the helicopter pilots decide not to fly, and now the transportation battalion tells me that the backup truck didn't go out to the ground pickup point this morning. The driver didn't get up on time."

The sergeant major picked up his phone. "Let me handle this, sir." He punched in a few numbers and waited while the traditionally faulty phone service tried to figure out where the connection was to be made. Mitchell got up from his desk and wandered over to the sergeant major's to listen in. Mitchell enjoyed watching Hooker in action.

Hooker stood only five feet two inches tall. Mitchell had always meant to look in the regulations to see if Special Forces had a height requirement, but he had never gotten around to it. Hooker was well known throughout the Pacific special operations community. When Mitchell first arrived in this assignment more than eighteen months ago, he had been told many stories about the diminutive DET-K sergeant major. Since moving up to the headquarters shed to be the DET-K operations officer, Mitchell had grown to really enjoy working with Hooker. He'd also started to believe many of the stories he'd been told about the man.

Hooker didn't tell war stories like a lot of the older NCOs did. When the sergeant major talked about his experiences, it was usually for the purpose of making a point or educating those around him. He had a lot of stories. Hooker had been around Special Forces for twenty-eight years, twenty-three of them in the Far East.

Mitchell was a contrast physically to the squat sergeant major. Eight inches taller and fair haired, Mitchell had the build of a lean, long-distance runner. This was his first tour of duty in this part of the world. He had nine years in the army, the first three with the 1st Infantry Division at Fort Riley, Kansas. Mitchell had then volunteered for Special Forces training. He'd wanted more challenge than riding around in the back of an armored personnel carrier through the Kansas countryside. Special Forces had given him that. The six-month Special Forces Qualification Course (Q

course) had introduced him to a new type of warfare and a
new type of soldier. The NCOs who taught the Q course had
impressed Mitchell from the start with their overall profes-
sionalism and depth of expertise in unconventional warfare.
The tactics taught at the John F. Kennedy Special Warfare
School made a lot more sense to Mitchell than those he'd
learned at the infantry school at Fort Benning.

The course at Fort Bragg, North Carolina, had also introduced him to something more than a new part of the army.
He'd met his wife there. During a practical exercise in rescu-
ing downed pilots and moving them through a resistance network, Mitchell's student team had picked up a female
helicopter pilot. Mitchell's first impression of the slender,
five-foot-six, dark-haired pilot was not favorable. He was the
serious type; she, on the other hand, made a joke of everything. At first he took her jabs personally. After being forced
to stay together in a safe house for almost thirty-six hours,
however, his opinion of Capt. Jean Long had slowly under-
gone a transformation. He realized that her teasing wasn't
meant to belittle him. It was simply her way of dealing with
the world. She laughed at the stupidity built into the exercise
and at the other ridiculous things life brought her way, and
she didn't really care if other people disapproved of her attitude.

By the time he was ready to pass her on to the next link
of the escape network, they had formed the basis of a friendship. Four months later they were married. Mitchell had
never thought he'd tie the knot that quickly, but he had never
regretted it. Life had certainly been an adventure since he'd
met Jean Long.

Mitchell's musings were interrupted by Hooker's roar into
the phone. "Sergeant, this is Sergeant Major Hooker. You got
ten minutes to kick that driver in the ass and get him over
here to my compound. I want to look into his beady little
eyeballs before he goes to pick up my people. I got troops
standing ass deep in a shit-filled rice paddy waiting on that
yo-yo. You read me loud and clear, Sergeant?"

Hooker slammed down the phone without waiting for an
answer. He smiled at Mitchell. "Sir, you just have to know
how to talk to these people. NCOs don't understand all those

fine manners and etiquette they taught you at West Point. You have to master the firm but gentle art of persuasion in a manner similar to mine."

Mitchell laughed. Hooker was a master of persuasion, but he didn't know much about being gentle. "Hey, Sergeant Major, tell the colonel I'm out with the deuce and a half. I'll go with the driver to make sure he gets to the right spot."

Hooker nodded. "All right. Better you than me facing down Dave Riley anyway. He's going to want an explanation for both the helicopter's no-show and the truck being late. Since your wife is one of them-there whirlybird drivers, you might be able to explain it better than me. By the way, are you going up or is she coming down here this weekend?"

Mitchell replied while grabbing his map and beret. "I'm going to take the train up there. Already got tickets on the 4:20. When I talked to her last night on the phone she said she's got to work again tomorrow. Got two birds she has to test-fly. If she finishes them today she might have the afternoon off tomorrow. We should have all day Sunday together."

Hooker shook his head. "Man, they're working her to death. When's the last time she had a weekend off?"

Mitchell had to think about that. "Probably about two months ago. When we went to Soraksan National Park for the weekend."

"Need a ride over to Chongyangni Station?"

"I'd appreciate it, but I can take the subway."

"No trouble, sir. We'll leave here at 1545."

Mitchell paused as a thought occurred to him. "You don't suppose we're going on alert because of all this stuff going down in China, do you, Sergeant Major?"

Hooker considered that. "I doubt it, sir. Everything seems to be pretty static."

Mitchell shook his head. "I don't know. On the news there was a story that they tried sending troops into Beijing and the troops didn't buy off on it."

Hooker shrugged. "Who knows what the hell is going on over there. I sure haven't been able to figure out this part of the world, and I've spent quite a few years running around here. China has always been the great enigma." Hooker smiled proudly. "Hey, you like that fancy word I used?"

Mitchell gave the sergeant major his thanks for the ride offer and went outside to wait by the gate of the small compound that housed DET-K. The compound consisted of six buildings, one for the headquarters and one for each of the five A teams that made up the unit. It was located on the south post portion of Yongsan Army Military Base, nestled in the heart of Seoul. On a day when the winds blew away the cloud of pollution that usually covered the city, you could see the Seoul Tower on a hilltop rising above the city to the north, and the tall 63-Building to the south on the other side of the Han-Gang River. Today wasn't one of those days—a foreboding gray cloud hovered above the city.

Mitchell saw a deuce-and-a-half truck swing around the corner, roar past the softball field, and come toward him. He knew that if he didn't go with the truck, there were better than even odds that the driver wouldn't make it out of the city. Seoul had not been designed with cars in mind. In fact, it hadn't even been designed at all; it had just grown. There was a definite shortage of road signs, although a big improvement had been made during the buildup for the Olympics. Mitchell could read Korean characters and make out most signs, although he was a long way from being fluent in the language.

The driver pulled the truck up and got out. "Sir, I'm supposed to report to a Sergeant Major Hooker."

Mitchell decided to have mercy on the young man. "Private, you don't want to talk to the sergeant major. He hasn't had his breakfast yet and he might make you the first course." He clambered up the passenger side. "Let's roll."

Pickup Point, 42 Kilometers Southeast of Seoul
Friday, 2 June, 0012 Zulu
Friday, 2 June, 9:12 A.M. Local
It was a long and tiring fifteen-kilometer walk back to the pickup point. Riley enforced strict tactical discipline the entire way. As he continued to control the operation, he could sense the captain getting irritated with him. That was all right with Riley. They could hash things out after they got back to the team room.

Riley drove himself and his team hard, because he'd seen

the results of half-assed efforts. In the peacetime army it was hard to keep the motivation level up. Occasionally, Riley just got tired of pushing. His soldiers sometimes resented his pickiness, what he called "attention to detail." But it was attention to detail that determined whether a soldier lived or died. Still, he tried to be fair, and his men respected him for that. Riley had two passions: his team and his martial arts training. Unlike many other soldiers serving a tour in Korea, Riley didn't have a mistress off post. Nor did he frequent the GI bars every evening. Riley dedicated himself to taking care of his team. The ten members of Team 3, Special Forces Detachment-Korea, were his family.

On the way to the pickup point, they reached a bridge spanning a small but deep stream. Riley stopped the team and signaled for Hoffman and Sfc. Lech Olinski, the team's intelligence sergeant, to come forward. Riley instructed them to emplace a one-rope bridge downstream from the road bridge for the team to cross on.

Hoffman stared at Riley for a second, then realized the futility of complaining. It would be much easier to go nontactical at this point and walk across the road bridge. But Riley didn't know the meaning of the word *nontactical.*

As the two moved off to the riverbank and broke out a 120-foot rope, Riley heard Hoffman mutter to Olinski. "Guess the man figures we need a bath, hey, Ski?"

Olinski grunted in reply. Riley smiled to himself. Olinski was not exactly verbose. As intelligence sergeant, he was the second-highest-ranking noncommissioned officer on the team, and Riley knew that he could count on Olinski's support for his strict training habits. Olinski had the same outlook Riley did.

Olinski was one of those people with a varied background that Special Forces seemed to attract. His parents were Polish and he himself had lived in Poland until he was eleven, when the family had escaped to West Germany. Olinski had spent three years there, then came to the United States to live with an uncle. At seventeen he enlisted in the army and joined the Rangers, where he rose to the rank of staff sergeant. When someone at the Department of the Army happened to see that Olinski spoke fluent Polish, German, and Russian, Olinski was asked to volunteer for Special Forces. After finishing his training, Olinski had spent several years in the 10th Special Forces Group, which had Europe as its area of orientation. When DET-K had picked up some responsibility for eastern Russia, Olinski had been sent to Korea for a one-year short tour.

Since his arrival, Olinski had maintained a reputation as a quiet but extremely competent intelligence sergeant. His knowledge of Soviet and Warsaw Pact armies and security forces came from more than just books. He also had his personal childhood experiences to draw on.

Olinski looked his name, with a broad Slavic face and tall lanky body. Besides the usual Polish jokes, Olinski was often the butt of other younger, and less experienced, team members' jibes for his willingness to be miserable when there might be an easier way out. In the Rangers, Olinski had learned to ignore the pain and discomfort that hard, realistic training entailed. This hard-core quality endeared the man to Riley, who was fond of saying that pain was weakness leaving the body.

Riley watched as Olinski lowered his body into the chilly mountain stream. This was the price one had to pay to be good, Riley thought. The easy way got you killed. With the rope tied around his waist, and his M16A2 held overhead, Olinski sidestroked to the far bank, being careful not to swallow water. Any water in the Korean countryside was extremely suspect: pollution and the Korean way of fertilizing fields with human waste ensured that. In his dripping uniform Olinski anchored the rope around a tree, then turned to provide far bank security.

Hoffman enlisted the aid of three other team members and they anchored the near end of the rope on a tree, then tightened it down as much as possible. Hoffman hooked Olinski's and his own rucksack onto the rope with snap links and started across. The natural stretch of the rope made the center section of the bridge sag so that Hoffman's head went underwater briefly, but he pulled himself over quickly. One by one, the rest of the team followed.

Sending his ruck over with Devito, Riley remained until last. He untied the near bank rope and swam it over. On the far bank, he coiled the rope and hung it on the outside of his ruck as the team moved out to cover the last kilometer back to their pickup point. When they reached the road junction where the truck was supposed to be, Riley sighed as he saw nothing there. He was too tired to get angry. Typical, he thought. He knew it would show up sooner or later. Between Hooker and Mitchell at the Operations Shop, one of the two would get things rolling.

Riley missed Mitchell. The captain had been Riley's team leader for sixteen months before moving up to the DET-K S-3 slot. Riley had enjoyed working with someone who was competent and also willing to learn. During those sixteen months, Riley had imparted as much knowledge as he could to Mitchell, and at the same time learned a few things himself. They had split the chore of running the team in an efficient manner.

The two had formed an extremely close professional and personal bond during their time together. Because of that bond, Team 3 had become what all Special Forces teams should be but few achieve: twelve individuals welded into an effective, cohesive fighting force. The team worked and played together. The Mobile Training Team (MTT) mission to Australia, six months ago, culminating in a successful joint training mission with the Australian Special Air Services (SAS), had put a fine edge on Team 3—an edge that Riley saw the new team leader threatening.

Besides the professional aspect, Riley enjoyed Mitchell's company and had even learned to like the captain's wife, although Riley questioned the idea of women in the army. He also didn't understand why she had kept her own last name, but he figured that was none of his business, and he knew that if he mentioned it, Captain Long would make that very clear to him. She was one of the most stubborn and self-reliant persons Riley had ever met. Riley and Jean Long had a mutual but wary respect for each other that was beginning to become a friendship.

Riley steeled himself as Captain Peterson came over and sat down next to him. Riley was tired, hungry, and wet. Add the lack of transportation, and he was in no mood to deal with a petulant captain.

Peterson wasted no time on small talk. "Sergeant Riley, I

did not appreciate the way you talked to me at the cache site."

Riley stood and gestured for the officer to follow him. He wasn't about to argue in front of the rest of the team. Riley led the captain to the other side of the road.

"Yes, sir. I can understand that. But to be honest I don't appreciate the way you've been treating me this past week. You haven't listened to my advice nor have you tried to seek it out. If we're going to work together, then you have to work with me. I'm willing to work with you."

Peterson didn't seem to be buying it. "I'm the commander of this team. If you can't go along with that, then I'm going to have to do something about it and go to the colonel."

Riley shook his head in wonderment at the captain's lack of common sense. "Sir, there's no need to get Colonel Hossey involved. I think you might find that's not so smart. He's not going to move people around just because they don't get along. I realize I can be kind of mule headed sometimes, but you need to realize where the expertise on this team lies. I've got ten years of Special Forces experience. There's a bunch more experience sitting across the road in the heads of the other enlisted people on this team." Riley turned and looked the young captain in the eyes. "You have six months of schooling and two weeks in country."

Peterson looked at Riley steadily for a few seconds, then walked away. Riley rubbed his eyes; he was getting a headache. He looked up as he heard the roar of a truck headed their way.

A U.S. Army two-and-a-half-ton truck rolled down the one-lane dirt farm road toward them. Riley stepped out in the road as the truck pulled over. He hid his smile as Captain Mitchell got out of the passenger side of the cab. "Where was our helicopter? And why the hell is the truck late?"

Mitchell flicked a half salute toward Riley. "Nice to see you too, Sergeant First Class Riley." Mitchell looked up at the sky. He pointed at a wisp of a cloud floating above the jagged peaks of the ridgeline to the south. "See that cloud? That's why the helicopter didn't fly. As far as the truck goes, I decided to do some sight-seeing on the way down. Took some beautiful pictures of a rice paddy."

"Keep it up, asshole," Riley grumbled as he signaled for the team to load their rucks on the truck. "The chutes are about fifteen k's that-a-way, right off the DZ. Hopefully some Korean farmer hasn't found them by now and used them to make four thousand new shirts."

Mitchell turned as Peterson came up. "Got room in the cab for me?"

Mitchell hesitated, looking briefly at Riley, then back at his fellow officer. "How about you navigate the driver up to where the chutes are cached and I'll ride in the back? We'll go to the target and recover the demo after we get the chutes." Peterson nodded and walked to the front of the truck.

"Looks like you two are getting along great," Mitchell whispered to Riley as they headed to the rear to join the rest of the team.

"He'd better pull his head out of his butt, Mitch," Riley muttered. Then, out of earshot of the team, he turned to Mitchell. "You believe the little shit actually has threatened to go to Colonel Hossey and complain about me?"

Mitchell could see that Riley was upset, so he answered seriously. "Yeah, well, if he does that, the Old Man will smoke him like a cheap cigar."

Riley shook his head, not so sure. "I'm getting tired of dealing with you officers. He's even dumber than you were," Riley said, smiling to show that he was getting over his anger. "Maybe it's easier to join than fight, and I'll go get my warrant after all."

Mitchell laughed. "You'd be part of the enemy then." He grabbed Olinski's outstretched hand, pulling him up into the truck. Looking at the familiar faces of Team 3, he felt a wave of sadness that he was no longer part of the team.

Fort Meade, Maryland
Friday, 2 June, 0400 Zulu
Thursday, 1 June, 11:00 P.M. Local
Meng put aside his work every half hour to listen to the latest CNN report regarding the situation in Tiananmen Square. He wasn't sure what to make of the unsubstantiated reports of fighting between elements of the 38th Army and the 27th Army on the outskirts of Beijing. He could well believe that

the 38th had turned back, refusing to enter the city to crush the students. The majority of the conscripts in the 38th were from the Beijing area and were probably sympathetic to the students.

Meng looked through one of the classified Defense Intelligence Agency (DIA) reports on the makeup of the Chinese Army. He could see why 27th Army had been brought in. It was from the Nei Monggol Military District, which meant that the soldiers in that army would have little in common with the students in the square.

Meng sensed that the tinder and firewood were all piled up in Tiananmen Square waiting for the match. It was just a matter of time before it was ignited. He said a silent prayer before turning back to his work.

Chongyangni Train Station, Seoul, Korea
Friday, 2 June, 0720 Zulu
Friday, 2 June, 4:20 P.M. Local
Mitchell scrunched up in his seat as the old Korean lady sat down next to him and jammed her large bundle between them. Mitchell smiled at her. She looked back passively for a moment, then turned her attention elsewhere.

It was a two-hour train ride from Seoul to ChunChon, where Mitchell's wife was stationed. They had come to Korea about eighteen months ago on a joint assignment. Korea was normally a short tour of one year for soldiers because it was unaccompanied, meaning that families and spouses stayed behind in the States. When Jean had gotten orders for an unaccompanied tour to Korea, Mitchell had volunteered to go over also so they could be together. In exchange, the army, which didn't know the meaning of the words *good deal,* lengthened their respective tours to two years.

As Mitchell reflected on it, he thought they might have been better off with Jean going on the short tour and him staying back in the States. For the first sixteen months in country Mitchell had been commander of Team 3; Jean had worked in the 17th Aviation Brigade headquarters at Yongsan. During that time, despite being stationed at the same post, they had seen little of each other. Mitchell had been gone more than 50 percent of the time on field training exercises and deployments around the Orient. Then, just two months ago, when he had finally moved up to staff, which meant he would have less field time, his wife had been offered command of an aviation company. Only it was in the 309th Aviation Battalion of the 17th Aviation Regiment, stationed up in ChunChon about ninety kilometers northeast of Seoul.

Jean had needed a command in an aviation unit and this was the only one available in her specialty, which was aircraft maintenance. She'd had little choice but to accept the job. Although the position was professionally rewarding for her, the separation made both of them miserable. She worked almost every weekend to keep up with the demands of being a company commander, on top of her duties as maintenance test pilot. Since she had taken the command, they had gotten to see each other for only about half of any weekend.

As the train pulled out of Chongyangni Station, Mitchell was contemplating the prospect of another eleven years in the army under such intolerable conditions. He already had nine years in, but somehow, ever since he and Jean had gotten married, an army career just didn't seem that bright any more. He knew that as they both reached higher rank, the number of jobs would become more limited. Therefore, opportunities for them to be assigned together would also be more difficult to find. It was a trade-off he wasn't sure he wanted to make.

Mitchell decided to squelch his negative thoughts and occupy himself more productively. A Korean girl of about three or four was peering at him over the seatback. Mitchell knew that his short blond hair and occidental facial features made him stand out to the Koreans. He stuck out his tongue and she promptly grabbed her mother and pointed at him, yelling excitedly, "Mi-Guk, Mi-Guk"—American.

Mitchell feigned surprise and pointed back at the little girl, saying, "Han-Guk, Han-Guk"—Korean. The girl squealed and stuck out her tongue at Mitchell. The old lady, next to Mitchell, smiled and said something to the mother. The mother passed the girl back to the old lady, who perched the child on top of her bundle on the seat. The rest of Mitchell's train ride was spent entertaining the young girl with a variety of facial distortions and pidgin Korean.

Camp Page, ChunChon, Korea
Friday, 2 June, 0800 Zulu
Friday, 2 June, 5:00 P.M. Local
Captain Jean Long was presently six thousand feet above ChunChon conducting a test flight of an OH-58 helicopter. The aircraft had just finished phase maintenance, and it was important to make sure that everything had been put back together correctly.

She sat in the right-hand seat, and a young lieutenant, new to the battalion, sat in the left. Jean liked taking up new lieutenants fresh out of flight school for test flights. It opened their eyes to what was required to check out a helicopter before it could be flown on missions. Sometimes line pilots treated their helicopters like toys, with little consideration for the amount of maintenance needed to keep them flying.

She was getting ready to do one of the more interesting tests. Slowly rolling off the throttle, she watched her N-1 indicator until the engine clutch disengaged. The rotor blades, no longer powered by the engine, began to autorotate. That meant the blades were turning free, slowing the aircraft's descent as it plummeted without power. This was an emergency procedure normally used in case of engine failure. Jean knew that the young pilot next to her had done maybe three or four autorotations during flight school. As a maintenance test pilot, she did them almost every day.

She watched as the altimeter unwound, briefly checking the lieutenant out of the corner of her eye. She could tell that he wanted to grab the controls and get the aircraft back under power. She waited until she was sure that the helicopter was working satisfactorily, then slowly increased throttle, slowing the descent. Bringing the aircraft to a hover, she then began the approach to the airstrip at Camp Page. Carefully maneuvering the helicopter down the flight line, she slipped in between two parked Blackhawk helicopters and touched the skids lightly to the ground.

As the blades slowed she turned to the lieutenant. "What

do you think? You want to go to maintenance school and become a test pilot?"

The young man shook his head. "Ma'am, it's all yours. I'd rather be in the line unit. We get to fly the real missions."

Yeah, right, Jean thought. What do you think we just did? That's why your knuckles were white from grabbing the side of your seat when I autorotated, she smiled to herself. Another manly man who wanted to do manly things. Thinking about men, her mind turned to her husband, who should be on his way right now. She looked at her watch and shook her head. She had so much paperwork left to do in her office that she doubted she'd be done by the time he arrived.

3

"Set the troops to their tasks without imparting your designs: use them to gain advantage without revealing the dangers involved."
Sun Tzu: *The Art of War*

Fort Meade, Maryland
Friday, 2 June, 1110 Zulu
Friday, 2 June, 6:10 A.M. Local

Brigadier General Sutton looked over the group of men arrayed in front of him. US-SOCOM hadn't brought very many people to run this exercise, he thought to himself. During some joint exercises, Tunnel 3 had been packed with up to forty various commanders and staff personnel, all of them tripping over each other. For Dragon Sim-13, the Tunnel looked almost empty, with just five people from the command at MacDill Air Force Base seated in front of him. The man in overall charge was the deputy commander for US-SOCOM, Major General Olson. It was to him that Sutton addressed his inbriefing. "Good morning, General. Welcome to Dragon Sim-13. Before we get started with the briefing that describes what you will be doing over the course of the next week, I'd like to introduce the members of my staff."

Sutton pointed out his people as they were introduced. "Although I'm the head of Strams, as we call the project here, the real brain behind this setup is Doctor Meng. He is also the program chief of the first shift." Meng inclined his head at the guests. "The man in charge of handling all your communications and message traffic is Major Tresome. He's also the second-shift communications chief. Our second-shift program chief is Doctor Wilson. The first-shift communications chief is Master Sergeant Burns.

"As you can tell, very few people are involved in the running of this exercise. There are two major reasons for this." Sutton gestured at the electronic billboard behind him and then at the computer consoles. "The first is that the majority of the exercise is automated and we simply don't need that many people. The second is due to the fact that we are using real war-plan oplans—every mission is highly classified. The fewer people involved the better."

Sutton looked down and slid his notes for the formal inbriefing to the top of the podium. "Gentlemen, you all have copies of US-SOCOM contingency oplan Typhoon 17-A. That is the oplan we will be using for Dragon Sim-13."

Sutton looked up at General Olson. "Sir, perhaps you could explain to us, so we're all on the same sheet of music, the significance behind this operational plan and why your staff developed it."

General Olson was a heavyset air force general with a ruddy complexion. He shifted in his seat as he handed off the question. "I'd like my operations man here to answer that. Colonel Moore?"

An army colonel with a Special Forces combat patch on his right shoulder fielded the inquiry. "I'm the assistant operations officer at US-SOCOM. Our Typhoon series oplans are contingency and wartime missions for our Special Operations Forces in the Pacific targeted against China. Every special ops unit in the Pacific has various wartime missions allocated to them. The alpha at the end of this oplan signifies that the unit is army. The seventeen means that it is the seventeenth mission assigned to army special operations in the Pacific."

They all watched as Moore got up, walked over to the electronic map, and pointed. "We have a limited number of Special Operations Forces permanently stationed in the Pacific. The air force has the 1st Special Operations Squadron at Clark Air Force Base in the Philippines, which consists of four MC-130 Combat Talon aircraft.

"As far as navy goes, they have a Special Warfare Group of SEALs dedicated to the theater. The army has the 1st Battalion, 1st Special Forces Group headquartered in Okinawa and the Special Forces Detachment-Korea, also known as DET-K, up here in Seoul.

"This mission, 17-A, is for a unit from DET-K. It was initially designed as a team's wartime mission in the event of all-out war between the United States and China. The way we come up with these missions is to give general taskings to the subordinate units and then ask them to develop missions they feel are within their capabilities. In this instance the general guidance was to inflict damage on the Chinese war-fighting ability by attacking their petroleum industry."

Moore seemed ready to continue, but Sutton held up a hand. "I think that's all we need for now. In this scenario, we're using the wartime mission as a Command Authority surgical strike to retaliate against the Chinese government. The political reasons for such a strike are not important, since we are merely testing the ability to command and control such a mission. In doing so we will also get a good idea of the feasibility of the mission. That data will be in our files. In case there is ever a need to consider any of these missions, the data will be available for study."

Sutton consulted his notes again. "I want to run through the tentative schedule and rules for the exercise so we can get started on time. The evaluated exercise formally begins today at 1200 Zulu. By the way, all times from here on will be in Zulu, or Greenwich mean time. That will help prevent any confusion with the various time zones we'll be working with. All your message traffic will go through the computer. The blank square in the lower right corner of the electronic map is where all the traffic going in and out will be displayed."

Sutton paused as Olson raised a hand. "You mean there's no way we can talk directly to the units?"

Sutton shook his head. "Not verbally. There are two reasons we run it this way. First, it is more secure because we are able to automatically encrypt and decrypt the message traffic. You will find, if you ever operate out of the Pentagon's Emergency Operations Center, that it works in the same way. There is the capability to talk voice in an emergency, but almost all traffic is handled through the keyboard.

"The second reason is that the computer in some cases will be making the responses for your subordinate and higher elements. For example, you will be receiving some input from the chairman of the Joint Chiefs of Staff as your link to the

National Command Authority. Naturally, we don't have the chairman standing by. The computer will simulate his responses and input along with that of other people and units."

Sutton turned to the map board. "In addition to the . . ."

In the back of the room, Meng tuned out the droning of Sutton's voice. He'd heard it all before. Grown men playing games. He looked at his watch. Almost 7:30. He slipped out of Tunnel 3 to catch the latest news on the TV.

Camp Page, ChunChon, Korea
Friday, 2 June, 1145 Zulu
Friday, 2 June, 8:45 P.M. Local

About ten soldiers were scattered about talking quietly in the bar area of the Page II All-Ranks Club. Mitchell looked around as he grabbed a bar stool. It was early yet for a Friday night. Mitchell knew most GIs went downtown to one of the five Korean clubs clustered around the post's main gate; these places offered bar girls and livelier entertainment.

He looked with irritation at his watch. Jean was really late tonight. He'd gone over to the hangar to see her as soon as he'd arrived at seven. She'd still been in her office, working on paperwork that she hadn't been able to get to in a day full of flying. She promised him she'd make it to the club by eight. Mitchell had dumped his overnight bag in the small room on the end of a Korean war–vintage Quonset hut that served as Jean's quarters and then come over to the club to wait for her.

He nodded as a warrant officer from his wife's unit came in and took the stool next to him. Chief Warrant Officer Third Class Colin Lassiter was his wife's main assistant in making sure the flow of aircraft went smoothly. Her company, D Company, 309th Aviation, was responsible for fixing all the helicopters in the battalion—a total of almost fifty aircraft.

Lassiter shook his head at Mitchell. "Captain Long working late again, sir?"

Mitchell nodded glumly. "She was supposed to be here at eight."

Lassiter ordered them both a beer. "I'm sure glad she's in command here. Things have gotten a lot better since she took over. We used to be totally screwed up. Now we're only half screwed up."

Mitchell was relieved to see Jean walk into the bar, still in uniform. She smiled as she saw him and strode over. "Hey, babe. Sorry I'm late."

He was still irritated. "Yeah, sure. Want a beer?"

She looked at her watch. "No, I've got to fly tomorrow morning." She turned to the warrant officer. "Keeping my husband out of trouble, Colin?"

"Yes, ma'am. You know me."

She laughed. "Yeah, I do. That's why I asked." She turned back to her husband. "I'm starved. Let's eat."

Mitchell slid off his bar stool and, saying good night to Lassiter, followed his wife to the other end of the club where the dining room was located. It was five minutes before the kitchen closed but the Korean waitress was more than happy to persuade the cook to scrape together something for her favorite captain and her husband. Mitchell was always impressed by how his wife could make people like her. A sense of humor was a valuable tool, he knew, but one he didn't have a good handle on. His wife was usually smiling and could laugh at anything. In the army this sometimes irritated people, who thought she might be laughing at them. It was the same mistake he had made when he'd first met her at Fort Bragg.

As they waited for the meal, they filled each other in on events of the past week. Mitchell let his wife do most of the talking, because he could sense she was upset about something. It took her a few minutes, but she finally got around to it. She reached into one of the numerous pockets on her flight suit, pulled out a photograph, and passed it across the table. "Someone in my company found that posted on the bulletin board at flight operations."

Mitchell checked out the picture. It showed his wife drinking out of a large tankard in front of a bunch of men. Someone had scrawled across the bottom: MUST BE HARD TRYING TO BE A MAN. "When was this taken?" he asked.

"During my hail to the battalion six weeks ago. They fill that tankard with beer and you have to drink all of it."

Mitchell looked at his wife. "You drank all of it?"

She nodded. "It was only four beers. I had to do it. It's the tradition for a new officer."

Mitchell didn't think much of the tradition. "That's a real professional unit you're in."

"Hey, it was only in fun. I thought it was kind of humorous."

Mitchell stabbed his finger at the printing. "Who the hell wrote this at the bottom?"

She shook her head. "I don't know. Someone from my company saw it on the board at flight ops and took it down and brought it to me."

Mitchell was pissed. The resentment that was continually directed toward his wife for being in the army grated on his nerves. He hated it when someone tried to hurt her. It made him want to find whoever had done it and hurt them. Not a very mature reaction, he knew. Jean could, and wanted to, fight her own battles. And she was good at it. She'd held her own for nine years. All she wanted from him was comfort and support.

"What are you going to do about it?"

She put the picture away. "I'm going to talk to the captain in charge over at flight ops. Even if he doesn't know who put it up, if he saw it there he should have taken it down. Then I'm going to talk to my colonel and show it to him."

"Why do people do things like that?"

Jean shook her head. "I'm the only female pilot in this battalion. I think it threatens the men to have me here. They think they're less of a man because a woman can do the same job." She slumped back in her chair exhausted. "I don't know. I just get tired of this shit. If someone has a problem with me I'd rather they come and talk to me rather than do childish stuff like this. This is such bullshit. I just want to do my job."

Mitchell tried to lighten the mood. "They won't face you because they're not man enough. Hell, even I don't like getting in an argument with you and I'm married to you. You always win." He slid his seat toward his wife and put his arm around her. "Listen, sweety-pie, don't let these idiots get to you." He hugged her tight.

Clark Air Force Base, Philippines
Friday, 2 June, 1300 Zulu
Friday, 2 June, 9:00 P.M. Local
The duty officer for the 1st Special Operations Squadron (1st SOS) looked up as the secure SATCOM terminal machine in

the corner hummed with an incoming message. He put down
his book and went over to the machine. After five seconds,
the humming stopped and the message was spit out. The
man's eyes widened as he read the message.

CLASSIFIED: TOP SECRET
ROUTING: FLASH
TO: CDR 1ST SOS/ 1ST SOW/ MSG 01
FROM: CDR USSOCOM/ SFOB FM
SUBJ: ALERT/ TANGO ROMEO/ AUTH CODE:
    FIERCE WIND
REF: OPLAN TYPHOON ONE SEVEN ALPHA
REQ: ONE MC130
START: FRIDAY/ 2 JUNE/ 1500 ZULU
DEST: OSAN AFB/ ROK
POINT OF CONTACT: LTC HOSSEY/ DET-K
END: TBD
CLASSIFIED: TOP SECRET

The duty officer grabbed the phone and punched in the
number for the commander's quarters. Damn, he thought.
1500 Zulu. That wasn't much time to preflight and get a crew
together.

Eighth Army Headquarters, Yongsan, Seoul, Korea
Friday, 2 June, 1332 Zulu
Friday, 2 June, 10:32 P.M. Local
Hossey pulled into the parking lot of the Eighth Army Headquarters on north post less than fifteen minutes after getting the
phone call from the duty officer about the Flash message.
Hossey showed his ID card to the guard and wound his way
through the building until he got to the duty office. The major
there checked his ID card again. Satisfied that Hossey was who
he claimed to be, the major handed over a sheet of paper.

Hossey put on his reading glasses and perused the contents.

CLASSIFIED: TOP SECRET
ROUTING: FLASH
TO: CDR DET-K/ MSG 01
FROM: CDR USSOCOM/ SFOB FM

SUBJ: ALERT/ TANGO ROMEO/ AUTH CODE:
        RIVER THUNDER
REF: OPLAN TYPHOON ONE SEVEN ALPHA
REQ: ONE OPERATIONAL DETACHMENT/ ONE
        FOB OSAN AFB
START: FRIDAY/ 2 JUNE/ 2000 ZULU
MISC: ONE MC130 DUE IN OSAN FRIDAY/
        2 JUNE/ 2000 ZULU FOR MISSION PLAN-
        NING AND INFILTRATION SUPPORT/ IN-
        FILTRATION WINDOW 1400Z TO 1800Z
        6 JUNE
END: TBD
CLASSIFIED: TOP SECRET

Hossey took a minute to consider the message. It was an
alert and the Typhoon 17-A referenced the war plan. Hossey
couldn't remember exactly which mission it was, but he knew
the target was China. Had to be either the nuclear power plant
or the pipeline, but he couldn't remember which. More importantly, he wondered if this was real or a training exercise.
The River Thunder authorization code was the real one, but
Hossey could see little reason why they would be running a
Typhoon mission for real. The ongoing events in China were
certainly serious but seemed more a political than a military
problem. He decided after a few moments of consideration
that it was most likely a training exercise to test their ability
to react, while at the same time giving the politicians a military option for a show of force.

Using the duty officer's phone, he started dialing. As the
phone began to ring on the other end, he shook his head. A
great time to call an alert—Saturday night on a payday weekend. Most every soldier would be off post in Itaewon getting
drunk and chasing women. He was surprised when the receiver was lifted.

"Riley here."

"Dave, this is Colonel Hossey. This is an alert. Get your
team together and meet me at the compound."

"All right, sir. I'm going to have to go downtown to track
most of them down. When do you need everyone?"

Hossey checked his watch and subtracted the drive down to

Osan. He added in the number of bars in Itaewon. "Try to get as many as you can by 0100. I'll have Hooker run the rest down as they come in. I'll meet you at the compound at 0200."

"Roger that, sir."

A thought struck Hossey. "You have any idea where Hooker might be right now?"

"Probably at the NCO club, sir. He usually gets fired up there and then heads downtown around midnight."

"Thanks. Out here." Hossey put down the phone and headed for his car to drive to the NCO club.

On the other end of the line, Dave Riley replaced the receiver. He quickly dialed the phone number of the one team member who didn't live in the barracks. Then he went out into the hallway and pounded on the doors of those who did. The only one to answer his door was Olinski.

"What's up, Top?"

"An alert. We need to go downtown and find the guys. I already got a hold of Chong at his *yobo*'s place. He's on his way to the team room. I told him to get our team and isolation gear ready to go."

Riley waited while Olinski threw on a shirt, then they headed for the gate. Riley led the way as he broke into a trot. He knew he could try for a cab, but the chance of getting one of the post-run cabs at this hour on a Saturday night was slim. The same was true for getting a Korean cab right outside the gate. They'd get to Itaewon quicker on foot than by standing around waiting for a taxi. Besides, Riley hated waiting.

With Olinski trailing behind him, Riley turned right on the main Korean street that separated North and South Post Yongsan. After a quarter mile, the cinder-block walls on either side that guarded the military post disappeared, and they arrived at a major four-way intersection. On the other side of the intersection, bright lights indicated the beginning of the Itaewon district. During the day, Itaewon was the mecca for shoppers in Seoul. The many stores and sidewalk vendors catered to both local and foreign browsers. At night, the district transformed itself into Western-style nightlife. Dozens of nightclubs blasted music into the streets, and the twenty-block area was garishly lit by hundreds of neon signs. Clusters of bar girls lurked inside most of those bars, waiting to fall on GIs with money in their pockets. Riley knew which of the clubs his team members frequented. He decided to start on the main street and then work his way south.

Clark Air Force Base, Philippines
Friday, 2 June, 1400 Zulu
Friday, 2 June, 10:00 P.M. Local
The crew was scraped together from whoever could be found on base. The 1st Special Operations Squadron didn't normally keep an alert crew. There hadn't been a need for one, since Talon missions usually required a few days of planning and advance notice. One of the hastily gathered-in crew members, Maj. Ed Kent, blinked as a pair of headlights turned in his direction. He opened the glass door to the base operations building and dragged his deployment flight bag outside. An air force station wagon pulled up next to him and a burly black enlisted man got out. "You the new EW officer?"

Kent nodded as he threw the bag in the backseat. "Major Kent."

"I'm Master Technical Sergeant Young. I'm the loadmaster for the aircraft you'll be flying on. You must be new. I've never seen you before. You can hop in the car with me and I'll take you over."

Kent got in the passenger side and Young started the car rolling slowly along the flight line. "I just got in country a couple of days ago."

Young looked him over. "How much time in Talons you got?"

Kent shook his head. "I just graduated from the electronics warfare school for them at Hurlburt. I was the EW man on an F-111 before this. You know what this is all about?"

"I don't know what the hell is going on, but it sure got the colonel hopping mad. Lieutenant Colonel Riggins, that is," Young explained. "He's the pilot for our bird. They're pre-flighting right now. He had to replace the copilot too, cause his usual had a few too many at the o club this evening." He glanced over at Kent. "There a fire we got to put out or something? We don't see too many two-hour notices for a deployment unless someone's shooting at somebody somewhere."

Kent didn't know either. "All I know is, I've got to go with you all. I don't even know where we're going."

"Uh-huh," Young noted. "This is it here," he said as he pulled up to a pickup truck with two air police in it. Young showed his ID and Kent followed suit. The police waved them on. "You see that red line we just crossed?"

Kent looked back at the lit tarmac where the pickup was parked. "Yes."

"We call that the line of death. If someone who isn't authorized crosses that line, those MPs will draw down on them. You're in a secure area of the flight line now." He pulled up next to an aircraft. "And this is my baby." Kent got out of the car and looked over the aircraft.

Kent knew the capabilities of the MC-130E, designated as the Combat Talon, from his classes and training at the home of the 1st Special Operations Wing at Hurlburt Field, Florida. The basic design was that of a Lockheed C-130. Using that airframe, the air force had built a plane unique in the world.

Seeing the fuselage in the harsh spotlights, Kent could note some of the more obvious external modifications. The nose of the airplane had a large bulbous protrusion under the cockpit that normal C-130s didn't possess; that bulb housed many of the additional navigational devices the airplane employed. Also in front, two "whiskers" scissored out from the point of the nose, forming an inverted v along the direction of flight. The whiskers were for the Fulton Recovery System, designed to retrieve either personnel or equipment from the ground. A balloon was used to stretch a cable up from the ground. The pilot flew the plane right into the cable and the whiskers snatched it between them. From the edge of the whiskers, a steel cable with wire cutters extended to the tips of the wings. This cable was protection in case the pilot missed; it would prevent the balloon cable from fouling the props.

In the center of the whiskers, the balloon cable was clamped, then the speed of the aircraft drew the cable up along the belly of the plane. Hanging off the open ramp in the back, another clamp caught the cable and rotated it onto a winch inside the aircraft. Once the winch was activated, the cable was pulled into the aircraft, reeling in whatever had been on the ground.

As he ran his eyes back along the craft, Kent noted the extra fuel pods slung under the wings, which increased the air-craft's range. In the rear, he could see Young ground-guiding the driver of a forklift, maneuvering a pallet into the back of the aircraft. Kent wandered around the back.

The rear of the aircraft opened up to allow such cargo to be put in and also for paradrops of personnel or equipment. The back split, with the bottom half coming down to form a ramp and the top half disappearing into the fuselage of the aircraft beneath the massive tail.

Young had positioned the pallet over the ramp. Using hand gestures, the loadmaster had the driver lower the pallet until it sat on a set of rollers. After the forklift driver backed off, Kent hopped up and helped Young roll the pallet into the main body of the aircraft.

The interior of the Combat Talon was the same size as a regular C-130 except that the front half of the cargo area was taken up with the banks of electronic equipment that were Kent's domain. Along with an assistant, Kent operated equip-ment that allowed them to detect enemy radar systems, a key factor in enabling the aircraft to penetrate hostile airspace without being detected. Another critical component to that ability was the navigational systems the pilots used to fly the aircraft. A precision ground-mapping radar laid out the terrain ahead, allowing the pilots to monitor the plane's location and anticipate upcoming obstacles as the aircraft hugged the ground to avoid radar. Cameras on the nose of the aircraft fed information back to a low-level light display in the cockpit, enabling the pilots to fly at night almost as if it were daylight.

Young was strapping down the pallet when several people climbed up into the aircraft through the front left crew door. Kent followed them up the short ladder that led into the cockpit.

He introduced himself to the airplane commander. "I'm your new EW chief, Ed Kent."

The pilot didn't seem too cheerful. "I'm Lieutenant Colo-nel Riggins. This is Major Bailey, the copilot. The navigator is still doing final flight planning over at base ops. You should meet Captain Bradley, the junior electronics warfare officer, in the back just before takeoff. You gentlemen might as well head on back and get comfortable. We've got a long flight on up to Korea."

Yongsan, Seoul, Republic of Korea
Friday, 2 June, 1700 Zulu
Saturday, 3 June, 2:00 A.M. Local

Riley had tracked down most of the team. He had them start loading out their gear into the two-and-a-half-ton truck that Sergeant Major Hooker had commandeered. Then he went in search of Colonel Hossey. He found the Old Man in his office.

"You got everyone, Dave?"

"No, sir. Comsky and Lalli are still missing, but I left Devito downtown looking for them. I think he'll find them unless they've already hooked up with a couple of bar girls and are spending the night somewhere."

Hossey nodded. He handed over the message that had started the alert.

Riley frowned as he read it. "What the hell is Typhoon 17 Alpha, sir?"

Hossey pulled out a folder with Top Secret stamped on it. "Part of our war plan. It's a direct action mission into China."

Riley considered that. "Is this for real?"

"I don't know," Hossey shrugged. "The authorization code is real. The oplan is real. My best guess is that it's just a readiness exercise, but I don't want to take any chances. By the way, on this operation US-SOCOM cuts Eighth Army and our army SOCOM out of the chain of command."

Riley was confused. "Can they do that, sir?"

"Yes. On strategic missions we're the regional reaction force. We work directly for the National Command Authority under those circumstances. You guys on the teams haven't been involved in it yet. It's just been me and the S-3 shop war-gaming and working out proposed missions like this one for various scenarios we've been sent by the US-SOCOM's G-3 section." Hossey handed Riley the mission folder. "But you're going to be involved now.

"I say *you* because, as you've already guessed, I've picked you to be team sergeant for this deal." Lieutenant Colonel Hossey peered closely at Riley to see if his announcement got any reaction.

Riley had already figured that one out when he'd noticed that none of the other teams had been alerted. Riley had done many strange things in Special Forces (SF). He'd take this one step at a time. "And the rest of the team, sir? How do you want to work that?"

The twelve-man Special Forces Operational Detachment Alpha (ODA), or A Team, was the core of Special Forces. Colonel Hossey had five teams in DET-K to choose from. None of the teams was up to authorized strength with twelve bodies, so whenever a mission requiring a full team came down, they pulled members off other teams to fill up the deploying one. Riley knew that Hossey had a couple of options. He could cannibalize all the teams in DET-K to pick the twelve best soldiers, or he could simply fill out Riley's team with two more bodies.

"Well, Dave, I thought I would humbly ask your opinion, seeing as you're the one who's going to have to live with it. I think you know my opinion on composite teams. I didn't like them in Vietnam and now that I'm in command, I'd prefer not to do that now. Plus, I don't have the time or the inclination to be pulling everyone in. I didn't want to alert the other teams because of security."

Riley and Hossey had discussed the concept of composite teams several times in the past. Hossey felt that esprit and cohesiveness, buzzwords that he truly believed in, were more important than having twelve outstanding individuals. Riley agreed with him. Twelve good people who could work together as a team would beat twelve outstanding individuals every time.

Hossey continued. "Now don't get a swelled head, but I happen to think that, besides you being the best team sergeant in this unit, Team 3 is also the best team. But you still need an executive officer and another weapons man to fill you out. Also, if you'd like to replace anybody on the team, we can work something out. What about your junior medic, Comsky? He seems a little slow at times."

Riley smiled. "Comsky's all right, sir. He's a good medic. He isn't any Einstein, but I've got Hoffman to fill that role for me. As far as executive officer goes, I'd like to take Jim Trapp with me. We've worked together some other places and he knows his stuff. For junior weapons man I'd like Pete Reese from Team 1. He was a machine gunner in the Ranger battalion before he came to SF and jumped into Grenada, so at least he's had somebody shoot at him before. He's one of the best with automatic weapons I've seen in a while."

Riley waited as Hossey considered his choices. He mentally reviewed the qualifications of the two men he had picked. Chief Warrant Officer Trapp was probably the best warrant officer in DET-K. Ever since Special Forces had allowed senior noncommissioned officers to get warrant commissions and become detachment executive officers, that position had become an important one. Before that it had been just a nominal job given to new lieutenants in Special Forces, so they could get some experience before becoming detachment commanders. Now lieutenants weren't allowed into Special Forces and warrants filled the executive officer slot.

Trapp had been a sergeant first class before getting his warrant. He was the only executive officer in the unit with Vietnam experience. Trapp had spent two years in Southeast Asia as a young sergeant in Special Forces. He'd gotten out of the army when he returned to the States, but, bored with civilian life, he'd come back in ten years ago. Despite his age, Trapp was in superb physical condition, constantly working out.

The weapons man, Reese, was a good choice also. He was a rotund man who hid surprising strength behind an appearance of being overweight. Despite his size, Reese consistently scored a maximum score on the army's physical fitness test, as did most of the members of DET-K. In his off-duty time, Reese competed in Eighth Army powerlifting competitions. Riley had seen him wield an M60 machine gun at a qualification range and had been impressed with the ease with which the young staff sergeant handled the twenty-two-pound gun. With the addition of these two men, Team 3 would be at full strength.

Hossey appeared to have made up his mind. "OK, I'll talk to their team leaders tomorrow. You go ahead and track them down now. Tell them that as of this minute they're yours. You'd better get your people moving to be ready to go into isolation—it's supposed to start at 0500 at our Osan isolation facility. You need to at least be ready to receive the warning order by then. Sergeant Major Hooker is coordinating your vehicle and the iso area down there."

Hossey sensed Riley had something else on his mind. "What's the matter? I know this whole thing seems strange, but we're going to have to wait for the warning order in isolation before we find out what's really going on."

Riley wasn't sure how to broach the subject. "It's not that, sir. I know this whole thing seems funny. It's about your asking if I wanted to replace someone."

"Yes?"

"Well, sir . . . I'd like to trade off Captain Peterson. It's not that I've got anything against him. Well, sir, it's just that . . . well, you know. He's new and he doesn't know our standard operating procedures and all that."

Hossey shook his head. "I knew there was something we were forgetting. Where the hell is the young captain? I haven't seen him around."

Riley hung his head. "I forgot to call him, sir."

"Shit!" Hossey exploded, and then saw the humor in the situation. "Don't tell me you forgot. You didn't alert him on purpose." Riley could see that Hossey was at least considering his proposal.

The colonel countered Riley's earlier explanation. "Trapp and Reese won't know your SOPs either. You've got to give me a better reason than that."

Riley sighed. He should have known that Hossey wasn't going to let him off that easily. "OK, sir. The bottom line is that he's not that good right now. Maybe with some team time behind him he'll come around. Now that's only my opinion, and I'm only a lowly E-7 and all that, but—" He stopped at the colonel's snort of derision. "Anyway, even though I don't know what this is we're going on, I don't want to go with someone who doesn't understand the situation. Why are you briefing me instead of him? Why didn't you notice he was missing until I brought it up? It's because you know as well as I do that in Special Forces the person who can get the job done best is the one who should do it. At least that's the way it should be. Captain Peterson doesn't know that yet, and if this is a live mission, it isn't the time for him to be learning."

Riley would not have talked this way to any other battalion commander he'd ever had. But he trusted Colonel Hossey. Riley had served under him when the colonel was only a major during a six-month mobile training team mission to Thailand in 1982. They had developed a mutual trust there that had carried over the years.

"I understand that, Dave. I hate to ask, because I already know the answer, but who do you want to go with you as detachment commander?"

"Let me have Captain Mitchell back, sir. Just for this mission. With him there'd be a real commander on the ground to handle things, and I could do my job right, without having to do the commander's too. We did OK in Australia on the joint mission with the SAS there, as you might remember. Also, if he's up to speed on this US-SOCOM planning you and he have been doing, he'd be a valuable asset."

Mitchell had been a team leader longer than any other captain in DET-K, until finally Hossey had had to move him. He had made Mitchell his battalion operations officer just two months ago, and he hated like hell to give him up now. But he had an uneasy feeling about this whole mission. He'd seen a lot of weird things in twenty-one years in the army, twelve of which had been in Special Forces. But he'd never seen a situation quite like this. China *was* hot right now. Hossey was smart enough to know that the situation in Beijing was not likely to end in victory for the democratic movements. He also read the daily classified intelligence bulletins that described troop movements in the country.

Despite his "just an exercise" theory, there was always the chance that this was the real thing. That meant this was probably not something to hedge on. Hossey felt that he needed to give it his best shot, even though it would hurt his headquarters to lose Mitchell as operations officer.

Hossey conceded. "All right. You call him. Anyway, ever since I moved him off the team he's been moping around my headquarters. This ought to bring a smile to his face. Now let me go make all these changes and place a few phone calls to Osan to get things ready down there."

Camp Page, ChunChon, Korea
Friday, 2 June, 1713 Zulu
Saturday, 3 June, 2:13 A.M. Local
The ringing of the phone woke Mitchell out of a sound sleep.

"It's for you," he mumbled to his wife, who was cuddled

up next to him on a single-sized army-issue bed. "Probably one of your soldiers got in a fight downtown and is in the lockup," he added as she groggily got up and padded across the small room to the phone near the door.

"Three three oh two, this line unsecure. Captain Long speaking."

She put the phone down on the cabinet and returned to the bed. "It's for you, wise guy."

Mitchell cursed as he got out of bed and grabbed the phone. "What?"

"Hey, bud. Get your butt on down here to the team room and start working for a living."

Mitchell immediately recognized Riley's voice.

"Hey listen, Dave, don't screw with me, OK? It's two in the morning if you haven't noticed. Are you out drunk with the guys?"

"Listen, Mitch, I'm not bullshitting you. I just talked to the Old Man. It's an alert and you're back in charge of the team for this one. The colonel's in his office right now if you want to call him and check. But hurry up, 'cause we got to get moving for isolation. This one's got a short fuse."

By now Mitchell knew that Riley was serious. He tried to get his alcohol- and sleep-fogged brain to wake up. "How the hell am I going to get from here down to Seoul at two in the morning?" He and his wife didn't have a car—they weren't allowed at ChunChon and Mitchell didn't need one at Yongsan. And the train had stopped running hours ago.

"I'll get the Old Man to call the MPs there and have them run you down in one of their cars."

"All right. I'll get my stuff and head over to the MP building. See you in a couple of hours." Mitchell looked across the darkened room at his wife, then went over and sat next to her on the bed. She was so tired that she had almost fallen back to sleep.

Mitchell shook her shoulder gently. "Hey, babe. It's an alert. I've got to go back down to Seoul."

Jean struggled to open her eyes. "Are you going to deploy?"

"I don't know. Go back to sleep. I'll give you a call when I find out what's going on." He got up and quickly dressed.

Jean wanted to get up and say good-bye, but she was completely exhausted from her eighty-hour work week. They'd both been through alerts like this many times before. "Take care," she whispered as her husband walked out the door.

FOB, Osan Air Force Base, Korea
Friday, 2 June, 2000 Zulu
Saturday, 3 June, 5:00 A.M. Local

Riley wandered around the isolation area. It was an old one-story building, barely big enough to isolate all five teams from DET-K at once. The building had no windows and was routinely swept for listening devices, since the North Koreans would have been very interested in hearing what went on inside. The facility was surrounded by a chain-link fence topped with razor wire. Armed air police guards manned the one gate, admitting authorized personnel only. Once a team entered isolation, they had no outside contact until the mission was complete.

Team 3 had commandeered one room as their main work area. It already had blank map boards and tables in it. Another room, with twelve bunks, would be their sleeping area. Colonel Hossey and Hooker, along with three other personnel from the S-3 shop, worked out of the forward operating base operations center (OPCEN), which also held the SATCOM terminal and radio equipment.

A forward operating base, or FOB, was a Special Forces headquarters, usually at battalion level, which was designed to run up to eighteen A teams through isolation and then be headquarters and radio base station on missions. Since Team 3 was the only team this FOB was isolating, Colonel Hossey could give it more personal attention. The FOB's mission was to isolate the team while the team prepared for the mission. Then the FOB commander would listen to the team's briefback, where the detachment presented its plan for conducting the mission. The FOB commander then would either approve or disapprove the plan. If the plan was approved, the team was launched on the infiltration. The FOB's mission from then on was mainly to monitor the team's radio traffic. The FOB also was the link to higher headquarters, which was usually called a Special Forces Operating Base, or SFOB. For this mission, the US-SOCOM element at Fort Meade would be their SFOB.

In the OPCEN Riley glanced up as someone opened the door. He smiled as he saw a bedraggled Captain Mitchell hauling his rucksack and duffel bag through the door. "Hey, partner, let me give you a hand."

Mitchell passed over his ruck. They threw the gear into the sleeping area and went back to the op center. Mitchell looked over the area. "Where's the team?"

Riley pointed at the door leading into the isolation work area. "I got them started getting the area ready. Comsky and Lalli got here just before you did. Hooker managed to track them down in Itaewon."

"What's the mission?"

Riley shook his head. "I don't know. All Colonel Hossey got was an alert notice from US-SOCOM and a reference to Typhoon 17 Alpha."

Mitchell nodded. "That's the war plan against China. But did it say which part of the plan or give any sort of time line?"

"Nope. Just be ready to go at 0500. Which we are."

Mitchell thought the whole thing was unusual and didn't mind saying so. "Is this real or just an exercise? Do you have an offset area?" He paused as Hossey came in the door on the far side of the room and gestured for the two of them to come over. "Glad you could make it, Mitch."

"What's going on, sir?"

Hossey pointed at three locked one-drawer metal file cabinets stacked on a table. "Typhoon 17 Alpha." He handed over a set of keys for the locks. "You should have most of what you need for planning in there. I haven't received the warning order yet. It should be coming through. We just got commo set up with the SFOB. They say we'll get the warning order about 2100 Zulu. They're operating out of Fort Meade, for some reason, so we should be able to get some good intel from NSA if they're willing to get off their asses and walk next door. In the meantime you might as well hang up the maps and get started with the stuff in those files."

4

> "Thus, what is of supreme importance in war is to attack the enemy's strategy."
> Sun Tzu: *The Art of War*

FOB, Osan Air Force Base, Korea
Friday, 2 June, 2100 Zulu
Friday, 2 June, 6:00 A.M. Local

Colonel Hossey read the warning order as it rolled out of the terminal, then looked over at Hooker. "Is this for real?"

Hooker shrugged. "As far as I know it is." He grabbed the paper. "I'll give it to Captain Mitchell."

Hossey took it out of the sergeant major's hands. "I'll do it."

Since DET-K was smaller than a normal Special Forces battalion, Hossey's FOB was also smaller. He had himself, Sergeant Major Hooker, and only three other enlisted men to run the shift work. Mitchell, as the S-3, would normally have been in charge of the operations center. Now that Mitchell was back with the team, Hossey had taken over that job himself. For the duration of this mission he would let his executive officer command the other four teams in DET-K who were doing normal training back in Yongsan. His top priority lay here, especially if this mission turned out to be real.

Hossey took the warning order and left the operations center, going into the isolation area. The team had already set up tables, chairs, and map boards. They were all staring at him expectantly as he walked to the front of the room. He beckoned to Captain Mitchell and Riley.

"I've got your warning order." He handed it to Mitchell, who read it and handed it to Riley without comment.

CLASSIFICATION: TOP SECRET
TO: CDR FOB K1/ MSG 02

FROM: CDR USSOCOM/ SFOB FM
SUBJ: WARNING ORDER
REF: OPLAN TYPHOON ONE SEVEN ALPHA
1. SITUATION/
    A/ ENEMY FORCES/ AS PER OPLAN ORDER
       OF BATTLE
    B/ FRIENDLY FORCES/ 1 ODA DETK/
       1 MC130 1ST SOS
2. MISSION/ ODA INFILTRATES VIA MC130
       PEOPLE'S   REPUBLIC   OF   CHINA/
       HEILONGJIANG PROVINCE/
    1500 ZULU 06 JUNE TO INTERDICT DAQING-
    FUSHUN PIPELINE
3. CRITICAL TIMES/ INITIAL CONCEPT OF OPER-
    ATIONS TO
    THIS HEADQUARTERS NLT 1200 ZULU
       03 JUNE/
    MUST INCLUDE INFIL/EXFIL LOCATIONS/
       INTERDICTION
    POINT
    FINAL BRIEFBACK 1000 ZULU 05 JUNE
4. GENERAL INSTRUCTIONS/
    A/ STATEMENT OF REQUIREMENTS/ STOP
       FLOW OF OIL FOR
MINIMUM 7/ REPEAT 7/ DAYS
    B/ EXFILTRATION/ 2 MH-60/ 2000 ZULU
       08 JUNE
CLASSIFICATION: TOP SECRET

Riley looked at the two officers. "Where did this target come from?"

"That pipeline is one of the targets from the Typhoon oplan," Hossey explained. "It's a strategic target that plays an important role in China's economy. You have the map sheets you need from the war plan files."

Mitchell reread the paper and calculated. "This doesn't give us much time. We've got to give them an initial concept of operations by tonight. Plus we have only two days on the ground. That's cutting it real close."

Hossey agreed. "Once you take a look at the target, work

out how much time you'll need and I'll send a request to the SFOB for an extension."

Riley asked the question that was uppermost in his mind. "Is this real or an exercise?"

Hossey sighed. It was the same thing he had asked Hooker. "The code word for the alert was real. I imagine we'll find out after the briefback whether this is real or not. At the very least, the infiltration itself can't start without another final authorization code word. I very much doubt that we'll see that."

Mitchell considered all that. He turned to the rest of the team members, who were engaged in various activities getting the room ready for work. "Everyone grab a seat."

He waited while the men sat down. Mitchell had always been the one to coordinate the overall isolation effort; Riley spread his expertise among the other team members and did the tactical plan. It was time to get things on track.

"All right. Listen up. We've been tasked with a direct action mission into China to destroy an oil pipeline, with a down time of at least seven days." He waited a few seconds to let that sink in. He could see questions start to take form on some of his men's faces and decided to forestall that for now.

"I know you're wondering if this is the real thing or just an exercise. I don't have the answer to that and neither does anyone else here. I want you all to work under the assumption that this is a live mission. That's the way we've always done it in the past, and I see no reason to change now.

"We also don't have much time. I'm going to request an additional day of isolation and another twenty-four hours on the ground. Right now we're scheduled to briefback Monday night and infiltrate Tuesday night. We're supposed to be exfiltrated on Thursday night. We've got a four-hour target window on the sixth. You know that's damn tight, even if we infil and exfil almost right on top of the target. We'll be lucky to get twenty-four hours' surveillance before having to do the hit. Despite my asking for more time, I want you to proceed under the assumption that we won't get any more."

Mitchell looked at the message again. "We also have to give a tentative concept of operations by 2100 tonight." He turned to Riley. "See if you agree with me on this. I feel that our priorities should be as follows: First we need to decide how we're going to hit the target. I want you to work with Hoffman and Smitty on that. Once you come up with where exactly we're going to attack, I'll get with you and we'll work out some infiltration drop zones and exfiltration pickup zones. As you all can guess, we're going in by Talon and coming out by helicopter."

Riley nodded his approval. Mitchell turned to the other members of the team and ticked off their tasks one by one in order of priority. By the time he was done the team was ready to get to work.

Fort Meade, Maryland
Friday, 2 June, 2400 Zulu
Friday, 2 June, 7:00 P.M. Local
General Sanders watched as Olson worked with his staff. The data link had been established with the FOB at Osan Air Force Base in Korea and the initial mission warning order had been forwarded. Sanders knew from the one previous Strams exercise they had run with Special Forces that it was now a question of waiting until the team and aircrew started sending back their tentative concept of operations. Once Meng got that, he could start working out the rest of the simulation for the actual execution. The computer was already set with the enemy situation, the target, and all the other known factors. The team's plan was the only missing ingredient.

In the meantime, it appeared that General Olson was going to occupy his staff's time by checking all details, to be sure they didn't have any screwups on this end. He'd just quizzed his operations officer, Colonel Moore, on the security of the mission. He also wanted to know whether it might be a problem that Eighth Army and 6th Air Force in Japan were being cut out of the operation—or, on the other hand, what would happen if they found out about the mission. It was obvious to Sanders that General Olson hadn't spent much time on operational planning prior to this exercise. That was typical of high-ranking staffs and officers and one of the reasons that these Strams were run. It was often the first taste of an operational mission for these people.

Moore was reassuring his boss. "It's not a problem, sir. We're authorized to run these types of missions without the various services' intermediate headquarters being involved. The chain of command runs directly from the National Command Authority, through us, to the FOB, to the employed elements. It's been streamlined that way as a result of the after-action reports from the Iranian hostage mission. We've cut out all the levels that could interfere with or confuse the flow of information.

"The only people who are in on this, besides us here, are the alerted team and aircrew of the Talon in isolation over at Osan. The airplane is presently in a secure hangar out of view. We've got some worker bees involved for the intelligence, communications, and logistics support over there, but they've been told only enough so they can do their job. The other military elements, such as the exfiltration aircraft, will know only enough to be able to accomplish what's needed. It's under wraps, sir."

Olson nodded. "It had better stay that way. And not just because part of our success in the simulation rests on keeping this secure. If it gets out that we're running a simulation exercise to plan an actual attack into Chinese territory, it would cause a scandal that would be the end of me, and you also. Give me an update on the plan as it stands now."

"OK, sir." Colonel Moore leafed through the printouts of the messages from Osan. "The team's been in isolation since 2000 Zulu, or five tomorrow morning their time. We sent the warning order at 2100 Zulu. They haven't had enough time to do much, other than try to digest the intelligence we're feeding them. NSA has provided some great imagery of the entire length of the pipeline, which we're also forwarding. We're going to let the team pick the actual target spot based on the intelligence and target vulnerability."

Olson interrupted. "What about aircraft range limitations?"

Moore let the air operations man on the US-SOCOM staff, Lieutenant Colonel Bishop, handle that. "Sir, there's no problem going in. The Talon has the range and then some to make the entire length of that pipe and back out. The problem will be the exfil helicopters' range. I'll see what they send us for exfil location and work something out. I have a few ideas as to how I can expand the range of the Blackhawks if I have to."

Olson nodded and signaled for Moore to continue.

"I'll be able to give you an update at our 0700 staff meeting tomorrow morning. I should have more information from the FOB by then. The time line is pretty compressed, but I think the team can get in a good plan under the wire."

Olson continued, returning to the issue of security. "Let's war-game this a little. What about the simulated mission? What if we get word that something's happened to the team and they're compromised once they've supposedly gone in?"

Colonel Moore fielded that question also. "The team and all their gear will be entirely sterile. They'll be drawing it from actual war stockage over there. There's not much we can do to stop them from talking if they're captured. I think there really isn't a high probability of that. It's much more likely that they'd get in a firefight and killed, if compromised on the ground. Other than the bodies, the Chinese won't have much to go on.

"I'm actually more concerned about the aircraft we'll be using to go in and out. We can always deny the team if they're caught. We'll look stupid, and people will know, but it won't be as bad as if we get a plane or chopper shot down over Chinese territory and they can parade the wreckage and crew." Sanders knew that everyone in the room would recognize the picture Moore was painting. Desert One all over again.

Olson pointed a thick finger at his subordinate. "That's the last thing we want to happen, Bill. Desert One was a mess. If something comes up and things get hairy, I'll abort before that happens."

Colonel Bishop added his thoughts on that. "Well, sir, you can do that going in, but it might be difficult once that team jumps out of the Talon. The only way we can pick them up is by helicopter. Like I said earlier, I'll be able to work out the details of that once I find out where they want to be picked up. Right now I'm planning to use two MH-60 helicopters out of the flight platoon of the 1st Battalion, 1st Special Forces Group on Okinawa. They've been alerted and are forward deploying up to Misawa Air Force Base in northern

Japan later today. The MH-60s are specially modified UH-60 Blackhawks. Those aircraft can be traced back to the United States if they go down intact, although the Chinese do have some regular UH-60s that Sikorsky sold them last year under a military aid contract."

Olson was getting into the play of things. "Couldn't we, for the sake of this problem, pretend we're using civilian helicopters, which couldn't be traced back?"

Sanders frowned at that suggestion, but before he had a chance to reply, Bishop shot down that idea. "No, sir. Not if we're going to be realistic. The exfiltration has got to be flown at night for security reasons, and it's going to be a long flight. You need a lot of special equipment to be able to do that. Forward-looking infrared radar, night-vision devices, and so on. With the rush we're in now, we wouldn't have the time to modify a civilian bird and get it over there. Also, the pilots are trained on that type of aircraft and we wouldn't be able to get them qualified on a civilian aircraft in time."

Sanders thought it was time to clear the air. General Olson was running into the same problem almost all the other commanders hit during the initial stage of a Strams exercise—the inability to separate what was real from what wasn't real on the other end, the tendency to want to play it as an exercise rather than as the real thing. "Sir, you need to treat everything involved in this mission as the real thing. Right now everything *is* the real thing. There is actually an FOB at Osan with a team in isolation. There is actually a Combat Talon sitting in that hangar. As far as those people are concerned, this is a real mission. You can't try to pretend or use something that doesn't exist."

Sanders pointed at the map and message screen. "You're receiving traffic from both the Command Authority and the FOB. You need to treat both as real. Everything between here and the FOB is hard copy in message format just as it would be if this were real."

Olson frowned. The whole thing was confusing. "Well, what about the other direction? I've got some questions for the Command Authority that I need answered. How do I go about that?"

Sanders pointed at the commo gear. "Like you would if this were real. Send a message like you were inbriefed to."

Olson gestured for Colonel Moore. He outlined the message he wanted sent. "I'm kind of unclear on the operational chain of this thing. I know from the oplan that the chairman gives the final go the night the plane takes off to send in the team, but what about after that? Does he want to give a final go to the team on the ground just prior to the target window? Does he want me to make all further decisions, especially concerning aborting, or does he want me to bounce them up to him?"

Moore took a few minutes to put the questions into the format and then fed it into the terminal. A few minutes later the message board lit up and the printer chattered out a hard copy of the reply.

There was a pause as everyone read the message. Sanders looked to the back of the room where Meng was seated. This was Olson's first taste of what the computer could do.

PORTER HERE/
I WANT TO GIVE THE FINAL GO THROUGH YOU/ BOTH WEDNESDAY AND JUST BEFORE ACTUAL DESTRUCTION ON THE GROUND/ YOU MAKE THE REST OF THE DECISIONS PETE/ REMEMBER THAT IF IT CONCERNS A POSSIBLE COMPROMISE TO ABORT/ I WANT TO KNOW AS SOON AS POSSIBLE IF SOMETHING GOES WRONG/
END/

Olson stared at the board in amazement. The machine's use of his first name had been as startling as the message itself. It was as if the chairman had actually written the message. The whole thing was much more realistic to him now. He turned to Sanders. "That was the computer answering me, pretending to be General Porter?"

For the first time, Doctor Meng spoke up from the back of the room. "No, General. As far as you are concerned, that *was* the chairman of the Joint Chiefs of Staff himself answering you. If you remember that, it will make this week much easier for all of us."

FOB, Osan Air Force Base, Korea
Saturday, 3 June, 0102 Zulu
Saturday, 3 June, 10:02 A.M. Local

It took Riley and the engineers less than two hours to come up with the actual point of attack on the pipeline. Using 1:64,000 scale maps of the pipeline area, and satellite imagery sent from Fort Meade, Riley had sat down with Hoffman and Smith and quickly traced the pipeline, looking over the whole length for possible target locations.

It didn't take them long to come up with the most promising target. They'd been instructed to put the pipeline out of operation for a minimum of a week; therefore, blowing a section would be insufficient. According to the intelligence, the Chinese maintained an adequate repair capability. Taking down a hundred-foot section would only put the pipe out of operation for forty-eight hours. Riley knew that something more vital to the pipe's operation had to be attacked. He asked Hoffman and Smith to search for a node critical to the operation of the pipe.

They had briefly considered destroying a pump station, but Riley had discarded that idea. Pump stations were staggered along the entire length to help maintain and regulate the flow of oil. Although pump stations were critical to the successful functioning of the pipe, intelligence indicated that they were also manned by a platoon-sized reaction force. The last thing Team 3 wanted to do, in Riley's opinion, was get into a battle. They wanted to do their job and get out without making any contact.

It was Hoffman who found the answer. The pipe crossed the Sungari River, more than nine hundred kilometers from the pipe's terminus on the Yellow Sea at the port of Qinhuangdao. The imagery blowup disclosed that the pipe was suspended by cables from pylons anchored on either shore. There were six cables, each two and a half inches in diameter. Cutting them would be a relatively simple operation for the team. Severing all six cables simultaneously would release the support for the suspended section of pipe, which, weighed down by the oil inside, would crash into the river. To repair the crossing would require extensive engineering work, including bringing a barge upriver. Hoffman conservatively estimated a down time of three weeks. That definitely met the requirements for the mission.

The tricky part, Riley mused as he looked at the satellite blowup of the river crossing, was getting into the compound that enclosed the pylon. Whoever had designed security for the pipe had also known that this river crossing was a critical point that needed extra attention. The pylons on either shore were surrounded by a fence topped with barbwire. The fence enclosed a rectangular area approximately 150 meters by 250 meters.

Hoffman, using a stereoscope on the satellite imagery, was able to make out other unwelcome features. He discovered at least three remotely controlled cameras deployed in the compound. Riley assumed that the cameras were monitored at the nearest pump station, which was pump station 5, only fourteen kilometers to the northwest. According to their intelligence, the remote-control cameras were probably part of the Scoot system sale a British firm had negotiated with the Chinese government a few years previously. The cameras were supposed to have been used in Beijing for traffic control. Apparently the government had decided to use them for other, more important, functions, one of which was guarding this pipeline.

Hoffman could also make out what appeared to be an inner fence consisting of three strands of wire, spaced barely four inches inside the main fence. Cross-referencing with other similar security setups, he deduced that this inner fence was an alarm system, called a T field. The T-field fence was sensitive to any cutting or tampering with the outer fence, including someone trying to climb it. They were beginning to appreciate the importance of this pipeline to the Chinese based solely on the security dedicated to it.

Keeping that in mind, Riley warned Hoffman and Smith to assume also that the inside of the compound was mined. To reach the berm anchoring the cables, they would have to be prepared to breach a mine field. Once the team got on the ground and put surveillance on the target, they could probably verify if it was mined or not, but Riley intended to worst-case the scenario. It was better to have the equipment and not have to use it, than to not be prepared. Additionally, Riley felt that they had to figure there were regular army patrols along the service road of the pipeline and possibly even over-flights by helicopters. It was a military axiom that an obstacle was not an obstacle unless checked and observed at least part of the time.

Riley was impressed with the quality of the satellite imagery they were getting from the NSA. It was top of the line, a vast improvement over what they normally received for training exercises through the Department of Defense. The NSA imagery looked as though the pictures had been taken with a zoom lens from an aircraft at three hundred feet. On a plywood board in the isolation area, Hoffman and Smith put together a 1:25 scale satellite imagery mosaic of the compound.

Stretching his shoulders, Riley took a break from working on the target. He knew that Mitchell was checking on the progress of the other team members, but he wanted to make sure that everything was going all right. As Riley moved about the isolation area, Hooker brought in another batch of messages with information from the FOB.

In his whole career Riley had never seen anything like this setup. Despite its efficiency, it made him a little nervous. Someone had gone to a lot of trouble to prepare all this data, and Riley doubted very much that this whole operation was being conducted just to test the reaction of one Special Forces team. He wondered if they were the only mission being mounted or if other forces were in action aimed against China.

Riley watched as Hooker dumped the messages into the in box that Comsky lorded over. The junior medic went through the papers, dutifully logging in each entry, then breaking them down into piles for the various team members who needed to see them. Since the initial mission tasking, the team had been overloaded with information. The hardest part of this phase of isolation was separating what was relevant and what wasn't: making intelligence out of information.

Olinski and Reese were working on the enemy situation in

the vicinity of the target, poring through classified documents from the Central Intelligence Agency (CIA), Defense Intelligence Agency (DIA), and National Security Agency (NSA) to determine the potential enemy threat.

One of the hardest jobs fell to Trapp. With Paul Lalli, the junior communications sergeant, and Chong, Trapp had begun the task of devising an escape and evasion (E & E) plan. One of the tenets of Special Forces planning was to always have a "go-to-shit" plan, in case the planned exfiltration became unfeasible or something else went wrong. Riley felt comfortable knowing that Trapp was working the E & E plan; whatever the warrant officer came up with would be the best possible strategy.

The senior communications sergeant, Walt O'Shaugnesy, was working with the communications man from the FOB staff to coordinate the satellite communications that the team would use as their electronic lifeline back to the forward operating base. O'Shaugnesy and the FOB man were checking times, message formats, codes to be used, and equipment. Riley watched the two for a few minutes as they worked.

O'Shaugnesy looked as Irish as his name. He had short, sandy hair and a ruddy complexion. He was slightly overweight and Riley was always after him to lose his spare tire and cut back on his off-duty drinking. The bottom line for Riley was whether someone could operate in the field, and O'Shaugnesy could. As long as O'Shaugnesy could perform out in the woods, Riley tolerated the weight and the drinking. But it had been made clear to O'Shaugnesy that if he ever showed up drunk for duty, Riley would have his ass. So far there had never been a problem.

The junior communications sergeant, Paul Lalli, was O'Shaugnesy's drinking buddy, but he was the physical opposite. Lalli was thin and had always pushed Captain Mitchell hard during the team's weekly ten-kilometer physical training runs. Lalli maintained the radios and other communications gear with a jealous passion that Riley liked. Lalli considered the team radios "his gear" and allowed only O'Shaugnesy to "borrow" them. The team normally used the PRC70 radio, which worked in both the FM and high-frequency (HF) ranges. For this mission, though, they would use the PSC3 radio, a satellite communications radio. This arrangement suited Riley, because satellite communications were more secure and reliable than high frequency. Unfortunately for the commo men, the PSC3 was no lighter than the PRC70. The bulky, twenty-three-pound radio added noticeable weight to the commo men's rucks.

Riley wandered over to where Pete Devito, the senior medic, was poring over an area study of China. This was Devito's first step in producing a medical profile of the mission and target area to ensure that each man carried the proper medical equipment for the dangers most likely to be faced. With all the other gear that needed to be carried, Devito and Comsky could not take the entire contents of their M-3 medical kits. Based on his best guess of the potential injuries and wounds, Devito would begin paring down the kits to a manageable size, bringing only the medical supplies and equipment he judged to be most critical.

Completing his circuit, Riley ended up at the table where Mitchell was comparing the maps with the satellite imagery, searching for a drop zone for the infiltration. "Got anything good yet?"

"I think so. Since we're pushed for time we're going to have to go in as close as possible. Plus we want to move around as little as possible for better security." Mitchell stabbed a finger down on the map. "What do you think?"

Riley looked at the indicated point. He started to nod his head slowly as the significance of the drop zone Mitchell had picked sank in. "I like it. Great idea." Mitchell's finger rested on a small patch of blue on the otherwise predominantly green map sheet. The blue represented a small lake, about three kilometers from the target site.

The more Riley thought about the team leader's choice, the more he liked it. There were many advantages to jumping into a water rather than a land drop zone. The first one that came to Riley's mind was ease of finding the drop zone. He knew that for the infil they'd be jumping "blind" from the Combat Talon. A blind jump entailed no spotting by a jumpmaster because there would be no ground marking from a reception party; instead, they would rely on air force navigation to release them over the right spot. The navigator of the

Talon had met with them earlier this morning, and had told them he could give them only a 90 percent probability of getting the team within two kilometers of a proposed land drop zone.

Using a large body of water greatly increased the chances of hitting the right location for two reasons: First, the MC-130 Talon navigated by reflected radar images. The smooth, flat surface of the lake would give an excellent radar image to the Talon's navigator, allowing him to zero in on it, as opposed to a land drop zone, which would give off the same image as the surrounding terrain. Second, Riley, as jumpmaster, would now be able to do some spotting from the aircraft; the team wouldn't jump unless he was positive that the plane was over the lake. From bitter experience, Riley knew that there were few things worse than landing not knowing where you were.

Riley thought about another aspect: The water drop zone would be more secure. There was much less chance of running into unfriendlies on a lake late at night than in an open field. Open fields usually had houses next to them. Riley looked over the operational area (OA) on the map. There didn't appear to be any open fields suitable for a drop zone within five kilometers of the target anyway. A second aspect of security was that the parachutes could be hidden by simply sinking them in the lake, precluding a repeat of the great digging exercise they had just conducted.

Riley felt very comfortable with Mitchell's choice. "What about exfil? Had any time to look at that?"

Mitchell scratched his jaw. "Well, Dave, that's another story. There are several places we can use for PZs. That's not a problem. What worries me, though, is that the warning order said we were going to have two MH-60s take us out. Now, I may not be the brightest guy in the world, but I do know a little about the Blackhawk. Jean is rated on that aircraft and I know from her that it doesn't have the range, even with external tanks, to make it from here to the target area and back. Not even close. I'm curious how they think they're going to do this, and who's flying the mission. Especially considering our track record in training with helicopter exfils."

"I couldn't agree more. I'd like to meet the pilots before we go. Makes it a little more personal for them if they see who their passengers are beforehand. And it will make me feel better to look into their eyeballs."

Mitchell smiled. "Yeah. I understand. Some of those fly-boys are too high up in the clouds and need to come down to earth. I'll hit the colonel up and see if I can't get us a meet with someone who can talk to us about exfil. Hopefully we'll get an answer on that today, along with the request for more time."

Fort Meade, Maryland
Saturday, 3 June, 0900 Zulu
Saturday, 3 June, 4:00 A.M. Local

Lieutenant Colonel Bishop was the duty officer on the night shift for the US-SOCOM SFOB exercise staff. He read the message from the FOB requesting an additional twenty-four hours in isolation and another twenty-four on the ground to surveil the target. He considered waking the general, who was sleeping in the billet area in Tunnel 1, to get his opinion, then decided against it.

Bishop looked at the calendar on his desk. If he OK'd this request, the whole exercise would last forty-eight hours longer than it was presently scheduled for. Bishop had no desire to be away from home an extra two days for the sake of a game. Then, he reasoned, Olson would have to relay the request and the "computer chief of staff" would probably disapprove it anyway. Bishop sat down at the keyboard and typed out a denial.

FOB, Osan Air Force Base, Korea
Saturday, 3 June, 0932 Zulu
Saturday, 3 June, 6:32 P.M. Local

Riley and Mitchell were both unhappy with the short amount of time the team would have on the ground prior to the target hit. Twenty-four hours of surveillance was not sufficient to establish a valid pattern of guard patrols and other security measures. Despite that, Riley had expected the denial from SFOB. This whole operation was so tightly organized that he had doubted there would be any latitude built in.

Something even more important was bothering him. He grabbed Mitchell and took him out into the corridor, where they couldn't be overheard.

"What's the matter, Dave? Worried about the time line?"

Riley shook his head. "Not really. It's tight, but we can do it. What's bugging me is whether this is real or not. The whole thing is kind of crazy, don't you think?"

Mitchell obviously felt the same way. "Yeah, it is strange. I've got a lot of questions about this whole setup. My primary concern, if this isn't just an exercise, is why the hell we're doing this. I mean, what's the purpose? As far as I know we aren't at war with China and they haven't done anything against the United States to warrant such an action by us."

Mitchell had keyed in on just what had been bugging Riley. The whole operation had the ring of an exercise about it. But it had a disturbing hint of reality too. The intelligence and imagery were top-notch, much better than what they normally received for training missions. The presence of the MC-130 aircraft in the hangar on the base said that it was very likely they were going to go somewhere at the end of isolation. From their meeting earlier in the day with the Talon crew, Riley and Mitchell knew that the aircrew was really planning an infiltration into China.

The air force navigator and the pilot, Lieutenant Colonel Riggins, had been happy with the choice of drop zone when Mitchell pointed it out to them. It would be easier than land for them to find. The crew of the Talon had not been told the reason the team was jumping into China; they just knew they had to get the team there. In another part of the building, in their isolation area, the aircrew was working just as hard as Team 3, plotting possible routes and examining the potential air defense threats along the way.

Riggins had told them that the Talon would fly to the target following the terrain at 250 feet above ground level and at 250 knots. (Riley had been on that type of gut-wrenching flight before, and he planned on not having anything in his stomach prior to takeoff.) One minute out from the drop zone, the plane would slow down to a safe jump speed of 125 knots and the ramp would be opened. Thirty seconds from the drop zone the plane would climb to 500 feet, which was the minimum safe jump altitude. The pilot had insisted that this was his maximum altitude, based on the radar threat in the area. At 500 feet, Riley knew that they would not even bother wearing reserve parachutes. If the main didn't deploy, the jumper wouldn't have time to pull his reserve anyway. Immediately after the last jumper was out, the plane would close the ramp, go back down to 250 feet, and head for home.

Mitchell voiced a new concern. "What about the weapons and other gear? That worries me."

They both knew that Sergeant Major Hooker had gone up to Yongsan to draw sterile equipment from the detachment's war stockage. The authorization had come direct from the SFOB. Hooker was also drawing live ammunition and explosives. They had never seen that done before.

Riley took a deep breath to clear himself of all these worries. "I don't know if this thing is real or not, Mitch. Most likely it's just an exercise, but we need to make sure everyone treats it like it's real."

Mitchell nodded his agreement to that philosophy. "Let's stay on top of everyone and make sure they do their best."

They both looked up as Hossey came down the hallway. "What are you two plotting?"

Riley held up his hands. "Nothing, sir. Just needed to clear our heads."

Hossey held out a sheet of paper. "You'll get a briefing on the helicopters, but it won't be from the pilots. They're over in Japan right now, and the powers-that-be have decided not to fly the pilots over here for security reasons. Some staff officer from the helicopter unit flying will be here at 1000 tomorrow morning."

Mitchell nodded. "Sounds good, sir."

Riley said nothing. What were the helicopters doing in Japan? As far as he knew, the target was northwest of where they were and Japan was east. Hopefully they'd find out tomorrow.

Fort Meade, Maryland
Saturday, 3 June, 1254 Zulu
Saturday, 3 June, 7:54 A.M. Local

Meng scrolled the message traffic on his screen in Tunnel 1 and perused it while he sipped his first cup of tea for the day. When he came across it, he printed out a copy of the concept of the operation, which had come in from the FOB only an hour ago. With that in hand, he could start the final programming for the exercise. It was simply a matter of filling in the blanks. He would take the team's plan and flowchart it against the various possibilities that could occur. The computer would rate the paths in terms of probability. Meng knew that he couldn't cover everything, but the success of the Strams program rested on its ability to present a statistically significant percentage of possibilities in a realistic manner.

Just prior to the team's departure for infiltration, Meng would control the exercise by cutting the real commo link with the FOB and substituting a simulated FOB link to the computer. The computer would then play out the team and FOB conducting the mission. When Meng switched from real to computer link, the people in Korea would have completed the exercise. Right now, Meng planned on notifying the FOB of mission completion just before the aircraft took off for infiltration. That would allow him to pick up any last-minute changes that the team or aircrew might make. The purpose of the exercise was to test the command structure at Fort Meade, not the team or aircraft in the field.

Meng took the concept with him and went back to his office in time to catch the 8:00 A.M. news. The exercise was forgotten as the TV screen caught his attention. A reporter was standing on the edge of a massive crowd near Tiananmen Square. Night had descended in China, but the Goddess of Democracy was well lit in the background.

"Early this morning, crowds estimated to be in the tens of thousands surged onto the streets of Beijing and turned back an army column attempting to reach the center of the city. Approximately two thousand troops attempted to pass along Changan Avenue, a main east-west street in Beijing, in a show of popular support. Workers joined the students in preventing passage of the soldiers.

"The incident that precipitated the troop movement occurred last night when a police van struck four bicyclists, killing two and seriously injuring the other two. Rumor has it that this was a deliberate act. When the troops attempted to pass, the largest crowd we have seen here in more than a week took to the streets. There have been reports of tear gas being fired near the Communist party headquarters, but I have seen no signs of violence here at Tiananmen Square. The rumors are that the troops were coming to seize the square back from the students."

The anchorman in Atlanta cut in.

"Jim, did you actually see the troops?"

"Yes. They were dressed in white undershirts with khaki uniform pants, and were unarmed. They didn't seem comfortable with what they were doing. When confronted by the students and workers they appeared disoriented. I saw soldiers simply sit down on the curb along the road and talk with the students, who exhorted them not to use violence since they were from the People's Army and the students were the voice of the people."

"Jim, what effect do you think this latest turn of events will have on the government?"

"That's uncertain at this time. There is the possibility it might help the more conciliatory attempts of Mister Zhao by discrediting Prime Minister Li Peng's hard-line approach to the student protest. It appears from today's actions that the army is unwilling to follow a hard-line approach."

The scene shifted back to Atlanta. "That was Jim Thomas in Beijing. On another front the Soviet Congress accused Andrei Sakharov of slandering his homeland and . . ."

Meng turned off the set. He knew quite a bit about the Chinese Army from his research for the Dragon Sims and from his personal experience. The fact that soldiers had seemed sympathetic to the students made him feel hopeful, but Meng also knew that the leaders of the army probably didn't share this sentiment.

There was a traditional Chinese saying that if the people

want the leaders to notice, then they must do something difficult. Obviously, Meng thought, the students' hunger strike had not been difficult enough.

Meng sighed and looked at the clocks on his wall that designated the time zones for various major cities in the world. It was 9 o'clock at night in Beijing. There would be no more news until tomorrow.

The picture of the woman and child drew his attention. She was dead now. He'd received word of that four years ago. The boy was now a young man—a student at the University of Beijing. In his heart Meng hoped his son was one of the protesters gathered in the square, but that same hope was overshadowed by fear. Meng closed his eyes briefly, forcing his mind to shift from the square, thousands of miles away, back to reality here, or rather this simulation of a reality that would probably never be used. He turned back to his work desks.

As Meng started working on the concept of operations, the first thing that caught his eye was the water drop zone. Meng smiled thinly—a major sign of emotion for him. The Special Forces men were very clever. He estimated that that choice dramatically increased their odds of surviving the infiltration. His initial program had indicated a 26 percent chance that the team would be compromised on infiltration, either by the aircraft being discovered or the team being caught on the drop zone. Off the top of his head, Meng figured that that was now down to probably no more than 15 percent. This whole mission was looking more feasible.

FOB, Osan Air Force Base, Korea
Saturday, 3 June, 1320 Zulu
Saturday, 3 June, 10:20 P.M. Local
Mitchell decided it was time for everyone to get some sleep. They'd been working nonstop all day, and sleep was important if they were going to continue to function at a high level of proficiency. He went to the podium in the front of the isolation workroom and got everyone's attention.

"Listen up. Everybody grab a chair." He waited until the team had settled in, facing him. "I want to do a little summarizing of what we got done today, and then I want everyone to rack out. Tomorrow's another day. You all have done a good job so far."

He turned to Riley. "Anything new on the tactical plan?"

Riley shook his head. "Not much has changed since we had the last team brief on the concept of operations three hours ago. We're still working on breaching the compound and taking out the security systems. Infil is as you briefed it earlier. Tomorrow I should be able to tell you how we're actually going to hit the target."

Mitchell nodded. He indicated another team member. "Pete, anything you need to tell us from your medical survey?"

Devito, the senior medic, stood up. "I've ordered the medical supplies that each man will carry. I also want everyone to leave their vest survival kits with me prior to going to bed and I'll make sure they're up to date." Devito sat down.

Mitchell moved on. "O'Shaugnesy, how's the commo going?"

"Good, sir. I've got our one-time pads and I've coordinated with the FOB on send and receive times."

Mitchell pointed at the two radios resting on the commo man's work desk. "I want you to give everyone a class tomorrow on the PSC3. I know that most of us have seen it before, but I for one could use a refresher on how to set it up and use it."

O'Shaugnesy nodded. "OK, sir. They're real easy to work. I won't need more than forty-five minutes to run you all through."

Mitchell penciled in the class on the team's isolation schedule, posted on the wall behind him. "All right. We'll do it at 1300 tomorrow." He moved on to the next specialty, which for this mission was the most important. "Dan, have you got your charges all calculated?"

Hoffman stood up. "Yes, sir. At least the ones for the actual target—you know, blowing the wires. We're still working on some other ones we might need to breach the fence and the mine field."

"I want you to be able to give a class to everyone, late tomorrow afternoon, on how to prime and emplace those charges. Will you be able to do it by then?"

"Yes, sir. No problem."

Mitchell addressed the rest of the room. "I want everyone to be able to use the radio and rig the charges. If just one of us makes it to the target, I want that person to be able to blow it." He glanced around the room. He hated holding long meetings and he could tell that everyone was tired. "That's all I've got for tonight, unless someone has a question or something they want to add."

Riley scratched his head. "One thing I would like to know is why we're hitting this pipeline. How important is it? Maybe that will give us an idea of why we're planning to do this."

Mitchell knew a little about the pipeline's significance from his initial work as the S-3 on the Typhoon oplan, but he wanted to let someone with more knowledge answer. "Dan, you've been working on this pipeline all day. What can you tell us about it?"

Hoffman pushed his thick glasses farther up on his nose and pulled a piece of yellow scratch-pad paper from the cargo pocket of his fatigue pants. "Well, sir, I think that someone did a damn good job in picking this pipeline as a strategic target, both for economic and psychological reasons. If you wanted to pick a target out of all of China to hurt them in both those areas, I really doubt that you could come up with a better one than this. Other than maybe the locks and dams that help control the Yellow River, but that's a target that fifty A teams couldn't hit.

"The Daqing-Fushun pipeline carries oil from the Daqing oil field to the port of, hell I can't pronounce it." Hoffman struggled with the name until Chong interrupted. "Spell it please."

"Q-i-n-h-u-a-n-g-d-a-o."

Chong pronounced it correctly for Hoffman, who continued. "Anyway, it runs from Daqing to the port Chong just named. That section alone is 1,150 kilometers long and was operational in 1974. In '75, they extended that pipe to run all the way to Beijing. Another portion coming out of the same trunk line branches off to North Korea."

Riley interrupted. "How much of that will be affected if we take it down at the point we plan on hitting?"

Hoffman walked over to the map. "We're taking down the main line prior to any branching. That means that the lines to Beijing and to North Korea will both go dry along with the one to the port." He ran his finger up the pipeline to its starting point.

"The Daqing oil field accounts for anywhere from one third to one half of all oil production in China. We're talking about at least an approximately million-barrel-a-day operation. That oil is not only critical to China's own industry, but they also export some of it. As best as I can make out from the data, one percent of Japan's oil imports comes from China, almost all of that out of the Daqing field."

"Wait a second," Mitchell halted Hoffman. "What effect will that have on Japan if we dry that up for a couple of weeks?"

"I don't know, sir. Hard to estimate. It's only one percent, but when you're talking the magnitude of the amount of oil Japan imports, that's quite a bit. I imagine they would be able to make up the loss by increasing their Middle East imports or their imports from other Asian sources. What I do know is that this will be a bad kick in the ass for the Chinese economy. Not only will they lose almost half their oil for the duration of the down time of the pipeline, but they'll lose valuable foreign currency that they need desperately."

Chief Trapp had obviously been doing his homework in the intelligence field, and he tried to put it into a clearer perspective. "They think so much of this oil field and pipe that they don't even put it on their maps. In other words, if we take this thing down, the leaders in China are going to sit up and notice."

Hoffman nodded his agreement. "This is a rough analogy, but it's almost as if some terrorist group attacked the Alaskan pipeline. It pumps more oil than the Daqing pipeline but contributes a much smaller percentage to our economy. Also, the U.S. economy is in a hell of a lot better shape than the Chinese economy. If we do this, it will hurt them bad where it counts—in the pocketbook."

Hoffman shifted from the economic aspect. "As important as the economic impact is, there is also a psychological one. The Daqing oil field was used extensively throughout the six-

ties and seventies as a model for the rest of the country."
Hoffman grabbed one of the books he had been using for research. "Let me read you something to give you an idea of
what I mean."

He flipped open to a marked spot. " 'Throughout the
twenty years since liberation, and particularly during the
Great Proletarian Cultural Revolution, the Chinese oil workers have displayed the revolutionary spirit of hard struggle,'
blah, blah, blah." He went down a few lines. " 'The workers
of the Daqing Oilfield, which is the model for developing the
oil industry by self-reliance and arduous struggle, have continued to display the revolutionary spirit they showed during
the battle to open up the oilfield. They have striven to catch
up with and surpass advanced world standards,' blah, blah,
blah. Oh yeah. Here's the good part. 'Using the invincible
Mao Tse-tung Thought as their weapon, they sharply criti-
cized,' that refers to the workers," Hoffman threw in, " 'the
poisonous influence of the counter-revolutionary revisionist
line, as* . . .' well, that's enough." Hoffman threw the book
on the table. "Get the picture? This isn't just a pipeline. It's
a symbol."

Mitchell looked over at Riley. He had a feeling that the
team sergeant was thinking the same thing he was: If this target is that significant, maybe this is for real.

Fort Meade, Maryland
Saturday, 3 June, 1330 Zulu
Saturday, 3 June, 8:30 A.M. Local
Colonel Bishop had been laboring over his charts ever since
the initial concept of operations arrived. He was trying to figure out a way to get the exfil helicopters to the pickup zone
that the team had designated and back out again. His main
problem was fuel. The closest land base from which he could
launch the aircraft was in either Korea or Japan. Right now
he was thinking of using Misawa Air Force Base in Japan.
For security reasons they were keeping the helicopters separate from the base where the team and infiltration aircraft

*From *The Petroleum Industry of The People's Republic of China*,
H. C. Ling, Hoover Institution Press, Stanford University, 1975, pp. 166–168.

were stationed. Misawa was the same distance as Osan, using the route from the Sea of Japan over either North Korea or Russia. Bishop had early on ruled out the route to the west of North Korea, shooting north up to the target. The Chinese air defense capabilities were much greater in that corridor. From Misawa, a straight shot to the PZ was 1,230 nautical miles one way. Even with the external tanks, the helicopters would still have only a total range of 1,090 nautical miles. Not even enough to make it one way.

Bishop was beginning to think that someone in his office had made a mistake in planning to use the Blackhawks. He usually assigned one of his young captains to work the supporting air annex to the contingency oplans. He couldn't believe that the captain had overlooked the range factor—the idiot should have realized that the Blackhawks couldn't reach any part of the pipeline and make it back with one load of gas.

Bishop considered the hand that his staff officer had dealt him. He thought about trying to get an air force HH-53 Pave Low out to Japan. The Pave Low had an inflight refuel capability, which would solve the fuel problem. Unfortunately, the Pave Lows were all stationed at Hurlburt Field in Florida, and he knew that it would cause quite a ruckus to get one loaded onto a C-5 transport and flown all the way to Japan. Besides, they'd already ordered the Blackhawks moved during the initial alert this morning.

Bishop scratched his head. There had to be a way out of this mess.

5

> "By moral influence I mean that which causes the people to be in harmony with their leaders, so that they will accompany them in life and unto death without fear of moral peril."
>
> Sun Tzu: *The Art of War*

Fort Meade, Maryland
Saturday, 3 June, 2030 Zulu
Saturday, 3 June, 3:30 P.M. Local

At the first report of trouble in Tiananmen Square, Meng had left word not to be disturbed and locked the door to his office. Now he sat mesmerized as the disjointed pictures from the few Western camera crews that had braved the events of the previous night in China's capital rolled across the screen. The anchorman was making the most he could of the little information he had.

"Thousands of Chinese Army troops supported by armored vehicles stormed Tiananmen Square early this morning Beijing time. Initial reports indicate that dozens were killed and hundreds wounded as troops opened fire with automatic weapons.

"Exact reports on the number killed are sketchy. The Associated Press reported that the state-run radio put the death toll in the thousands and denounced the crackdown. Shortly after that, the station changed announcers and began broadcasting reports supporting the Communist government. Our man in Beijing, Jim Thomas, is presently on the telephone. Hello, Jim. Can you hear me?"

"I can barely make you out, Tom."

"What can you tell us regarding the number of people killed in this crackdown?"

" 'Crackdown' is a mild word for it, Tom. I think massacre would be more appropriate. It's difficult to get even a good estimate because there is still firing going on in the square and along Changan Avenue, where most of the killing has taken place. Soldiers are firing at anything that moves, so naturally most of us are reluctant to move out and about. I have been on the phone to local hospitals and they give me reports of at least sixty-eight corpses being received. Students I've talked with who were present in Tiananmen Square when the shooting began claim that at least five hundred were killed.

"The official news program now claims that more than one thousand police officers and troops have been injured and some killed. The report also says that an undisclosed number of civilians were killed but did not give any more detail. This was after an initial report of thousands killed."

"Can you tell us how all this began?"

"Well, it's difficult to say, Tom. It probably started yesterday afternoon about 2:15 local time when protesters overturned and set fire to several army vehicles that were attempting to move along Changan Avenue toward Tiananmen Square from the west. Troops retaliated by firing tear gas and beating protesters. Then, around 4:00 in the afternoon, a group of protesters threw stones at the Great Hall of the People. This may or may not have driven those in power to try to move more troops in. At about 6:00 another convoy was stopped trying to come into the square from the east. For the next six hours it was unclear what was happening, but it was obvious that the military was preparing for some sort of large-scale move. At midnight, there were the first reports of shots being fired. Then, at 12:30 this morning, troops entered the square from all directions. These troops were not the same ones who had tried on Saturday to enter the square. These were troops from the provinces who the government apparently felt would not hesitate to follow orders—and, as events have turned out, rightly so. Another change was that these soldiers came in armed with AK-47 assault rifles loaded with live ammunition. Once the firing began, the situation turned to chaos. I can still hear shots being fired as we speak."

"Thank you, Jim. We'll be keeping in touch with Jim

Thomas to give you the latest information as the situation sorts itself out over there.

"The initial reaction from the United States government has been one of caution. President Bush made a brief statement from his retreat in Maine, where he is spending the weekend."

The scene shifted to President Bush at his house in Kennebunkport.

"I deeply deplore the decision to use force against peaceful demonstrators and the consequent loss of life. We have been urging and continue to urge nonviolence, restraint, and dialogue. Tragically, another course has been chosen. Again, I urge a return to nonviolent means for dealing with the current situation."

"That was the president—"

Meng turned off the volume on his set using the remote control. He was disgusted with Bush's comments. He didn't want to hear any more. He stared as the station replayed the few video clips they had. Meng stood up and talked to the TV. "What does 'nonviolent means' entail, Mister Bush? Against tanks and bullets? It is too late for that. The Old Men have spoken and they will not listen to your prattling."

He slumped back into his chair. Staring at the pictures of bloody bodies being carried from the square by other students, Meng felt rage burn through his veins. A flickering shot of a lifeless body being tossed onto the back of a hand-held cart caused Meng to leap out of his chair and run to the TV. The scene shifted to a view of tanks rolling across the square, but the slack face of the young man being put in the back of the cart was fused in Meng's mind. It was the face he had been looking for on every broadcast since this whole crisis began.

FOB, Osan Air Force Base, Korea
Saturday, 3 June, 2100 Zulu
Sunday, 4 June, 6:00 A.M. Local
Mitchell opened an eye as he felt someone tap him on the shoulder. "Hey, bud. Get up. The shit has hit the fan across the water in China."

He leaned up on an elbow and focused in on Riley. "What do you mean?"

"The government cracked down on those students in Tiananmen Square. There are reports of hundreds having been killed."

Mitchell processed that slowly. "Anything from Hossey or the SFOB on whether this changes the mission?"

Riley shook his head. "Not a peep. I'm having Lalli write up a message asking that question, plus a request for information on how much this has affected their army. I sure don't like the idea of going into a country in the middle of a rebellion if that's what this turns into."

Mitchell found his glasses and put them on. "It's a hell of a coincidence that we're planning this mission during all this."

Riley agreed. "I think we need to crank down another turn on the guys and make sure they really have their shit together for this mission. I still haven't seen anything on a training offset area. Maybe somebody in Washington knows something we don't about China."

Fort Meade, Maryland
Saturday, 3 June, 2400 Zulu
Saturday, 3 June, 7:00 P.M. Local

Meng sat in his usual position in the back of the room as General Olson and his staff held their meeting. With the rational part of his mind he listened in. They were trying to decide whether the events in Tiananmen Square would have any effect on this mission. Meng himself was not concerned. The operational area was far enough away from Beijing, or for that matter any other big city, that it would not make any difference. He did not plan on making any changes to his program. If anything, he would estimate that it improved the team's chances of infiltration because the Chinese military was sure to be in some degree of disarray. There was a good chance of troops being moved from the Shenyang Military Region, where the target was, down to Beijing, reducing the enemy threat for the mission. There was also less possibility of the Combat Talon being picked up on the way in, since the Chinese military would have its eyes focused inward.

Meng's first run-through using the team's proposed concept of operation had yielded a surprising 58 percent chance of success with no losses or discovery. Meng thought that number quite high, considering how deep the target area was in China and the difficulties in infiltration and exfiltration. That success percentage included destruction of the pipeline for the indicated period of seven days. Meng thought, on the whole, that the percentage of risk was quite acceptable for such a high-profit target.

Meng was somewhat surprised that his mind could still function on the task at hand while his emotions tore at him. His son was dead—the son he had never told the Americans about when he'd come to them in Hong Kong twenty-three years ago. If he had told the intelligence officer that he had family back in China, they would never have accepted him. He would have been sent back. This lie was the foundation upon which Meng's freedom and career had been built.

Even having the picture on his desk had been risky. He'd always been afraid that someone would ask who they were and he would have had to lie. It seemed such a trivial thing now that they were both dead. He would no longer have to lie.

FOB, Osan Air Force Base, Korea
Sunday, 4 June, 0003 Zulu
Sunday, 4 June, 9:03 A.M. Local

Riley was working on the tactical plan for the actual assault when Hossey entered the isolation area and signaled to both Mitchell and him.

"I've got the staff officer from the aviation unit that will be flying the exfil birds. He's in the operations center, and I don't want to bring him in here because he has no need to know your mission. He's got what he needs to answer your questions."

Hossey led the way to the op center, where an army captain wearing a flight suit and a green beret was waiting. Riley was immediately annoyed. The least the idiot could have done was to wear a nondistinctive uniform, Riley thought. Between the Talon being rolled into a hangar on post and this guy showing up, any North Korean spies—who were surely watching the air base—were probably curious about what was happening. Security and espionage were two very serious subjects between the two Koreas.

Hossey didn't bother with introductions. There was no need for the pilot to know who they were. Riley could see the velcro on the man's flight suit where he had removed his patches. Despite that, Riley had no doubt that the man was from the 1st Special Forces Group aviation detachment—the yellow flash on his beret signaled that. God save me from pilots who think they're hot stuff, Riley thought. Even though this pilot isn't Special Forces qualified, he gets to wear the Green Beret because he is assigned to a Special Forces group. A Green Beret aviator must be the ultimate in cool at the o club bar, Riley mused bitterly. Rambo and Top Gun combined. But this wasn't an o club bar, and it was obvious that the aviator didn't know the first thing about mission security.

"Afternoon, gentlemen. The colonel tells me you have some questions about the mission my men are supposed to fly for you."

Mitchell let Riley take the lead. "Sir, I don't have a warm fuzzy feeling about this exfiltration. Can you tell us who the pilots are going to be?"

"We're going to be using four of my own. Men with extensive flying experience. Both primary pilots have more than a thousand hours of blade time in the Blackhawk."

"Are we going to be able to meet with them for coordination prior to infiltration?" Riley asked.

"I'm afraid not. The aircraft are already in place at the forward launch site at Misawa Air Force Base in Japan. If you need to give them any information, I'll relay it. You've got the frequencies, call signs, and recognition signals. We've got your pickup zones, both primary and alternate. What more do you need?"

"Well," Mitchell intervened, "we haven't had much luck with helicopters. We'd just feel a little more comfortable if we could talk to the pilots."

"What's the problem? Maybe I can answer it for you."

Mitchell pointed at the chart in the man's hand. "The first question we have is that from Misawa to the target area and back is a little long for a UH-60 to be flying. I know you all have thought of that, but we'd like to know what the plan is."

The captain unrolled his chart and laid it on the table. The four of them gathered around it. "The operational range of the UH-60 is two hundred and sixty nautical miles on internal fuel. We're going to put four external tanks on the outside of the birds on pylons above the cargo bay. These will increase the range to a total of one thousand and ninety nautical miles. A straight shot from Misawa to your pickup zone is eight hundred and fifty-one nautical miles. As you've noted, the aircraft aren't going to be able to do the round-trip without refueling.

"Additionally, they're not going to be flying straight in and out. We've planned a low-level route over land, avoiding the known radar, that we figure will add around fifty to a hundred miles each way. To accommodate that, on the way in they'll refuel off the U.S. Navy frigate *Rathburne,* which will be located here at checkpoint 2, in international waters in the Sea of Japan. Topping off there will give them enough fuel to make the trip from the *Rathburne* to your pickup zone and back. On the return trip they'll refuel again on the *Rathburne* and fly you back here to Osan. We're also ready to fly on a twenty-four-hour weather delay if the primary exfil day doesn't go."

The captain rubbed his chin. "The only tricky part is going to be the weight. With four full external tanks, a Blackhawk can't lift any cargo. We figure that the aircraft will have burned enough weight in fuel by the time they get to your pickup zone to just be able to put six men with no equipment aboard each bird. Even then it's going to be real close to the weight limits."

Riley interrupted him. "What if only one bird makes it? Are you telling me I'm going to have to leave half my team behind?"

"That's the way it is, Sergeant. With that much fuel the helicopter can lift only so much weight. You could fit all twelve of your people on board with no problem, but the bird wouldn't lift. It's a trade-off we've had to make."

Captain Mitchell and Riley were not at all happy. Mitchell stood up. "What you're telling me is that there's no backup. How many aircraft do you have over at Misawa?"

"Just the two."

Captain Mitchell wasn't satisfied. He knew from his wife's stories that helicopters were terribly prone to being down for maintenance. "What if one breaks down? There's no latitude here for any problems."

"That's not my decision." The captain didn't seem too concerned. "We've got only the two anyway. There are no more." The aviator smiled at them. "What's the big deal? We haven't even gotten the offset mission yet. Maybe the training area will be closer and we won't have to put on so much fuel; then we'll be able to put all twelve of you on one bird."

Hossey jumped in with both feet before Riley or Mitchell could. "Captain, you have a problem, and that problem is your attitude. As far as I know this mission is real, and your men will be flying to that pickup zone in China. If you're thinking this is a game, you've got your head up your ass, and you'd better pull it out.".

The captain quickly realized he had made a mistake. "Yes, sir. I want to assure you that both birds are up now and I can damn near guarantee that they'll be up for this mission. They were test flown last night and both worked fine. We're not going to crank them again until it's time to go."

Mitchell wasn't buying it. "Why can't you get other army or air force helicopters to back you up?"

"Like I said, both birds will lift. Based on the enemy threat, we feel we can't get more than two birds into the airspace anyway. Putting more aircraft on the mission will just increase the chances of being detected."

Hossey decided to intervene. "All right. I'll contact the SFOB at Meade and ask for helicopter backup, but I doubt that we'll get it at this late notice." He turned to the aviator. "I hope you tell your men to take this seriously. Until we find out different, this whole mission is to be treated like the real thing."

"Yes, sir."

Mitchell and Riley were still not satisfied, but they knew they were hitting a stone wall. Maybe Hossey's request would get some action through the SFOB. Otherwise they'd have to go with what they had.

The news that a navy ship was now involved further increased the reality of the situation, Riley thought. The SFOB was sure pulling a lot of strings.

1:23 P.M. Local

Down the hall from the Special Forces isolation area, the aircrew was laboring over charts and wading through the intelligence they'd been fed by the SFOB.

Major Kent, the Talon's electronics warfare officer, was

concerned primarily with the electronic threat that the aircraft would face. In his opinion, from an aviation viewpoint, the target was in an extremely difficult location to reach. The routes in and out were fraught with numerous problems.

Kent had quickly ruled out going over the Korean demilitarized zone (DMZ) and flying the length of North Korea. The DMZ was one of the hottest spots in the world and was heavily guarded. Despite the Talon's capabilities, Kent knew that their odds were poor of making it over the DMZ without being detected.

That meant they had to make an end run either east or west. Both were about equidistant from Osan. Kent looked at a classified map that listed the various radar and air defense installations in the area. It was obvious that the western route, up over the Yellow Sea, was the more heavily guarded, both by the North Koreans along their west coast and by the Chinese.

Kent studied the eastern route over the Sea of Japan. It looked good except for one major problem—China didn't have a seacoast there. To go in, the Talon would have to cross a strip of land that belonged to either Russia or North Korea. Kent shook his head. Vladivostok was a major Russian port. Although Kent felt that they could avoid its ground air defense radar system, he was concerned about the possibility of Russian ships in the Sea of Japan.

Next he studied the North Korean radar array. Then he examined reports on the alert status of the North Korean and Russian air forces. His conclusion: The scale tilted toward the North Koreans being the greatest threat to alert and launch. Kent decided to make the primary route a shore crossing over Russia rather than North Korea.

Kent lifted his gaze from the maps and leaned back in his chair. Time to put it all on the overlays. He got up and headed over to the navigator to start working on their route options.

5:00 P.M. Local

Mitchell felt it had been a profitable day. The team had gotten a lot accomplished and was ready to try its first practice run of the briefback. He took his place in front of the team and quickly looked through his notes.

"All right. Listen up. Before we start this practice there are a couple of things I want you to remember about both the briefback and this mission. The primary thing is to treat the mission like it's real. For all we know, right now it is. Every plan you come up with, every little thing you say you're going to do, you damn well better be able to do it."

He swung his gaze to O'Shaugnesy. "If you say you're going to blow the radios in case of compromise, you'd better have requested thermite grenades from the engineers to do just that. Since the sergeant major is giving us the real shit for this mission, I'd also better see a thermite grenade with your radio's name on it among the gear you're packing."

Mitchell took in the entire room. "Saying something during a briefback that you don't really mean or couldn't really do is one of the worst mistakes any of us can make. So when you all listen to each other in this practice, I want you to sharpshoot. If I brief that I'm going to wear yellow underwear with purple stripes, someone better ask to see it."

"No thanks," Riley laughed. The team sergeant turned serious. "Let me add something to what the captain is saying. I know I beat you guys to death on this, but remember first and foremost we're a team. If a fellow team member gets up there in the real briefback before the colonel and says something stupid or answers a question wrong, I don't want to see anybody correcting or contradicting him. To take the captain's analogy a step further, if I brief that every member of the team is going to wear yellow underwear with purple stripes, I'd better see eleven heads sitting here nodding, saying, 'Yes, sir, that's what we're going to be wearing.'"

Riley looked around the room. "We're a team. We stick together no matter what."

6

"Therefore I say: Know the enemy and know yourself; in a hundred battles you will never be in peril."
Sun Tzu: *The Art of War*

FOB, Osan Air Force Base, Korea
Monday, 5 June, 1000 Zulu
Monday, 5 June, 7:00 P.M. Local

"Good evening, Colonel Hossey, Sergeant Major Hooker. I'm Captain Mitchell, commander of Team 3. This briefing is classified top secret. Team 3's mission is to infiltrate Operational Area Dustey, located in Manchuria in northeastern China, at 1600 Zulu time, 6 June 1989, and destroy target Dagger, between 1600Z and 1900Z on the eighth. The purpose of this mission is to stop the flow of oil through the Daqing-Fushun pipeline for a minimum of seven days. We will be exfiltrated at 2000 Zulu time, 8 June.

"First, I'd like to introduce the members of Team 3 and give you a brief operational overview. I'll be followed by the members of the detachment, each briefing their own specialized areas." Hossey and Hooker knew everyone on the team, but Mitchell wanted to follow the standard format for a briefback. It was good training.

For three hours after the introductions the team presented its plan and then defended it. Mitchell led off by giving an overview of the concept of operations. He was followed by Olinski, who briefed terrain, weather, and the enemy situation in excruciating detail. At the conclusion of his portion Olinski handed Colonel Hossey the team's E & E plan.

Hoffman then stood up to give his portion. "Sir, I'll be briefing our demolitions plan for destruction of the target. The actual tactical plan at the target will be covered after me by Sergeant First Class Riley. First I will cover the target analysis we did on the pipeline, so you can understand why we chose to destroy this portion, and then the actual actions at the target.

"The trunk line of the Daqing-Fushun pipeline is eleven hundred and fifty kilometers long and runs from . . ."

Mitchell tuned out the history lesson on the pipeline as he'd heard it several times before. The entire demolition plan had been formulated by Hoffman and his assistant, Corporal Smith. When they had briefed Mitchell and Riley on the plan, Mitchell had understood only about half of what they'd said. He'd turned to Riley, who had nodded his approval. That was good enough for Mitchell. But the captain had had the two engineers explain things again to the entire team, and in language everyone could understand. Then the team had rehearsed, as well as they could in the isolation area, the actual placement of charges, until every team member could do it.

Hoffman was on a roll. He pointed at a grid he had drawn on a sheet of butcher paper. "I analyzed the entire length of pipeline inside operational range of infiltration and exfiltration aircraft using the CARVE formula. This acronym stands for criticality, accessibility, recuperability, vulnerability, and effect. As a result of this analysis, we have chosen this portion, where the pipe crosses the Sungari River, as a critical node and our target. As you can see on this satellite imagery, the pipe is suspended above the river by means of cables running over these pylons on opposite shores—in effect a suspension bridge of pipe similar to the Golden Gate Bridge."

Mitchell always insisted that every briefback be given in the simplest terms possible. Everyone had to understand every part of the plan; in fact every member on the team had to be able to get up and give any portion of the briefback from memory. One person missing one critical part could spell disaster. They'd rehearsed for this briefback by randomly choosing people to give the different parts.

"Each pylon has six, 2.5-inch-diameter steel cables running over it. These cables are anchored here at these berms, if I can draw your attention to the mock-up over here. We will attack the northern compound. We will place two and a half pounds of C-4, configured in a diamond charge, on each cable approximately four feet from its anchor point on the berm. Blowing these cables simultaneously will release the support and drop the pipeline into the river. This will cause that section of pipe to be torn away and dragged downriver.

"For a bonus effect, we will punch a hole in this section of pipe inside the compound with a platter charge, which is basically a shaped charge that focuses a cone of intense heat approximately four feet away from it. We will have two thermite charges on small wood rafts near the hole. The purpose of this secondary explosion is to start a fire in the northern compound, which will delay discovery of exactly what happened."

Hoffman looked up and smiled. "The concept is to add to the general mayhem and confusion in the first hours after the attack. This should aid in our exfiltration. The hole will allow residual oil to flow out into the compound. There will still be fourteen kilometers of oil between the hole and pump station 5, even if the pump station ceases operating immediately. The rafts will float on top of the oil and burn, igniting the oil."

Hoffman wound up. "This target, which we have codenamed Dagger, fits the acceptable criteria of the CARVE formula. Dagger is critical to the successful function of the pipeline. There are only eight places on the entire length of the pipeline that are as critical. The others are either in a heavily populated area or too strongly defended. This target is accessible. Sergeant First Class Riley will describe how we will access the target.

"For the enemy to repair the damage will take an estimated minimum of three weeks. They will have to bring a barge, with crane, from Harbin, one hundred and fifty kilometers downriver, to repair it. Dagger is vulnerable to this detachment and the amount of explosives we can carry in. The effect on the local population will be minimal in the immediate vicinity. The effect on the Chinese economy is beyond the scope of this detachment to estimate. This concludes my portion of the briefback. I'll be followed by Sergeant First Class Riley."

"How long is all this going to take you, Sergeant Hoffman?" Hossey demanded, halting the engineer before he could regain his seat.

"Sir, we have given ourselves five minutes from start of action to completion of destruction."

Hossey shook his head. "That's not much time. You sure you won't take more than that?"

Hoffman gestured toward his team sergeant. "Sergeant Riley will give you the sequence of action and show you why we believe we can keep it under five minutes."

Riley stood in front of the maps and covered the tactical conduct of the mission from the moment the Talon's wheels would leave the ground at Osan, through the arrival of the exfiltration helicopters. He paid particular attention to the actions at the objective for Hossey's benefit.

Finished, Riley yielded his place as Devito got up and briefed the potential medical problems and how the team was prepared to deal with them. Riley knew they were as ready for medical problems as they could be. Every team member could run an IV and handle basic medical emergencies. The team medics were carrying a variety of medical equipment, including controlled drugs.

After Devito was done, O'Shaugnesy got up to explain the communications systems, both internal to the team, and the link back to the forward operating base. Riley tried to pay attention as Staff Sergeant O'Shaugnesy droned on in a monotone. "We will be using satellite communications back to the FOB. We will make our initial entry report, an ANGLER report. After that we will make one contact every twelve hours, according to schedule, with a situation report or SITREP. We will receive a confirmation of mission 'go' two hours prior to target destruction at 1600Z on the eighth, and we will broadcast an estimate of target destruction—a PONDER report—within one hour of target destruction.

"Internal to the team we will have four PRC68 FM radios to use between the ORP, the target surveillance, and the pickup zone surveillance element. The FM radios will be turned on every hour on the hour for five minutes by all three sites for monitoring. If any message needs to be passed, it will be done then. This will reduce battery consumption. The PRC68 FM radio has an effective range of only four kilometers. It will be keyed only in case of emergency. This is to reduce the possibility of enemy radio direction finding, known as RDFing, picking up the transmission.

"We feel that the possibility of being RDF'd is minimal. Enemy RDF equipment in that area is oriented mainly to the north, and also northeast toward Russia. Although intercepting satellite communications is not impossible, it is extremely difficult since the transmission is directional up and down. If we have to go FM communications on the internal net, the possibility of being RDF'd increases slightly. There are a lot of unknowns involved, but I'd estimate there's about a ten percent chance of being picked up on the FM if we have to use it and if the enemy is looking for us.

"I have all codes and frequencies needed. We will refer to all team members and locations by their code names in transmissions. As you may have noticed, all code names have been given a six-letter designation starting with the letter *D*. This is because our operational area has been given the D designation and we encode in six-letter groups for transmission.

"All team members are trained in the use of the PSC3 SATCOM radio and the PRC68 FM radio. If for some reason we have to go manual, all detachment members are trained to a minimum standard of five words per minute in Morse code, both sending and receiving. It is not likely that this will occur, since we will be carrying in two DMDGs."

O'Shaugnesy looked up. "If there are no questions, this finishes my portion of the briefback, and I'll be followed by Captain Mitchell."

Mitchell stood up. "Sir, this concludes the briefback, pending further questions. However, there is one point I'd like to bring up. As you know, we've been briefed on the helicopter exfiltration by the representative from that unit, and the plan looks well thought out with the exception of one area—there is no backup at all. There are only the two helicopters. If one breaks, or is shot down coming to pick us up, I'll have to leave behind half my team and that is unacceptable. We think there ought to be more helicopters for backup."

Hossey pulled out a message. "I just received an answer from the SFOB to our request on that just before coming in here. It's been denied. They say there are no other units in the area that could support the operation and they don't have time to move more birds up to Japan."

Hossey pointed a finger at the team sergeant. "I've got a few questions, Sergeant Riley. First off, why are you carrying in these SAWs? They're American weapons, aren't they?"

"Sir, we'll be carrying, between the twelve of us, the following as primary armament: three SVD sniper systems; four squad automatic weapons, or SAWs; two SPAS 12 shotguns, and three MP5 SD3 silenced 9mm submachine guns. The SVD is Soviet, the MP5 is manufactured by Heckler and Kock in Germany, and the SPAS 12 is manufactured in Italy. The SAWs are made by FN—Fabrique Nationale—of Belgium. The U.S. Army uses the same model. All the weapons we will be carrying can't be traced because the serial numbers have been removed. The ammunition and demolitions cannot be traced either."

Hossey seemed satisfied with the weapons issue. "What if someone drowns on the drop zone, or you're missing someone? Will you still be able to destroy the target?"

"Sir, we've planned as best we can for those contingencies. Ultimately, one man with the explosives could destroy this target. With twelve of us, we have a lot of redundancy built in. If someone drowns or is killed, we bury them and drive on. If someone is missing we have several alternate assembly points, as already briefed, and if push comes to shove, the pickup zone is our 'go-to-shit' rally point. Pardon the expression, sir, but if the shit does hit the fan, that's where everyone will head to regroup and reconsider options."

For another hour, Hossey and Hooker bombarded the team with questions, what-iffing every stage of the operation. Finally Hossey turned to Sergeant Major Hooker. "Any questions for the team, Sergeant Major?"

Hooker indicated negatively. "Looks good to me."

Hossey stood up. "I'll be sending a summary of the briefback to the SFOB. We should get their reaction in a few hours."

Mitchell nodded. Maybe then they'd find out if this was real or if they would have to start planning for an offset mission. He glanced toward the back of the room where their rucksacks and weapons were stacked. Regardless of how this turned out, the presence of live ammunition and explosives, combined with the Combat Talon parked outside and the high-level intelligence they were receiving, had certainly made this the most realistic isolation in which he had ever participated.

7

"All warfare is based on deception."
Sun Tzu: *The Art of War*

Meng stared in amazement at the scene on the television screen. A single man, dressed in a white shirt, walked into the street with his right hand raised. He stood slightly taller than the sloping front of the tank, eye level with the invisible driver seated in its bowels in front of the turret.

The man placed his body in front of the first armored beast in the long column and signaled for it to halt. Amazingly it did, the treads of the lead tank clattering to a halt just a few feet in front of him. The man was yelling something at the tank, but whatever it was, the words were lost in the shouts of students from the sidewalks and the sound of gunfire that still crackled through the air.

The tank moved again, angling to the right, attempting to go around the man. He sidestepped to his left. The tank pivoted left. The man went right. The tank gunned its engine. The man stood fast. Tanks that were bottled up behind the first one gunned their engines, spewing diesel exhaust into the street. Then the man bounded onto the lead tank and leaned over the hatch, yelling at the crew inside.

The man stood on top of the tank for a little while, then climbed down. Two other men ran out into the street, their arms raised as if to say, Don't shoot. They grabbed the man and hustled him off the street. The armored snake crept forward again toward the center of Beijing.

Meng felt his heart torn. Pride at the man's actions was overwhelmed by shame at his own position, safe in America.

He had never seen a more brave gesture than the one he had just watched. If an ordinary man could risk everything like that, why couldn't he do the same?

Seeing his dead son had caused him to reevaluate his position. He had always tried to justify his life in the United States with a belief that he was aiding a country that one day would help the people of China achieve freedom. He now knew that that was a shallow and misdirected concept.

The news shifted to a report that the American president was resisting suggestions of stronger sanctions against the Chinese government. The president apparently didn't want a total break in relations. Meng knew that that was the wrong course. The Old Men would see it as weakness. The Americans had to take a stronger stand or more would die. The news also reported rumored clashes between units of the Chinese Army.

The Old Men were doing it again. He rubbed his forehead, feeling an itch from the scar that was much deeper psychologically than physically. An idea had been plaguing Meng for the last twenty-four hours. Now he knew what he must do. He turned from the TV to the computer terminal behind his desk. His decision had been triggered by emotion, but Meng was an intelligent man. He would act on his decision with all his knowledge and expertise. After twenty-three years, it was time.

FOB, Osan Air Force Base, Korea
Tuesday, 6 June, 0900 Zulu
Tuesday, 6 June, 6:00 P.M. Local

Riley and Mitchell had spent the day drilling the team on every aspect of the plan, running through their SOPs, practicing actions at the objective, simulating the placement of the charges on the cables. The lurking feeling that this was just an exercise was fading—this was the real thing and that somber fact was sinking in.

"Thinking about what's going to happen?" Jim Trapp sat down on Riley's ruck in front of him in the darkened hangar where the Talon awaited them.

"Yeah. How'd you know?"

"I was thinking about it, too. You had that faraway look.

Remember, I've been there before. Of course, we don't know that this is real. You've got to admit they've supported us pretty well so far, though. Enough to make you believe it's real. I think we can do it."

Trapp surveyed the team in various stages of sleeping and equipment preparation. "They're good soldiers," Trapp said. "Other than my second team in Vietnam, this is the best team I've ever been associated with. I appreciate your asking for me. Of course if this goes tits up, I'm gonna deny I ever said that."

Riley looked around. "Yeah, they are good. Exfiltration is the one part that really worries me. It's always been the weak link. You and I both know what happens when you don't leave yourself any slack with helicopters."

Trapp nodded in agreement. "For what it's worth I'm not happy about the chopper thing, either. Not much we can do about it. We've got to depend on the SFOB to a certain extent. They've got their hands on the aircraft and communications, which means they control our lives."

Trapp stood up and stretched. He looked at his friend and tapped him on the shoulder. "Hey, get some sleep, OK? We all should be thinking with clear heads when we hit the ground tonight. Murphy's going to be waiting on the drop zone, and who knows what he's thought up. We've done all we could do in the time we had. I'll tell you one thing I learned a long time ago: Always stick with the plan. Believe in the plan." Trapp gave Riley a thumbs-up as he walked off toward his gear.

Riley tried to nap but couldn't. Thoughts kept flitting through his head—live border missions early in his career in Thailand, various training missions to other countries. Soldiering was a profession—a way of life. A soldier didn't just get up in the morning and punch the time clock in at eight and out at five. A soldier's life was funny, Riley thought to himself. In other professions people *wanted* to do what they had been trained to do. A soldier spent years training to do something he hoped and prayed he'd never have to do. At least Riley did. He knew others, like Trapp, who liked going on live missions. They felt that it was the only time they really came alive. They enjoyed living on the edge.

Riley started running the operation through his mind from start to finish, trying to find something he hadn't thought of. Something they'd missed in their planning. He could imagine a thousand ways this mission could get messed up and a thousand ways he could end up dying. Too much imagination was dangerous. "I think too damn much," Riley muttered to himself.

Fort Meade, Maryland
Tuesday, 6 June, 1000 Zulu
Tuesday, 6 June, 5:00 A.M. Local

Meng had not slept. He'd been too busy modifying the Dragon and Sim-13 programs. He was finally done. With a perverse sense of pride, he knew that it was his greatest creation yet. He pressed the send key. It was started.

Meng stood up and left his office, heading down to Tunnel 3. Wilson was at the tail end of his night shift as Meng came in. "How's it going? Want me to stick around for the infil simulation?"

Meng shook his head. "You can go home now. I'll cover everything."

Wilson pointed at the map board. "When do you want to send the mission termination message to the FOB? They're probably pretty anxious right now." Wilson checked the clock. "It's only two and a half hours before they're supposed to lift off."

Meng waved a hand. "I just sent that from my office. Kept it off the screen in here so it wouldn't confuse them more than they already are."

Wilson frowned briefly. He hadn't seen the message go by on his console. Still, he knew that Meng could bypass the master console from his office. He stood up. "The program ready?"

Meng replaced Wilson at the master console. "Everything is quite ready. We will find out shortly how well prepared these people are."

"See you tonight, then." Wilson stretched his back and wandered down toward the front of the Tunnel. A thought occurred to him. He walked over to Major Tresome, the communications specialist, sitting at his console in the front row. "Did you see the mission termination message just go out?" he asked in a low voice.

Tresome shook his head. "Just the normal mission traffic between SFOB and FOB. No administrative stuff."

Wilson looked back up the Tunnel at Meng and then back at Tresome. "Meng says he sent it."

Tresome shrugged. "He probably did. Meng usually does a lot of stuff from his office. He doesn't like using this terminal for admin traffic. Whatever goes through here comes up on the screen and in the printouts. That means the exercise participants here in the Tunnel see it. Meng can bypass all that from his office or from the master console."

"But wouldn't you or I have seen it go by?"

Tresome shook his head. "Nope. There's no record of that. Like I said, Meng can bypass."

Wilson was too tired to pursue it any further. "Well, you might as well shut down the SATCOM link with the FOB if Meng has already closed down with them."

Tresome reached forward and flipped a switch. "We're on the computer now." Tresome scanned the board. "Hell, Meng's damn office terminal is still linked into the FOB." He looked up at Wilson. "Should I shut that down too?"

Wilson thought about it. "No reason not to. We've nothing more for them. He probably just forgot to shut it down."

FOB, Osan Air Force Base, Korea
Tuesday, 6 June, 1000 Zulu
Tuesday, 6 June, 7:00 P.M. Local
Hossey grabbed the message as it came out of the machine. He felt his heartbeat pick up as he read the message.

```
CLASSIFICATION: TOP SECRET
TO: CDR FOB K1/ MSG 38
FROM: CDR USSOCOM/ SFOB FM
SUBJ: INFILTRATION
AUTHORIZATION CODE: BLAZING THUNDER/
   REPEAT/ BLAZING THUNDER
CLASSIFICATION: TOP SECRET
```

Hossey took the message and drove to the hangar. The team had spent most of the day there trying to relax and re-hearse various tactics. He pulled up to the personnel door and

Hooker, who was standing guard just inside, opened it. Hossey showed the sergeant major the message. Hooker whistled lightly and commented, "I didn't think they had the balls in D.C. to do this."

Hossey shook his head. "I guess the massacre pushed the powers-that-be over the line."

He headed across to Riley and Mitchell, who were leaning back against their rucks. He handed the message to Mitchell, who read it, then silently passed it across to Riley.

Riley looked at his team leader. "Does this mean what I think it does?"

Mitchell nodded. "Get the team together."

Riley whistled to wake up everyone. "Gather around."

While they waited for the men to assemble, Hossey went over to alert the Talon crew. Mitchell took a deep breath, then addressed the team. "The mission's a go, men. We just got infiltration authorization. No offset or cancelation. This is the real thing." Mitchell looked at his watch. "We load in two hours."

Without a word the team members turned and went back to their rucks, each man absorbing the information in his own way. All day long the tension in the air in the hangar had grown as the uncertainty dragged on. Now the uncertainty was replaced by apprehension. They were really going.

The men reacted to the news in different ways. A few, such as Mitchell and Olinski, seemed to withdraw and become even quieter. Others, such as Lalli and Reese, got louder, even cracking jokes. Both reactions were a way of dealing with the stress.

Each man did final weapons checks. Rucksacks were rigged for jumping. They were going in heavy, equipment-wise, for a three-day operation, but they were prepared for almost any eventuality.

The men were dressed in jungle fatigues dyed black. Over the fatigues each soldier wore his combat vest, configured to carry extra magazines and ammunition for the weapon he carried. The vest had straps that were buckled around each thigh through the crotch, so the vest could serve as a safety harness if no pickup zone was readily available for the helicopter, and extraction became necessary. The extraction harness consisted of two snap links fitted into the shoulders of the vest, which would hook into ropes hung below a helicopter.

Riley, along with Trapp and Comsky, carried the Soviet SVD sniper rifle. It fired the Soviet 7.62 by 54mm cartridge. All three men were school-trained snipers and could hit a two-inch circle out to twelve hundred meters, under favorable conditions. Riley felt that the use of the Soviet rounds to take out the cameras would shift suspicion for the raid to the Soviets. The Soviet-Chinese border had been the sight of numerous border clashes since the end of World War II. The Chinese might even suspect a Soviet Spetsnaz, or Special Forces, team.

Additionally, Riley and Trapp carried cutoff M79 grenade launchers, attached to their combat vests with a snap link. Hooker had a hard time tracking down the M79s for them. They supposedly had been made obsolete years ago and replaced by the M203, a weapon that combined the M16 rifle with a 40mm grenade launcher, which was hung below the M16 barrel. But Trapp remembered the effectiveness of a cutoff M79 from his Vietnam days. The short, stubby weapon could be attached to the vest, out of the way, until needed. The 40mm grenade launcher acted in effect like a large shotgun. The M79 used high explosive (HE), and special flechette rounds, which consisted of hundreds of sharp little metal slivers. Riley and Trapp each carried twenty mixed rounds for the M79s.

The captain, and the two communications men, Walt O'Shaugnesy and Paul Lalli, each carried MP5 SD3 submachine guns—silenced 9mm guns that held a thirty-round magazine. They could be fired on semiautomatic or full automatic with a flip of the selection lever. Although accurate only out to about a hundred meters, the guns would be effective for silent, close-in killing of enemy security personnel if needed.

Olinski and Hoffman each carried the Italian-manufactured SPAS 12 semiautomatic shotgun. These twelve-gauge shotguns were carried because they could be used without leaving a distinctive signature. They were in limited use by the local population throughout the target area. A corpse riddled with twelve-gauge 00 buckshot or slugs would not immediately point to a foreign source. Additionally, Riley liked them because a shotgun was a very effective weapon during an ambush. It was an area weapon with devastating results at close range. Each shotgun could be loaded with nine shells, which could be fired as fast as the trigger was pulled. To add to their effectiveness, the gun's magazines were loaded with alternating double-aught buckshot rounds and solid slug rounds. The twelve-gauge slug round was guaranteed to put a man down permanently if it hit him.

Chong, Reese, Smitty, and Devito all carried the squad automatic weapon. The SAW fired 5.56mm rounds from a hundred-round drum magazine. Not as heavy as the more commonly used M60 machine gun, the SAW could still reach out nine hundred meters with an effective field of fire. Riley was counting on these for suppression of the enemy if they did make contact or had to fight off a reaction force. With the SAWs providing area suppression, and the SVDs giving accurate, long-range fire, Riley felt that they had a good chance of beating off a reaction force, at least for a little while. For close-in work, the M79s, shotguns, SAWs, and submachine guns would do the job.

Each man also carried two pistols. One was a 9mm automatic of choice, either Beretta or Browning High Power, in a holster on his vest. Strapped inside his shirt in a shoulder holster, each man also carried a .22-caliber High Standard semiautomatic pistol equipped with a silencer. These were last-resort weapons, carried more for survival use than anything else: Using the silenced .22 pistol, team members could kill small animals for food if they had to evade for an extended period. To use a .22 on a person required a high degree of accuracy and luck, because the small-caliber round could not be counted on to stop whatever it hit.

Every man also carried one thermite grenade and three small M18 high-explosive grenades, which had an effective bursting radius of five meters. A Claymore mine was packed in the top flap of each rucksack. The Claymore was a crescent-shaped mine full of small ball bearings. When fired, it exploded thousands of these balls on a wide front, out to a range of twenty meters. The effect was devastating on anyone caught inside that arc.

O'Shaugnesy and Devito each carried a Soviet-made RPG rocket launcher and five rounds, since they would be the security team on the service road during the actual target hit. The RPG could fire accurately out to five hundred meters and disable most vehicles. The shaped charge in the rocket warhead could even penetrate a tank if it hit in a vulnerable spot.

In addition to the demolitions, the team carried an assortment of special equipment. Every other man carried PVS-5 night-vision goggles. The men would work the goggles in pairs, switching off every hour. Extended wear of the goggles caused eye strain and diminished their usefulness.

O'Shaugnesy and Lalli each packed a PSC3 satellite communication radio, which weighed twenty-seven pounds when combined with its antenna and digital message device group sender (DMDG). This made their rucksacks significantly heavier than the rest of the team's. Once the men were on the ground, the SATCOM radios would be rigged with thermite grenades for emergency destruction. Four PRC68 FM radios were carried for internal communications among the team, if needed.

Two 120-foot ropes were carried. Riley had long ago discovered that he always found a lot of potential uses for a rope whenever he didn't bring one, so now Team 3 always carried two. Every other man also carried a small vial of CN powder, which was a condensed form of the powder used to generate tear gas. This powder could be sprinkled along a trail behind a person if dogs were tracking. A good whiff of CN and a dog would be done tracking for a long time.

The basic food load was five meals, each dehydrated and weighing less than a pound. Heat tabs were carried, which could be used to heat water in canteen cups. A Goretex poncho and bungee cords were taken for shelter if needed, and to sleep the men could crawl into a waterproof Goretex bivy sack.

Each man wore an internationally manufactured brown Goretex boot. Goretex gloves and black watchcaps completed their outfits.

Colonel Hossey had questioned the relatively large load

each man was carrying for a three-day mission, but Mitchell and Riley had stood by their decision. Fully loaded, each man had an approximately forty-pound rucksack. Their combat vests weighed almost thirty pounds apiece when filled out with spare magazines, pistols, grenades, survival kit, butt pack, and two full one-quart canteens.

While heavy, the seventy pounds of total gear each team member carried was actually far lighter than the load carried on training exercises. Picking up his ruck with one hand, Comsky referred to it as a "nerf" ruck, it was so light compared to what he was used to. The team had once deployed for thirty days without resupply—just one meal a day added up to thirty pounds of food alone. Riley remembered an exercise they had conducted the previous winter in the mountains of Korea when the team had carried almost a hundred and thirty pounds of gear apiece.

Mitchell and Riley felt satisfied with the choice of weapons and equipment. They had prepared for the worst possible scenario, which they envisioned as making contact and/or having to escape and evade for several days before being picked up. Despite all the ammunition they carried, Riley hoped only three rounds would be fired—the three rounds needed to blind the surveillance cameras.

Riley checked his watch. Two hours until the Combat Talon took off. He considered doing one last verbal run-through of the mission but decided against it. He'd allow the men to spend this remaining time with their own thoughts.

8

"Nothing is more difficult than the art of maneuver. What is difficult about maneuver is to make the devious route the most direct and to turn misfortune to advantage."
Sun Tzu: *The Art of War*

FOB, Osan Air Force Base, Korea
Tuesday, 6 June, 1200 Zulu
Tuesday, 6 June, 9:00 P.M. Local

The members of Team 3 completed loading their rucksacks onto the floor of the Talon and seated themselves along the right side of the plane on the cargo webbing seats. Wearing black rubber dry suits, with hoods and camouflage face paint, the men looked like seals out of water. The one-piece black dry suits, manufactured by the Viking Company of Norway, covered the entire body except hands and face. It was entered through a zipper in the back; latex seals around the wrists and neck kept out water. Theoretically the person inside would remain completely dry, although Riley had gotten soaked more than once inside a leaky suit. They had triple-checked these suits, and all seemed to be functioning properly. To keep their hands warm in the chilly water, each man wore diving gloves. A dive compass on one wrist would help in navigation once they were in the water. A dive knife was strapped to each soldier's right calf.

Riley had coordinated six checkpoints en route to the drop zone. The loadmaster in the back of the aircraft would relay the checkpoint number from the navigator to Mitchell as they crossed each checkpoint, keeping the team oriented as to where they were on the route. At checkpoint 1, where the aircraft dropped altitude and headed north, Riley would have the team start their inflight rig; at the last checkpoint, six minutes from the drop zone, Riley would start his jump commands.

Every team member felt a surge of adrenaline as the loud whine of the four powerful turboprop engines filled the air. It was a sound that any person who was ever on airborne status would never forget. It meant you were going: no weather delays, no broken airplane, no last-minute cancellation. You were taking off, and the only way you could land was with the parachute on your back.

Fort Meade, Maryland
Tuesday, 6 June, 1220 Zulu
Tuesday, 6 June, 7:20 A.M. Local
Meng could sense a slight increase in tension in Tunnel 3. For the members of the SFOB, the simulation was about to start. For Meng, something much more vital was beginning. He had linked up the main console with his office terminal. The link with the FOB no longer existed here in Tunnel 3 because the computer simulation was taking over, but Meng's reprogramming the previous night had kept open the line from his personal program to the FOB. If the real FOB made a call to the SFOB, the message would be routed to Meng's office terminal and stored in a locked data file that only Meng could open. His plan was to monitor his office terminal and answer the FOB using a reverse of the simulation.

In other words, Meng had set up a double simulation. He was running the expected Dragon Sim-13 for members of the SFOB here in the Tunnel. That in itself should not be a major problem. The difficult part for Meng would be keeping up the pretense to the FOB in Korea. He felt that he had worked out most of the bugs the previous night. Both jobs consisted exclusively of monitoring and replying to message traffic.

Meng scanned his locked data file. No messages from the FOB since they had rogered receipt of the go authorization. Meng really didn't expect any traffic from the FOB until infiltration was accomplished. He settled into his chair at the master console. It was going to be a long day.

FOB, Osan Air Force Base, Korea
Tuesday, 6 June, 1237 Zulu
Tuesday, 6 June, 9:37 P.M. Local

Riley checked his watch. Right on time. The wheels of the MC-130 lifted off the tarmac and the plane roared into the night sky, exactly at 1237 Zulu. The plane, listed by Korean aviation authorities as a normal U.S. Air Force run to Misawa Air Force Base in Japan, powered its way up to five thousand feet.

Devito, the senior medic, started passing out motion-sickness pills to those who wanted them. All the men had experienced rides on Combat Talons before and knew that once the plane penetrated the shoreline, the terrain-following flight would cause extreme discomfort. Motion sickness was an integral part of any Talon flight.

Riley smiled as he glanced down the side of the plane. Comsky was already asleep with his head against the cargo netting and his mouth wide open. Riley couldn't hear the snoring over the roar of the engines, but he had no doubt that it was loud. Comsky could sleep through anything. The other members of the team tried to get as comfortable as their bulky equipment and dry suit would allow. For the next three and a half hours it was the air force's show.

9:46 P.M. Local

Hossey had watched the Talon drill a hole into the eastern night sky until it was no longer visible. Then he had slowly driven back to the operations center. After writing a message to the SFOB detailing the successful departure of the aircraft, he settled in to wait. The next communication he should receive from the team—barring any last-minute problems en route—would be their ANGLER report after they were on the ground in China. Hossey could make contact with the Talon, but he would do so only in an emergency. Even though the odds of the aircraft's SATCOM being picked up were very low, it was still considered poor procedure to make any sort of broadcast. Besides, Hossey reflected, he had nothing to say to the team or the aircraft now. They were on their way. All he could do was sit here and wish them well.

Fort Meade, Maryland
Tuesday, 6 June, 1340 Zulu
Tuesday, 6 June, 8:40 A.M. Local

The staff of the SFOB was tracking the simulated progress of
the Talon on the electronic map. The aircraft was just about
at checkpoint 1. Meng had computed in no problems with
the infiltration simulation. The less fuss, the better, as far as
he was concerned. He accessed his locked message file for
the FOB. Still nothing. No news was good news, as the
Americans were fond of saying.

Checkpoint 1, Sea of Japan
Tuesday, 6 June, 1343 Zulu
Tuesday, 6 June, 10:43 P.M. Local

Riley felt the aircraft bank and the air pressure change
slightly as the plane rapidly descended. He unbuckled his seat
belt and staggered down the center of the plane. Leaning over
Mitchell, he signaled and then yelled in the officer's ear.
"Time to rig."

Mitchell started rousing the team members. Riley and the
loadmaster moved to the back of the plane and undid the
cargo straps holding down the parachutes and rucksacks.
They passed out the chutes, a main and reserve to each man.

Riley and Mitchell buddy-rigged each other. Riley went
first, slipping the harness of the main chute over his shoulders
and settling it on his back. Mitchell helped him fasten the leg
straps and attach the reserve to the front of the rig. The SVD
sniper rifle was cinched down over Riley's left shoulder using
the rifle's sling and cord. The rucksack was added last,
hooked on with quick release straps below the reserve in the
front.

Finished, Mitchell tapped Riley on the rear and gave him
a thumbs-up, signaling he was good to go. Riley then helped
Mitchell rig and "jumpmaster-inspected" his team leader.
When he was done with Mitchell, Riley moved on to the
other team members, making sure all were properly jumpmaster inspected.

All the team members' weapons had been waterproofed
and tied off. Swim fins were stuck in the waistband of each
parachute and attached to the jumper with cord. After thirty

minutes of checking, Riley was satisfied. They were ready to jump.

In the front half of the cargo bay, Major Kent was watching his screens diligently. He was catching reflections of some shore-based radar up in Vladivostok, but he knew that the Talon was too low to be picked up by that. He ran through the various wave bands, searching for any invisible groping finger that might pinpoint them.

Checkpoint 2, Sea of Japan
Tuesday, 6 June, 1420 Zulu
Tuesday, 6 June, 11:20 P.M. Local
The loadmaster leaned over to Captain Mitchell. "The navigator wants to talk to you," he screamed above the plane's roar and passed his headset to the captain.

"Hey, Captain, we're picking up radar echoes along the flight route, up by Vladivostok. We think it might be a Soviet warship. We don't want to take any chances. We're switching on the spiderweb to another leg. The new route comes pretty close to going straight from checkpoint 2 to checkpoint 5. We'll pass almost right over the North Korean–Soviet border now. The EW officer isn't picking up too much radar activity there and he thinks it's safe. We'll be going over the shore in about fourteen minutes. We want to get lost in among the mountains there, so this ship won't pick us up. This is going to cut off some time. I figure on getting to the drop zone about ten minutes early, give or take a minute or two."

Mitchell acknowledged and turned to Riley to pass the word along. This often happened on a Talon flight. The crew planned not one route, but an entire spiderweb of routes. That gave them options, depending on the enemy threat. If Team 3 got to the drop zone a few minutes earlier, that was fine with Riley. The more minutes of darkness they had, the better.

Everyone was awake now and fidgeting. No matter how much they had trained, it couldn't prepare them for the fear and uncertainty of the real thing. They were only a few minutes from the shoreline. Once they hit that, the ride would get extremely bumpy as the pilots used their sophisticated electronics to keep the aircraft down in the radar cluster of the terrain. The tension in the aircraft was palpable.

Riley was sweating under his dry suit. He hated waiting, and he hated having his destiny in someone else's hands. He'd feel a lot better once they were on the ground.

FOB, Osan Air Force Base, Korea
Tuesday, 6 June, 1540 Zulu
Wednesday, 7 June, 12:40 A.M. Local

Hossey was trying to work a crossword puzzle but couldn't help glancing at the clock every few minutes. The team was twenty minutes out. He knew what it must feel like in the back of that Talon. The team members would all be rigged, ready to go. At this point, Hossey knew, all they wanted to do was get out of the aircraft and start the operation.

He looked up at Sergeant Major Hooker, who was pacing nervously around the room. Hooker didn't like sitting on his butt in an FOB. The sergeant major was a person who'd rather be at the doing end.

Hooker stamped out his cigarette, then went over to the commo terminal and looked restlessly through the message logs. He frowned. "Didn't you get a roger on the departure message?"

The commo man shook his head. "Negative, Sergeant Major. I haven't heard anything from the SFOB in more than four hours."

Hooker knew that wasn't unusual—the FOB and SFOB really had nothing to say to each other at this point. Everything was in the team's hands right now. Still, though, there should have been an acknowledgment of their last message saying that the Talon had departed for infiltration.

"Send a message to the SFOB and ask them for acknowledgment of," Hooker looked through the out log, "message number forty-three."

"Yes, Sergeant Major."

Hooker lit another cigarette as he waited, then took another stroll around the room, ending back where he had started from. "Well?"

The communications man shook his head. "I'm not getting anything from the SFOB."

Hooker frowned. "Go to backup."

He waited while the man switched to the backup terminal and sent the message. "Nothing, Sergeant Major. It's like they're not even on the air. I'm getting good bounce-backs off the satellite, so I know it's not on this end."

"Colonel," Hooker called out. "You'd better be aware of this. We've got no commo with the SFOB."

Hossey got out of his chair and hurried over. "What about backup?"

"We've tried it. Nothing. It's not this end. Our stuff is working."

Hossey bit his lip. What the hell was going on? "When was the last time you heard from the SFOB?"

"There's been nothing for more than four hours." Hooker showed him the log. "They didn't acknowledge our message that the Talon had departed."

Hossey looked at the clock. Fifteen minutes out. His gut feeling told him something was wrong. "Go clear voice to the SFOB. Maybe their decrypter is down."

He waited impatiently as the comm man called the SFOB in the clear. Still no answer. He looked at Hooker. "What do you think?"

Hooker shook his head worriedly. "Something's wrong. If they didn't acknowledge that departure message, it means they might not even know the team is on the way."

"They would have gotten ahold of us by now if their SATCOM was down, don't you think?"

Hooker shrugged. "I don't know, sir. You know how difficult it is getting through from the States to here on the phone lines."

"Shit!" Hossey exclaimed. Loss of communications with the SFOB didn't mean they had to abort, but it made him suspicious. This whole mission was flaky. He didn't like the idea of his team going into China.

Hossey grabbed the phone. He'd try the emergency phone number they'd been given for the SFOB at Fort Meade.

Fort Meade, Maryland
Tuesday, 6 June, 1544 Zulu
Tuesday, 6 June, 10:44 A.M. Local

Meng looked up as a warning light flashed on his console. Someone was trying to get through from the FOB on the phone line. His initial reaction was relief that he had programmed the comm system to switch all such calls over to his computer—then he began to worry. Why would someone from the FOB try calling on the emergency number when they could use the SATCOM? There hadn't been a message from the FOB over the SATCOM for more than four hours, according to Meng's restricted message file.

A possible reason occurred to Meng in a moment of sickening realization. His fingers flew over the keyboard as he checked. The answer popped onto his screen. Someone here had shut down his SATCOM link with the FOB. Meng's mind rewound. He remembered telling Wilson that he had switched over the program. He pictured Wilson leaving. Damn! Meng thought. Wilson had stopped by the comm desk prior to leaving. Meng had seen him do it. The idiot had probably told Tresome to cut the link.

Meng shut down the emergency phone line and went to work to reopen the SATCOM link to his terminal.

Checkpoint 6, Operational Area Dustey, China
Tuesday, 6 June, 1544 Zulu
Tuesday, 6 June, 11:44 P.M. Local

Riley held six fingers aloft. "Six minutes!" He extended both hands, palms out. "Get ready!" The team members unbuckled their safety straps.

With both arms Riley pointed at the men seated along the outside of the aircraft. He pointed up. "Outboard personnel stand up."

The members of Team 3 staggered to their feet in the wildly swaying aircraft, using the static line cable and the side of the aircraft for support.

Curling his index fingers over his head, representing hooks, Riley pumped his arms up and down. "Hook up!"

Riley watched as each man hooked into the static line cable. As jumpmaster, Riley was already hooked up and facing the team as he screamed the jumpmaster commands. The loadmaster was holding onto Riley's static line and trying to keep him from falling over as Riley used both hands to pantomime the jump commands.

"Check static lines!"

Each jumper checked his snap link hooking into the cable and traced the static line from the snap link to where it disappeared over his shoulder. He then checked the static line of the man in front, from where it came over his shoulder to where it disappeared into his parachute.

"Check equipment!"

Each man made sure one last time that all his equipment was secured and his connections made fast on his parachute harness.

Riley cupped his hands over his ears. "Sound off for equipment check!"

Starting from Captain Mitchell, who slapped the man in front on the rear and yelled "OK," the yell and slap were passed from man to man until Comsky, who was to be the jumper behind Riley, yelled "All OK, Jumpmaster," giving the thumbs-up.

With all his jump commands done except the final "GO," Riley gained control of his static line from the loadmaster and turned toward the rear of the aircraft. He swayed to the front as the aircraft slowed down from 250 knots to 125 knots. Three minutes out. Then the ramp would open and he would lead the team off into the dark night.

FOB, Osan Air Force Base, Korea
Tuesday, 6 June, 1548 Zulu
Wednesday, 7 June, 12:48 A.M. Local

Hossey slammed down the phone in anger. "The operator says I was connected to the number but it went dead." He looked at the clock and made a decision. "Cancel it. Call them back. This whole situation is too uncertain. It's better if we do nothing than go when it looks like our SFOB has disappeared. I'll take responsibility. We can always go again tomorrow night. Get me the Talon on voice. We still have twelve minutes."

"Yes, sir." The communications man went to work on his equipment.

One Minute Out, Operational Area Dustey, China
Tuesday, 6 June, 1549 Zulu
Tuesday, 6 June, 11:49 P.M. Local

The loadmaster leaned over Riley's shoulder and stuck an index finger in his face. Riley looked over his shoulder at the team and screamed: "One minute!"

Ten seconds later his knees buckled as the plane rapidly climbed the 250 feet to the minimum safe drop altitude. The noise level increased abruptly as a crack appeared in the ramp, growing into a gaping mouth. As the ramp leveled off, Riley stared out into the night. It was hard for him to believe that he was actually over China.

Fighting the bulging rucksack hanging in front of his legs, Riley got to his knees. Grabbing the hydraulic arm on the right side of the ramp, he peered around the edge of the aircraft, looking forward and blinking in the fierce wind. It took a few seconds to get oriented, but there it was in the moonlight. Only about twenty seconds away loomed a lake. It had the right shape. He could see a river—it had to be the Sungari—to the left of the lake. Despite himself, Riley was impressed. More than two hours of low-level flying, an en route change, and they were right on target.

He stood up awkwardly and yelled over his shoulder as he shuffled out to within three feet of the edge of the ramp. "Stand by!"

Riley stared at the red light burning above the top of the ramp. As soon as the light turned green he'd go. He moved a few inches closer to the edge. Looking down he could see the leading shore of the lake below.

The green light flashed. Riley yelled "GO!" over his shoulder and was gone. Comsky followed. Then Chong.

As the sixth jumper approached, the light turned red. Olinski ignored the stop signal. If one went, all went. The rest of the team did the same. The loadmaster lunged forward from the side of the plane and tried to grab the last jumper as he went by. Captain Mitchell shrugged off with a surge of adrenaline and stepped off into the swirling air.

FOB, Osan Air Force Base, Korea
Tuesday, 6 June, 1551 Zulu
Wednesday, 7 June, 12:51 A.M. Local

Hossey was livid. "What do you mean they're *gone*?"

Through the static of the scrambler, the pilot of the Talon patiently explained. "They jumped about a minute ago. We had to change course to avoid Soviet radar we picked up along the way. The new route was more direct and cut about ten minutes off the drop time. We got the message just after we turned on the green light. The first several jumpers were already gone. The loadmaster tried to stop the rest but couldn't."

Hossey considered the situation. The plane was still over Chinese airspace and it wasn't a bright idea to keep them on the air too long anyway. "All right. Out here." Hossey put down the mike.

Hooker summed up the situation. "The bottom line is that the team is on the ground now. In about five hours we should get their ANGLER report, giving us their status. Our first scheduled contact going to them is in eight hours. Do you want me to tell them to abort then?"

Hossey's mind raced. What a screwup. There was nothing he could do about it now. The team was in. He looked up as the SATCOM terminal came alive for the first time in several hours. Hossey snatched the message as soon as it cleared the printer.

```
CLASSIFICATION: TOP SECRET
TO: CDR FOB K1/ MSG 45
FROM: CDR USSOCOM/ SFOB FM
REF: FOB MESSAGE 43
    ROGER YOUR MSG 43/ SATCOM PROBLEMS
    ON THIS END/ LOST COMMO/ UP NOW/
    SORRY WHAT IS TEAM STATUS
CLASSIFICATION: TOP SECRET
```

"Bullshit," Hossey muttered to himself. "Get out of the way." The comm man moved while Hossey sat down and typed in his own message for reply.

CLASSIFICATION: TOP SECRET
TO: CDR USSOCOM/ SFOB FM/ MSG 44
FROM: CDR FOB K1
REF: SFOB MESSAGE 45
   TEAM INFILTRATED/ COMMO PROBLEMS
   SERIOUS/ ALMOST ABORTED INFIL
   BECAUSE OF/ EMERGENCY PHONE LINE
   DEAD/ SATCOM DEAD/ NO ROGER MY 43/
   WHAT IS GOING ON
CLASSIFICATION: TOP SECRET

Fort Meade, Maryland
Tuesday, 6 June, 1555 Zulu
Tuesday, 6 June, 10:55 A.M. Local
Meng almost smiled as he saw the message from the FOB
run across his screen. It had been a close call and a stupid
mistake on his part. He tapped out his response.

   CLASSIFICATION: TOP SECRET
TO: CDR FOB K1
FROM: CDR USSOCOM/ SFOB FM/ MSG 46
REF: FOB MESSAGE 44
   AGAIN/ COMMO PROBLEMS SOLVED/
   MISSION A GO/ SORRY
CLASSIFICATION: TOP SECRET

Operational Area Dustey, China
Tuesday, 6 June, 1555 Zulu
Tuesday, 6 June, 11:55 P.M. Local
Jumping at 500 feet left little time for anything other than
landing. Riley was only 250 feet above the water of the lake
when his main parachute finished deploying. He barely had
time to check his canopy before he was in the water. The natural buoyancy of the air trapped under his dry suit popped
him back to the surface after a brief dunking.

The parachute settled into the water away from him where
the wind had blown it. As the pull of his two weight belts
tried to draw him back under, Riley quickly pulled his fins
out from under his waistband and put them on to tread water.

He worked rapidly to get out of the parachute harness. Unhooking his leg straps, he then pulled the quick release on his waistband. He pulled out the parachute kit bag, which had been folded flat under those straps, and held onto it while he shrugged out of the shoulder straps.

With the harness off, Riley pulled in on the lines to his parachute. Holding one handle of the kit bag with his teeth, he used his hands to stuff large billows of wet parachute into the bag. After two minutes of struggling, Riley succeeded in getting the chute inside and the kit bag snapped shut. Riley took off the second weight belt he wore and, attaching it to the handles of the kit bag, let it go. The waterlogged chute and kit bag disappeared into the dark depths.

Allowing his rucksack to drag behind him on a five-foot line, Riley turned to swim in the direction he believed the aircraft had been heading. As he lay on his back and started finning, he checked his wrist compass to confirm the direction, straight along the azimuth the Talon had flown over the DZ. Soon he heard muffled splashing ahead, which verified that he was heading in the right direction.

This was the first time that most team members had ever conducted a water jump under these kinds of circumstances. In training, safety requirements, combined with the cost of parachutes, required one safety boat per jumper to assist in recovery of the jumper and parachute. There was no one to assist in recovery now. The lack of realistic training was showing itself in the noise and time it was taking the other team members to derig. For Paul Lalli, a disaster seemed in the making.

Lalli came down facing directly into the six-knot wind. When he popped to the surface after landing, he found his parachute descending on top of him. The two weight belts he wore gave him an almost neutral buoyancy and, without his fins on, he found it difficult to keep his head above water. When Lalli reached up to push away the nylon so he could breathe, the movement caused his head to slip underwater. In the dark, with the chute bearing down on him, Lalli became disoriented and panicky.

The first thing he needed to do was get his fins on. That's what Riley had emphasized during the jumpmaster briefing at

Osan, but Lalli had forgotten this in his initial panic. Now he reached down, pulled out his fins, and tried putting them on. He got his right one on, but as he was maneuvering the left one, the suspension cord from the parachute got caught around his arm and leg. He was momentarily trapped two feet below the surface. In his panic, Lalli dropped the fin and it was swallowed by the cold water. Struggling even harder, he got himself more entangled. Using his right leg he stroked vigorously and broke surface underneath the canopy. Taking a gulp of air, Lalli sank back underwater, wrestling with his parachute.

Fort Meade, Maryland
Tuesday, 6 June, 1600 Zulu
Tuesday, 6 June, 11:00 A.M. Local
Meng looked up as the words scrolled by on the message board.

> CLASSIFICATION: TOP SECRET
> TO: CDR USSOCOM/ SFOB FM
> FROM: CDR FOB K1/ MSG 45
> TEAM INFILTRATED/ NO REPORTS
> OF PROBLEM/
> AIRCRAFT RETURNING
> CLASSIFICATION: TOP SECRET

The reaction in the Tunnel from the US-SOCOM staff was one of relief. Meng watched as General Olson turned to his operations officer. "That's one hurdle crossed."

If only they knew, Meng thought.

Operational Area Dustey, China
Tuesday, 6 June, 1600 Zulu
Tuesday, 6 June, 12:00 P.M. Local
Riley couldn't see the chem light the captain was supposed to hold up for the assembly point. He figured that Mitchell was still struggling with his parachute. Riley continued swimming until he came upon the next jumper in the water. It was Comsky, who had followed him off the ramp. He helped Comsky finish stuffing his parachute in the kit bag and sink

it. They hooked together with a six-foot buddy line and, trailing their rucksacks behind, slowly finned on their backs along the compass heading.

Wednesday, 7 June, 12:01 A.M. Local

Lalli was losing his battle. The parachute was becoming waterlogged and he knew it would stay afloat for only about ten minutes. He estimated he had been in the water more than five minutes now. Using his one free leg to struggle to the surface and grab quick breaths, he was tiring. The sodden nylon was suffocating him, pressing down like a cold, wet blanket.

Then Lalli remembered something that Riley had told them to do in such an emergency. He reached down his right leg to where his dive knife was strapped, pulled it out, and started hacking wildly at the suspension cord that entangled him. On his third slash he managed to drive the point of the dive knife into his left thigh almost an inch. Despite the pain, he yanked it out and continued his efforts. He was rewarded by his left leg finally coming free. Treading water, Lalli pushed out against the wet silk and took a few seconds to catch his breath. Then he used his knife to cut through the parachute to open air.

12:05 A.M. Local

Slowly, Riley gathered in the members of the team as he swam. After meeting up with the third jumper he saw the blue chem light come on ahead. It was then that he came across Lalli treading water in the middle of a half-submerged parachute. With the other three team members, Riley pulled Lalli free of his chute and finished sinking it. As Lalli treaded water next to Riley, he told him of his self-inflicted wound and loss of a fin.

"Can you make it to shore?" Riley asked.

"It really doesn't hurt. I'm not sure how much it's bleeding or how bad it is. I can use the leg. The only problem right now is that my suit is filling with water and with only one fin I can't swim as fast as the rest of you."

"Drop your weight belt and use your ruck for buoyancy if

you need to. Don't worry, we aren't gonna leave you. We got plenty of time." Riley hissed at Comsky to come over.

Riley told Comsky what had happened. "You stay with Lalli the whole way in. As soon as we get to the changing area, check him out."

"Right, Top." Comsky hooked himself to Lalli with his buddy line and peered at him in the dark.

"You hurt, Comsky fix," he grunted. Just the hulking presence of Comsky in the water next to him made Lalli feel better.

Riley picked up only two more jumpers; the rest of the team headed toward the captain on their own. When he arrived at Mitchell's position, he found the entire team accounted for. That in itself was a major hurdle crossed, Riley knew: infiltrated in the right place with all people accounted for.

With some difficulty, they organized themselves into their team formation for swimming. Lining up in pairs they started finning, Riley and Hoffman, the second-strongest swimmer after the team sergeant, in the lead. They finned slowly, on their backs, arms tight to their sides, not allowing the tips of their fins to break the surface. The weight belts kept their bodies submerged except for their camouflaged faces, which looked up into the night sky. Waterproof rucksacks bobbed in the water behind each swimmer. From the air the formation appeared to be a long, swimming centipede, edging its way toward shore.

After only five minutes of finning, they felt the lake bottom, quickly discovering that the shore was not solid but swampy. Unhooking their buddy lines and taking off their fins, Team 3 stood up and trudged through the swamp for two hundred meters until they hit a patch of firm ground. The buddy teams formed a circular perimeter, and as one man took off his dry suit, the other readied his weapon and provided security.

Each man's dry suit, weight belt, buddy and rucksack lines, dive knife and fins all came off and were stuffed into a sack. Captain Mitchell had decided that they would not cache this equipment, but carry it with them. The extra twenty pounds were a burden, but the captain didn't want to take the chance of a cache site being discovered. Also, the dry suits could become part of one of the variations of their escape and evasion plan if that became necessary.

Comsky peered at Lalli's leg in the dark. Using his fingers he probed the gash. Lalli's sharp intake of breath alerted him that he had found the edges. From his probing, Comsky thought it wasn't too bad. The biggest danger with the wound would be infection.

"Does it hurt?" Comsky solicited kindly, as he pressed the edges of the slash together.

"Yes."

"It ought to. It's going to hurt even more in about two seconds, as I take this armed suture and stick it here, and push it through to here."

Lalli gritted his teeth with the pain. Comsky could be downright nasty and ghoulish when he worked on a patient. Actually, his apparent lack of bedside manner was calculated; it served the purpose of getting the patient so mad at him that they tended to forget their own troubles for a little while—at least that was Comsky's theory.

Finished, Comsky reported to the captain and Riley. "Ape Man fix. No more bleed." Turning serious he added, "The wound itself isn't too bad. It'll start hurting him but he can walk on it if he ain't a wimp. The suture will pull out on the walk and he'll start bleeding again. I'll have to redo it at the base camp. I'm not going to give him any painkiller, considering the walk we have to make. Actually what worries me right now is that he's wet. As long as we keep moving he'll be all right, but if we stop too long he might start getting hypothermic."

Riley considered this. They hadn't brought any change of clothes with them. It wasn't that cold out. In the mid-fifties. But the combination of being wet and wounded could be dangerous. Riley consulted with Mitchell and they walked over to see Lalli.

Mitchell knelt down next to the wounded soldier. "Hey, wild man. How you doing?"

"All right, sir. Comsky did a good job. I think he enjoyed himself."

Riley and Mitchell smiled. Comsky and Devito divided the

medical chores between them. Devito considered himself the internal medicine man because he preferred handing out pills to team members when they were sick. Comsky liked the more dramatic injuries. If a detachment member wasn't bleeding, he wasn't hurt, according to the Ape.

Mitchell decided to cut their rest halts down to only five minutes instead of the normal ten on the hour. That would give Lalli less of a chance to cool down. Carrying a ruck through the woods would keep all of them warm. The captain told Comsky to monitor the wounded man and inform him immediately if there were any problems.

With dry suits tied off on top of their rucks, weapons at the ready, and half the men wearing night-vision goggles, the team struck out on a 195-degree azimuth south-southwest. They had more than four kilometers to go before they reached the pipeline. Then they would cross under it, turn south, slide along the pipeline a few hundred meters, and move to their objective rally point.

Fort Meade, Maryland
Tuesday, 6 June, 1630 Zulu
Tuesday, 6 June, 11:30 A.M. Local

As far as Meng could tell, everything was proceeding smoothly. There had been no more messages from the FOB, so apparently the commander there was mollified about the earlier communication problem. Meng allowed himself to relax slightly. The next time they should hear anything would be the FOB forwarding the team's ANGLER report.

In the last five minutes, Meng had reprogrammed the computer to alert him whenever a real message from the FOB went to his office terminal. It would sound a tone on the computer in his office when he was in there. For the master console here, all Meng had to do was type in a code word at the start of his shift and the message would be forwarded here; he would be alerted by a special code word appearing on the terminal screen, and he could then access the message. That would hopefully prevent him from being slow in answering any future messages. He didn't want to have any more trouble with the FOB over communications.

He glanced up as he heard General Olson talking to his operations officer about something that concerned Meng also. "Is the ship for the refuel moving?"

Colonel Moore nodded. "Yes, sir."

The general's next words demonstrated that he still wasn't getting into the play of the problem.

"I mean is it *really* moving? I know you deployed those Blackhawk helicopters up to Misawa, but are we really going to have the navy move one of their guided missile frigates just for this exercise?"

General Sanders fielded that question. "Yes, we are. This is a test of command and control. The *Rathburne* is not a unit that normally falls under US-SOCOM authority. Actually getting the ship to move to the point where it would do the mission is a test of how well the tasking authority of this headquarters works. You have authorization from the chairman of the Joint Chiefs to task any element of the armed services to support this operation. The problem is that you also have to keep this whole operation secure."

Colonel Moore nodded. "I had a hell of a time getting the navy to release the ship to conduct the mission. It's moving now, but there's probably going to be a stink about it. The navy is real big on chain of command, and this mission requires that we short-circuit that as much as possible. I have several recommendations I'll put in the afteraction report that would help improve the system for interservice taskings in the future."

Sanders nodded his approval. "That's part of the reason we run this. To learn before we do the real thing."

Meng was relieved. The SFOB staff was doing the majority of the work for him. All he had to do was push the units one step further to actually do the tasks they were assigned. In every case all that consisted of was using the authorization code words listed in the oplans.

9

"To be certain to take what you attack is to attack a place the enemy does not protect."
Sun Tzu: *The Art of War*

FOB, Osan Air Force Base, Korea
Tuesday, 6 June, 1700 Zulu
Wednesday, 7 June, 2:00 A.M. Local

Hossey was tired. It would be another two hours before the first scheduled broadcast from the team, their ANGLER report, should come in. Hossey was still angry over the SATCOM communications screwup by the SFOB, but he was smart enough to know there wasn't anything he could do about it. US-SOCOM was on the other end at the SFOB, and they had more rank there than he cared to shake a stick at. Besides, Hossey reasoned, they had apologized.

What concerned him more was his own attempt to abort the mission based solely on the lack of communication with the SFOB. Upon reflection, Hossey realized he had acted presumptuously. No commo with the SFOB was not sufficient reason to have made that abort decision. He could account for his actions with only two possible explanations. The first was that he was tired and had reacted poorly under stress. The second, and more ominous, was his gut feeling that something was rotten about this whole mission. He wanted to start dissecting that feeling to see if he could come up with something tangible, but he was too tired to think that hard.

After leaving instructions with the commo man on duty to wake him when the ANGLER came in, Hossey went to the small office he had been using and threw himself onto the cot for a short nap.

Operational Area Dustey, China
Tuesday, 6 June, 1700–1900 Zulu
Wednesday, 7 June, 1:00–3:00 A.M. Local

Trudging through the swampy forest, the team found the going much harder than they had anticipated. The ground was spongy moss that sucked in the foot almost to the top of the boot. Each step was an effort. It took them an exhausting forty-five minutes to cover the first kilometer, even though the terrain was relatively flat. Mitchell halted the team for a five-minute break after the first hour and moved up next to Riley.

"If it stays like this, we could have a problem. We'll make it to the objective rally point in time, but it's going to be tight for Olinski and his guys to make it to the pickup zone before first light. When we get to the pipeline, I'm going to cut them loose there and have them go straight to the pickup zone instead of coming to the objective rally point. We can use the team linkup SOP if they need to come back to the objective rally point for any reason."

Riley considered this. "With Lalli being hurt we probably ought to keep him with the main body so the medics can look after him. How about switching him and O'Shaugnesy? That way we still have a communications man with each cell. They're carrying the same weapons, too, so Lalli can pull O'Shaugnesy's job at the target site."

Mitchell nodded in concurrence. In isolation they had considered the option of letting Olinski head off early, and agreed to use that plan if necessary. The second change with Lalli and O'Shaugnesy made sense.

Mitchell went to check on Lalli's condition and inform him of the change. When he returned, he gave Riley the night-vision goggles he'd been wearing. For the second hour, the buddy teams switched goggles. The team continued their march.

After three hours, Team 3 had covered an estimated three and a half kilometers, making better time as the men got used to walking in the muck. Riley figured another thirty minutes until they reached the pipeline. The lack of any sign of civilization was comforting, since they stood little chance of walking into anyone in the middle of this vast forest at night, but it was also unnerving to Americans unused to such vast uninhabited spaces.

At 1840Z they halted to allow O'Shaugnesy to send the initial entry message. While O'Shaugnesy set up the antenna dish and oriented it, Captain Mitchell pulled out his message format pad and started writing the ANGLER report.

Translated, using the message format, his report read:

01: (First message the team was sending.)

ANGLER: (Name of the format used.)

AAA: (Infiltration location) DUSTER.

BBB: (Infiltration time) 2355Z 6 June.

CCC: (Wounded) none. Mitchell had thought about this one for a few minutes. Lalli's cut wasn't that serious, and he didn't want to give the FOB the mistaken idea that they had made contact with the enemy.

DDD: (Killed in action) none.

EEE: (Mission status) go.

FFF: (Present location) grid 361487.

DOUBLE: (Detachment's code word.) Lack of this code word in a message would indicate that the message was being sent under duress.

Mitchell then placed the message into final form, eliminating any excess, and writing in segments. He hated this part: writing in six-letter blocks. It made for mistakes and was a pain to read. He double-checked his unencrypted message:

ZEROON   EANGLE   RAAADU   STERBB
BTWOTH   REEFIV   EFIVEZ   ULUSIX
JUNECC   CDDDEE   EGOXXX   GOFFFT
HREESI   XONEFO   UREIGH   TSEVEN
XXDOUB   LEXXXX

With this done, Mitchell used his one-time pad to encrypt the message. He first wrote the message letters on top of the six-block groups on the page of the one-time pad; then, using a trigraph, which linked all the letters in the alphabet in three-letter combinations, he matched the original message letter with the one-time pad letter to come up with a third letter. The final message he handed to Lalli was unintelligible:

MWKERR   WLSORN   QNDPTM   RHEMWL
THRNWL   ELWPMD   WHRZAQ   MAEOTY
PALTMR   ZXDSTY   KTHRUE   WOSLRJ
WQARWP   THRMWL   POIWER   MERTTS
EKDWIW   WHTISM

Lalli sat down at the keyboard of his digital message data group device and typed in the coded message. The DMDG took the coded message and, transcribing it into Morse code, placed it on a spool of tape. Lalli then hooked up the DMDG to the SATCOM radio with a cable. O'Shaugnesy had gotten a successful bounce-back from the satellite they were to use. He'd aimed the antenna at the proper angle and elevation and sent out a brief squelch. He'd received the same squelch bounced back to him from the satellite, which confirmed that the antenna was properly aligned. Now they waited.

When it was time to send the message, the tape would be run at many times normal speed, transmitting the message in a short burst. The purpose of the burst was to reduce transmit time, which correspondingly minimized the possibility of being intercepted and RDF'd. The base station would receive the burst and copy it on tape. The tape would be slowed down and run across the small screen of the FOB's DMDG. The message would then be broken out by reversing the process Mitchell had used. A duplicate of the one-time pad that Mitchell carried was in Colonel Hossey's hands. Even if someone else intercepted the message and slowed it down, there was no way it could be read without that matching one-time pad. Olinski carried the team's backup one-time pad and would use it to monitor the radio traffic from his position at the pickup zone.

At exactly 1900Z O'Shaugnesy pushed the send on the DMDG and the encoded message was burst-transmitted in less than one second. O'Shaugnesy then broke down the equipment and repacked it.

Acknowledgment of the message would come at the team's first scheduled receive in three hours. The whole communication setup between the team and the FOB was a series of scheduled receives and sends. There was no such thing as getting on the radio and carrying on a conversation, or bursting messages back and forth. The necessity to encode and burst made that impossible. This built-in delay in acknowledgment of information could cause problems. For those not used to the delays of Special Forces long-range communication, Mitchell knew that the process was frustrating.

FOB, Osan Air Force Base, Korea
Tuesday, 6 June, 1900 Zulu
Wednesday, 7 June, 4:00 A.M. Local

Hossey quickly wrote out the letters as the encoded message worked its way across the display on the DMDG. When it got to the end, he took out his one-time pad and copied the groups onto the first page. Using the trigraph, he broke the message out. He sighed with relief as he saw the legible words. Everything was good to go so far.

Hossey then transcribed the ANGLER into the terminal for transmission to the SFOB.

Operational Area Dustey, China
Tuesday, 6 June, 1900–2200 Zulu
Wednesday, 7 June, 3:00–6:00 A.M. Local

It was just an hour and a half prior to first light when Chong stepped out of the woods and saw the pipeline ten feet in front of him. The long silver pipe stretched as far as he could see in either direction. He halted the team and went back to consult with the captain and Riley.

The first glimpse of the pipeline was impressive. The team had studied pictures and knew the dimensions, but the shiny four-foot-diameter pipe, standing three feet above the ground, was much more striking when actually faced. This large pipe stretching for miles on end, from the oil fields in the north down to Beijing, indicated the price the Chinese placed on their black gold. Every thirty feet, the pipe was held up by two stanchions that had conductors on them to prevent the pipe from freezing in the harsh winter. The forest was cut back ten feet on either side of the pipe.

The team quickly crossed underneath the metal snake. Trapp, as last man across, checked to make sure they hadn't left a noticeable trail. As soon as the entire team was in the woods on the far side, Mitchell gave a last briefing to Olinski.

"Monitor all our broadcasts from the forward operating base so you know as much as we do. Every hour turn on your FM radio for any messages we might send. We'll be monitoring for any you might have. If you need to come back and link up with us at the objective rally point, we'll use our link-up SOP along the pipe here, to the south, on the west side. Any questions?"

Olinski didn't mind being reminded of things he already knew. It never hurt to be sure. "No, sir. Good luck."

"Good luck to you, Ski." Olinski, Reese, and O'Shaugnesy faded into the dark woods as they headed west.

Chong led the remaining members of the team on a course paralleling the pipeline forty meters in the forest. The absence of a service road on this side of the pipe told him that they had run into the pipe south of the point where the service road zigged off to the west, heading toward its bridge over the Sungari. Team 3 followed the pipe for four hundred meters, then turned farther west into the woods. They went less than half a kilometer into the dark forest and halted. Mitchell signaled for the men to drop their rucksacks. Team 3 had arrived at the objective rally point. This was to be their home for the next couple of days, until the actual target hit.

Mitchell, Riley, Chong, and Hoffman, after noting the location of the ORP, moved off to take a look at the target. Chong and Hoffman carried their rucksacks, since they would be staying at the target to do surveillance. The five members of the team remaining at the ORP broke out their bivy sacks, and, with two men providing security, the rest tried to get some sleep.

Chong led the three men cautiously along the tree line paralleling the pipe. The first indication that they were close to the target came from the glow of lights ahead. Riley remembered Hoffman briefing that the compound most likely had high-power lights on top of the pylon to enable the surveillance cameras to see at night. The tree line drew back and they had their first glimpse of the target.

Fort Meade, Maryland
Tuesday, 6 June, 2045 Zulu
Tuesday, 6 June, 3:45 P.M. Local
Meng knew that Wilson would be here soon to take over. So
far everything was going well on both sides of Meng's computer operation. The staff in the SFOB was caught up in the
simulation they were playing; the ANGLER from the real
FOB had told Meng that in the Far East the mission was proceeding without a hitch.

Meng shifted the FOB communications to his office and
locked out the master console from his FOB program. He had
just finished when Wilson strode up the center aisle of Tunnel 3.

"Everything going all right?"

Meng nodded. "The team has infiltrated. The refuel ship is
on course and on time. The exfil helicopters are ready."

Wilson took Meng's place. "Anything I need to know
about?"

Meng shook his head. "No. I'll be in my office resting if
you need me."

ORP, Operational Area Dustey, China
Tuesday, 6 June, 2300 Zulu
Wednesday, 7 June, 7:00 A.M. Local
Riley and Mitchell returned to the ORP, having left Chong
and Hoffman at Dagger pulling surveillance. Their initial daylight look at the compound had confirmed everything the satellite imagery had told them: three cameras, an eight-foot
fence topped with barbwire, and an inner T-field fence. It
didn't appear to Riley that the compound was mined, but unless the surveillance could confirm that, they must assume
that it was.

Chong and Hoffman would remain hidden near the target,
switching on and off—one resting, the other pulling surveillance. Tomorrow morning, at 0600 local, Mitchell would send
Smith and Riley up to confer with Hoffman to see if the plan
had to be modified in any way, and to pick up the surveillance team's notes on security patrols and any other pertinent
information.

Riley checked in with Lalli to see if he'd copied the transmission that should have been received an hour ago.

"Copied it five-by-five, Top. No problem. Here's the message, hot off the DMDG."

Riley took it over and handed it to Mitchell. While the captain decoded the message, Riley brewed up a cup of coffee for them, using his canteen cup and a heat tab.

Although they were only five hundred meters from the pipeline and six hundred meters from the service road, Riley felt they might as well have been miles from both. The vegetation was so thick they could hardly see twenty-five meters. The team's biggest concern was to prevent any loud noises. The odds were miniscule, in Riley's opinion, that someone would come wandering through the swamp and find the objective rally point. He had yet to see any sign of man, other than the pipe, in the immediate area.

The surveillance teams at the pipeline and pickup zone were in greater danger of being spotted. Both surveillance teams were emplaced well back in tree lines, and both had a small camouflage net they would string up and peer through to further conceal their positions.

Riley felt uneasy with his team broken into three segments, but that was an operational necessity. The day and a half of waiting would be nerve-racking. Hopefully they could catch up on their sleep. Smith also had to do final preparation of the charges. With communications working well, all they needed now was a little bit of luck and things should go fine.

It took Mitchell only five minutes to break the message out. "Nothing exciting here."

Riley took the decrypted message from the captain and read it:

```
ZEROON     EROGER     ANGLER     XXWEAT
HERLOO     KSGOOD     GOODLU     CKXXDR
ATTSXX
```

The code word they had agreed on with Hossey was there—DRATTS, which meant that the message was legitimate. Riley handed the message back to Mitchell, who burned it along with the page from his one-time pad.

PZ Drable, Operational Area Dustey, China
Tuesday, 6 June, 2315 Zulu
Wednesday, 7 June, 7:15 A.M. Local

When O'Shaugnesy handed him the encrypted copy, Olinski broke the message out and scanned it briefly. Nothing new. He burned the message and pad page, then looked over the pickup zone one more time.

Mitchell and Riley would know that PZ Drable was adequate since he hadn't called on the FM radio and told them otherwise. At first glance, Olinski had thought the clearing wouldn't be big enough. The small opening was bordered by tall pine trees on all sides. In the field itself, several small trees struggled to grow. After stepping off the area to measure it, Olinski figured he could easily land one helicopter there, if they cleaned up some of the trees and brush. There was no way two could land at the same time—but one at a time would be sufficient. Just after dark tomorrow night, he, Reese, and O'Shaugnesy would clear away the small trees, and they'd be good to go.

Target Surveillance, Operational Area Dustey, China
Wednesday, 7 June, 0300 Zulu
Wednesday, 7 June, 11:00 A.M. Local

Hoffman studied the compound for the hundredth time through his binoculars. Chong was quietly sleeping ten feet behind him, underneath the branches of a dead pine tree.

They had picked a spot to the northeast of the compound, in the wood line. The compound's access road came out of the tree line more than two hundred meters to the southwest. The northeast corner of the fence was about fifty meters away, directly in front of him. Sitting on his ruck, ten feet into the tree line, with the camouflage net in front of him, Hoffman knew that he was virtually invisible from the compound and service road. Also, he had seen something that made him feel less vulnerable. He noted what he called "Chinese mistake number one": The Scoot cameras were all inner directed. The cameras obviously were remotely controlled by someone at pump station 12. They scanned the compound randomly, but had never yet looked outside the fence. The two on the opposite fence corners looked along the fence and inside the compound. The one on the berm looked down the pipe, then turned back into the compound to surveil the pylon and the pipe as it crossed the river.

Another good sign, Chinese mistake number two, was that the compound didn't seem to be mined. Hoffman couldn't guarantee it, but he'd bet on it. The grass was too high inside. Mines would have to be checked and serviced at least every six months, and the grass couldn't have grown that high in that short a time period. Also, more convincingly, there were random vehicle tracks throughout the compound, probably left by maintenance vehicles.

Chong had pulled the first three hours of surveillance; now it was almost the end of Hoffman's three hours. He woke up Chong to replace him. Just as Hoffman lay down to catch some sleep, they both heard a sound they had hoped they wouldn't—the beat of rotor blades.

Hoffman rolled out of his bivy sack and joined Chong. They both spotted the helicopter coming out of the north. From their training they quickly recognized it as an old Russian MI-4 Hound model that the Chinese had redesignated the H-5. Memorized specifications flashed through both soldiers' minds. The Hound had a crew of two and could carry up to fourteen soldiers in its cargo bay. It was an unarmed helicopter used for transport or scouting.

The H-5 was flying about fifty meters above the pipe. As the helicopter drew up to the compound, it flared to a hover and slowly settled down to land inside the fence on the west side of the berm. A Chinese soldier jumped out the door on the left side of the cargo compartment and started walking the inside perimeter of the compound.

"Now we know it isn't mined," Hoffman whispered to Chong as the blades of the H-5 slowed and the noise level dropped. The soldier appeared to be calling to someone on a hand-held radio. He was tapping the strands of the T-sensor fence every ten meters or so, obviously checking its functioning. When the soldier got to the eastern side of the fence it became apparent that something was wrong. He hit the same location several times, each time talking into his radio and apparently getting a negative response. Finally he threw up his hands in disgust and continued on with his inspection.

"Now that's mighty interesting," Hoffman muttered. "Looks like their stuff breaks down as much as ours does. Chinese mistake number three."

When the soldier finished his inspection, he got back into the helicopter, which lifted and flew to the south compound across the river, where the same procedure was followed. Finally the H-5 lifted and headed south.

ORP, Operational Area Dustey, China
Wednesday, 7 June, 0300 Zulu
Wednesday, 7 June, 11:00 A.M. Local

Riley was shaken awake from his sleep by Mitchell, who was pulling security. "Listen," Mitchell hissed.

They heard the helicopter and tracked it by sound. When they heard it die down to their southeast they knew that the aircraft had landed near the target site.

"There's no way they could have spotted those guys," whispered Riley as he and Mitchell exchanged questioning looks. "It's got to be a normal security flight."

After ten minutes, they heard the whine of the chopper pick up again for a minute, then die down. Ten minutes later they heard it pick up and fly off to the south.

"They must check each compound," Riley deduced. "I wonder what kind of helicopter that was. I hope it wasn't one of their attack helicopters."

"And I hope those guys don't fly at night," Mitchell said. "If there's a helicopter in the air when we do the exfiltration, that could cause some trouble."

They both knew that the big advantage American helicopter aviation held over the Chinese was superiority at night operations. American pilots had been flying for years with night-vision goggles, whereas the Chinese had only very recently introduced night flying and were still inexperienced. They also didn't have night-vision goggles.

Riley settled back in his bivy sack and tried to catch a couple more hours of sleep before it was his turn to pull security.

Target Surveillance, Operational Area Dustey, China
Wednesday, 7 June, 0500 Zulu
Wednesday, 7 June, 1:00 P.M. Local

Chong was just starting his last hour of surveillance when he heard the rumble of a vehicle engine to his left. He peered along the tree line. A small BJ-212 four-by-four utility truck pulled out of the woods, following the service road, and drove up to the locked gate of the compound.

The sound of the engine died, and three men got out. Two, with slung Chinese Type 56 automatic rifles, started walking around the fence in a clockwise direction. The third stood by the jeep and waited.

Chong watched as the soldiers passed only fifty meters in front of him. He could see their faces and the bored expressions. Even the helicopter hadn't made it all seem as real as these Chinese soldiers walking only a short distance away. Somehow, up until now, the mission had still seemed like some sort of sophisticated training exercise. The armed Chinese soldiers brought home the truth of the situation.

Chong's heart stopped when one of the soldiers came to a halt almost directly across from him at the northeast corner of the compound and turned toward the wood line. The other kept going, turning the corner of the fence.

Chong swore that the man was looking straight at him. Every muscle in Chong's body was tensed. He fingered his SAW machine gun with his right hand and his grip tightened. He figured he could take out the man in front of him and the other going around the compound. Then he and Hoffman would have to shoot the third guy at the jeep before he could call on the radio. Chong shifted his glance and saw the third soldier sitting on the hood of the truck.

The man directly in front of Chong reached down, opened his fly, and sighed as he began to urinate. When he was done he turned and caught up with his comrade on the far side. They continued their inspection. After completing the circumference of the compound, they returned to the jeep. All three climbed in and the jeep drove off.

Chong slowly relaxed. He pulled out his notebook to enter the incident in his surveillance notes. After two attempts he realized he couldn't write because his hands were shaking so hard.

ORP, Operational Area Dustey, China
Wednesday, 7 June, 1130 Zulu
Wednesday, 7 June, 7:30 P.M. Local

The sun was low in the western sky. Riley lay next to his ruck on the edge of the seven-man encampment and peered out into the darkening forest. He'd already been on security for forty-five minutes. Before Mitchell turned in to get a few hours of needed sleep, he had given Riley the encoded message for the next send. He got up and took the message to Lalli.

The commo man was leaning back against his ruck, already hooking up his equipment.

"How's the leg?"

Lalli looked up at his team sergeant. "Pretty good, Top. Comsky had to resew it, because all the stitches pulled out on the walk here, but it's doing OK now. Devito gave me a whole bunch of antibiotics to swallow. I'm trying not to move it too much. I'll be all right."

"Think you'll have any trouble making it to the pickup zone?"

"No, shouldn't be a problem. What about at the target? You want me to take O'Shaugnesy's place, right?"

"Yep. Take it easy and get some rest after this send."

Riley left him and went over to the northwestern side of the camp, which was his security responsibility. Devito was awake ten meters away on the southeastern side. They were keeping up two men at a time for security, leaving Lalli out of the rotation so he could make all the radio contacts.

Riley started war-gaming again in his mind, trying to look ahead for possible problems. The exfil still worried him, but there wasn't a thing he could do about those logistics. There was an added problem with the exfil that had not come up during the briefback. Depending on how quickly the Chinese reacted after the pipe was blown, the airspace on the way out could become very dangerous. Additionally, they still had to go over either North Korean or Soviet terrain to make it to the ocean. If the Chinese called a military alert along the border after the attack, it could set off a corresponding alert with the Koreans or the Russians. Neither would look kindly upon a helicopter coming out of Chinese airspace and violating its borders.

That was one of the main reasons Riley had kept to a minimum the time between the actual attack and the pickup at the PZ. The less time between the two, the less time the enemy would have to react.

FOB, Osan Air Force Base, Korea
Wednesday, 7 June, 1145 Zulu
Wednesday, 7 June, 8:45 P.M. Local
Hossey considered his situation. They'd received a "roger" from the team, reference the first message fifteen minutes ago. Everything seemed to be secure on that end. The only thing left for him to worry about was the exfiltration the next night. So far that was looking good, except for one potential problem.

The debriefing of the MC-130 crew after their return had brought out the information about the radar in the vicinity of Vladivostok—the radar that had caused them to switch on their spider leg and hit the drop zone ten minutes early. Hossey had relayed that information to the SFOB with an advisory that this same radar might affect the exfil helicopters. Following the debrief, the Talon crew was catching a few hours of sleep, then would fly back to the Philippines later in the day, with strict instructions not to discuss the mission they had just participated in.

Other than the intruding radar, Hossey was relatively satisfied. The message traffic from the SFOB was back up to normal and it was just a matter of waiting.

Fort Meade, Maryland
Wednesday, 7 June, 1155 Zulu
Wednesday, 7 June, 6:55 A.M. Local
Meng pondered the issue of the radar mentioned in the FOB's message. He had no idea whether or not it would be able to pick up the inbound helicopters. He looked around Tunnel 3. The men who would have the answers were seated down below him. Meng was considering how he could ask them,

when the answer suddenly came to him. His fingers flew over his keyboard and he pressed the enter key.

In the front of the room on the message board a new communication from the FOB appeared. The SFOB staff watched it carefully. Since the initial confirmation of the ANGLER report on the team's infiltration, things had slowed down.

CLASSIFICATION: TOP SECRET
TO: CDR USSOCOM/ SFOB FM/ MSG 52
FROM: FOB K-1
REF: MC130 DEBRIEF
1. TALON CREW INDICATED RADAR SOURCE VICINITY132 DEGREES LONG/ 42 DEGREES 40 MINUTES LAT/POSSIBLE RADAR MAY AFFECT EXFIL AIRCRAFT/
2. WAVELENGTH OF RADAR INDICATES MOST LIKELY POT DRUM TYPE/
3. TALON DEPARTED 0900 ZULU TO RETURN TO HOME BASE
CLASSIFICATION: TOP SECRET

Meng smiled to himself as Olson reacted to the message by ordering his air operations officer and intelligence officer to get on top of the situation and brief him in one hour. The air operations officer ordered imagery of the area while the intelligence officer started scouring his data, searching for Soviet ships that carried the Pot Drum–type radar along with information on the radar capabilities.

Meng settled back to wait. He'd let the SFOB do their job.

PZ Drable, Operational Area Dustey, China
Wednesday, 7 June, 1200 Zulu
Wednesday, 7 June, 8:00 P.M. Local
O'Shaugnesy had the radio set up and pointing at the designated satellite. At exactly 1200Z he heard the hiss of the burst through his headphones, and the DMDG indicated message successfully received. He turned off the PSC3 radio. O'Shaugnesy hand-copied the unintelligible letters flowing

across the screen of the DMDG. He handed the encrypted message to Olinski, who was pulling security, and then crawled back into his bivy sack for a few hours of sleep before it was his turn at security and surveillance.

Olinski pulled his poncho liner over his head and, using a red-lens flashlight, copied the message onto his one-time pad. Below the letters on the pad, he slowly broke out the message.

ZEROTW	OMSGRO	GERZER	TWOXXC
ONFIRM	PZXXXP	ZXXYOU	RSHOSS
EYXXDR	ATTSXX		

Olinski hated reading messages in their six-digit blocks. This one told him nothing new. The forward operating base rogered the team's second send, and this was the second one the FOB had sent. No change in weather, and the FOB wanted a confirmation on the location of the pickup zone. The captain should confirm pickup zone Drable on his next send, since Olinski hadn't gotten back to him, either over the PRC68 FM radio, or in person, with a negative report. Mitchell was probably reading this message right now.

Turning off his light, Olinski put his SPAS 12 shotgun across his knees and leaned back against his ruck. He scanned the open area encompassing the pickup zone. Odds are that nothing will happen here, Olinski thought. But then he had heard a helicopter earlier in the day. Since this area had so few open fields, there was always the possibility that the Chinese might use this one for something—practice landings maybe. A slim possibility, but that's why they were here.

In the dark of the night Olinski watched the stars appear. This is beautiful country, he thought. Relatively uninhabited, at least in this area. Plenty of game, and miles of unspoiled wilderness. Too bad this is the only way you could come visit—with the United States Air Force travel service, he chuckled.

Fort Meade, Maryland
Wednesday, 7 June, 1300 Zulu
Wednesday, 7 June, 8:00 A.M. Local

The satellite imagery had arrived and Meng listened with interest as General Olson was briefed by his staff. Colonel Moore, who seemed more and more to Meng to be the key man on the US-SOCOM SFOB staff, was handling the talking.

"We've got pretty good imagery of the area the Talon said they were receiving the radar output from. The pictures show a Komar-class Soviet patrol boat moving roughly in a northeast direction along the coast. Plotting the ship's course out, if it keeps going at the same speed and in the same direction, it will be four hundred kilometers north of the point where the Blackhawks plan on crossing the coast."

Olson nodded. "What do you have on the ship?"

The SFOB S-2 handled that. "Our intelligence on that ship indicates it does have the Pot Drum early warning radar. That system is rated out to less than twenty kilometers and definitely has no over-the-horizon capability. They shouldn't be able to pick up the birds going in or out. Besides, the Soviet radar is so lousy, they could be only ten kilometers away and I don't think they'd pick out those birds coming in over the wave tops."

"What kind of armament on the ship?" asked Olson.

"It's pretty outdated. Two launchers for SS-N-2A, which are surface-to-surface missiles, and one twin 25mm cannon in the front. The cannon can be radar controlled against air targets by the Pot Drum, but it has to acquire first. The Komar-class boats are mainly used for close-in coastal patrolling or attacking surface targets. They're the oldest active patrol boats in the Soviet fleet."

Meng was relieved to learn that the potential problem could be discounted. The last thing he wanted was to lose one of those aircraft. They had to get the team out on the first try. If they didn't succeed on the first attempt they wouldn't have another chance, because the Chinese would be alerted after destruction of the pipeline.

Olson seemed relieved too. He ordered his staff to tell the FOB not to worry about the radar. He also commented that he was quite impressed with the simulation's realism—finding that Soviet ship and using it in the play of the problem.

PZ Drable, Operational Area Dustey, China
Wednesday, 7 June, 1400 Zulu
Wednesday, 7 June, 10:00 P.M. Local

At the end of his two-hour shift, Olinski woke up O'Shaugnesy and handed him the night-vision goggles. Olinski wearily crawled into his bivy sack and was asleep in minutes.

O'Shaugnesy was tired. He hung the goggles around his neck and lay his MP5 down at his side as he leaned back on his rucksack and looked out into the darkened pickup zone. Between pulling security and making contacts, O'Shaugnesy had had only two hours of sleep since leaving the FOB more than twenty-four hours ago. He slowly scanned the open area.

An hour had gone by and O'Shaugnesy felt himself nodding off. He jerked himself awake, then cocked his head to one side. He thought he'd heard something. There it was again. Something was moving behind him in the trees. O'Shaugnesy turned slowly and peered through the woods.

The meager light from the stars and moon didn't penetrate the foliage. O'Shaugnesy couldn't see anything, but he could hear it. Something big was moving out there and it was damn close. He reached down, picked up his MP5, and slipped the safety off, placing the weapon on semiautomatic.

He peered into the darkness. Whatever was out there was big, man-sized, and it was coming this way. One-handed, he reached down, grabbed the night-vision goggles where they rested on his chest, and slowly brought them up to his eyes. He turned them on. The darkness disappeared and the area in front of him suddenly became clear.

O'Shaugnesy swung up his MP5 and pulled the trigger. Whoever was standing there was only five feet away, on the other side of the sleeping bodies of Reese and Olinski. The gun made a soft chunk as the first round fired. There was a yell of pain and the figure leapt at O'Shaugnesy. He got off one more shot before he was overwhelmed.

Olinski awoke as he was knocked aside by the figure charging O'Shaugnesy. O'Shaugnesy screamed as Olinski

swung up his shotgun. In the moonlight Olinski saw two figures, the smaller of whom had the outline of an MP5 in his
outstretched arm.

Olinski hesitated briefly, then fired. The initial buckshot
round separated the two figures. Olinski fired the rest of his
shotgun rounds into the larger figure as fast as he could pull
the trigger.

ORP, Operational Area Dustey, China
Wednesday, 7 June, 1531 Zulu
Wednesday, 7 June, 11:31 P.M. Local

Riley was shaken awake. Trapp put his head next to the team
sergeant's and whispered in his ear, "I think I heard shots."

Riley's senses swung into full gear. "How long ago, how
many, and what direction?" he asked.

"Just about a minute ago. I waited before waking you to
see if there were any more, but there haven't been. I think I
heard seven or eight. They were real faint. I'd say a couple
of klicks. Off to the west maybe. I really can't be sure."

"Who's on security with you?"

"Comsky."

"Get him over here," Riley ordered. He pulled himself
clear of his bivy sack and put on his shirt against the chill
night air. He woke Mitchell.

West, Riley thought. That's the direction of the pickup
zone. There's nothing else out there. Trapp had said a couple
of kilometers away. That ruled out someone on the service
road, which was only four hundred meters away.

Comsky made his way over to Riley in the dark.

"Did you hear anything, Comsky?" Riley asked. Mitchell
sat up, trying to clear his head.

"Shots, I'd say eight or nine. Pretty far away. If it wasn't
such a clear night I never would have heard them. They were
real faint. I really couldn't tell what direction. Sounded to me
like a shotgun. There was one, about a second pause, and
then all the rest came real fast, like someone blasting away as
fast as they could pull a trigger."

"OK, thanks. Get back to your post."

Riley turned to the captain. "Jim heard the same thing and
woke me up. He thinks the shots came from the west. If you

add it all up, it sounds like Olinski. He has the SPAS 12 and
it's the right direction and distance. Hell, O'Shaugnesy could
have fired a thousand rounds, too, and we'd never have heard
it. I don't think anybody is going to be up in the middle of
the night hunting here."

Mitchell looked at Trapp in the dark. "What do you think?
Could it have been the pickup zone team?"

Trapp thought for a few seconds. "Sir, it's been a long time
since I've heard firing in the distance like that. In Vietnam,
I could have told you the azimuth, distance, and type of
weapons involved with no problem. But it's been awhile.

"I think Comsky is right. It was a shotgun. Definitely
wasn't an AK; I've heard enough of them fired at me to remember what they sound like. Wasn't a SAW, even fired on
semiautomatic. Shotgun sounds right, and, as fast as those
rounds were fired, it was either a semiautomatic or two guys
firing pumps as fast as they could in succession. Most likely
a semi. Which I very much doubt anyone in this area has."

Mitchell and Riley considered this. Riley stirred. "Damn!
What the hell was he shooting at? You heard no return fire,
yet it sounds like Olinski emptied the entire magazine. No
explosions, no nothing. Maybe he pulled off a very effective
ambush. But then why use the shotgun and not the MP5? Or
maybe they used them both? But who the hell would they be
ambushing in the middle of the night down there?"

Mitchell spoke slowly. "All right. This is what we'll do.
Before we go blundering off in the dark, we'll see if they
come up on the FM radio at," he looked at the glowing dials
of his watch, "2400, in twenty-five minutes. Hell, turn the
damn thing on now, in case they're trying to reach us. Even
if they aren't, we'll come up and ask them if they're OK and
what the hell happened. If we get no answer at 2400, we'll
send some people over right away. I'll go with Comsky in
case they might need a medic. Trapp too. We'll leave Smith
here with the demo, Lalli to make commo, and Devito to take
care of Lalli. What do you think, Dave? I need to leave you
here 'cause one of us has to stay. I want to confirm the
pickup zone anyway."

"All right, sir. Jim, you trade in your SVD for an MP5.

That way you'll have two silenced subs if you do have to go."

PZ Drable, Operational Area Dustey, China
Wednesday, 7 June, 1545 Zulu
Wednesday, 7 June, 11:45 P.M. Local

"Fuck the red light. Take the lens off so I can see," Olinski hissed at Reese, who was holding the light. Olinski continued to work on O'Shaugnesy. He knew that white light could be seen for a long way, in the unlikely event someone was in the area to see it, but if he didn't get O'Shaugnesy to stop bleeding soon they were going to have a corpse on their hands. A red light doesn't do much good when you're trying to find where all the blood is coming from.

Olinski had already bandaged some of the more obvious places. O'Shaugnesy is really screwed up, Olinski thought. He'd already given the wounded man a syringe of morphine, and he was still moaning in pain. Damn! We need a medic and we need him fast. He looked at his watch—another fifteen minutes until he could call the ORP.

"Hey, Ski," Reese whispered.

Not now, thought Olinski, as he probed a gash on O'Shaugnesy's stomach. "What?"

"Maybe they heard the shots at the base camp and are monitoring."

Why hadn't he thought of that? Olinski chided himself. In all the excitement it hadn't occurred to him that they might have heard the shots over at the ORP. "Get the radio and see if they're monitoring," he told Reese.

ORP, Operational Area Dustey, China
Wednesday, 7 June, 1547 Zulu
Wednesday, 7 June, 11:47 P.M. Local

"ORP, this is PZ. Over."

Mitchell grabbed the radio. "This is ORP. Over."

"We need a medic over here ASAP. Denser is all screwed up. Over."

"Roger, what happened and what's the extent of his injuries? Over," Mitchell replied calmly as he hand-signaled Riley to get Comsky and Devito.

"He got attacked by a bear. He's got lacerations all over; his stomach was torn open and Ski just finished strapping his guts in place. He's got bites on his arms and shoulders and face. It's real hard to tell. Ski's been bandaging him for twenty minutes now and there's blood all over the place. We need that medic real fast. Over."

Mitchell turned to Comsky, who had come over from his security position. "Got that?" he asked. Comsky nodded. "Get your stuff together. I'm sending you and Trapp. As soon as you're ready, go. Take Riley's 68 with you, too. Keep it on until you link up with those guys." Comsky moved out.

Mitchell punched the send button. "Roger, you've got a medic and help on the way now. They're monitoring a radio, so if you need any professional advice, go ahead and ask. I'll also have the other doc here monitoring this radio. Put out an IR chem light for them to home in on. Over."

"Roger. Right now we got white light down here. It's the only way we can work on him. But we'll pop the IR and turn the light out as soon as we can. Over."

Mitchell looked at Riley. They both shared the same thought: a bear?

The more Riley thought about it, the more he realized the high probability of such an occurrence. During the briefback Devito had said that brown bears were dangerous wildlife endemic to the operational area. The pickup zone team probably had left food out, or done something else that attracted the bear. Normally, bears didn't attack unless provoked.

Riley watched as Comsky and Trapp moved out, wearing night-vision goggles. In a little more than six hours, Riley knew he would have to go forward and check the target security in preparation for the hit. At least O'Shaugnesy was already at the PZ. We won't have to carry him there, Riley thought—about the only bright spot in the situation.

10

"And as water has no constant form, there
are in war no constant conditions."
Sun Tzu: *The Art of War*

Camp Page, ChunChon, Korea
Wednesday, 7 June, 1745 Zulu
Thursday, 8 June, 2:45 A.M. Local

Jean Long slid her night-vision goggles down on her helmet,
twisting the on switch when they were in place. She adjusted
the focus of each eyepiece separately, looking around the darkened flight line to make sure they were set correctly. Satisfied,
she peered underneath the bottom edge of the goggles at the
dimly lit instrument panel and checked the gauges. All good to
go.

The 309th Battalion was presently out in the field on maneuvers about forty kilometers from Camp Page, due to return the next day. Jean had flown back to Page from the field
site three hours ago on a parts run. In the back of the helicopter a mechanic was sitting with the critical parts they needed
to fix one of the battalion's aircraft.

As she watched the engine rpm's increase on the gauge, she
briefly thought about her husband. She hadn't heard anything
from him since he'd been alerted. She felt bad that she hadn't
gotten out of bed to say good-bye when he left, but she knew
he understood. She was just grateful he was on staff now and
wouldn't be doing anything dangerous. He'd joked with her,
shortly after moving up to the S-3 shop, that the most dangerous
thing he did there was staple together oporders.

With sufficient engine power, Jean lifted collective and
pushed forward on the cyclic. The Blackhawk shuddered,
then lifted. Jean turned the aircraft to the southeast and accelerated, thoughts of her husband forgotten as she concentrated
on the job at hand.

USS *Rathburne*, La Perouse Strait
Wednesday, 7 June, 1800 Zulu
Thursday, 8 June, 3:00 A.M. Local

On the bridge of the *Rathburne* Comdr. Rich Lemester shifted his weight nervously as he looked over the shoulder of his chief radar operator. His ship was threading a needle and Lemester didn't like the eyehole. To the north, the radar blipped the outline of the southern tip of Sakhalin Island, only twenty-one miles away. To the south he didn't need radar to tell him where the land was—lights on Hokkaido Island could easily be seen twinkling in the dark. Those two pieces of land on either side squarely placed the *Rathburne* in La Perouse Strait, separating Japan and the Soviet Union. Cruising at twenty knots, Lemester knew they had another hour before they'd break out into the Sea of Japan.

Lemester was uncomfortable with the whole situation. His orders had told him where he was to go, what he was to do, and how long he would be doing it, but they had not answered the nagging question of why. The *Rathburne* was sailing into a Soviet bathtub and, like any sane U.S. naval officer, he didn't like it. While the rest of *Rathburne*'s battle group was sailing southeast around Japan to the waters off South Korea to participate in naval exercises, he'd been ordered to break off on this course two days ago. Following his orders he had gone in the opposite direction, northeast around Japan.

For ultimate destination all he had been given was a set of coordinates, 132 degrees longitude and 42 degrees latitude. The *Rathburne* was to stay within a one-kilometer circle of that point on the ocean. It was most unusual—Lemester had never done or heard of anything like this.

Be there, and be prepared to land and refuel two helicopters between 1500Z on the eighth and 1500Z on the tenth, the orders read. When Lemester had radioed his battle group commander to ask for more information, he was told that there wasn't any more. When he'd protested about sitting still, surrounded to the north and east by Soviet territorial waters and to the southeast by the North Koreans, who were known not to be friendly to American ships, his commander had been unsympathetic, informing Lemester that he didn't know what was going on either, but that these orders had come from very high. The commander's bottom line had been blunt: Get moving.

Outstanding, thought Lemester as he watched the water flow by on either side. I'm going to go sit there, surrounded by Soviet territorial waters on two sides, North Koreans on the third, no room to maneuver, and wait for some helicopters. Obviously he wasn't cleared to know what the helicopters were doing. Just refuel them and do whatever else the pilots ask.

Lemester turned his gaze to the north. He knew that his ship had already been picked up by shore-based radar on Sakhalin Island and pretty soon he could expect to be shadowed, at least electronically. Once he reached his destination and started circling in place, he had a feeling that the *Rathburne* might get a visitor or two, curious about what the hell they were doing. He'd rather have Soviet visitors than North Korean. *Pueblo II* was a nightmare Lemester could live without.

ORP, Operational Area Dustey, China
Wednesday, 7 June, 2300 Zulu
Thursday, 8 June, 7:00 A.M. Local

Riley returned from the meeting with the target surveillance just as Lalli burst out the 2300 Zulu send. Riley checked in with the captain. It had been a long night for all of them, ever since Trapp had woken them up after hearing the shots. Just before Riley left to link up with Chong and Hoffman, they'd finally received a radio call from Comsky and Trapp. The two had reached the pickup zone a little less than an hour after leaving the objective rally point. Comsky had worked on O'Shaugnesy for almost three hours and then radioed a brief summary of his condition, trying to stay on the air as little as possible.

The bottom line of Comsky's report was that O'Shaugnesy had lost a lot of blood. There wasn't anything they could do other than run a transfusion, which Comsky wanted to avoid unless absolutely necessary. O'Shaugnesy was stable, but that could change. Comsky had pumped the wounded man full of antibiotics but wasn't too optimistic about the chances of preventing infection. Some of the wounds were deep. The best medicine for O'Shaugnesy would be to get him on the birds tonight and into a hospital.

In the 2300 Zulu send, the captain had written the following:

ZEROTH	REEROG	ERZERO	TWODEN
SERXXX	DENSER	HURTBY	BEARXX
SERIOU	SBUTST	ABLEXX	URGENT
HEGETT	OHOSPI	TALXXB	RINGWH
OLEBLO	ODXXXW	HOLEBL	OODONE
XFILCH	OPPERX	XTARGE	TSTILL
LOOKSG	OODXXS	EEYOUT	ONIGHT
XXDOUB	LEXXXX		

Denser was O'Shaugnesy's code name. Riley knew that message would cause a bit of an uproar at the forward operating base. They'd say the same thing he and the captain had said the previous night: a bear?

Well, that's the way it goes, Riley thought angrily. He could sense a depression settling over the team. With O'Shaugnesy hurt, the team's mood was low.

As soon as it got dark, they'd pull out of the ORP and link up with the target surveillance. Hopefully all the talking on the FM radio hadn't been picked up.

FOB, Osan Air Force Base, Korea
Wednesday, 7 June, 2310 Zulu
Thursday, 8 June, 8:10 A.M. Local
Hooker looked up from the message. "A bear? What the hell did they do, try and pet it?"

Hossey was upset. One of his men was hurt. Mitchell having written serious meant that O'Shaugnesy was really messed up. Hossey didn't know how it happened and it really didn't matter. What was important now was that they get them out tonight. He told Hooker as much.

Hooker held up his hands in defense. "Hey, sir. I care as much as you do about this. I'll contact the SFOB and make sure both birds have the blood on board. We've got his type from the isolation information. The weather looks good for the exfil flight. Let's hope nothing else goes wrong. This thing has been screwed up from the start."

PZ Drable, Operational Area Dustey, China
Wednesday, 7 June, 2320 Zulu
Thursday, 8 June, 7:20 A.M. Local

Olinski wearily watched the sun come up and start chasing away the night's chill. His uniform was covered with dried blood. Comsky came by and squatted down next to him.

"How's he doing, Doc?"

Comsky stretched his arms and back. "He's screwed up bad. If he isn't in a hospital in forty-eight hours, he's going to be in real bad shape. You did good last night, stopping the bleeding. If he'd lost any more, we'd be burying him right now. What the hell happened?"

Olinski wasn't sure himself. Going over the ground in the morning light, they'd found a few clues. "The bear must have smelled the food we ate last night, or maybe it just scented us and was curious. I don't think it would have attacked. But O'Shaugnesy must have been startled. He got off two shots on semi from his sub. I figure he shot the bear and all the 9mm did was piss off the bear and make it go after him.

"It took all nine of my shotgun rounds to put it down. And every other round in my gun is a solid slug. That thing took four 12-gauge slugs and five double-aught."

Olinski looked over at the bear carcass and shuddered. It was a big one. It had stood over six feet tall on its hind legs.

O'Shaugnesy had caught a few pellets from Olinski's first shot, but Olinski figured if he hadn't shot when he did, the bear would have finished tearing O'Shaugnesy apart. By the time Reese got out of his bivy sack, Olinski had managed to put the thing down with his last round. Otherwise the carcass would have had a hundred rounds of 5.56mm from Reese's SAW in it too.

Fort Meade, Maryland
Wednesday, 7 June, 2345 Zulu
Wednesday, 7 June, 6:45 P.M. Local

Meng was napping in his office when his computer chimed, waking him up. He snapped alert and keyed in his personal access code. He stared in disbelief at the latest message from the FOB.

CLASSIFICATION: TOP SECRET
TO: CDR USSOCOM/ SFOB FM/ MSG 56
FROM: FOB K1
DENSER HURT BY BEAR/ CONDITION SERIOUS/
REQUIRE O POSITIVE/ REPEAT O POSITIVE/
WHOLE BLOOD ON EXFIL HELICOPTERS/
CLASSIFICATION: TOP SECRET

For the first time, Meng wasn't really sure about the decision he had made. He realized with a sudden chill that he had never stopped to consider there were real men at the other end of the terminal, men who could lose their lives. He had been so used to playing the game here in Tunnel 3 that none of it seemed real. Punching keyboards and reading computer screens was a strong insulation from reality.

Meng knew the seriousness of his actions and was prepared to face the consequences—probably the end of his career. Theoretically, he had known quite well that there was a chance that members of the team would be killed or injured—after all, he was the one who had written the Dragon program.

Was it worth a human life to send a message to the Old Men? Meng shook his head angrily, dismissing that question—many lives had already been lost, his son's among them. They were a small price to pay for freedom for a nation. The small chance that this mission might seriously shake up the Chinese government and cause change was worth everything.

Meng looked at the clock. Less than nineteen hours to go until the team hit the target. That is *if* they hit the target now, Meng suddenly realized. He tapped into his keyboard. First he wrote out a message to the helicopter crews at the launch site at Misawa Air Force Base, telling them to take the blood. Then he wrote one to the FOB.

FOB, Osan Air Force Base, Korea
Wednesday, 7 June, 2354 Zulu
Thursday, 8 June, 8:54 A.M. Local
Hossey looked at the message from the SFOB with confusion. They were asking if the team was still mission capable. He looked up at Hooker. "Don't these assholes think I would have told them if the team wasn't mission capable?"

Hooker shrugged. "Hey, sir. Remember you're dealing with staff wienies. They don't know what a team can or can't do."

Hossey considered the question seriously. Mission capable meant whether the team was capable of blowing the pipe. The team still had the explosives. They were within reach of the target. They had enough healthy bodies to do the mission.

He shook his head and tapped out a message to the SFOB, assuring them that the team was still able to conduct the mission—and reminding them about the blood.

ORP, Operational Area Dustey, China
Thursday, 8 June, 0100 Zulu
Thursday, 8 June, 9:00 A.M. Local

Riley reviewed the situation. There had been no enemy activity in the area so far. If those FM transmissions or shots had been heard last night, they would have seen something by now. So our luck isn't all bad, he reflected. Although two injured, one seriously, without any enemy contact wasn't too good.

In the light of day, he looked around the small patrol base. With five men at the exfiltration pickup zone and the surveillance still at the target, only the remaining five team members were gathered here. Everyone was awake. Riley could feel the anxiety that permeated the camp. The accident with O'Shaugnesy had underscored the seriousness of the situation. They'd trained for years for something like this; now they were going to put it all on the line. It was difficult to train men to such a high level of preparedness, then keep them on a leash, waiting to go. Team 3 had been let off its leash.

When they got back, the men would never be able to tell anyone where they'd been or what they'd done on this mission. They would be provided with a cover story and would have to stick with it. O'Shaugnesy would be listed as having been injured during training. It sucked, Riley thought, but it was the way things had to be.

Riley imagined that the Department of Defense had a good cover story all prepared in case some of them didn't come back from this mission. "I'm sorry, ma'am, but your husband was killed during an aircraft crash over water and we haven't been able to recover the bodies." It had been done before and it would be done again.

Riley watched as Lalli limped about, setting up his radio to receive the next send. Riley went over to the captain and sat down on the ground next to him. "Hey, Mitch, we having fun yet? Aren't you glad I asked for you to go with us on this mission?"

Mitchell looked over at his team sergeant and grinned wryly. "Yeah, the old fun meter is all pegged out. Sure beats sitting up there in the S-3 shop fighting paperwork." The team leader turned serious. "I've been thinking about the helicopter lifts. We probably ought to rearrange the exfiltration aircraft loads based on the new situation. Here's the way I see it. Shift O'Shaugnesy forward to the first bird. Devito will be on board to take care of him. Then we'll move Lalli back to the second with us and Comsky can be in charge of him."

It hadn't occurred to Riley that both the team's communications men had been hurt. It made sense to put O'Shaugnesy on the first aircraft. They always tried to cross-load the team as much as possible, putting one man of each specialty on each aircraft just in case an aircraft crashed. The main reason for the shift was that if only one aircraft made it to the pickup zone, they definitely wanted O'Shaugnesy to be on it.

That made the first lift: Trapp in charge, O'Shaugnesy as commo man, Devito as medic, Reese as weapons, Smitty as engineer, and Olinski to round out the six. The second aircraft would have Riley and the captain, Comsky, Hoffman, Chong, and Lalli. Riley considered this mixture, using factors such as the weapons each man was carrying and his skills. Something else occurred to him. "Let's switch Lalli and Olinski. Any of us can handle the radio. O'Shaugnesy sure doesn't count as an effective commo man now anyway. If we get only one bird, then Lalli, who can't walk that well, will go out; Olinski, who can speak Russian, will stay with us. Hell, if we don't get two birds we might as well have Olinski. We can use him as an interpreter when we marry some local girls over the border and settle down in the area. Either that or Chong can take care of us here with his Chinese, 'cause it's a goddamn long walk if we can't fly."

Mitchell agreed to the change. "Good idea."

The captain reached into his ruck and pulled out a freeze-dried meal. "Breakfast for the day. Lunch and dinner also, if you want to get technical. Shall we dine? Or shall we see what wondrous news the FOB sends us, prior to our repast?" Mitchell added, as he watched Lalli limp over with his sheet of paper.

Mitchell pulled his one-time pad and trigraph out of the cargo pocket of his pants. He started transcribing and decrypting.

ZEROTW   OROGER   ZEROTW   OBLOOD
ONEXFI   LBIRDS   XXGOOD   LUCKXX
DRATTSX

Mitchell handed the message to Riley. "The colonel wishes us well. We need to get organized to make the hit. We're going to have to make some adjustments with O'Shaugnesy down and Trapp and Comsky at the PZ."

Riley thought a minute. "All right. We've still got the surveillance in place. We've got O'Shaugnesy torn to pieces down at the pickup zone. Trapp and Comsky are also at the PZ, and they're two of the snipers we need to take the cameras out. We'll have to get them back up."

"Yeah," Mitchell agreed. "But I think Trapp will figure that out, don't you?"

Riley smiled. "Yeah, Jim's pretty sharp."

PZ Drable, Operational Area Dustey, China
Thursday, 8 June, 0112 Zulu
Thursday, 8 June, 9:12 A.M. Local
Olinski had set the radio for the 2400Z receive and then decrypted the message. He looked at it for a few seconds, then called Trapp over and handed it to him. "Blood will be on the birds."

"Comsky will be glad to hear that."

Trapp scratched his head as he worked the tactical situation. "Comsky and I are going to have to go back up there. We can wait for dark. I guess we ought to call the guys on the hour and make sure the plan's the same. Hey, Ape." Trapp called Comsky over. "Do you think you can leave O'Shaugnesy without a medic?"

Comsky considered. "Yeah, for a couple of hours. I've done all I can do for him. Ski here can do as much as I can at this point."

"Good, 'cause we got a hot date with a pipeline and I don't want to miss it."

Naryn, **Peter the Great Bay**
Thursday, 8 June, 0200 Zulu
Thursday, 8 June, 11:00 A.M. Local
Senior Lieutenant Chelyabinsk of the Soviet Navy ordered the speed of the *Naryn* diminished from the twenty-five knots she had been doing to five knots. With the change, the small patrol boat was barely making headway against the current that surged north out of the Sea of Japan toward the Tatar Strait.

Chelyabinsk was disappointed. He'd been enjoying his leisurely patrol along the coastline. The *Naryn*'s usual job was to watch for smugglers running the coast from North Korea into the Soviet Union. As always, there were people on both sides of the border willing to make deals. Chelyabinsk usually stayed in tight along the shore, cruising in and out of the many rocky bays, searching for signs of criminal activity. But several hours previously, shore-based radar on Sakhalin Island had picked up the radar image of an American missile frigate of the Knox class moving through La Perouse Strait. A patrol plane out of Vladivostok had been sent to investigate and had found that the American ship had turned south, once it passed through the strait. They expected the ship to join the other American warships participating in the annual naval exercises with the South Koreans. Still, the operations officer of the Joint Naval Forces at Vladivostok had obviously decided that the American ship needed to be watched.

That had resulted in the order to the *Naryn*; they were to reduce speed so they would be in position to move out from the coast to investigate if needed. If the American ship stayed on course, the *Naryn* should pick it up on surface radar in a couple of hours.

The patrol plane was sent back to Vladivostok. Where else could the Americans go but south? Soon the American ship would come in range of the *Naryn*. It was not important enough to keep a plane circling for hours.

ORP, Operational Area Dustey, China
Thursday, 8 June, 0222 Zulu
Thursday, 8 June, 10:22 A.M. Local

Riley tilted his head and listened. The beat of rotor blades sounded off to the east. He checked the surveillance notes. Pretty close. Yesterday it had come at 0300Z. Within an hour wasn't bad. The next time the Chinese helicopter came they'd be long gone.

Trapp had called at ten from the pickup zone and they'd briefly confirmed the message and the updated plan.

The mood was growing more tense at the rally point. Riley could feel it. Adrenaline was starting to flow. Hoffman and Smith were starting final preparation of the charges. Everyone was checking his weapons and cleaning them. Reloading magazines to make sure every round was properly seated. Repacking rucksacks and tying everything down. Hoffman and Smitty had run six lines of rope from rocks on the ground up to a nearby tree and were practicing placing their charges.

In isolation, Hoffman had come up with a simple device to speed up the emplacement process. Each charge was taped to a piece of rubber from an inner tube. The rubber was wrapped around the wire, holding the charge tight against the cable, and then fastened there by hooking the end of the rubber on a nail embedded in the plastique charge itself. It took less than three seconds per cable to attach the charges.

Riley reread the security notes and discussed them with Mitchell. Together, they decided on two slight modifications of the tactical plan. They'd have Hoffman and Smith blow the hole in the fence on the east side of the compound instead of the north. It appeared that the T-field fence system wasn't working over there. Every little bit of advantage would be needed. Additionally, they would not have to use the line charge to blow a path to the berm, because the landing of the helicopter inside the compound had confirmed that the ground was not mined.

Riley just hoped they'd receive the final go. He hated to think of the effect a no-go would have on the team.

11

**"Thus, those skilled in war subdue the
enemy's army without battle."
Sun Tzu: *The Art of War***

Misawa Air Force Base, Japan
Thursday, 8 June, 0600 Zulu
Thursday, 8 June, 3:00 P.M. Local

Chief Warrant Officer C. J. McIntire pulled in collective with
his left hand and felt the Blackhawk's wheels leave the
ground. He climbed to five hundred feet and then waited until
the other Blackhawk, with his friend Luke Hawkins at the
controls, slid into place to his left rear.

While his copilot updated the Blackhawk's Doppler navigating device with their present location, C.J. pushed his cyclic control forward and turned on an azimuth of due west.

The Doppler is a navigating device that theoretically would
allow them to find the *Rathburne* in the middle of the ocean.
C.J. was worried because in his experience the Doppler was
unreliable over water. He hoped that a combination of staying
on the proper headings for the designated amounts of time,
and interpreting what information the Doppler did give,
would allow them to locate the ship. If absolutely necessary
they could call the *Rathburne* and have it turn on an electronic beacon. They had already planned on doing that for the
return trip, but C.J. preferred not to rely on that going in. The
fewer electronic transmissions, the less the chance of alerting
the North Koreans or Russians.

C.J. estimated a 3.7-hour flight to the *Rathburne*, arriving
about 6:43 P.M. local time. That would give them a six-hour
rest on board before having to fly the rest of the mission. Just
as important, it allowed them to fly this leg in daylight, sav-
ing their goggle time for the actual penetration of the hostile
airspace.

Once he was sure everything was working, C.J. let his co-pilot, Tim Yost, take the controls. C.J. leaned back in his seat and closed his eyes. He was trying to control his nervousness. Despite all his flight hours, this was the first time he was flying a mission like this—into hostile airspace with state-of-the-art detection devices. Between the Soviets, North Koreans, and Chinese, there was a pretty impressive array of air defense systems waiting up ahead.

Once they left the *Rathburne* and got down into the wave tops, C.J. felt confident they'd make the shoreline. From there to the pickup zone, it would be terrain flying under goggles. Terrain flying consisted of following the contour of the earth with a margin of safety of only twenty-five feet above the highest object. At that altitude they should avoid getting picked up on radar, yet be high enough to avoid crashing into an obstacle.

The trip out was going to be the hairy part, C.J. figured. It all depended on whether or not they were spotted. He didn't know what the people he was picking up were doing, but he had a feeling it was something that probably would upset the natives. C.J. shook his head—flying under goggles at any time was dangerous work. Those mountains were going to require some good flying tonight.

Naryn, **Peter the Great Bay**
Thursday, 8 June, 0800 Zulu
Thursday, 8 June, 5:00 P.M. Local
Senior Lieutenant Chelyabinsk peered at the green haze on his surface radar screen. There in the center sat the brightly glowing dot that indicated the American warship, more than one hundred kilometers to the east. The Komar-class missile boats had a curious radar setup: They could see farther on the surface of the ocean than they could into the sky. The ship was designed to attack surface ships, not air targets. According to the radar, the American ship had been steaming in a tight circle for the past hour. Chelyabinsk didn't know what it was doing out there and frankly he didn't care. It was a nice, clear, crisp day. As long as the ship didn't come any closer he was happy.

Chelyabinsk looked to the west at the shoreline. The

Changbai Mountain Range loomed in the distance. It was at times like this that he was glad he had joined the navy and not the army. Imagine being out in those hills looking across the border at the Chinese or North Korean pigs, he thought. Much nicer here aboard ship, where a man could always get hot food and stay out of the rain and snow.

He glanced forward along the short deck of his ship. Seamen Second Class Aksha and Kachung were manning the forward, twin 25mm antiaircraft gun. Chelyabinsk looked at the two Mongolians with undisguised loathing. The riffraff he had to work with. Those two idiots hadn't even known what boots were until they'd been drafted into the navy to do their obligatory two years of service. Chelyabinsk wasn't even sure they knew how to fire the 25mm.

In his three months in command, the crew had never had an opportunity to conduct a live-fire exercise. The cost of ammunition was too high, they'd been told. Chelyabinsk could only assume that the two gunners had been taught how to shoot in their basic naval training, but he wasn't confident of that. The men spoke only the most basic Russian.

ORP, Operational Area Dustey, China
Thursday, 8 June, 0900 Zulu
Thursday, 8 June, 5:00 P.M. Local

The shadows were lengthening. Riley glanced around—everyone had their gear packed. Lalli finished bursting out what would hopefully be their last send before the PONDER report and exfiltration. The message rogered the last FOB message and reconfirmed the location and time of the exfiltration.

Hoffman and Smith had finished priming the demolitions and placed them on top of their rucksacks. Everyone would move from the objective rally point to the target as soon as Trapp and Comsky rejoined them. Riley figured that the two would show up about 2030 local. Then a half hour up to the target, arriving about 2100. That would give them five hours prior to the actual hit.

It was going to be a cool, clear night, Riley observed. Should be good weather for the exfiltration. The ride home

was the only thing that was out of their hands right now—
they simply had to be in the right place at the right time.

Riley sat on his packed ruck next to the team leader. "Let's
play what if, Mitch. What do you want to do if the birds
don't show?"

There were several options in their escape and evasion
packet. As long as they had a radio, they could keep communications with the base station and rearrange their exfiltration
somewhere along the evasion route chosen.

The first option was northeast: Use the Sungari River itself.
Wearing their dry suits and taking advantage of the river's
fast current, they could float downriver each night and hole
up on shore during the day. With the current at 2.2 meters a
second, it would quickly get them out of the immediate area.
There were two major problems with that plan. First, they
would have to pass through the city of Harbin, where the
odds of being spotted were very high. The second was that
after 750 kilometers, and an estimated sixteen nights in the
water, they would only get to the border with Russia and the
Sungari's junction with the Amur River. If they stayed on
the Amur, it was more than 1,000 kilometers to the Tatar
Strait. There things would get even more difficult, and the options more vague. Perhaps getting picked up off the coast by
submarine. Perhaps stealing a boat and making it into international waters. They'd known in isolation that the river option
wasn't the greatest, but its one advantage was that it got them
out of the target area relatively quickly and unobtrusively.

The second option was to evade to the southeast by foot
and strike out directly for the coast. This would entail a land
trip of almost 250 kilometers. If they had to walk the whole
way, Riley conservatively estimated a minimum of thirty to
forty days. Probably more, since the Changbai Mountain
Range lay in the way, 150 kilometers from the coast. The
mountains were a significant obstacle. At its highest, the
range was close to sixteen thousand feet. The planned route
called for them to skirt the highest part of the range by going
around to the north and crossing the Russian rather than
North Korean border.

On the southeastern route there was always the possibility
of getting helicopters to pick them up along the way, if they

were still in communication with the FOB. They'd listed several potential pickup points in the escape and evasion packet. Every step they took toward the southeast would make the flight shorter.

If they didn't get picked up by helicopter en route and had to walk the whole way to the coast, then the plan was either to coordinate getting picked up by a submarine or ship, or to steal a boat. The southeastern route was more viable than up north in the restricted Tatar Strait because they would be closer to Japan and more open water. Unfortunately, this direction would be most closely watched if the Chinese suspected American involvement. Riley believed firmly in the military tenet that the direct route was always the most dangerous.

Heading west wasn't feasible. Not unless they wanted to spend the rest of their lives strolling across the expanse of China, Mongolia, and then Russia proper.

The last option they had considered was heading southwest, following the pipe to its southern terminal and the coast seven hundred kilometers away on the Yellow Sea. That way was ranked last in choice for two reasons. First, the population increased as you went south, and the chance of being spotted increased correspondingly. The second problem was that the Yellow Sea terminated in the north in either Korea Bay or the Gulf of Chihli. Both bodies of water were surrounded on three sides by either China or North Korea. It was an area that the U.S. Navy and Air Force avoided. The Sea of Japan might be dangerous, but at least it led somewhere other than a dead end. If Team 3 went southwest, the odds of getting picked up were greatly diminished. Any foreign intrusion into the sea or airspace would almost certainly be detected.

Riley and Mitchell ran all these options through their minds, weighing them against the current team situation. After a few minutes Mitchell expressed his thoughts. "The first thing we have to consider is that O'Shaugnesy is hurt. Unless we want to carry him a long way, I think we have only two options. One is to go northeast using the river. We can put O'Shaugnesy in a dry suit and float him along with us without too much trouble. We'd never make it out if we went southeast or southwest, trying to walk and carry him.

"The only other option that seems feasible is staying in place for a while until things cool down and see if the FOB will retry the original PZ. Hunker down for a couple of weeks in the area." Mitchell held up his hand as Riley started to protest.

"Yeah, Dave, I know that doesn't seem too smart. The Chinese are going to be over this place like stink on shit after we blow the pipe. But if we escape their initial sweep, I don't think they would figure that whoever did it would stay in the area."

Riley considered that. He could easily imagine how the Chinese would search the area. Their army certainly had the manpower to do it thoroughly. They would bring in large numbers of troops and make a long search line. Everything and everybody in its path would be found. Riley didn't fancy the idea of trying to evade one of those sweeps. Maybe they could put on their dry suits and hide in the swamp, but he still didn't think they'd escape detection.

Floating down the river didn't appeal to him either, though. True, it would get them out of the immediate area quickly. And it was the one way they could move O'Shaugnesy without having to carry him. But they would be heading in the wrong direction. The team was already on the outer fringes of the range for exfiltration helicopters from Japan. If they went northeast it would further diminish that possibility. Trying to steal a boat or make a water pickup way up there wasn't too likely either. Low probability of success, Riley calculated.

"Yeah, you're right. With O'Shaugnesy hurt we don't have many choices. If the birds don't come tonight, what do you say we head southeast as far as we can carry O'Shaugnesy in the dark, then hole up. See what the FOB has to say about reflying the exfiltration later on."

The unspoken option—one that Riley and Mitchell would not even consider—was leaving O'Shaugnesy. During training exercises, Riley had evaluated teams during their mission planning, and he had actually seen a few teams talk about leaving a wounded man behind if taking him meant the rest of the team wouldn't make exfiltration. That Special Forces soldiers would even discuss such a thing made Riley's blood boil. His early indoctrination into Special Forces had impressed one rule upon him above all: Never leave anyone behind. A team was just that—a team. It should live or die as a team.

The argument Riley heard from those who talked of leaving a wounded man behind was that it was practical. Why trade eleven lives for one? Riley's counterpoint to this kind of reasoning was to ask each person that one important question: "How would you feel if *you* were the one they were going to leave behind? Think about it real hard before you answer. How would you feel if you were the one who was going to be abandoned?"

Beyond the moral considerations, Riley felt there was also a practical aspect. If a soldier knew that he might be left behind if he was wounded, he'd be much less willing to take chances—potentially to the detriment of the mission.

On Team 3, Riley and Mitchell emphasized teamwork in everything they did. During physical training runs, Team 3 always finished as an intact group. If someone fell behind, the rest would go back and get him. Riley was proud that no one on this team had even brought up the possibility of leaving a team member—not in planning, or even now, when faced with the grim reality of the situation. That might change if the birds didn't show, but Riley doubted it.

Checkpoint 2, USS *Rathburne*
Thursday, 8 June, 0943 Zulu
Thursday, 8 June, 6:43 P.M. Local
Captain Lemester squinted into the wind as the second helicopter settled down on the helipad located on the fantail of the ship. He waited until the blades on both birds stopped turning, then walked out to the lead one. He was already disquieted by the fact that the helicopters bore no marking. He recognized the type: Sikorsky UH-60. But he'd never seen a UH-60 Blackhawk with a flat black paint job and extra fuel tanks hung on the small wings above the cargo bay.

With those extra tanks they must be flying an awfully long way, Lemester conjectured. That made him feel even more uneasy. The only countries in two directions were Russia and

North Korea. And those birds had come from the third direction: west. He didn't think the navy would go to all the trouble of moving his ship up here to refuel two helicopters if the aircraft were just going to turn around and go back.

Lemester watched warily as the pilot got out of the first chopper and walked over to him.

"Evening, sir. We'd appreciate it if your men could top off our birds and if you could find the four of us a quiet place to get some rest for a few hours. We're not leaving again until about a quarter after midnight local time. We'd also sure appreciate it if you could detail a couple of marines to keep people away from the inside of the birds. We've got a lot of classified gear on board."

Lemester designated one of his ensigns to escort the pilots to a stateroom. The short conversation with the pilot had done little to ease his disquiet. Lemester was also annoyed. First of all, the pilot hadn't introduced himself. Second, he wasn't wearing any identifying insignia, just a plain flight suit. Third, the man obviously felt that the captain of this ship didn't have a need to know what the hell was going on. Fourth, one of the pilots was setting up what looked to be a portable SATCOM radio and sending a message right from the flight deck—without even asking. Lemester didn't fancy being treated as a floating gas station and hotel.

The pilot could have acted more friendly, Lemester fumed. He might have asked if Lemester had any pertinent information for them. For instance, it might be helpful to know about the radar along the Soviet coast off to the west. But if the pilot was too important and high speed to ask, then the hell with him. The captain turned and went back to his bridge.

Fort Meade, Maryland
Thursday, 8 June, 1000 Zulu
Thursday, 8 June, 5:00 A.M. Local
The buzzer on the computer woke Meng out of a fitful nap. He accessed the file and perused the message from the FOB.

CLASSIFICATION: TOP SECRET
TO: CDR USSOCOM/ SFOB FM/ MSG 56
FROM: FOB K1

TEAM CONFIRMS PZ/ SAME PLACE/ SAME
TIME/
READY FOR MISSION/ AWAIT FINAL GO/
DENSER STABLE/
CLASSIFICATION: TOP SECRET

Things sounded as though they were finally starting to go
right. Meng had already received a message that the helicopters had arrived at the *Rathburne* almost twenty minutes ago.
He typed in the confirmation of the PZ and transmitted it to
the launch site in Misawa to be forwarded to the aircraft.

PZ Drable, Operational Area Dustey, China
Thursday, 8 June, 1100 Zulu
Thursday, 8 June, 7:00 P.M. Local
Olinski led Reese out into the open field. They left
O'Shaugnesy back at the tree line in a morphine-induced un-
consciousness. Despite the best efforts of Comsky, blood was
still seeping through the bandages covering O'Shaugnesy's
stomach.

Using knives and a small folding saw, they began cutting
down all the small trees and bushes more than a foot high.
After an hour's work they had succeeded in clearing an area
large enough for one helicopter to land safely. They gathered
all the loose debris from the field and disposed of it twenty-
five meters into the tree line, so it wouldn't be blown about
when the helicopter landed.

Olinski then checked the wind direction. Out of the west.
Using his knife he dug four small holes in the ground in the
shape of an inverted *Y*, with the stem pointing into the wind.
There was a hole at the end of each stem and at the joint. A
half hour prior to the scheduled exfiltration, Olinski would
stake down an infrared chem light in each hole to mark the
landing zone.

The team had an FM frequency and call signs for the aircraft, but they would be used only if absolutely necessary.
Hopefully, the pilots would be able to find this small open
area. Olinski didn't have much confidence in the navigational
abilities of pilots, however. He'd have the PRC68 radio

hooked to his vest, ready just in case he had to guide the aircraft.

Fort Meade, Maryland
Thursday, 8 June, 1520 Zulu
Thursday, 8 June, 10:20 A.M. Local
Meng knew he must send the final authorization code. Everything and everyone involved was committed. To back out at this point would simply result in his disgrace and punishment without any result. Looking at the headline on the front page of today's *New York Times* strengthened his resolve: "ARTILLERY FIRING IN SUBURBS ADDS TO TENSION IN BEIJING; MYSTERY ON LEADERS GROWS. ARMY CLASH DENIED." Meng scanned the article for the twentieth time, focusing on what he felt to be the critical parts.

> The evening news program denounced as "purely rumor" the reports of fighting between military units near the military airport in southern Beijing. It also offered an unusual denial of a report that Deng Xiaoping, China's senior leader, had died.
>
> "That's a sheer fabrication intended to poison people's minds," the newscaster said, without shedding any light on Mr. Deng's situation or whereabouts.
>
> Not since the end of the Maoist period more than a dozen years ago has there been such confusion about the situation in the world's most populous nation. Today, even the most basic information—such as whether anyone at all is running China, or whether Mr. Deng is alive—is contested. None of China's leaders have been seen for 12 days or more, and there have been rumors of coups or assassination attempts against both Mr. Deng and Prime Minister Li Peng.

Meng put down the paper. The Old Men were teetering—he could feel it. Maybe all that was needed was a final push. Meng sat down at his computer keyboard and typed in the final authorization code word to the FOB.

Checkpoint 2, USS *Rathburne*
Thursday, 8 June, 1530 Zulu
Friday, 9 June, 12:30 A.M. Local

Right on schedule the two Blackhawks crawled into the sky, laboring under the load of more than sixteen hundred gallons of fuel. C.J.'s right hand was wrapped around the cyclic, which poked upright between his legs from the floor. With his left hand he held the collective, a lever set into the floor on the left side of his seat. Pulling up on the collective basically increased power, making the helicopter climb. Dropping it decreased power, making the helicopter descend. The cyclic controlled the attitude of the blades and was used for maneuvering. To add to the fun there were pedals (one for each foot) controlling the rear vertical rotor blades, which kept the aircraft in trim and flying straight, along with a throttle, which adjusted the fuel rate. Juggling cyclic, collective, pedals, and throttle made the helicopter perform. Each affected the others, which was why a helicopter was much more difficult to fly than a plane. Let go of the controls of an airplane and the plane will glide along, held aloft by the lift of its wings. A helicopter's wings are its rotor blades; let go of the controls and the helicopter tries to turn upside down and beat itself to death.

C.J. banked his aircraft smoothly to the northwest and headed for the shore. He adjusted the throttle for maximum fuel conservation, and they were on their way, skimming along at 130 knots fifty feet above the waves. One hundred and twenty kilometers of ocean and then the real fun would begin.

Surveillance, Target Dagger, Operational Area Dustey
Thursday, 8 June, 1600 Zulu
Friday, 9 June, 12:00 P.M. Local

ZEROFO	URROGE	RZEROF	OURXXG
OXXXGO	XXXGOX	XXGOXX	CMOPPE
RSENRO	UTEXXX	CMOPPE	RSENRO
UTEXXB	ESTWIS	MESAND	GOODLU
CKDRAT	TSXXXX		

Riley read the message and smiled. They had the final go and the birds were coming. Outstanding, Riley thought. He had been afraid of a last-minute cancellation.

Everybody was in place. Devito and Lalli, armed with their RPGs, were positioned where the compound service road ran into the pipeline's service road. Chong and Trapp were along the tree line, off to the west. Trapp, with his SVD, would shoot out the southwest camera; Chong would provide local security for Trapp.

Riley, Comsky, and Mitchell would stay here at the surveillance point—Riley to shoot out the berm camera and Comsky to shoot out the southeast one. Hoffman and Smith were waiting with them, prepared to hit the target as soon as the snipers finished firing.

In the glow of the security lights from the compound, Riley could see the gleam of anticipation in the others' eyes. He was nervous but wouldn't show it in front of the team. He knew that everyone was nervous—and scared. Once they hit the target, the clock started. The hunt would be on. And Team 3 would be the hunted.

Naryn, **Peter the Great Bay**
Thursday, 8 June, 1605 Zulu
Friday, 9 June, 1:05 A.M. Local
Junior Lieutenant Omsk took his duties as watch officer very seriously. Senior Lieutenant Chelyabinsk had impressed upon him the importance of maintaining a vigilant watch, since the American ship was circling farther out to sea.

"You never know. The Americans may attack you!" Chelyabinsk had told Omsk, laughing, before he retired to his captain's quarters for the night, leaving strict orders not to be disturbed.

Omsk didn't think it was amusing. He was a commissioned officer in the navy of the Soviet Socialist Republic. Enemies of the state were only one hundred kilometers away. Certainly that was nothing to laugh at.

Omsk had grown even more serious a minute ago, when the radar operator reported picking up two low-flying objects moving directly toward the *Naryn*. Objects coming from the direction of the American ship. The two blips would be flying by in only a few seconds. Omsk glanced down quickly at the 25mm-gun crew. He yelled at them to be prepared. They stared back at him stupidly.

As Omsk was debating about waking up Chelyabinsk, the first helicopter flew by only fifty meters off the port bow. Omsk didn't know what to do. He hadn't recognized the outline of the helicopter and didn't know if it was friendly or not. Then they saw the second helicopter.

Exfiltration Aircraft, Peter the Great Bay
Thursday, 8 June, 1606 Zulu
Friday, 9 June, 1:06 A.M. Local

Hawkins didn't even see the patrol boat as he flew by it. Flying lead for this leg, he was concentrating on trying to make out the shoreline through his goggles. His instruments told him that the coast should be coming up any second. The two helicopters had been switching off lead every thirty minutes to reduce fatigue.

He saw the ship only when its searchlight came on and probed the sky. The flare of the light exploded in his computer-enhanced goggles, causing them to shut down momentarily to prevent overload. At first, Hawkins thought he was being fired at. His helicopter dropped toward the surface of the ocean before he regained control. He turned slightly left to see what was going on, then saw the ship and the searchlight.

Jesus Christ! Hawkins thought. What the hell was a patrol boat doing here? Hawkins hit his right pedal, swung the tail of his aircraft toward the ship, and opened his throttle all the way, heading for the safety of the shore.

C.J., piloting the trail bird, had also been blinded. He'd seen the patrol boat in his goggles just a second before they blacked out. His first thought concerning the flash of light was missile launch!

C.J. immediately took the proper evasive action, diving down and toward the direction of the missile. This pointed his helicopter directly at the ship. The purposes of this maneuver were to turn the hot exhaust of the helicopter away from a heat-seeking missile, to present a smaller target, and to give the missile less time to react.

In the two seconds it took to tear off his goggles, he'd closed the two hundred meters between his aircraft and the ship. Looming in front of him were the searchlight and mast of the ship. C.J. frantically hauled back on his collective and jerked the cyclic to the right. He felt, rather than saw, his aircraft hit something. It shuddered momentarily, then the power was back and he was gone, slowly gaining altitude. He yelled at Yost to take the controls so he could put his goggles back on.

Naryn, **Peter the Great Bay**
Thursday, 8 June, 1608 Zulu
Friday, 9 June, 1:08 A.M. Local

Omsk stared in amazement as the second helicopter flew off into the dark night. He would have sworn that the helicopter was going to crash into the ship after he turned on the searchlight. It had passed only ten feet above his head, striking the radar mast. Looking up, Omsk could see that the mast had been severed just below the tip. Who were those fools? he thought, just as Chelyabinsk staggered onto the deck.

"What the hell was that?" Chelyabinsk roared.

"A helicopter," Omsk replied.

"What helicopter? Whose helicopter? What hit us?" Chelyabinsk barked out questions.

"I don't know, sir. There were two of them. They had no lights on. The first one kept going. The second dove right at us when I turned on the searchlight. We'd picked them up only a minute ago, coming from the direction of the American ship."

Chelyabinsk stopped yelling at his junior lieutenant. It was obvious that the man was ignorant. He ordered the ship's searchlight turned off.

Back in his cabin, Chelyabinsk sat down and tried to figure out what he would report. How the hell can I put together a report when nobody seems to know what happened? Probably some army pilots out of Vladivostok in training—maybe buzzing the American ship. That fool Omsk must have blinded the pilot by turning on the searchlight. I'm surrounded by idiots. Well, Omsk would pay dearly for the damage to the ship. I'll file the report when we get back to port, Chelyabinsk thought. The captain turned off the light and went back to sleep.

Changbai Mountain Range, China
Thursday, 8 June, 1630 Zulu
Friday, 9 June, 12:30 A.M. Local
"Fuck this shit. Let's go home."

C.J. turned his eyes momentarily from the mountains flashing by and glanced at his copilot through the goggles. He knew that the little wimp would chicken out when things got tough. He'd never liked flying with Yost and had complained to the captain several times, saying he didn't think Yost had the right stuff to make a flight like this.

"Listen, Yost, we're only three and a half hours out. Those guys will be waiting for us. We're going in."

"Bullshit, C.J. We had a blade strike at least. This thing could shake apart on us any minute. Plus somebody knows we're here now. We'll never get out. That ship will be waiting for us when we come back."

"So we come back south of there. No big deal."

"Come on, C.J. We'll never make it. Fuck those guys. Nobody will blame us for turning around. Not after hitting that ship."

As he flew, C.J. considered what Yost was saying. True, no one would blame them for turning around now. In training, a blade strike is considered an emergency that requires immediate landing, followed by replacement of the entire transmission of the helicopter, since a blade strike can cause damage to the gears. If the transmission seized up while they were flying, the UH-60 would have all the aerodynamics of a rock and would land accordingly.

If that ship reported them, the Soviets would be alerted, which meant they might have lost almost three hours in reaction time. C.J. figured that the Soviets must be on alert—hell, that asshole was missing part of his mast. If that was so, then they would just have to come out over North Korea.

C.J. carefully felt the controls, playing with them slightly. Everything felt normal—no unusual vibrations, just that brief loss of power when they hit. At least they didn't shoot at us. Probably means they had no idea who we were, C.J. reasoned.

He really couldn't blame Yost for being scared. They all knew that the Blackhawks, loaded with more than sixteen hundred gallons of fuel, were an explosion waiting to happen. If they crashed or were shot down, they wouldn't have to worry about the Chinese finding any wreckage. There wouldn't be enough left of the aircraft to make an ashtray. Yost was probably envisioning that fate.

C.J. laughed to himself. I've never heard of a helicopter having a midair collision with a ship. That was a first. It'll make a great bar story when I get back. *If* I get back.

Ah, screw it, C.J. thought. He turned to his copilot. "OK, Bud. Let me put it to you in terms you can understand. I'm flying this bad boy and I'm taking it in. If you don't want to go, the door is to your right and you're welcome to leave at any time." The senior pilot brought the helicopter even closer to the earth, negotiating the mountain passes.

12

"His potential is that of a fully drawn
crossbow: his timing, the release of a
trigger."
Sun Tzu: *The Art of War*

Target, Operational Area Dustey, China
Thursday, 8 June, 1805 Zulu
Friday, 9 June, 2:05 A.M. Local

Mitchell counted down for Riley and Comsky; Chong
counted down for Trapp. "Five, four, three, two, one."
The three SVD shots sounded as one in the clear night air.

At pump station 5, the watchman stared at his screens in
confusion as all three cameras at compound 8 went black. He
cursed. It had to be another system malfunction.

"Go," Mitchell hissed.
Hoffman and Smith leapt from the tree line and sprinted.
Eighteen seconds later they were at the eastern fence. Hoffman
hooked the line charge onto the fence while Smith unreeled the
firing wire. Eight seconds later Smith fired the charge and a six-
foot gap opened up in the fence, beckoning them in.

Nothing registered at pump station 5. The T sensor on the
eastern side of compound 8 had been broken for a week now.
As required by the rules, a work order had been submitted for
its repair.

2:06 A.M. Local
Twenty seconds after the hole appeared, Hoffman and Smith
were at the berm. They began strapping the charges on the
wires. It took them forty-five seconds to put on all six. Hoffman then connected the fuses while Smith placed the platter

charge beneath the pipe and laid out the two thermite grenade rafts. The two engineers ran their respective detonating cord back to each other and hooked the wires together.

They turned and ran back toward the hole in the fence, unreeling the det cord. At the fence Hoffman placed the end of the cord into the fuse ignitor. He muttered "boom" as he pulled the ignitor.

2:07 A.M. Local
At pump station 5 an alarm bell rang stridently. Something was wrong—pressure was dropping rapidly. Pumping was automatically stopped and word relayed along the line: Complete pipe failure somewhere between pump stations 5 and 6.

2:09 A.M. Local
The team walked quickly through the woods, Chong in the lead wearing goggles.

Hooker had wanted to know if the pipe would drop, Riley remembered. He couldn't wait to tell his battalion commander. *Dropped* was too simple a word to describe the destruction they had just wrought. Even now the glow from burning oil lit up the sky behind them.

The explosion had worked perfectly. The six wires snapped like rubber bands. The pipe held still for a few seconds, then collapsed into the Sungari River with a roar. While the suspended pipe was going down, the platter charge had exploded, burning a hole cleanly through the bottom of the still-standing section of pipe in the compound. As oil poured out, it was ignited immediately by the thermite grenades.

Perfect, Riley thought. Less than three minutes from start to finish. Perfect.

PZ Drable, Operational Area Dustey, China
Thursday, 8 June, 1900 Zulu
Friday, 9 June, 3:00 A.M. Local
Olinski had heard the explosion at 2:07 A.M. Thirty minutes ago, as planned, he'd gotten a radio call from Captain Mitchell over the PRC68.

"We're on the way. Everything went according to plan. Complete destruction. Send the PONDER. Out."

Olinski had carefully encrypted the message and now it was ready to go. He burst it out at exactly 1900Z.

Putting the PSC3 radio back in his rucksack, Olinski left Reese watching O'Shaugnesy while he went out to place infrared chem lights into each small depression of the inverted Y.

FOB, Osan Air Force Base, Korea
Thursday, 8 June, 1905 Zulu
Friday, 9 June, 4:05 A.M. Local
Hossey anxiously decrypted the message:

ZEROFI	VEPOND	ERXXXP	ONDERX
XAAADA	GGERBB	BCOMPL	ETECCC
DDDEEE	TELLYO	UKNOWW	HOITDR
OPPEDX	XDOUBL	EXXXXX	

Using the message format book, he interpreted the codes:
Type: (Target destruction report) PONDER.
AAA: (Target name) DAGGER.
BBB: (Extent of destruction) COMPLETE.
CCC: (Wounded) none.
DDD: (Killed) none.
EEE: (remarks) TELL YOU KNOW WHO IT DROPPED.
DOUBLE.

Hossey felt some of the tension in his body ease, and he allowed himself a small smile. "Sergeant Major," he said, handing the message to Hooker.

Hooker protested the remarks with a grin on his face. "I never doubted that it would drop, sir. I just wanted to see if they had done their homework. Now all we need is a successful exfiltration and we'll be home free. They done good so far."

Fort Meade, Maryland
Thursday, 8 June, 1930 Zulu
Thursday, 8 June, 2:30 P.M. Local
Finally Meng allowed himself a sigh of relief. The team had interdicted the pipe and, based on his other data, the exfiltration looked good. Both helicopters had left the *Rathburne* on time. A blow had been struck to an artery of the Dragon. The Old Men would have to notice.

PZ Drable, Operational Area Dustey, China
Thursday, 8 June, 1915 Zulu
Friday, 9 June, 3:15 A.M. Local

Team 3 was whole again. All twelve members were in the
same place for the first time since they had separated at the
pipeline three days ago. That made Dave Riley feel a whole
lot better. But looking at O'Shaugnesy dampened his spirits.

The man was in bad shape. Comsky had told them, when
he'd come up to the rally point, that O'Shaugnesy's condition
was deteriorating. Keeping him out of shock was a full-time
job for Reese, who was lying with the wounded man in a
bivy sack to give him his body warmth. O'Shaugnesy's
wounds were starting to smell, which meant that infection
had gotten a foothold.

At least the birds were en route, thought Riley. We'll get
him out and to a hospital tonight. The man would be scarred
for life, but at least he'd be alive.

Riley checked his watch. Forty-five minutes until the birds
showed up. They still had heard no activity in reaction to the
explosion. More than an hour and nothing. Riley was surprised. But he figured that the Chinese still didn't know what
was happening. Riley hoped that by the time they figured it
out, Team 3 would be long gone.

Pump Station 5, China
Thursday, 8 June, 1930 Zulu
Friday, 9 June, 3:30 A.M. Local

The foreman of the pump station had alerted the reaction platoon within a minute of the first indication of trouble. It had
taken the platoon more than thirty minutes to get everyone
awake and prepared to depart the pump station. The foreman
was still waiting for a radio call back from the platoon leader.

He had just received a call from the duty officer of the
118th Division, whose area of responsibility included this
section of pipeline. The duty officer reported that the 3d Aviation Regiment, in response to the division's request, had dispatched a helicopter to investigate.

Airspace, China

C.J. didn't really trust the Doppler. As he liked to put it—the Doppler might tell you what street you were on, but when you've got to knock on somebody's door, you need to do better. In preparation for this mission, C.J. had memorized the satellite imagery and the location of PZ Drable.

Because of his distrust of the navigational device, C.J. made his plan for getting to the PZ as simple as possible. Fly on azimuth until he hit the Songhua River, then follow it northwest. When he reached the fork where the Songhua split from the Sungari, he knew he'd be about seven minutes out from where the Daqing-Fushun pipeline crossed the Sungari. Prior to that crossing he'd slide north about a kilometer from the river and parallel it west. Two kilometers after crossing the pipeline, he should see the infrared chem lights and strobe on the pickup zone.

They'd hit the Songhua River twelve minutes ago and were still heading northwest. There was danger in following the river, but C.J. figured at 125 knots the helicopter would be past anybody on the ground before it could be identified.

The route heading back was also as simple as he could make it. They'd reverse the route in, flying back down the Sungari and taking the right fork along the Songhua. Then C.J. planned on deviating slightly from the inbound route. He didn't want to cross Soviet airspace, so he would go a little farther south. At the end of the Songhua they would fly over the Sungari Reservoir, which was almost 150 kilometers long. C.J. liked the idea of using the reservoir because he could open up the throttle and go faster over the water. They'd skim the surface of the reservoir to its southern end, then follow an unnamed stream up into the Changbai Mountains. They'd crest the mountains just short of the North Korean border and then it would be a straight shot, due east to the coast and the *Rathburne*.

C.J. decided to let Hawkins land first when they reached the PZ. When Hawkins took off, he would land and, while the rest of the team was loading, he could hop out and quickly inspect the helicopter to see if he could figure out what damage they'd done during the collision with the ship.

PZ Drable, Operational Area Dustey, China
Thursday, 8 June, 1945 Zulu
Friday, 9 June, 3:45 A.M. Local

Fifteen minutes. They collected their rucksacks into a large pile and Riley lay three primed thermite grenades on top. They'd been briefed to reduce the weight as much as possible. Everyone would keep their weapon and vest, but the rucks would be torched. If found, there would be a mass of melted equipment—which had been sterile to start with. Riley would ignite the grenades as he went forward to get on the second bird.

Team 3 was clustered on the edge of the pickup zone in two groups of six. The members of the first lift had O'Shaugnesy wrapped in a bivy sack; they would carry him using a poncho. Everyone's ears were straining, listening for the sound of rotor blades.

At 3:47 A.M. they heard blades off to the east. Too soon, thought Riley. But maybe they're ahead of schedule. Olinski stood next to him with the earplug for the PRC68 FM radio pressed against his ear, listening in case the pilots called them.

The blades were getting closer. Still off to the south. Was the idiot following the pipeline this close? Riley wondered. Then he realized what the sound probably was—a reaction force to check out the pipe. As long as the Chinese aircraft stayed down there, it would be okay. Only ten more minutes.

Airspace, China
Thursday, 8 June, 1953 Zulu
Friday, 9 June, 3:53 A.M. Local

The fork of the two rivers appeared right on schedule. C.J. slid the Blackhawk to the north of the Sungari River. Seven minutes out.

The kilometers flashed by beneath them. Five minutes. C.J. could see a glow off to the southwest. Those sons of bitches must have blown up something big, he thought.

Two minutes. The pipeline flashed by beneath them. C.J. slowed down. He started scanning to the right as Yost scanned to the left, looking for the IR chem lights and strobe.

PZ Drable, Operational Area Dustey, China
Thursday, 8 June, 1958 Zulu
Friday, 9 June, 3:58 A.M. Local

Trapp stood at the junction of the Y and turned on his IR strobe. He could hear helicopters coming from the east. The one that had come by earlier, to the south, had quieted down.

A minute and a half later the helicopters were very close.

4:00 A.M. Local

C.J. could see the strobe and the inverted Y. Perfect. Seven hundred and fifty kilometers from the *Rathburne* and a flawless linkup. He slid over the pickup zone to let Hawkins land first.

Hawkins flared his Blackhawk and started to settle in. C.J. could see the figure with the strobe extinguish it. Damn, this is a tight pickup zone, C.J. thought, as he watched Hawkins maneuver. We wouldn't have been able to fit in both birds anyway.

Hawkins brought the helicopter to a halt on the ground. Five men carrying a sixth came running forward. They slid in the bivy sack, then clambered on board.

The first Blackhawk started to lift.

Target Dagger, Operational Area Dustey, China
Thursday, 8 June, 2000 Zulu
Friday, 9 June, 4:00 A.M. Local

Captain Lu was senior officer on board the MI-4 helicopter that had flown up to investigate the drop in pressure. It hadn't been hard to find the cause, even in the dark. A fire was still burning in the northern compound of the Sungari River crossing, and the pipe across the river was gone. He ordered the pilot to land near the service road.

Soldiers from the pump station platoon were gathered around their trucks at the service road, watching the fire. They weren't getting any closer than they had to. The men scattered as the helicopter settled down and the officer got out.

Lu cursed to himself. He didn't know what could have caused such a tremendous accident. Probably another engineering screwup. It would be their job to find the cause and fix it. Then Lu scanned the area with his binoculars and saw the hole in the fence. And, as his own aircraft shut down, he heard the sound of helicopters off to the north.

PZ Drable, Operational Area Dustey, China
Thursday, 8 June, 2001 Zulu
Friday, 9 June, 4:01 A.M. Local
Riley watched the first helicopter lift. He pulled the fuse running into the thermite grenades. After ensuring that the fuse was burning properly, he ran forward as the second bird landed.

Riley jumped on board, then stared in disbelief as the pilot hopped out and started running around the aircraft. What the hell was he doing?

Target Dagger
Lu screamed at the pilot of the helicopter to get it back into the air. Slowly the blades started turning. Lu was elated and scared at the same time. Elated at the thought of actually capturing the saboteurs; scared of what would happen to him if he didn't.

PZ Drable, Operational Area Dustey, China
Thursday, 8 June, 2002 Zulu
Friday, 9 June, 4:02 A.M. Local
C.J. leapt back in as Yost lifted the bird. With the blades still turning, it had been impossible for C.J. to see if they were notched or damaged. The outside external fuel tank on the right side pylon had some scratches on it, but that was all he could see in the dark. What C.J. hadn't noticed was the slight split in the seam of the outside right tank. Drop by drop, JP4 fuel was leaking out, dripping to the ground.

C.J. took the controls from Yost and did a quick scan of the area as he turned east. "We got company," he said, as the navigational lights of the MI-4 rose from the vicinity of the fire, two kilometers away.

C.J. knew that the Chinese helicopter couldn't have seen him yet. The Blackhawk was blacked out and Chinese pilots didn't have goggles. He wasn't about to give the aircraft a chance to find him. C.J. knew that the MI-4 Hound had a maximum speed of 155 miles an hour. C.J. chuckled—that was in the bright sunshine with the wind at its back.

"Come on, asshole. Let's race." Yost glanced over at the man talking to himself and shook his head.

C.J. opened up the throttle and pushed the cyclic forward.

The Blackhawk shot forward past the startled Hawkins, who immediately followed.

Thursday, 8 June, 2007 Zulu
Friday, 9 June, 4:07 A.M. Local
Lu could see a fire in the tree line at the edge of the small open field, but no sign of helicopters. Flying at night by searchlight was a risky proposition at best. The pilot was afraid to move too far away from the navigational security of the pipeline or the river.

Lu cursed. If only he had been quicker in reacting to the lost pressure on the pipeline. He'd never thought it could actually be a terrorist action. Now he knew that it was too late to catch whoever had done it. And too late for him. He picked up the radio microphone and called headquarters.

Airspace, China
Thursday, 8 June, 2045 Zulu
Friday, 9 June, 4:45 A.M. Local
Riley was still a little surprised. He'd mentally prepared himself for the exfiltration to be screwed up. But things had worked out. They were actually on board a helicopter and heading for home. The target hit had been a success. Team 3 had two injured, but both would recover. He knew it was premature, but Riley began to allow himself to feel good.

In the front of the helicopter, C.J. had opposite feelings. He started sensing a slightly abnormal vibration in the controls. Yost felt it, too. They exchanged worried looks.

Don't do this to me, C.J. thought savagely. We finally won one. Come on baby, hang in there. If there was a way to will a helicopter to stay in the air, C.J. was going to do it.

The seam on number 4 external tank also reacted to the strange vibration. Instead of just a drip, a trickle of highly flammable fuel was now leaking out.

118th Division Headquarters, Harbin, China
Thursday, 8 June, 2053 Zulu
Friday, 9 June, 4:53 A.M. Local
Once the division commander, General Haotian, was awakened, the Chinese reaction speeded up dramatically. It had

been almost three hours since the explosion. In that time only one MI-4 helicopter and the pump station platoon had been dispatched to investigate.

With Lu's report of apparent sabotage, General Haotian contacted the 3d Aviation Regiment in Shenyang and asked for help. In response to the request, six Z-9 gunship helicopters lifted out of Shenyang and headed north. Haotian realized, based on Lu's report and the distances involved, that they were probably too late, but he wanted nothing left to chance. When he had to explain to his superior, he wanted to be able to say. he had done everything possible.

If only that idiot Lu had moved quicker, Haotian thought. By now, the terrorists were probably out of the area he controlled with his division. Haotian reluctantly called his higher headquarters—Shenyang Military Region headquarters located in the city of Shenyang to the southwest. They'd find out what was happening anyway when the 3d Aviation Regiment reported its search mission.

Airspace, China
Thursday, 8 June, 2100 Zulu
Friday, 9 June, 5:00 A.M. Local

The vibration hadn't gotten any worse. It was so slight that C.J. could almost fool himself into believing it wasn't there. But he knew it was. Hang in there, C.J. prayed. Another hour and a half to the coast.

In the trailing helicopter, Devito had whole blood flowing into O'Shaugnesy. The sense of security inside the aircraft was comforting. The high of the target hit and exfiltration was wearing off, and everyone slumped wearily against the back and doors of the cargo compartments.

In the lead aircraft, Riley sat with his back against the pilot's seat, surveying the five other members of his team. Comsky, as expected, appeared to be sleeping, although Riley suspected it might be an act. Mitchell was sitting with his back against the copilot's seat with his eyes closed. Probably thinking about the FOB debrief. Olinski, Chong, and Hoffman were peering out the windows at the terrain flashing by.

They ought to market this as a ride at an amusement park, Riley thought as he glanced out the side window. They were flying barely twenty feet above the surface of a large lake. Riley had flown in numerous helicopters and he felt a grudging admiration for the man flying this one. The pilot was good, whoever he was. Occasionally, as they turned to follow the bend of the lake, Riley could catch glimpses of the second aircraft following a hundred meters behind.

Riley felt good. All in all, a successful mission. What had happened with O'Shaugnesy was unfortunate, but you couldn't plan for everything on a mission.

Riley wasn't sure what they had accomplished by blowing up the pipe. Sent a message to the Chinese government that the U.S. meant business, Riley supposed, but the whole thing still didn't make sense. Sometimes the way countries interacted seemed like such a game. Like two kids in the alley, shoving each other back and forth, trying to see who was the toughest. Riley closed his eyes. Now wasn't the time to ask those questions. Now was the time to be happy to be alive. To be going home.

Thursday, 8 June, 2130 Zulu
Friday, 9 June, 5:30 A.M. Local
The six Z-9s flew over the destroyed pipe, then broke into two sets of three. The first set spread and flew due east. The second set fanned out and flew to the south. They could fly those azimuths for only another twenty minutes before they would have to return to Shenyang to refuel. The spiderweb had been spun too late. The fly was gone.

Thursday, 8 June, 2155 Zulu
Friday, 9 June, 5:55 A.M. Local
C.J. carefully climbed the helicopter farther up the streambed into the Changbai Mountains. He could see the ridgeline just ahead. In a few minutes they'd be across it and heading down. Just another fifty minutes and they'd be over the ocean. The Blackhawk was still holding together. Just another hour and thirty-five minutes and they'd be at the *Rathburne*.

C.J. was startled by a blazing flash of light to his right.

5:56 A.M. Local

C.J.'s helicopter exploded right in front of Hawkins. Before his goggles shut down, Hawkins thought he saw the entire aircraft disintegrate. In the two seconds it took his goggles to recover, he was past the explosion. There was no sign of the other aircraft.

In the cargo compartment, Trapp leapt to the door and peered out the window into the darkness below. A ball of fire settled into the trees as they flew by. It looked like part of a helicopter.

"Goddamn, Goddamn," Trapp muttered in shock. "We were almost there. We almost had it made." He didn't know what had caused the helicopter to explode, but the effect had obviously been catastrophic. He looked at the others' shocked faces.

As his goggles cleared and he could see again, Hawkins swung around and headed back to where C.J.'s bird had disappeared. Cruising just above the trees, he couldn't see the other helicopter. There was a fire burning in the trees below but nothing else. Considering the amount of fuel the aircraft had been carrying, Hawkins knew that was understandable. There was also no place nearby to land.

Looking at his fuel gauge, Hawkins turned and started heading east again. He climbed and crossed the crest of the Changbai Mountains. Those on board the lone helicopter could see the first gray light of dawn tingeing the ocean off in the distance.

13

"Secret operations are essential in war; upon them the army relies to make its every move."
Sun Tzu: *The Art of War*

USS *Rathburne*, Tatar Strait
Friday, 9 June, 0003 Zulu
Friday, 9 June, 9:03 A.M. Local

Commander Lemester watched the lone Blackhawk waver above the fantail of his ship and then slam down on it.

Son of a bitch almost crashed into my ship, he thought angrily as he strode forward to confront the pilot. He stopped in amazement as the cargo doors slid open and five dirty men, dressed in black and carrying weapons, hopped off. Four of them reached back in and started pulling out a man wrapped in a poncho. The fifth man ran over to Lemester.

"We need a stretcher up here right now to take this man to your infirmary."

"Who the hell are you?" Lemester shouted over the whine of the helicopter engine shutting down.

"Listen, we've got a wounded American here. Just get the damn stretcher!" the tall, powerful-looking man yelled back.

Lemester had had enough of taking orders on board his own ship. "First, I want to know who you people are."

Trapp glared at the officer standing in front of him in his clean white uniform. He grabbed his M79 grenade launcher from his vest and pointed the gaping 40mm muzzle at the navy man's face. "You've got ten seconds to get me a stretcher and get that man to your infirmary."

Behind Trapp, the four other members of Team 3, standing under the slowing rotor blades, brought their weapons to the ready.

Lemester was a by-the-book man, but he wasn't stupid. His

curiosity was rapidly diminishing. These men didn't look like they were bluffing. He ordered the stretcher brought up, then confronted the tall man. "What about the other helicopter? When is it going to be here? My orders are to wait for it, then I can get out of here."

"There isn't going to be another helicopter."

9:23 A.M. Local

Trapp cornered Hawkins in the small stateroom that Lemester had provided the team. They waited there while O'Shaugnesy was being worked on in the infirmary. Devito was also down in the infirmary to make sure that the wounded man didn't say anything about the mission while the navy doctor was treating him.

"What the hell happened to the other bird, and where are we going now? I thought you were supposed to fly us back to Osan from here."

"We are supposed to fly you there, but neither me nor my copilot are up to it right now. I've got to wait until my nerve comes back. Give us an hour or so, then we'll take off again.

"Also, I figured you'd want to get your man into the infirmary here rather than let him wait another four hours in the air. C.J.—he's the guy who was piloting the other bird—and I, before we left Japan, decided that if we had any wounded, we'd drop them off here. That isn't what our captain told us to do, but screw that jerk. I'm not going to fly wounded men four extra hours when they can get taken care of sooner."

Trapp agreed with Hawkins' logic, and his respect for the pilot rose another notch. That had been some damn fine flying back there. The pilot's reasoning concerning O'Shaugnesy had mirrored his. If Hawkins hadn't shut down once he landed, Trapp had been prepared to do some weapon pointing at him also, so they could off-load O'Shaugnesy and get him some proper care as soon as possible.

"Yeah, OK. What about the other bird though? What the hell happened to it? I didn't see any ground fire. How come you didn't hang around longer searching?"

Hawkins sighed. Since the explosion he'd thought about the same thing, replaying the scene in his mind innumerable times. He hadn't seen any fire from the ground either. C.J.'s

bird had just exploded. He gave Trapp the only explanation
that fit. "Going in we damn near ran into a Soviet patrol boat.
As a matter of fact, the other bird *did* run into it. It looked
to me like it hit the ship's mast. Any number of things could
have been damaged that would lead to an explosion.

"I figure it was one of two things. They probably had a
blade strike, which means that the transmission might have
momentarily seized up, causing some damage to the gears.
That damage could have become catastrophic and the transmission finally seized up for good, causing the rotor blades to
stop immediately. Centrifugal force would have caused the
transmission to separate from the aircraft, and the shrapnel
would have punctured the external fuel tanks, causing the explosion we saw."

Hawkins considered what he had just proposed and ran the
explosion through his mind one more time. Somehow that explanation still didn't feel right. "I'm not sure if that would
have caused the type of explosion we saw, though. Another,
more likely, possibility is that one of the external fuel tanks
or lines might have been damaged in the collision and developed a small leak. The reason it took so long to blow is that
the fuel probably got ignited by static electricity."

Trapp didn't believe it. "You're telling me they flew for almost six hours with a fuel leak and it took that long to explode?"

Hawkins tried to explain. "Static electricity builds on a
helicopter as it flies. Sometimes it discharges into the atmosphere. Sometimes into the helicopter itself. That may have
happened this time. With all the fuel we were carrying, both
aircraft were an explosion waiting to happen. I don't think
we'll ever know what really occurred.

"I didn't have the fuel to hang around searching. All I
could see was a fire under the trees. There wasn't enough left
of the other bird to search for. That thing disintegrated in
midair. Plus, there was no place to land around the crash
site."

Trapp had to accept the inevitable—the explanation didn't
really matter. The bottom line was that the other aircraft
hadn't made it out. He grabbed Lalli and the two of them
went out to the fantail where the helicopter was sitting. While

Lalli set up the SATCOM, Trapp wrote out the hardest message he ever had to write.

FOB, Osan Air Force Base, Korea
Friday, 9 June, 0102 Zulu
Friday, 9 June, 10:02 P.M. Local
The brief, coded message had come in from the team two minutes ago. Hossey reread it and felt the chill settle deeper into his gut.

ZEROFI	VEEXFI	LONTIM	EONEAI
RCRAFT	LOSTON	WAYOUT	XXREPE
ATONEA	IRCRAF	TLOSTO	NWAYOU
TVICLO	NGONET	WOEIGH	TDEGRE
ESTWOT	HREEMI	NUTESL	ATFOUR
TWODEG	REESTH	REEZER	OMINUT
ESXXAL	LPRESU	MEDKIL	LEDXXR
EFUELI	NGDEPA	RTZERO	TWOONE
FIVEZU	LUXXXX		

Hossey's trained eye broke out the message from the six-letter groups. MESSAGE: NUMBER 05. Exfil on time, one aircraft lost on way out, repeat, one aircraft lost on way out, vicinity longitude 128 degrees 23 minutes, latitude 42 degrees 30 minutes. All presumed killed. Refueling, depart 0215 Zulu.

One aircraft, Hossey thought. Half the team and two pilots dead. Eight men. Hossey listlessly handed the message to Hooker, then sat down at his desk. He knew he should immediately forward the information to the SFOB, but he needed a few moments to let the reality of the loss sink in. They wouldn't find out who had been killed until the survivors landed here in three and a half hours.

Fort Meade, Maryland
Friday, 9 June, 0200 Zulu
Thursday, 8 June, 9:00 P.M. Local
Down the corridor in Tunnel 3, General Olson and his staff were celebrating the successful exfiltration of the Special

Forces team and the completion of their exercise. All had gone well in the simulation; the mission had been a success.

In Meng's office, the emotions were much different. Meng looked at the message about the lost aircraft another time. This was real. Eight men were dead because of his manipulations. He wasn't sure what to do. It was only a matter of time before the curtain of his deception was torn asunder. Questions would be asked. Meng thought he could control the FOB relatively well for a while yet. The surviving Blackhawk would drop the rest of the team at Osan and then, after a debrief and some rest, fly back to Misawa and down to Okinawa. Meng wondered how well the cover stories would work that had been concocted in the oplan against the possible loss of a helicopter. Would they work against the people who had written them?

Meng considered the situation. The aviation detachment commander from the 1st Special Forces Group was supposed to report the aircraft lost at sea during classified training. The FOB commander was supposed to back him up on that. The problem would come when someone at US-SOCOM put two and two together and came up with five. Meng ran the scenario through his computer. The answer was that he had anywhere from thirty-six to seventy-two hours, with a statistical mean of forty-eight, before someone started asking questions.

Meng rubbed his eyes wearily. He had that much time before the walls came crumbling down. He prayed the attack had moved the Old Men, even if just a little.

USS *Rathburne*, Tatar Strait
Friday, 9 June, 0200 Zulu
Friday, 9 June, 11:00 A.M. Local
The ship's doctor finished examining and cleaning the wounds. He'd never seen anything like them. The tall, silent man who'd accompanied the patient into the infirmary had been uncommunicative so far.

"What the hell happened to you?" the doctor asked as the patient finally came out of his drug-induced unconsciousness.

Despite being fuzzy headed from the morphine and loss of blood, O'Shaugnesy managed a weak smile. "I tripped over my rucksack."

Devito smiled and turned to the doctor. "He got mauled by a bear. I've got him on morphine, last injection was one hour ago. He's been taking whole blood for the last two hours. We need you to finish rebandaging him and give him some more antibiotics. We're taking off in a little while to take him to Korea and get him into a regular hospital."

The doctor was just finishing those procedures when three other men, dressed in the same black outfits and carrying exotic-looking weapons, came into the infirmary. They looked at the tall man, who shifted his gaze to the doctor. "Well, Doc? What do you think? Can he take another four-hour chopper ride back to a real hospital?"

The doctor considered. The tall man definitely knew something about medicine, the doctor could tell from what had been done so far, and had probably made up his own mind about the answer to that question. He was most likely just asking out of professional courtesy.

"I think getting him to a hospital as soon as possible is the best treatment he can receive right now. I really don't have the facilities here to do much more for him. Whoever's been treating him so far has done a super job. I've done as much as I can do."

"Let's take him on up, guys."

The doctor wondered where these men were going, and where they had come from. But he had a feeling he really didn't want to know.

Trapp supervised as they carefully loaded O'Shaugnesy onto the bird. The cleanly dressed naval officer who had met them when they landed was nowhere to be seen. Trapp expected as much. He climbed on board. The refueled Blackhawk lifted into the sky and turned to the southwest.

FOB, Osan Air Force Base, Korea
Friday, 9 June, 0545 Zulu
Friday, 9 June, 2:45 P.M. Local
Hooker and Hossey watched the Blackhawk touch down and roll toward the hangar. The cover story had already been released by the aviation detachment commander at Misawa Air Force Base in Japan. In fact, the U.S. and Japanese navies and air forces were presently conducting a search for survi-

vors in the location where the helicopter supposedly had been lost.

In the hangar, with the doors shut behind it, the Blackhawk rolled to a halt. The ambulance crew, which Hossey had called, ran forward as the cargo doors opened. They loaded O'Shaugnesy onto a stretcher for his final ride to the hospital.

Hossey ticked off the faces in his mind as he watched the men off-load: O'Shaugnesy, Trapp, Devito, Reese, Lalli, and Smith. Both Mitchell and Riley, he thought. Goddamn, not both. Which sparked a new thought in the colonel's mind: I'm going to have to see Mitchell's wife and tell her. He didn't look forward to that.

He looked at the dejected, beaten faces of the six who had made it home. Hossey walked over to Trapp. "What happened, Jim?"

Hooker edged up next to the two of them, forestalling Trapp's reply. "Sir, why don't we wait until we're in the isolation area and get some hot coffee and food."

Hossey nodded. As always the sergeant major made sense. The group walked across the hangar to a van. The team loaded their gear on board, and Hooker drove them and the pilots to the isolation area.

Hooker had dismissed the communications men, and the only ones now in the room were the six team members, the two pilots, and Hooker and Hossey. In the center of the operations center was a large table; on it were the maps Team 3 had used to plan the mission.

After the team members and pilots grabbed a cup of hot coffee, Hossey stood up to begin the debrief. "My first concern is what happened to the other aircraft." He turned to the chief pilot. "Where did they go down, how, and is there any chance of survivors?"

Hawkins leaned over the map and pointed. "They went down somewhere along here."

Hossey winced as he saw that it was over land. Hopefully, there were no identifiable pieces left, which also meant that the team members wouldn't be identifiable. He berated himself sharply in his own mind for such a coldhearted thought.

Hawkins continued. "We were flying up a draw, following it into the Changbai Mountains, where we figured we'd punch over the top, then drop right down and sprint for the sea. C.J. was leading me by about a hundred meters. You've got to remember that we were all under goggles." Hawkins described what had happened and his suspicions as to cause.

When he was done, it was Hooker who repeated the question nearest to Hossey's heart. "Do you think there might be survivors?"

Hawkins' answer was blunt. "No. That thing exploded as far as I could tell. We weren't too high up, probably eighty feet AGL. If it had just been an engine failure, C.J. probably could have autorotated into the trees. But an explosion, with all that fuel we had on board. . . ." Hawkins shook his head. "I did a sweep back across where they should have gone down and all I could see was a fire under the trees."

Hossey asked the next question that had to be asked from the point of view of mission success. "What about wreckage? Do you think it will be identifiable?"

Hawkins was exasperated. Didn't these idiots understand what he was telling them? "The damn helicopter blew up, sir. There probably aren't enough pieces left to figure out what the hell type of aircraft it was, never mind identify its source."

Hossey hung his head. Trapp spoke for the first time. "What are you going to do about the wreckage, sir?"

Hossey looked up. "What do you mean, what am I going to do?"

"You're not going to check on it? There still could be somebody alive back there."

Hossey rubbed his head as he considered the problem. "Now that we have a good fix on location, I'll have the SFOB run satellite imagery on the next pass over, which will probably be in a couple of hours. There's not much else we can do right now." He turned to Hooker. "Finish the debrief while I contact the SFOB and give them the grids for the crash site."

Fort Meade, Maryland
Friday, 9 June, 0600 Zulu
Friday, 9 June, 1:00 A.M. Local

Meng sat at the master console. Tunnel 3 was quiet. The SFOB staff was down to only a watch officer. All that was left for the US-SOCOM people to do was the debrief the next day. Meng had sent Wilson home with instructions to handle that tomorrow. He looked as a new message from the real FOB appeared on his screen. He transcribed the location of the crash and sent a request next door to the NSA for the imagery to be forwarded to the FOB. There was no sense in alarming the FOB commander, Meng reasoned, by not answering this request.

FOB, Osan Air Force Base, Korea
Friday, 9 June, 0717 Zulu
Friday, 9 June, 4:17 P.M. Local

Hossey looked over the faxed imagery with Trapp. The resolution and quality were unbelievable. Even so, the remains of the helicopter were hard to distinguish. The only reason they knew it was the location where the helicopter had gone down was because of the burn marks. There was no large piece of wreckage, just a few burned fragments barely visible through the trees. If that had happened before landing, then no one could have survived, Hossey knew.

He looked up and addressed Trapp. "Tell me again what you told me after the debriefing."

Trapp had pulled the colonel aside, fifteen minutes ago, at the conclusion of the debriefing, and he had clearly been agitated. "Sir, we're kissing those guys off too easy. That pilot was under goggles and all he saw was the initial explosion. I watched something go down in flames into the trees, but I don't think it was big enough to be the whole bird. Maybe something blew off it and the rest of the bird came down intact."

Now, Trapp looked at the colonel. "I'm sorry, sir. After seeing this I guess I was wrong."

Hossey rubbed the stubble of growth that had grown on his chin over the past thirty-six hours. "I'm not sure, Jim. I'm just not sure. What about the radio, either SATCOM or 70? Did the guys on the other bird have that?"

Not totally trusting the SATCOM, the detachment had made a private agreement with Hossey. Unknown to the SFOB, Team 3 had carried an extra radio, the Special Forces standard high-frequency PRC70, on the mission.

They had carried it in fear that the SATCOM might be cut off for whatever reason, most particularly if they weren't exfiltrated on time. If the SATCOM channel was shut down, Hossey was supposed to have the DET-K commo people set up a high-frequency base station and monitor an emergency guard net.

The team was to use the PRC70 only in emergencies, and only after they weren't receiving any more messages on the SATCOM, or if the messages received on the SATCOM lacked Hossey's authenticator. The 70 had been the team's ace in the hole against a loss of the primary means of communication.

The plan had been Riley's idea and Hossey had agreed with the team sergeant's reasoning. It was always good to have an alternate means of communications. Now Hossey wanted to know what had happened to that radio.

Trapp looked embarrassed. "We torched it, sir. We burned everything at the pickup zone before getting on the helicopters. You know we were briefed to get rid of everything to reduce the weight. Riley and Mitchell had figured that if we made it on the helicopters we wouldn't need that stuff anymore."

Hossey shook his head. That had been a mistake. He looked at the pictures again. "I guess it doesn't matter now anyway."

Everything here was shutting down. The Blackhawk crew would spend the night, then fly back to Misawa to link up with their support element there. O'Shaugnesy would remain in the hospital another week before being transferred back to the States for further care. Hossey ordered the remaining members of Team 3 to go up to Yongsan and stay on post for the next few days. He had already fed them the oplan cover story.

Jim Trapp had volunteered to accompany Hossey on his

next task. They would drive up to ChunChon the next morning to inform Mitchell's wife of his death. None of the other people lost had been married, as far as Hossey knew. Hooker had reported that Chong had had a local girl in Seoul with whom he'd been close, and volunteered to break the news to her the next day.

Hossey wrote out his last message to the SFOB, then transmitted it. Immediately afterward, the commo equipment was broken down and they started loading up for the ride back up to Seoul and home.

14

"They die away and are reborn; recurrent,
as are the passing seasons."
Sun Tzu: *The Art of War*

Western Slope, Changbai Mountains, China
Thursday, 8 June, 2155 Zulu
Friday, 9 June, 5:55 A.M. Local

The explosion of the number 4 external fuel tank blew the flaming pod away from the helicopter and sprayed the entire top right side of the aircraft with pieces of metal. The shrapnel tore through the turbine engines, simultaneously causing both engines to fail.

C.J. felt a total loss of power as he was trying to regain control of the wildly careening helicopter. He had three seconds from the initial explosion before the Blackhawk hit the trees, and he utilized that scant time as best he could. Automatically he brought the cyclic all the way up to its stops while pushing the cyclic forward to level the aircraft. With the loss of hydraulics, the stick responded sluggishly. The Blackhawk hit the trees nose down and rolled to the left. Bones cracked in C.J.'s right hand as he made a final desperate effort to keep the aircraft from flipping over before impact.

The aircraft tore through the thick tree cover and came to a halt on the ground. The combination of the original forward speed of ninety knots and the sudden drop in altitude produced a collision that crumpled the left front of the helicopter. Shattered glass, twisted metal, and foliage filled the cockpit.

On impact all the occupants of the cargo bay were thrown forward in a pile. Buried under the bodies of the rest of the team, Riley lay still until the helicopter came to a rest. He could feel the others stirring as they tried to get up. He heard someone in the front screaming in pain, but his first priority was to get himself untangled, then get a door opened and his people out before the helicopter exploded. Riley could smell jet fuel leaking. As soon as that fuel touched part of the hot engine, the helicopter would burst into flames.

In the confused darkness, it was Comsky who got the right cargo door open. Using all the strength in his short, powerful body, he wrenched the door off its rollers and shoved it aside. Then he proceeded to get people out by the expedient method of picking them up and throwing them through the open door. Olinski, Hoffman, and Chong were propelled out the door. He looked next at Riley, who signaled that he was all right.

Riley turned to help Mitchell, who was trying to tear through the wreckage and free the copilot. The pilot, in the right front seat, was trying to unbuckle his copilot but was able to use only one arm. The copilot was in bad shape. The whole left front of the helicopter was pressed against his seat. Blood was splattered about—a darker color than the flat gray of the interior paint.

As he leaned over the copilot's seat and tried to unfasten his seat belt, Riley saw something that turned his stomach. The front instrument console had been twisted back by the impact and had torn into the copilot's legs. Jagged metal had cut his thighs to the bone, pinning him to his armored seat. Riley could see the white bone against the console's edge.

Riley slid back and grabbed Mitchell by the shoulders. He pointed at the copilot's legs and then at the flowing fuel. He shouted at both Mitchell and the pilot. "Get out! He's a goner. We can't get him out in time before it blows. GO! GO!"

Riley shoved Mitchell toward the open cargo door, where Comsky waited patiently. With one large paw, Comsky grabbed Mitchell and hauled the team leader out. Riley saw that Hoffman had climbed back into the helicopter during all this and was hammering away at something in the rear of the cargo compartment.

"Get out!" Riley yelled at Hoffman. He didn't know what Hoffman was doing, but he didn't have time to find out. Fuel finally reached the hot engine exhausts and burst into flames. Instantly, the entire left side of the helicopter became an inferno. Riley clambered away from the flames as the copilot screamed in agony. The pilot paused in his door on the way out. Looking back at Riley, he pointed with his right hand. Riley quickly understood and nodded. The pilot rolled free out of the right front door.

Riley held himself steady in the right cargo door, ignoring the flames licking at his feet. He drew his 9mm pistol, aimed quickly, and fired twice. Then he jumped out, closely followed by Hoffman, who was cradling something in his arms.

Comsky, Chong, and Mitchell were dragging Olinski away from the burning helicopter as Riley and Hoffman caught up with them. The pilot was fleeing off to their left. They were thirty meters away when the helicopter exploded.

The impact threw them all to the ground, and Mitchell screamed in agony. Riley picked himself up and ran over to his team leader. The captain's entire right side was covered with blood where a fragment of the exploding helicopter had laid it open.

6:45 A.M. Local
An hour later Riley took stock of the situation in the growing daylight. They were still only thirty meters away from where the helicopter had crashed, but there was little to indicate that a helicopter had impacted on that spot. The explosion had scattered pieces in a hundred-meter circle and had scorched the forest.

Comsky finished sewing up the captain as best he could. Earlier, the medic had set Olinski's broken leg and arm. These two men had sustained the only serious injuries from the accident. The other team members were banged up but functional. Somehow, training and instinct had held fast and everyone had their weapons in hand. Those, in combination with the ammunition and grenades on their vests, meant that the beat-up outfit still had some bite left.

Riley walked over to Hoffman, who had been working with the insides of the black box for which he had risked his life. "What do you think? You gonna be able to do anything with that?"

Hoffman squinted up at Riley from behind his slightly bent glasses. "Hmm. I think so. Olinski still had the PRC68 on his vest, so I've cannibalized some stuff off that. There'll be two main problems. The biggest is that we don't have a power source. It takes a lot of juice to transmit high-frequency radio. The battery from the 68 won't even warm the wires of this thing. The second problem is we'll only be able to send, even if it does work. We won't be able to receive. I'll send using two wires as a kind of telegraph key. It's rigged to go now, if we only had a power source. I don't think it will be good for much beyond one shot."

Riley nodded. "That was real good thinking, Dan."

Hoffman was pleased with the compliment and the unexpected use of his first name. Riley really meant it. In the excitement of the crash, Hoffman had had the presence of mind to leap back into the helicopter and tear the aircraft's high-frequency transmitter out of the right rear panel of the cargo compartment. Using the transmitter, in combination with the small FM radio that Olinski had kept, Hoffman had jury-rigged something they could possibly use to send out a message. Where they'd send, and to whom, and on what frequency, Riley wasn't quite sure yet. He'd worry about that when they found a power source.

Riley turned his attention to the wounded. He walked over to the tree stump where Comsky was now setting the broken right arm and hand of the pilot. All the bones in that hand were fractured from the tremendous force C.J. had tried to exert on the cyclic during the crash. The arm had snapped during the helicopter's impact with the ground.

The pilot extended his left hand to Riley. "We haven't had the opportunity. I'm C.J. McIntire. You all can call me C.J." He looked at the lean sergeant. "I appreciate what you did back in the bird. I'd have done it myself but with this arm I couldn't get at my holster."

Riley accepted the hand and the thanks. Shooting the co-pilot had been an act of mercy. Burning alive wasn't a fate Riley would wish on anyone. There was no body to recover and bury. The fire and explosion had taken care of that. "I'm Dave Riley. That's Comsky who's doing the honors on you. The man messing with the radio is Dan Hoffman. Tom Chong is up there on that outcropping keeping an eye out for visitors. The man with the splints on his leg and arm next to you is Lech Olinski. And this over here is our team leader, Captain Mitchell." Mitchell painfully raised himself slightly on one arm and nodded.

C.J. returned the nod. "Well, Captain, what now?"

Mitchell gingerly sat up. He was pale from loss of blood. A twelve-inch gash ran from just under his right arm to above his hip. Although not deep, it was painful, and the sutures Comsky had put in threatened to tear open with any movement, starting the bleeding again.

"I thought you might be able to tell us what we'd do next. Were you able to get anything out over the radio before we crashed?"

"Hell, sir, I had about three seconds before impact, and my time was kind of full, what with keeping us from inverting and landing on the blades. If we'd turned over, none of us would be alive now."

Riley persisted for Mitchell. "What was the backup plan? The other bird saw us go down. What was the plan for a downed aircraft? They going to send another bird in here to the crash site?"

C.J. sighed. "There isn't a plan. There is no backup. We're on our own, unless we can get ahold of somebody. The way that fuel tank exploded, they probably think we're all dead. We should be, too. We're just lucky it blew away and didn't ignite all the rest of the fuel." C.J. shot the problem back to the team leader. "What was your backup plan for this?"

Mitchell shrugged. "We had a lot of contingency plans. Unfortunately, we didn't have one for the helicopter crashing on the way out. Since we didn't know what your flight route was going to be, and didn't even get a chance to talk to you all during isolation, it was kind of hard to plan."

The words sank in to everyone in the clearing.

Riley broke the silence. "We need to think this through. The Chinese definitely have a reaction force moving by this time. Now that it's daylight we can expect to see choppers pretty soon. It might take them awhile to work this far to the southeast, but they will eventually."

He reached into his pants cargo pocket and pulled out his 1:250,000 large-scale map of Manchuria. He unfolded the map and handed it to C.J. "Show me where you think we are."

C.J. studied the map, then pointed. "We're right here. We were flying up this draw."

Riley looked around. The terrain fit in with the location that C.J. had pointed out. "OK, this means we're about three kilometers west of the crest of the Changbai Mountain Range. We've got it downhill all the way, once we make it over the top. That's the good news. The bad news is that once we get over the top we'll still have a hundred and fifty kilometers to the coast."

He checked with Mitchell. "Can you walk?"

"Hell, yeah. It only hurts when I laugh or Comsky touches it. As long as we don't try to move too fast, I think I can make it."

Riley looked at Olinski. "We'll have to carry you, Ski. We need to get out of here. We've already been here too long. Let's sterilize the area. Maybe the Chinese will think everyone died in the crash when they find it, but we can't count on it. Comsky, make a litter for Olinski. You and I will start out carrying it and rotate with Chong and Hoffman. It's 0700 now. I want to put as much mileage between us and this spot as we can before we start spotting Chinese helicopters. Let's go!"

7:35 A.M. Local

Carrying Olinski, they moved very slowly up the mountainside. Comsky had made a stretcher out of two long branches and a poncho he always carried in his vest butt pack.

Chong scouted ahead to make sure the way was clear. Riley didn't like moving in daylight, but he knew they needed to get away from the crash site. He also knew that carrying Olinski at night, over rough terrain, would be a tricky proposition at best.

It took more than four hours, scrambling over the rocks and keeping under the cover of trees as much as possible, to make it to the crest. As they crossed over the top, Riley took a last look back to the west. He still couldn't see any sign of a search in that direction.

He led the team a kilometer down the eastern slope, then stopped under a thick stand of pine for a rest. Moving downhill was a bit easier; it had taken them a little less than an hour to do the last kilometer.

Shenyang Military Region Headquarters, China
Friday, 9 June, 0100 Zulu
Friday, 9 June, 9:00 A.M. Local

General Yang carefully examined the information available on the Daqing pipeline explosion. The most glaring fact was that General Haotian's duty officer had bungled things, but that would be dealt with later. The more immediate and pressing problem was tracking down the terrorists who had done this.

The evidence was disturbing. The most intriguing piece was Captain Lu's report of hearing helicopters off to the north of the explosion area. If there were helicopters involved, that meant somebody with more resources than a group of dissidents was involved. Yang had initially suspected the students or their supporters had been behind the explosion. The helicopter report changed that suspicion. Now, much as Yang disliked considering it, the most likely culprits were revolting Chinese soldiers. Ever since the killings in Tiananmen Square, the entire country had been in a state of flux. In this region, Yang had had no killings like they had in Beijing. The students had marched in Harbin, but it had been peaceful. Yang had already dispatched three of his divisions to Beijing at the request of the Communist party secretary, Zhao Ziyang, to aid in control there.

Yang was frankly more worried about that situation than this pipeline problem. With the dispatch of those troops, he had extended his hand into the power play going on in Beijing. The whole situation down there was very murky. He didn't need trouble in his own region.

Yang evaluated the likely possibilities and figured that the troops who had done the deed were probably trying to escape. He briefly considered the possibility that foreigners were involved. He doubted it, but had to admit there was a slight chance. Either the Russians, Americans, or Japanese. He very much doubted the Japanese. They used some of the oil from the pipe. He didn't think the Americans had the guts. They were making a lot of noise about the events in Tiananmen

Square, but they would never back up their words. But the Russians were another story, Yang knew from past experience along the border. He wouldn't put it past them to have done this.

Yang looked at his map. The fool Haotian had limited his search to the immediate area of the explosion. With the larger assets of the entire Shenyang Military Region at his command, Yang had the men and vehicles to correct that.

Yang swiveled his chair around to face his staff and subordinate commanders, who had been waiting quietly while he thought. "I want all aviation assets to be used in the search. Ground forces of a regiment from each division will also be used to patrol all roads. You will look in this area." He outlined an area on the map on his desk. His finger ran from Qiqihar to the Russian border in the north, down that border to North Korea in the east, and then along the North Korean border back to their present location in Shenyang.

"Somewhere in there you will find the terrorists if they are still in the country. I want the majority of forces concentrated to the east along the border with Russia."

Yang looked over his staff. "I also want the political officers of every unit to question each helicopter pilot and account for every one of our helicopters during the time of the attack. I want to know whether one of our own did this. Check with the neighboring military districts also. I will be immediately notified of any information or new development." Yang indicated they were dismissed.

Checkpoint 2, USS *Rathburne*
Friday, 9 June, 0304 Zulu
Friday, 9 June, 12:04 P.M. Local
Commander Lemester had been very happy to see the helicopter disappear off to the west. He was glad to be done with the whole operation. Hopefully things would get back to normal now. The only thing he didn't like was that his orders specified staying until 1500 Zulu on the tenth. He had to sit here another thirty-four hours. Lemester decided not to waste his crew's time. They could get in a lot of training before heading off to the southwest to rejoin the battle group.

Changbai Mountains, China
Friday, 9 June, 0400 Zulu
Friday, 9 June, 12:00 P.M. Local

The going was easier downhill, but not much. Olinski's 175 pounds were beginning to wear down the four healthy team members. Mitchell was in obvious pain. Comsky had tied the captain's right arm to his side to keep the sutures from tearing. The pilot, C.J., wasn't complaining, but the jarring downhill scramble was sending jolts of pain up his smashed right hand and arm.

Despite this, Riley pushed them unmercifully. They had to get out of the less thickly vegetated high ground as soon as possible. Having crossed the top of the mountain range at almost nine thousand feet, they slowly but steadily were dropping in altitude on their way to the North Korean border.

Riley's mind was working as they walked, trying to develop a plan. If they could find a power source for the transmitter Hoffman had rigged, Riley had to figure out what message to send. They had never considered this occurrence in their escape and evasion plan. The eastern escape route would have taken the team to the north of this part of the mountain range, up near the Russian border; that meant Riley couldn't use any of the pickup zones along the E & E eastern route.

On the ten-minute rest halts he allowed every hour, Riley pored over the map and searched the terrain ahead. He used a small monocular, which Olinski always carried in the butt pack of his combat vest, to check out the lay of the land below. While not as good as binoculars, the instrument allowed him to gain a perspective on what lay ahead.

From the map, Riley chose a tentative pickup zone twenty kilometers east of the crest they had crossed. He had to pick a terrain feature that would be relatively easy for pilots to find at night. His choice was a clearing about five hundred meters northwest of the intersection of an unnamed river, which would cut across their path, and what looked on the map to be an unimproved dirt road. With luck, a scarce commodity on this mission so far, Riley estimated they could make it there by the next night.

Riley shook his head as he considered the bigger picture.

Getting to the new PZ would help them only if they could find a power source to send out the information. If the transmitter worked. And if they could come up with a frequency to send on. And if someone happened to be listening. And if that someone could get the information to the proper people in time. And if the proper people decided to mount a rescue attempt. And if the rescue attempt made it to the pickup zone. Riley tried to keep down a rising tide of despair. He'd been in bad situations before, but none had seemed as hopeless as this one.

He didn't think they could make it across the border into North Korea and then to the coast. Not in the shape they were in. Not with the wounded. They had no food, no shelter, and no warm clothes—only what was on their backs and in their vests. Riley was furious with himself for having destroyed the rucksacks. That had been a stupid mistake and was going to prove costly. Most particularly galling was having destroyed the PRC70 high-frequency radio. If there was one thing they should have taken, it was the radio. If the other helicopter had made it out—and there was no reason to think it didn't— then Trapp would have told Hossey they had destroyed the 70 on the pickup zone. Which meant the colonel would most likely not go with the backup plan to monitor the HF net.

Riley thought about that. Maybe the colonel would monitor the radio. Or if he didn't, maybe Trapp or someone else from the team would. A tenet he and Mitchell had hammered into everyone on Team 3 was to always stick with a plan, even though the situation might appear hopeless. It was a slim chance at best.

3:00 P.M. Local
By three in the afternoon they had progressed five kilometers from the crest and dropped almost two thousand feet in altitude. Riley called a halt and gratefully put down Olinski's makeshift stretcher. Riley knew that if he was this tired, everyone must be. He walked over to Mitchell, who was slumped against a rock. "How's it going, Mitch?"

Mitchell grinned weakly at Riley. "I could lie to you and say great, but I won't. Is good OK?"

Riley hated to see his team leader and the other members hurting so bad. He felt responsible.

Mitchell stirred. "Hey, I've been thinking. If we can get that transmitter working, you got any idea what to send?"

"Based on a map recon, I've tentatively picked an exfiltration pickup zone. It's about fifteen klicks ahead of us. As far as the radio goes, I'm not sure yet what frequency to send on."

Mitchell considered that. "If the other bird made it, Hossey'll know we burned the 70. There's no reason for him to get someone to monitor the guard net."

"I know," Riley responded. "I guess there's some sort of international distress band the pilot may know. Of course, the Chinese, North Koreans, and Russians will probably monitor that, too."

Mitchell looked his team sergeant in the eye. "Things aren't too positive, are they, Dave? I mean, I know you don't want to say it, but the rest of us aren't stupid. The transmitter is a hell of a long shot. Without any gear, we're going to be getting kind of hungry soon, to put it mildly, and cold. I definitely screwed up when I let us destroy all that equipment on the pickup zone. We should have taken some of it, particularly the 70, with us. That was a bad mistake. I let the team down."

Obviously, Mitchell had been thinking along the same lines as Riley. The team leader gingerly picked himself up and forced a grin. "Crying about it isn't going to do us any good, I guess." Mitchell looked at the other men sprawled around the halt area. "Hey, Comsky. I got first rights on cuddling up with you tonight when it gets chillish. I've always had a thing for short, ugly guys with real hairy bodies. Let's go, folks, time's a wasting."

Mitchell led the way as the rest of the team picked themselves off the ground and moved out. Mitchell's example shook Riley out of his apathy. He'd been getting too down. As long as they were alive, they had a chance.

5:00 P.M. Local

Senior Lieutenant Wei was having fun. Any time he was allowed to fly, he had fun. At the moment, he was flying at sixty knots airspeed above the terrain. He kept his Z-9 at two hundred feet above ground level as he climbed into the mountains.

The air was thinner up here, and Wei had to apply extra power to keep his helicopter airborne. The Z-9 was the only rotary-wing aircraft the Chinese Air Force possessed other than the S-70s that could fly up here like he was doing. The French certainly knew how to build, he marveled. This helicopter was as good as anything the Russians had. Wei's ship was one of the thirty-five Z-9s the Chinese government had bought from Aerospatiale. The six in Wei's squadron had been modified into gunships with the addition of 7.62mm miniguns on either side.

Chinese Air Force pilots normally didn't get to fly often. Fuel and repair parts cost money. Wei knew that the recent American embargo on military equipment would eventually cause all the S-70s to be grounded for lack of repair parts. The French hadn't announced an embargo yet. Wei swooped down into a draw. He'd worry about that when it happened.

He wasn't sure what had caused the alert today, putting all the flyable helicopters in the air. They'd just been told to look for an armed band of dissidents. The whole thing was very unusual. Especially the questioning by the political officer prior to takeoff. Wei and his fellow pilots had been forced to account for their whereabouts the previous evening. Wei didn't care what this was all about, as long as he got to put in more flying hours.

Wei's sector of search was this part of the mountain range southwest of Yanji. His unit of six helicopters from the 3d Aviation Regiment was working out of a forward base in Yanji. He had flown up the river out of Yanji and around the highest part of the mountains; now he would fly over the crest of the Changbai Mountains on his way back.

It was one of the more difficult sectors. Many of his fellow pilots didn't like flying the mountains. The winds were sometimes perilous. Wei enjoyed the challenge.

Another three or four kilometers and he would be over the crest, heading for home. It would be dark soon anyway. At this rate he'd make it back to base just as it got completely black. He was looking forward to a nice hot meal tonight.

Then he saw the burned area.

5:10 P.M. Local

They were switching off carrying Olinski every twenty minutes now. Chong was scouting about fifty meters ahead, picking the easiest path for the team. The vegetation was growing
thicker as they descended, but they still had to cross occa-
sional open spots.

The men had just started across one of these spots when
they heard the sound they'd been dreading—the beat of helicopter blades in the air. Riley tried to figure out what direction the sound was coming from, as he gestured for everyone
to move faster.

They were halfway across. Hoffman and Comsky were
walking as fast as they could with Olinski. Another seventy-
five meters and they'd be under the cover of a stand of trees.

Riley had been peering downhill looking for the helicopter
when it occurred to him to check behind. As he turned, he
saw the Z-9 coming swiftly down the mountainside about
three kilometers back.

An aircraft had gone down back there. Whatever it was had
crashed and exploded, scorching the earth for more than a
hundred meters in every direction. Wei had spent about five
minutes flying over the site. There had been no place close
by to land and investigate, so he turned and headed for the
crest. Once he was over the top, he'd be able to radio in his
report without the mountains in the way.

The engines were straining as the Z-9 crested the ridge.
Wei slid over the top and, as he rapidly descended, keyed his
radio.

"Let's go!" Riley yelled. Hoffman and Comsky started running awkwardly with the stretcher. Riley reached over and
grabbed the pole nearest Comsky while Mitchell grabbed the
other side. Together the four of them sprinted toward the tree
line, followed closely by the pilot.

Chong had already reached the tree line. Resting the muzzle of his SAW on a tree branch, he started to take aim at the
point where the helicopter should appear over the far tree
line. It was getting closer.

They were ten meters from the tree line when C.J. lost his

balance and fell. With his right arm in a sling, he'd had trouble running, and now he couldn't break his fall. He landed heavily on his broken arm.

The Z-9 came over the far tree line, flying only fifty feet above the ground. Chong sighted in on the cockpit and began applying pressure to the trigger.

Wei thought he saw something as he flew over the small open area. He keyed the intercom and asked his copilot and the crew chief in the back if they had seen anything. They replied negatively. Wei considered going back for a look, but the impending darkness and low fuel supply prompted him to continue on home.

The pain in his shattered arm was so intense that it caused C.J. to vomit. Riley and Comsky ran out and dragged him back into the tree line. Chong waited a second, then joined the rest of the team.

If the helicopter had made the slightest hostile move, Chong had been prepared to fire. He had spotted the miniguns hung on either side of the bird. Chong hadn't fired because he thought there was a chance that C.J. might not have been seen, and firing definitely would have given away their location. That decision appeared to be vindicated as the sound of the Chinese helicopter faded into the distance.

Riley had to look away as Comsky tore the splint off C.J.'s arm. The fall had turned the simple fracture into a compound one. Pieces of white bone stuck out of the skin in two places.

Comsky took off his jacket and wrapped it around the pilot. Then he tenderly started rewrapping the man's arm, using the last of his sterile bandages. C.J. screamed from the pain.

What the hell else is going to happen? Riley wondered.

Camp Page, ChunChon, Korea
Friday, 9 June, 0930 Zulu
Friday, 9 June, 6:30 P.M. Local
Jean Long was eating her dinner in the dining room of the Page II Club when the news of the lost helicopter in the Sea of Japan was announced by the Armed Forces Korean Network (AFKN) news show. She watched the brief story on the

large-screen TV in the corner of the dining room. The report didn't indicate what unit the aircraft was from, only that eight soldiers were known to be on board.

Jean shook her head. Wherever her husband was, she hoped he didn't see the report; he'd be sure to get on her case about how dangerous flying was. Over the past nine years, several of Jean's aviation acquaintances had been killed in various accidents. Every time a helicopter went down, it struck close to home.

Mitch had never asked her not to fly, probably because he knew how important it was to her. Thinking about her husband made her wonder where he was. It had been a week since he'd left and she hadn't heard a word. She knew better than to try to call Yongsan. If Mitch hadn't called her, that meant he was doing something classified.

As she finished her meal, Jean said a silent prayer for whoever had been in that aircraft. She hoped the pilots were no one she knew.

Yongsan Army Base, Seoul, Korea
Friday, 9 June, 0943 Zulu
Friday, 9 June, 6:43 P.M. Local

Hossey put on his beret and left his office. He had done all he could today in wrapping up loose ends from the mission. The hard part would come tomorrow. He got in his car and drove to the officers' club.

Walking into the pub, he spotted Jim Trapp and the other four healthy members of Team 3 sitting at a table in the corner. Dressed in clean uniforms they looked better than they had getting off the helicopter this morning, but as he drew close, Hossey noticed that their eyes were shadowed from fatigue and their faces were tight with anger and grief.

As Hossey approached their table he was intercepted by the club manager. "Sir, I see you're wearing the same patch as those men. Are they yours?"

"Yeah. Why?" Hossey bristled.

"Sir, some of them aren't officers, so we can't allow them in here. I asked them to leave, but they've ignored me. Perhaps you could tell them to leave."

Hossey glared at the civilian in front of him. "They can

drink any goddamn place they want. If they choose to drink here then I think I'll join them. You going to kick me out, too?"

The manager backed away from the angry colonel, deciding he could overlook the isolated table in the corner. "No, sir."

"Thanks," Hossey said dryly. He walked over to his men. "Mind if I sit down?"

"All yours, sir." Jim Trapp pulled over another chair. The tabletop was littered with empty beer cans and shot glasses.

That's one way to deal with it, Hossey thought. Seems like a good one, too, right now. "How's O'Shaugnesy?"

Devito glanced up from his mug. "He's doing fine. Going to have some pretty ugly scars, though. They've got the infection under control. Should be able to fly him back to the States in about a week for recuperation."

Hossey looked at Lalli. "How's the leg, Paul?"

"A little stiff, sir, but other than that, it's OK."

He turned to Trapp next, who was obviously well on his way to a major drunk. "You going to be all right to travel with me tomorrow?"

Trapp glared at the colonel with bleary eyes. "Sure, sir. Just celebrating our successful mission, is all."

Hossey glanced around at the rest of the room. Nobody was paying them any attention. "I'm awfully sorry about those guys. If there was anything that could have been done to prevent it, or anything we could do now, you know I'd do it."

Trapp nodded slowly. His glare had been directed at the situation, not at the colonel. "I know that, sir. It's just that I've been doing this shit for more than twenty years now. I just don't know what the purpose is anymore. We lost some good men back there. Dave Riley was the best damn team sergeant I ever worked with. I don't know what he died for."

Hossey had to agree. "I don't know what he, or the rest of them, died for either. But I tell you one thing we can do. We can have a toast."

He raised his shot glass. The survivors of Team 3 all raised theirs.

Hossey said it for all of them: "To those we left behind."

The team's junior engineer, Smitty, looked up angrily. "Bullshit," he slurred. "Why are we kissing those guys off? We don't know for sure they're dead. Remember what top and the captain always said? Never quit on a plan. Always follow through, even though it looks like a waste of time. The plan, if someone wasn't exfilled, was to monitor the high frequency. How come we aren't doing it?"

Hossey felt tired. "Mister Trapp and I saw the imagery of the crash site. There was nothing in one piece on the ground. The helicopter must have disintegrated in midair. No one could have survived the explosion."

"Besides," Lalli added, "we torched the PRC70 on the pickup zone, Smitty. You know that. How the hell are they going to come up high frequency if they don't have an HF radio?"

Smith sank sullenly back in his chair.

Trapp stood up abruptly. "If you gentlemen would excuse me, I need to rack out to be prepared for the fun and games tomorrow." They watched as Trapp walked unsteadily out into the dark night.

The chilly night air slapped Trapp in the face as he scrunched his beret down on his head. He thought about what had been said inside. He turned and looked at the stars.

To those we left behind, Trapp thought. I agree with Smitty. Bullshit.

Shenyang Military Region Headquarters, China
Friday, 9 June, 1500 Zulu
Friday, 9 June, 11:00 P.M. Local

General Yang was upset. It had taken the idiots in the 3d Aviation Regiment five hours to get the information concerning the crash site to his office. He turned to his chief of staff, Colonel Tugur, who had just had the unfortunate responsibility of relaying the late information. "Obviously, the fool in command of that unit needs help. This information should have been here *hours* ago. First thing tomorrow we must search the wreckage. Maybe we will find the bodies of our so-called terrorists. But maybe some of those terrorists survived the crash and are even now still in the area."

Yang looked at the dark features of the Mongol officer. It

was difficult for someone of Tugur's ethnic background to make such a high rank as colonel in the Chinese Army. But Yang appreciated and rewarded ruthless efficiency and competence. Tugur excelled in both areas. He was the right man for this job.

"You will fly out tomorrow morning to personally supervise the search down there. Arrange for your plane to depart at first light."

15

"He selects his men and they exploit the situation."
Sun Tzu: *The Art of War*

Fort Meade, Maryland
Friday, 9 June, 1500 Zulu
Friday, 9 June, 10:00 A.M. Local

Hearing the knock on his door, Meng turned down the image on his computer screen so it could not be seen. "Come in." He relaxed slightly when he saw it was only Wilson carrying the debrief file.

"All done in Tunnel 3. Those US-SOCOM guys about broke down the door heading out. I guess they have an early flight down home to Florida."

Meng took the file. "Everything shut down?"

"Yeah." Wilson sat down on the other side of the desk. "This was a pretty straightforward mission. The computer didn't throw them any curves. I guess US-SOCOM will look pretty good over at the Pentagon when they see the after-action report on Dragon Sim-13."

Wilson noticed something on the desktop. He picked up the copies of the imagery that Meng had ordered the previous day from NSA. "What's this?"

Meng thought quickly. "It's part of a variation of the sim-ulation. One of the possibilities called for one of the exfiltra-tion helicopters to be lost on the way out. That picture is supposed to represent the crash site."

Wilson whistled. "Damn. Nothing could have lived through this. You can't even see there was a helicopter there. Where'd you get these pictures? Is this some real crash site?"

Meng shrugged casually. "I don't know. NSA sent over satellite pictures when I requested them during the initial programming for 13. I imagine it's an old crash site they drew out of their files."

Wilson dropped the imagery back onto Meng's desk. "Well, that wraps up 13. We've got a whole five days before we do 14. When do you want to start the programming for it?"

Meng wasn't really worried about 14. He didn't think it would ever run. "Come in tomorrow and we'll do some work on the Medusa program. I'll knock off 14 on Sunday and Monday." He could tell that Wilson wasn't happy about working on Saturday. But Meng also knew that he didn't have much time left. His sense of duty urged him to get as much done on the Medusa program as he could, before the facts on Dragon Sim-13 surfaced.

Wilson headed for the door. "All right, see you tomorrow."

After the door closed, Meng locked it. He slowly walked back to his desk and looked at the imagery one last time. No one could have survived the crash, and there had been no SATCOM radio calls from survivors. Meng said a brief prayer for the dead men, then fed the imagery through his shredder. He sat back down at his desk and shut down the SFOB program.

Changbai Mountains, China
Friday, 9 June, 1900 Zulu
Saturday, 10 June, 3:00 A.M. Local

The survivors of Team 3 were huddled together beneath the low branches of a weatherbeaten pine tree. The night stretched ahead endlessly. A night spent freezing, high in the mountains, did not possess the same sense of time as a normal night. The hands on a watch slowed down, moving sluggishly. Sleep never came. Instead, there were bouts of a shivering unconsciousness, lasting only a few brief moments, ending with a start.

For the hundredth time, Riley adjusted his meager clothing, trying to get better insulation. He was pressed between Mitchell and the pilot. Riley estimated the temperature to be in the high forties and dropping. With no equipment or extra clothing, and not able to build a fire for fear of discovery, the team was suffering through a long, cold night. Riley had briefly considered building a fire, but he'd decided that being cold was better than being dead. At this point some of the team members might have been willing to argue that point, if they could have spared the energy.

Riley could feel Mitchell shivering in the dark and pressed his body closer, trying to give his team leader what little body warmth he had. During the dash across the open field, the captain's sutures had pulled out and the wound had begun bleeding again. Comsky had used all the sutures in the survival kit to sew up the wound again. Riley didn't think Mitchell could make it much farther.

They had to assume the helicopter crash site had been found by now. That Z-9 must have seen the burned area on its way up the draw. That meant they would begin to see search parties tomorrow. Riley very much doubted the team's ability to make it across the border into North Korea. In fact, he wasn't sure North Korea would be any better than China. The farther down the mountains they got, the more populated the countryside would get—and the greater the likelihood of being found. Already they had passed the first signs of man— two dirt roads leading to old mines on the wall of the draw they were descending.

Riley felt despair seep through him. It was a cold, hollow feeling, chilling his soul as much as the air was chilling his body. He'd been pushing the team ever since the crash, but he was running out of mental energy.

They'd continued walking for three hours after sunset, until finally Riley had been forced to call a halt. They were stumbling along and he was afraid someone else would get hurt in the dark. And they needed some rest. Everyone was exhausted.

Riley still couldn't sleep. It wasn't just the cold. Despite his exhaustion, he wouldn't allow himself to lapse into unconsciousness. He was trying to figure a way out of this mess. Then he saw the lights.

It looked like a car or truck. He watched the headlights until they were turned off about a kilometer and a half away. He hadn't heard the engine, but he was positive it was a vehicle. He woke up Hoffman and Comsky. "I saw a set of headlights over there." Riley pointed in the dark. They all turned and looked.

"Maybe we can steal the vehicle and drive to the coast," Comsky offered hopefully.

Riley shook his head. "As soon as it got reported, they'd be down on us in a heartbeat. Plus, what are we going to do at the border? Wave at the North Koreans while we break down the barrier? And what are we going to do at the coast?"

Hoffman spoke slowly. "Hey, Top. We don't need to take the truck. We just steal the battery. That will get reported, but it won't make them as suspicious as the whole vehicle missing."

Riley immediately understood what Hoffman meant. He woke up Mitchell and told him the plan. After a few minutes of preparation, Riley, accompanied by Hoffman and Chong, left the little camp under the pine tree. Comsky stayed behind to take care of the wounded. Riley took Mitchell's MP5 silenced submachine gun, just in case.

3:45 A.M. Local

It took the three of them thirty minutes, in the dark, to reach the small dirt road. Bending down and running his numbed fingers over the surface, Chong could feel recent tire tracks. They followed them, and five minutes later the dim lights of a shack came into view. A pickup-style truck was parked outside. Riley halted them briefly while he considered the setup. There was one shuttered window in the front, to the right of the door. A rutted road ran to the right of the shack. Probably heads toward a mine in the valley wall, he figured.

Riley whispered the improvised plan to Hoffman and Chong. Together, they crept up to the derelict truck. Riley crawled to a position from which he could cover the front, while Chong slipped around back. Hoffman slid up to the old truck. Riley angled the submachine gun at the door while Hoffman carefully opened the hood. The old metal obliged grudgingly. Riley tightened his grip on the gun. He didn't want to kill a civilian if he could help it, but they couldn't risk being discovered.

Hoffman was messing around in the engine. Come on, come on, Riley urged silently. Hoffman finally pulled out the battery and slowly lowered the hood. Riley couldn't believe the people inside didn't hear the creaking of metal. Hoffman laid the hood as far closed as it would go without slamming it, then turned and hurried back into the trees.

Chong appeared from behind the house and joined him. Once the two were out of sight, Riley backed off and joined them. They retraced their steps back to the rest of the team.

Comsky softly challenged them as they loomed up in the dark. Giving their mission code names, the three men crawled in under the tree.

"Go ahead and set that thing up, Dan," Riley indicated to Hoffman.

As the engineer busied himself arranging the transmitter and wires, Riley spoke to the rest of the team in a low voice. "Anyone have any idea what frequency to send on and who to send this message to?" He turned to C.J. "Is there some sort of international distress band that's always monitored on high frequency?"

C.J. considered this. "Yeah, there is, but the Chinese and Russians monitor it, too. Unless you want them to hear the message, you probably don't want to use that."

Mitchell stirred. "Hey, you're forgetting something you taught me, Dave. You must be getting senile in your old age. Let's stick with the plan and use the guard net frequency we agreed on with Hossey."

Riley shook his head. "They won't be monitoring that, sir. Trapp will have told the Old Man that we torched the 70. They think we're all dead."

"That may be so," Mitchell agreed, "but we're still going to stick with the plan. It's as good as anything else."

Riley looked at Mitchell and decided. "Yes, sir. Let's go for it. I'll use a DET-K3 in the clear to start it and then put the rest in code."

Riley pulled out the small New Testament he carried, and began leafing through the pages. Chong held a red-lens flashlight so he could see. Riley wasn't carrying the Bible because he was particularly religious; this Bible was the key to their coding. He'd write out the message, then transcribe it using a trigraph and the letters on a designated page of the Bible. A trigraph was simply a listing of three-letter groups. Riley would take the first letter from the message he wrote in clear text, the second letter from the page in the Bible, and, finding the three-letter combination on the trigraph, write the third into the message. Using the same Bible page and trigraph, Hossey would be able to decode the message by reversing the process.

It was a long shot but better than nothing. Shakily, blowing on his hands every few seconds to get some warmth back in them, Riley wrote the message and transcribed it. Hoffman finished his final adjustments with the transmitter and strung an antenna wire between two trees.

Riley looked at the luminous dial of his watch. It was almost five forty-five in the morning in Korea. If someone was monitoring, he hoped that person was awake.

"Ready?" Riley asked.

Hoffman nodded and hooked the twelve-volt battery into the transmitter. Riley slowly read the letters to Hoffman, who tapped out the message using two wires. They made it through the message.

"Again," said Riley.

Fort Meade, Maryland
Friday, 9 June, 2055 Zulu
Friday, 9 June, 3:55 P.M. Local
Meng's spirits sank as he looked at the day's headline from the *New York Times:*

CHINA'S PREMIER APPEARS; ARMY SEEMS TO TIGHTEN GRIP; BUSH BARS NORMAL TIES NOW

BEIJING IS WARNED	PRAISE FOR TROOPS
PRESIDENT SAYS RELATIONS DEPEND ON ITS STANCE TOWARD STUDENTS	PROTESTERS ARE CALLED ON TO SURRENDER OR FACE HEAVY PUNISHMENT

It is too late, Mister President Bush, Meng thought. Soon the word will be out on the attack on the pipeline. What will *you* do then? Meng looked at the paper again. Between the two columns was a large picture of Prime Minister Li Peng. Meng stared at it with undisguised hatred. What will you do then, Mister Premier?

Changbai Mountains, China
Friday, 9 June, 2105 Zulu
Saturday, 10 June, 5:05 A.M. Local
Hoffman was in the middle of his fourth repeat of the message when the transmitter started to smoke and sparks flew. He quickly disconnected the battery. Opening up the transmitter, he peered inside with the red-lens flashlight.

"It's fried," he announced mournfully.

16

> "By terrain I mean distances, whether the ground is traversed with ease or difficulty, whether it is open or constricted, and the chances of life or death."
> Sun Tzu: *The Art of War*

Yongsan Army Base, Seoul, Korea
Friday, 9 June, 2100 Zulu
Saturday, 10 June, 6:00 A.M. Local

Colonel Hossey cracked an eye as the pounding on his BOQ door intruded on his sleep. "Who's there?"

"It's me, sir—Chief Trapp."

Hossey threw on a bathrobe and opened the door. The blood in his head was pounding against his skull. He'd stayed much too long at the club last night with the remaining members of Team 3, drowning his sorrows.

"You're a little early, Chief."

Trapp slumped into an armchair as he waited for Hossey to get dressed. "We're going to have a hell of a time getting through traffic, sir. I thought we'd leave a little earlier than planned."

Hossey threw on his fatigue shirt. "You going to drive?"

Trapp shook his head. "The sergeant major is. He dropped me off here and went to the compound to check on something. He should be back in a few minutes."

Hossey quickly buzzed his face with an electric razor, then grabbed his beret. "All right, let's go."

Hossey could think of a lot of things he'd rather be doing today than going to Camp Page to tell Jean Long her husband was dead. Even the timing of the notification of death was governed by the oplan, Hossey mused bitterly. He had wanted to tell her last night, but the cover story required that they wait until this morning, when the air force and navy would call off the search for the missing helicopter and declare the helicopter officially lost.

Carrying their overnight bags, the two men clattered down the stairs and went out front. In less than a minute they spotted Sergeant Major Hooker's old battered Mustang pulling up in front of the BOQ. The two men hopped in, Hossey in the back, Trapp up front with Hooker. The sergeant major pulled out of the parking lot and headed back toward south post.

Trapp was confused. "Where you going?"

Hooker glanced over at Trapp and shook his head. "I don't know what the fuck is going on, Jim. I did what you asked me to do and had one of the commo dinks up all night monitoring that frequency you gave me. I just went and checked on that idiot."

He threw a piece of paper into the shocked warrant officer's lap. "Maybe you or the colonel can break that out." Trapp picked it up and looked at it.

DETKTH	REEDET	KTHREE	AKEOWK
WJRLTP	EHRTTY	RHTKYL	RHTNWM
QZMLGF	QJWEJE	QMSTPF	QCHTYU
ADGJLO	WCXZGH	POERLK	EHSMIT
ENDHTI	EHRMCN	QNWHDS	SETHYU
ERDCBJ	POWSVY	WHEKRL	THENAO
RHRYIO	AHEYCN	WHJLTY	EHTUEO
QHWYES	WHTIRJ	SNEHTY	QKDKDJ
YMEJTU	LEJFUR	MZNXBC	HFGDSA
PTOYIW	ZHEYRI	FHRYEK	AGEJYO
GHFJDK	TYRUEI	VBCNXM	EHDUTP
XCVBNM	EHWUCQ	OYTLFD	EHDNUE
NDKWSL	LSMWKE	NABXGH	EHRYTT
WHEUTR	HEYSNN	TJRUWE	

"I don't believe it! When did you get this?"

"The commo man picked it up just before I checked in on him. In fact, he was on the phone trying to call me when I walked in. He said it was sent four times manual. About midway through the fourth time it disappeared. The kid also said it sounded like somebody who wasn't a commo man was sending, because it was real slow—about seven words a minute."

Trapp handed the sheet of paper to the colonel. Hossey's hand was shaking as he took it. He looked at Trapp. "So somebody's alive."

"How the hell did they transmit without a radio?" Hooker asked.

Trapp shrugged. "Obviously they got a radio somehow. We're talking about some pretty smart fellows. You got the Bible, sir?"

Hossey dug into his overnight bag and pulled out the tattered New Testament. Turning to the agreed-upon page, he started transcribing the message.

Hooker glanced at the backseat. "You didn't tell me you had worked out a backup commo system with the team, sir."

"Riley thought it up," Hossey mumbled as he concentrated on the letters. "You must have been out when we talked about it."

Hossey worked slowly through the groups, using the Bible and his trigraph. "It's a Flight report. Damn. Jim, you got a message format book?"

"Sir, I've been doing this stuff for twenty years. I've got that Flight report memorized. You just break it out and I'll tell you what it all means."

When Hossey was done he handed the decoded message to Trapp. He hadn't even tried to read the six-letter groups. He was afraid of what they would say. Trapp took the sheet and studied it.

DETKTH	REEXXD	ETKTHR	EEXXFL
IGHTAA	APAPAL	IMAONE	SIXEIG
HTTWOF	IVETHR	EEXXXP	APALIM
AONESI	XEIGHT	TWOFIV	ETHREE
BBBTEN	JUNEXX	XTENJU	NEXXZE
ROONEU	NTILZE	ROFIVE	LOCALX
XXZERO	ONEUNT	ILZERO	FIVELO
CALCCC	DDDIRS	TROBEX	XIRSTR
OBEEEE	SIXTYT	WOPOIN	TZEROX
XXSIXT	YTWOPO	INTZER	OXXCOD

ENAMES	FFFCRA	SHSITE	FOUNDE
XPECTE	NEMYTO	MORROW	GGGONE
DEADTH	REEWOU	NDEDMU	STGETO
UTTOMO	RROWNI	GHTXXX	

"All right, sir. We got a Flight, which is an exfiltration pickup zone report. AAA is location. PAPA LIMA 168253—that's the grid. BBB is time of pickup. Says 10 June, 0100 local until 0500. CCC is heading off exfiltration aircraft. There's nothing there, so they mustn't have had one.

"DDD is markings on the pickup zone—infrared strobe," he continued. "EEE is radio frequency and call signs. We got sixty-two hundred on FM for frequency and to use team code names for authentication. FFF is the enemy situation. Says crash site was found. Expect more enemy activity tomorrow. I guess that means today."

"GGG is remarks. Shit. It says one dead and three wounded. It ends with 'Must get out tomorrow night.' Damn, that means tonight, if we go by the 10 June pickup date." Trapp slumped back in the passenger seat and stared at the message. One dead.

Hooker turned into the DET-K compound. "That's why I'm bringing you here. We need to see what we can figure out." Hooker pulled the car up in front of the headquarters building.

They hurried into the Quonset hut that housed the operations offices for the unit. Hooker beckoned them into an empty office, closing the door tightly behind him. "What now, sir? According to the message, we've got to get them out tonight."

Hossey considered their options out loud. "I don't have the assets to run the exfiltration. I can't exactly go to the commander of the Eighth Army here in Korea and ask him to run it. I'd get laughed out of the office. By the time we get through to US-SOCOM and get them to authorize the mission, it will probably be too late. We don't have the time to mess around. That bird has got to lift this evening." He turned to Hooker. "What about the Blackhawk from 1st Group that made it out on the first exfil?"

Hooker shook his head. "It's already back down in Okinawa."

Hossey made his decision. "I'm going to get ahold of US-SOCOM and see what they can do. Hell, they started this damn thing, they can finish it. Maybe they can get that bird sent back up or task Eighth Army to shit us one."

Changbai Mountains, China
Friday, 9 June, 2300 Zulu
Saturday, 10 June, 7:00 A.M. Local

The survivors watched the ball of fire rise slowly out of the east. Cold didn't accurately describe how they felt. Neither did frozen, but it was closer. Riley knew that they had to get moving in order to warm everyone up. Since the transmitter had burned up at one in the morning, they had spent a long, restless night, shivering, looking at the hands on the watch, willing them to go by faster so dawn would come.

Most of the men were already awake. Comsky nudged the captain, who was huddled at his side. "Hey, sir. Was it as good for you as it was for me?"

Mitchell smiled. "I've had better, but, considering the circumstances, you'll do. Just don't tell my wife when we get back, OK? I'm not sure she'd understand."

Comsky chuckled as he left to check Olinski and C.J. He then reported back to Riley and the captain. "They're both getting worse. We'll start seeing some infection in the pilot's arm today. Without my medical kit, I've got only what I carry on my vest, and that isn't enough to deal with all this. Olinski's insisting he wants to try to walk. He wants me to make him a crutch. He's been feeling bad about us having to carry him. I told him if he got up I'd break his other leg. I think that worked."

Mitchell walked over to Olinski and knelt beside him. "Hey, wild man." Olinski looked over at the captain. "You and I both know you aren't walking anywhere. Right?"

Olinski looked away. "I know that, sir. But I feel like I'm dragging the team down. You guys would be twice as far if you hadn't been carrying me. I feel so useless."

"I know that. I feel useless, too, with my side the way it is. I can't help the others carry you. But suppose somebody else was hurt. You'd be the first person in line to carry them. We're a team, remember? We're going to finish this as a team. We're in no big rush anyway. The pickup zone is only about ten klicks away and we've got all day to make it. OK?"

Olinski nodded.

Mitchell went over to the pilot. "How you doing?"

"Sir, did you go to West Point?"

"Yeah, why?"

"I thought so. They must teach people to ask dumb questions there. How the hell do you think I'm doing? My arm hurts like a son of a bitch. I'm freezing my butt off. I'm hungry. I didn't sleep more than five minutes last night. I'm in the middle of China. My helicopter crashed yesterday and I lost my copilot. Anything I forgot?"

Mitchell smiled. "Yeah. I think Comsky needs to check your bandages again. Hey, Comsky!"

C.J. held up his good hand. "I was only joking. Things are going great. Never felt better. Just can't wait for us to get moving. No need for Comsky to waste his time."

Mitchell nodded. "Much better. See how different things can appear, depending on your perspective? You're part of Team 3 now. That's quite an honor to have bestowed on you."

C.J. gestured at his traveling companions. "Does every prospective member have to go through this same initiation?"

"No, only the ones we really like."

Now that it was light enough to see the way, Riley got them moving. They moved slowly, like old men. Riley directed the team's course along the northern edge of a draw heading east. The vegetation was thick enough now to hide them from the helicopter overflights that Riley expected to start proliferating today. What worried him more was ground troops. Carrying Olinski, they wouldn't be able to outrun anybody.

As they moved along, Riley felt his stiff muscles loosening up and his limbs grow warm. He hadn't heard anyone complain yet. They had to make the pickup zone tonight, by midnight at the latest. Everyone was moving slower than yesterday, but they should still make it to the site in time. If they weren't picked up by dawn tomorrow, they had

only one choice. Keep moving, get across the border somehow, then make it to the coast. Once they got there, they'd do
whatever they had to. Steal a radio. Find a boat and kill the
crew. Whatever was necessary to get home.

46th Army Headquarters, Yanji, China
Friday, 9 June, 2345 Zulu
Saturday, 10 June, 7:45 A.M. Local
When Colonel Tugur arrived, he took the 46th Army Headquarters by storm. He ranted and raved and screamed. The
normally quiet headquarters reeled under the impact of his
anger.

The senior commanders and staff of the 46th Army weath-
ered this storm for fifteen minutes in the headquarters conference room. Technically, the army commander outranked
Tugur. Realistically, as General Yang's aide, Tugur held the
power in the room. Finally the Mongol officer stopped yelling and faced the cowering officers. "Enough. You all have
managed to bungle this terribly so far. We must change that
now. Listen closely and follow the orders I relay from General Yang. If any of you fail again, it will be your last failure
in the army."

Tugur turned to the map. "You found the wreckage here."
He tapped the location. "I have just sent your assistant army
commander up there, with the pilot of the helicopter who
found the wreckage. Until they report back, we must assume
there are survivors.

"Since the terrorist act was committed here, along the
Sungari River, and the terrorists were fleeing to the east, as
we can tell from the wreckage, we must assume they will
continue to the east toward the border. I want this entire army
to be moving in one hour. We are going to stretch a net for
the criminals from here at Yanji down to Mount Paektu on
the border." Tugur swept his arm across the map. "Once the
net is in place, we will move it to the west and catch our fish.

"You all have a copy of your orders. Subunit areas are assigned in them. Are there any questions?" As expected, there
were none. "*One hour,* gentlemen."

Tugur left the conference room and went to an adjoining
office, where he dialed Yang's personal number in Shenyang.

Yang wasted no time in preamble once Tugur identified himself. "Were there any questions?"

"No, General. They are too scared to think. But they will be moving out on time and be in place by 1200 today."

"Good. Anything else?"

"No, sir."

There was a click as the phone was hung up on the other end. Tugur looked at the dead phone in his hand. He'd been with General Yang a long time and knew him well. Tugur felt his superior was taking a foolish chance now. They'd reported the pipeline explosion to Beijing—it would have been impossible to hide that. But Yang was keeping quiet the news of the crash site, and possible foreign involvement. The general wanted all the potential glory of capturing the foreigners. But Tugur knew that that was a two-edged sword. Yang would also get all the blame if the foreigners escaped. And as Yang's fortunes went, so went Tugur's.

Yongsan Army Base, Seoul, Korea
Saturday, 10 June, 0030 Zulu
Saturday, 10 June, 9:30 A.M. Local

Hossey stared at the phone in disbelief. It had taken him more than an hour to get through the notoriously screwed-up Korean autovon military system to talk to the duty officer at US-SOCOM, and the man had just hung up on him. It was eight at night at MacDill Air Force Base in Florida, and the only person Hossey could talk to was the duty officer, a Major Mills, who had almost laughed at Hossey's assertion that he had men on the ground in China who needed exfil tonight. The major said he worked in the S-3 shop and would know if US-SOCOM was running a live operation.

Hossey had referred him to the SFOB they had been working with up at Fort Meade. Then the major did laugh. "You mean the exercise up there?" The major turned serious. "That's a classified exercise and we shouldn't be talking about it over an open line." There had been a second of silence. Then Major Mills swore. "You're with the exercise team, aren't you? You're trying to test our security." That was when he had hung up.

Hossey looked at the other two men in the room. "What the hell is going on?"

Changbai Mountains, China
Saturday, 10 June, 0100 Zulu
Saturday, 10 June, 9:00 A.M. Local
They'd been moving for two hours and had covered three kilometers. Already there had been two overflights by helicopters. The hunt was picking up pace. A Z-9 had flown by thirty minutes after first light and gone up the draw over the crest. An S-70 had flown by only ten minutes ago, heading in the same direction. Riley knew that the Chinese were serious about this operation if they were using their most advanced helicopters in the search.

All four healthy team members were now carrying the stretcher. It had gotten to be too much for just two of them. Mitchell was moving about twenty-five meters ahead of them, through the trees, to provide early warning. He carried his MP5 submachine gun in his left hand and would fire it one-handed if needed.

Riley was halting the team for rest every thirty minutes. After only two hours he could feel the strain of carrying Olinski.

Riley doubted very much that their message had been received. They'd angled Hoffman's wire antenna so that the message would go south toward Korea. But the more Riley thought about it, the more pessimistic he became. He started chiding himself again for burning all the equipment at the pickup zone. Team 3 had had a lot of bad luck on this mission, but that had been a poor decision, not bad luck.

Riley knew that Mitchell was also blaming himself. As the commander, he was technically responsible for everything the detachment did or failed to do. There's too much self-recrimination going on, Riley thought, and he was one of the worst. He vowed to put an end to it. Moping over mistakes of the past wasn't going to do anyone any good. It was draining energy that was needed to solve the problems of the present.

Riley halted the team for the next break. They slumped to the ground as Mitchell came back and rejoined them. Riley looked at the faces etched with fatigue. He got up on one knee and faced the discouraged men.

"Listen up. There's some of us walking around, and being carried around," he glanced at Olinski, "who are spending a lot of mental energy bitching at themselves for what's happened so far. I know that the captain and I both feel real bad about burning the rucks on exfiltration. If we had brought them along we'd be a lot better off right now."

Riley looked each person in the eye as he talked to them. "C.J., you're getting down on yourself for losing your aircraft and copilot. Olinski, you're feeling bad because we have to carry you. Comsky, you're probably feeling bad because you don't have the supplies to help the hurt people. Hoffman, you're down because we burned out the transmitter. Tom, I don't know if anything is bugging you or not," Riley said, looking at Chong.

"But this bullshit has got to stop. We've got to get our heads out of our butts and think about the here and now. We succeeded in blowing the target. We're alive when we should be dead. We're moving. We have the possibility of exfiltration tonight. Yeah, I'll be honest and admit it's not a sure thing, but it's something. If we don't get out tonight, we make it across the border and to the coast and steal a boat or whatever. This life is the only one you got. If you all want to roll over and play dead, then we might as well go stand in the middle of a field and give the finger to the next helicopter that flies by. But that's not the way *I'm* going. I'm going to the pickup zone. Every one of you has to decide right now whether you want to go on or stay here and roll over."

Riley got up and looked at the team. It was the longest speech he'd ever made in his life.

Slowly, one by one, the men got to their feet. Olinski looked up from his stretcher. "You guys might as well carry me along. Comsky wouldn't be happy if he didn't have enough injuries to play with."

Yongsan Army Base, Seoul, Korea
Saturday, 10 June, 0130 Zulu
Saturday, 10 June, 10:30 A.M. Local

Hossey was running into a stone wall. No one seemed to know anything about the mission they had just run. He had tried Fort Meade and been told by the post duty officer that US-SOCOM was not running an operational headquarters anywhere. The emergency phone number for the FOB was now listed as no longer in service. The duty officer had referred him to the National Security Agency, which also had pleaded ignorance.

Hossey was weaponless in his fight against the entrenched bureaucracy. He couldn't tell people exactly why he was calling because they weren't cleared to know, and since he couldn't tell them, they weren't very interested in his "very sensitive and urgent matter." Even when he tried being explicit about the reason for the urgency, he had been ignored—it was too preposterous. Hossey felt that eventually he would get through to someone who could take some action. But it could take the rest of the day. Time was running out. He had even tried 1st Battalion, 1st Special Forces Group, in Okinawa and encountered the same disbelief.

Trapp looked up from the maps he was poring over as Hossey slammed down the phone in disgust. "Listen, sir. Even if you got through to someone, you know they aren't going to be able to do a damn thing. Not by tonight at least. It's the middle of a Friday night over there." Trapp stabbed a finger at the maps. "Even if you did get someone to act, there isn't an aircraft handy that can do the mission. The range is too great. If anybody is going to do anything, it's got to be us."

Hooker had been watching Hossey's fruitless phone calls, and now he stood up. "Show me on the map where the pickup zone is."

Trapp pointed out the location. Hooker looked at it and then at the large-scale map on the wall that showed Korea, Japan, and southeastern China. He took out a scale ruler and started measuring distance, then shook his head.

"They're a hell of a long way away. I don't know. The 2d Infantry Division up at Camp Casey has Blackhawks, but I

kind of doubt we can talk the division commander out of one
to fly this mission. You've seen what kind of results we get
when we call up someone." Hooker rubbed his face. "I don't
suppose either of you are helicopter pilots. We could go steal
one. Hell, even then, a Blackhawk can't make it from Korea
to China and back out, even going to Japan. It's too far. It
would have to refuel somewhere."

Something clicked in Trapp's mind. He stood up suddenly.
"I know what we can do. I don't know if it will work, but it's
a start in the right direction. At least it beats sitting around
here wasting our time on the phone. Hook, we're going to
need your help. We need you to get us some things first, then
we're going to need you to drive."

17

"And if in all respects unequal, be capable of eluding him, for a small force is but booty for one more powerful."
Sun Tzu: *The Art of War*

46th Army Headquarters, Yanji, China
Saturday, 10 June, 0200 Zulu
Saturday, 10 June, 10:00 A.M. Local

Tugur had taken over the army commander's office. He sat behind the desk, wreathed in cigarette smoke, with maps of the area spread out in front of him. He glanced up as the army commander walked in. The man seated himself across the desk and peered at the colonel for a few seconds before beginning his situation report. Tugur could tell that the man resented his presence but was too afraid of Yang to make an issue of it.

"All units are in place, Colonel. Two hours early. They are ready to move out when you give the order. We have also received a report from the crash site. They say that the explosion and fire make it impossible to determine the type or nationality of the aircraft. It appears to have been a helicopter. There are some human remains scattered about the area. Again, it is impossible to determine the number or nationalities of casualties."

Tugur shook his head. "Unacceptable! Tell that idiot up there I want to know how many casualties and the type and nationality of the aircraft. I don't care if he has to put the pieces together, both the aircraft and bodies, by hand."

"Yes, Colonel. I told him that they must remain up there all night if need be, until they have the answers we require. Since it will be cold tonight, I am sure they will work somewhat harder."

Tugur allowed himself the ghost of a smile. "Good. Anything else?"

"Should we not begin the sweep now? All units are in place and awaiting your command."

"Go ahead and get them started." Tugur stirred. "I need to make some phone calls." He waited until the army commander was out of the office, then dialed Yang's number.

"Sir, this is Tugur. The search has started."

Yang's voice acknowledged the news. "Good. We have another problem. I have an eyes-only message from Prime Minister Li Peng demanding any information I have on the terrorists who committed this act. It asks specifically for any indication that students might have been involved."

Tugur digested this new information. His fears grew stronger and more defined. Obviously Yang had not forwarded word on the helicopter. Knowledge is power, Tugur knew. But getting caught withholding knowledge could be very dangerous. They were in over their heads here.

Apparently Yang had come to the same conclusion. "I sent the prime minister a message telling him of the recent discovery of a crash site and also detailing our efforts to catch the terrorists. I hope that will satisfy him." There was a pause and Tugur could almost hear Yang thinking over the phone line. "Why would Li Peng be so interested in this situation? I would think he has enough problems in Beijing to occupy him. None of this makes very much sense. Why would foreigners destroy our pipeline?"

"I do not know, sir." Tugur had no answers and felt that it was a waste of time to speculate. He did not want to mention his personal fear—that the sabotage had been conducted by dissident Chinese soldiers trying to destabilize the government. The only things Tugur didn't understand were where the men had stolen the helicopter, and where they had been fleeing to when they crashed.

Yang hung up the phone. Tugur was more disturbed than ever by Yang's scheming. It was much easier being a simple soldier. Yang was trying to use this incident to advance his career, a move that could easily backfire. There was quite a bit of political maneuvering going on in Beijing, with some of the more liberal generals trying to lever out the Old Men. Despite their long association, Tugur didn't know where Yang's allegiances lay. Yang had sent divisions down to

Beijing to help settle the unrest there, so he was at least putting up the appearance of supporting the current regime. Tugur shook his head. He didn't like it.

Tugur entered the operations center for the army. The radio calls were going out, and the three divisions of the 46th Army had begun moving. From Yanji, down two hundred kilometers to Mount Paektu, the roughly thirty thousand men of the army turned to the west, away from the North Korean border, and moved toward the mountains.

**Camp Page, ChunChon, Korea
Saturday, 10 June, 0430 Zulu
Saturday, 10 June, 1:30 P.M. Local**
The last people Jean Long expected to see in the doorway of her office were Lieutenant Colonel Hossey and Sergeant Major Hooker, accompanied by a Special Forces warrant officer. The surprise on her face was evident as her first sergeant knocked on the door and escorted them in. Her company was working this Saturday, which wasn't unusual, since they had worked nine Saturdays in a row, trying desperately to keep up with Department of the Army standards for operational readiness.

The ride to ChunChon from Seoul had been harrowing. Hooker had negotiated the narrow mountain road with a skill that any native-born Korean would have been proud of. The normal two-hour ride had taken them only an hour and a half. Five minutes ago they had finally driven down the bustling main street of ChunChon and, at the end of the street, arrived at the only gate to Camp Page.

Jean stood up and greeted them. Hossey introduced her to Warrant Officer Trapp.

"John didn't tell me you were coming up here on an exercise when I talked to him last, sir."

Hossey shut the door behind the departing first sergeant. "I'm not here on a training exercise."

Jean took in the three men's haggard faces and somber expressions. "Did something happen to John? Is he all right?"

"We don't know," Trapp answered.

Jean stood stock-still. "You don't know! What do you mean you don't know? Where is he?"

Hossey fielded that one. "He's in China."

Captain Long sat back in her chair and let that sink in.

Hossey turned to Trapp. "Give her a brief summary of what's happened."

Hooker held up his hand. "I think I'd better go out and stay by my car, just in case some roving MP decides to get a little nosy and check out what's under the blankets in the back seat." He slipped out the door and shut it behind him.

Trapp began a quick narration of events. Jean remained composed throughout the story, occasionally asking a question for clarification. When Trapp finished, she sat silently for a few seconds. Then she reached into her desk and started to rummage through the drawers. She pulled out a large-scale aviator's map. "Give me those grids again."

As Trapp repeated the numbers, she plotted them out. Then she pulled out a ruler and started calculating.

"I've already done some plotting," Trapp told her, "and there's no way to get in and back without a refuel. And that was using the 1st Group's special ops Blackhawks with external tanks. It's too far."

Jean agreed. "I figure almost five hundred and fifty-nine nautical miles in from here, then the same coming back. Hell, our Blackhawks can only go two hundred and sixty total miles on their normal fuel tanks." She was struck by a thought. Getting up, she walked to the door and called to her first sergeant. "Top, what's the status on 579?"

First Sergeant Lucky spit a stream of tobacco juice into the Coke can he carried. "Ma'am, she's ready to go for that goddamn dog and pony show down at Tango Range tomorrow. I didn't get to tell you earlier this morning, but the colonel ordered everything put on that damn bird. This morning our armament guys wasted three hours loading that thing up with those new Stingers. They just finished about a half hour ago. It's sitting over in the secure holding area now."

"What about the internal auxiliary tanks?"

The first sergeant looked at his commander as if she'd grown wings. "Ma'am, we weren't told to put in the auxiliary tanks."

"I just got off the phone with the colonel, and he says he wants them in."

The first sergeant cursed resignedly. "Damn, ma'am!

We've haven't put those things in since we deployed last year to Okinawa. That's going to waste another two hours of maintenance time."

"I told the colonel that, but he insisted. This is one of those arguments we're not going to win."

The first sergeant spit another gob into the can. "Yes, ma'am. I'll get them started on it. Make it look real purty for the colonel. You know how many hours of good maintenance time we've wasted getting 579 ready for this display? I'm surprised they didn't have us paint and wax the damn thing."

"Don't say that too loud or someone might hear. Thanks, Top."

Jean closed the door and looked at the two men who had been following the conversation without much comprehension. She explained. "We've got an aircraft going down to Tango Range tomorrow to be part of a military display for a bunch of high-ranking Korean officers. I'm going to have my people put in the four internal auxiliary tanks. Normally we don't use them."

She pulled a manual off the bookcase behind her. "With internal auxiliary tanks we add quite a bit of range. That gives us, let's see, nine hundred and thirty-six nautical miles total. Still not enough. Plus, the internal tanks fill up the entire cargo bay."

She shut her eyes in thought for a second and mused out loud. "The internal tanks are basically rubber fuel bladders in a metal frame. If we drain two or three on the way in, the people we're going to pick up could deflate the tanks and cram aboard. We'd have to get down pretty low on fuel anyway because of the weight problem. Damn! All we need is one refuel on the way in or out, and I think I could fly it."

Hossey protested. "Hold on a second there, Jean. We didn't come here to get you to fly the mission. We wanted you to go with us to your battalion commander and convince him to give us an aircraft and crew."

Jean barked a short laugh. "With all due respect, sir— bullshit! Let's be real. We have a snowball's chance in hell of convincing my colonel to give up a helicopter to violate North Korean and Chinese airspace to rescue some Special Forces soldiers trapped there. Do you think he'd believe you? What would you do if someone came into your office with that kind of story? This is the 'real army.' We don't do things without orders in triplicate. Even if he halfway believed us, which I doubt, he'd have to confer with his boss, who'd have to confer with his boss, and so on. Look at all the trouble you've been having dealing with your own special operations people.

"Besides, what's the matter with me flying? Just because I don't have a certain bodily appendage doesn't mean I can't fly a helicopter as well as, if not better than, most men. The only problem we've got is convincing someone else to be as stupid as me. Stupider actually. I've got a definite reason for flying this mission.

"I can't fly alone. The Blackhawk is a two-pilot bird. You can't reach all the switches from one seat. Besides, that's much too long a flight to try with one pilot. I'm going to have to find another fool to go along." She looked at her calculations and started doing some more figuring.

Trapp had a small smile on his face. This female captain sure was damned spunky, he thought. He'd never worked with women in the army before. In fact, he had never been particularly fond of the whole concept. But he had to admit he admired the way the captain had answered the colonel. She was right, too. He glanced over at the colonel. Hossey raised his eyebrows and shrugged at Trapp, as if to say, I'm not going to argue with her anymore.

Jean looked up. "It's roughly a five-hour flight from here to the pickup zone, then five hours back out. That means we'd have to leave early this evening to make it in and out during darkness. By eight at the latest. I've never flown that long continuously. Nobody here has."

She shook her head irritably. "None of that matters anyway if we don't find a way to refuel on the way in. Even flying over to Japan won't work. China is closer to the north and east than Japan is. I'd have to fly south to Japan and then hop north. That would add more than eight hundred miles to the trip. We'd never make it by tonight. Besides, we'd never get fuel. Once we steal the bird we won't have an authorized flight plan."

Trapp suddenly jerked forward in his chair. "I know where we can get refueled."

Changbai Mountains, China
Saturday, 10 June, 0500 Zulu
Saturday, 10 June, 1:00 P.M. Local

Three more kilometers and they'd be at the pickup zone. Going downhill was much easier. The terrain had become less steep, and the bright sun and hard walking had warmed up everyone. Riley called a rest halt beneath a tall tree. He took out Olinski's monocular and climbed up the tree to get a look around.

Looking ahead to the east from his perch, Riley tried to spot the pickup zone. As the elevation dropped, the vegetation had gotten thicker, and he couldn't tell whether there was a clearing where the map said it should be. He could see the river off to their left front, sloping down toward Yanji in the north. The unimproved dirt road was there also—Riley could catch glimpses of the brown snake crossing the undulating terrain.

Riley looked farther to the east and froze. He spotted a plume of dust. Then another. And another. He spent five minutes studying the activity, then carefully shimmied down the tree.

Mitchell was waiting for him. "What you got? See the pickup zone?"

Riley shook his head. "But I can see the river and the road, so we're only about three kilometers away from where it's supposed to be. We've got visitors coming." Riley had immediately captured the entire team's attention. "I can see dust raised by vehicles heading this way. About ten kilometers past where the pickup zone is supposed to be. They seem to be moving real slow. I'd say we've got a cordon of troops heading toward us. They must have definitely found the crash site and figured out we were somewhere around. Really didn't take any genius on their part to figure out we'd head for the coast."

Comsky was the first to grasp the obvious implication. "Do you think we'll make the PZ before them?"

"Yeah, we can definitely make the PZ before them," Riley assured him, "that's not the problem. The problem is to keep them from seeing us when they sweep by. They're moving pretty slow—I'd say about two kilometers an hour. It gets dark in about five hours, so it's going to be close."

Olinski raised himself slightly on his good arm. "They'll stop for the night. I don't think they'll keep up their sweep in the dark. They'll stop and set up a guard line, then move out tomorrow morning at first light."

Mitchell considered this. "So it's a question of whether they make it to the pickup zone before dark. If they don't, we're OK because we'll be there. If the Chinese do make it there, or farther, we're going to have to go through their lines tonight."

Riley nodded. "I think we ought to hold up here and keep watch on the search line. Wait until dark and then move down. With a little luck the Chinese will stop before the PZ."

C.J. was tired and irritable. "All that's nice and fine, but what happens if we make it to the PZ and no bird comes tonight? We'll still have to deal with the Chinese tomorrow. Maybe we ought to head back the way we came and try to evade them."

Riley disagreed. "No way. It kicked our ass coming down here. We can't go back up. Besides, what's up there? They'll catch up with us eventually. We might as well go for broke tonight. If the aircraft doesn't come tonight, we'll try to slip through and head on down to the coast like originally planned. We can't run forever."

Camp Page, ChunChon, Korea
Saturday, 10 June, 0600 Zulu
Saturday, 10 June, 3:00 P.M. Local

Chief Warrant Officer Colin Lassiter was finishing running up a Blackhawk on the flight line when Captain Long finally tracked him down. He watched the approach of the captain through the windshield. She was with another warrant officer. Lassiter did a quick scrutiny of the man's uniform badges—you could learn a lot from a man's badges. No flight wings above the man's left shirt pocket: a warrant officer who wasn't an aviator. He noted the Special Forces patch on the man's left shoulder and the same patch on his right shoulder, indicating combat service in Special Forces. He wondered if that meant he had been in Vietnam.

Lassiter was too young to have been in Vietnam. He'd been in the army sixteen years, twelve of them as an aviator. He'd taken up flying because he liked excitement and he loved flying. He still loved flying but the excitement had worn thin. He was fed up with the army and planned on getting out after this tour in Korea. He was tired of all the games he had to play. He didn't know what he was going to do when he got out, and he really didn't care as long as he could fly.

He watched the captain and Special Forces warrant come up to the aircraft as he started to shut the bird down. Lassiter respected Captain Long. None of the warrants in D Company had been thrilled when they got a female commander, but their original antipathy had grudgingly given way to acceptance. Some still didn't like having a woman in command and never would, but after only two months in command, the captain had earned the respect of most of the men in her unit. Lassiter respected Long because she made decisions and didn't bullshit people. She told the truth as she saw it and was fair. That was unusual in officers, in Lassiter's experience—which was another one of the many reasons he was getting out of the army. On top of her command abilities, Lassiter also respected Captain Long's flying skill. She was one of the best pilots he had ever flown with.

With the engine finally shut down, Lassiter stepped out of the aircraft.

Long introduced the two warrants. "Jim Trapp, this is Colin Lassiter." She turned her direct gaze on Colin. "Jim is in my husband's unit down in Yongsan. He's come to me with a problem. I might be able to help him out but I need some assistance. I came to you first because I thought you might be willing to give us a hand."

Lassiter gathered together his flight gear, throwing his helmet in its bag. "What do you need?"

"I need a copilot to help me steal a helicopter and fly it to China to rescue my husband and some of his team members."

Lassiter put down the bag. Captain Long had a good sense of humor, but this was a little strange. "Come on, ma'am. That's pretty good. What do you all need?"

Trapp looked Lassiter in the eye. "She isn't joking. We were in China on a classified mission. Their helicopter crashed. Mine made it out. They've been written off as far as everyone else is concerned, but we know that some of them are alive. We can't get anyone else to react in time. We have to go in tonight."

Lassiter looked from one to the other. It sounded like dialogue from a bad movie. But he could tell they weren't joking. "You're serious," he said incredulously.

Jean Long looked at him piercingly. "Please, Colin. My husband is there. They've got three wounded men. We've got to go tonight to get them out."

Colin shook his head. "Why me? Why'd you come to me?"

"Because I know you're getting out and are fed up with this stuff. You're bored. You aren't married. You're a good pilot. And truthfully because you're probably the only one crazy enough to do this with me."

Colin considered this. "The last one is certainly true. I'd have to be crazy as hell to do this." He rubbed his chin in thought—things were looking more exciting by the second. "China, heh? I've always wanted to see China. What's the plan?"

"Let's go to my office and we'll show you."

Changbai Mountains, China
Saturday, 10 June, 0600 Zulu
Saturday, 10 June, 2:00 P.M. Local

The plan had been done scientifically. The 46th Army had five divisions. Two had been sent to Beijing. That left three infantry divisions at an authorized strength of ten thousand men each. Minus those sick or injured, the few on leave, and those slots that were unfilled, 26,345 were left to participate in the search. One wheeled vehicle per company was authorized to carry equipment and for radio control. Everyone else was on foot.

Taking out the truck drivers, division staffs, and various other support people, there were 24,395 soldiers on foot. Dividing the two hundred kilometers they were to cover by that many soldiers gave each man a search area approximately eight meters wide. With this gap between soldiers, the 46th People's Liberation Army marched toward the mountains.

The cordon already had run into twelve hunters and two trucks from mines in the mountains. The army commander was taking no chances. All had been taken into custody until their identification could be verified. Each regimental commander checked off the phase lines as their units crossed them. The pace had been set at two kilometers an hour.

Like a rising olive-green tide, the army swept the foothills of the mountains.

Camp Page, ChunChon, Korea
Saturday, 10 June, 0800 Zulu
Saturday, 10 June, 5:00 P.M. Local

Hossey, Trapp, and Hooker had spent the hours profitably. They war-gamed the situations they might face and devised plans to meet them. They decided that Trapp and Hooker would fly with the Blackhawk until the refuel point. Hossey wanted to go with them, but Trapp convinced the colonel that he had another important mission.

"Sir, you need to stay on the phone and get someone to believe that those men are really on the ground. I don't know what the hell is going on at US-SOCOM with them denying any knowledge of the operation, but you have to try to get to the bottom of it. We also need you to prepare for the return of the helicopter so it doesn't get shot down trying to get back into South Korean airspace."

Hossey was forced to agree with Trapp's logic. He took Hooker's car and headed back to Yongsan.

It had taken Lassiter and Long an hour to finish their flight plan for the mission. They plotted their route in and out of the target area and studied the maps they had available. The lack of good imagery was a handicap. Luckily the pickup zone appeared to be located just by the intersection of a river and an unimproved road. The plan was simple. They'd fly up the coast and turn left when they saw the lights of the North Korean town of Najin on its promontory. Circumnavigating the town, they'd fly almost due east until they saw the river, then turn left and fly until they hit the dirt road. Jean felt that they would have enough points over land to be able to update the Doppler en route and get them close to the PZ.

They planned to lift off just prior to 9:00 P.M. local. In the hours remaining they had a lot to accomplish. The internal tanks had to be filled on 579, the helicopter they would be using. They had to file a false flight plan with base operations so they could take off. They had to draw their night-vision goggles. Trapp and the sergeant major had to load some equipment on board the bird. And all this had to be done without arousing the suspicions of anyone in the unit.

Fortunately, the military mind-set aided them in their endeavors. No one questioned them as they went about preparing for the mission. The fact that it was a quiet Saturday afternoon helped. Jean let Lassiter handle the helicopter while she went over to flight operations and filed a flight plan. She told the NCO on duty the same story she had used on her first sergeant: She and Lassiter were taking 579 down to the range early and would spend the night there. Jean knew the story would last long enough for them to make the east coast of Korea. After that she wasn't sure what the reaction would be, but hopefully by then they would have disappeared from all radar screens as they hit the wave tops.

Lassiter had the support platoon bring over a fuel truck and pour in JP4 fuel until all four internal tanks were bulging. When that was done, he started preflighting the aircraft. As he was checking the engine fluid levels, Hooker and Trapp arrived, carrying a bulky duffel bag. Lassiter eyed the bag and the two Special Forces soldiers. "What's in there?"

Hooker tapped the bag knowingly. "Just some what-if stuff."

46th Army Headquarters, Yanji, China
Saturday, 10 June, 0800 Zulu
Saturday, 10 June, 4:00 P.M. Local

The army commander updated Tugur on the latest situation report. "The sweep has progressed twelve kilometers from the border road. They are making approximately two kilometers an hour." He turned to the map. "We estimate they will be somewhere along this trace by dark. So far they have managed to turn up some hunters and miners. There has been no sign of the terrorists."

Tugur grunted his acknowledgment.

The commander continued. "I have a recommendation to make." Tugur gave him an encouraging nod. "Since we found the wreckage in this location, I think we ought to narrow the search in order to concentrate our forces. The terrorists are on foot. They cannot be moving fast enough to have gone much farther than, say, from here to here." The commander outlined his estimate on the map. "I suggest we pull our forces from these areas here to the north and south and concentrate them in this center area, from twenty kilometers north of the indicated point to twenty-five kilometers below it. This will allow us to have a much better net."

Tugur agreed with the officer. "Your reasoning is valid. Give the orders."

Changbai Mountains, China
Saturday, 10 June, 0900 Zulu
Saturday, 10 June, 5:00 P.M. Local
Watching the search line creep forward had been agonizing. From his perch Riley watched in growing dismay as more trucks pulled into the area, dropping off additional troops. He climbed down from the tree and reported to Mitchell. "They're going to make the pickup zone before dark. They're only two kilometers away from it now. I figure they'll go maybe another kilometer beyond by dark. And there's more bad news. Looks like the search is being concentrated here. For the last hour more troops have been coming into this area. The density of the search line has almost doubled."

Mitchell sighed. "Do you think we can break through to-night?"

Riley shook his head. "Before these reinforcements I would have said maybe. Now I doubt it. We're definitely going to make contact. I don't relish the idea of running toward the pickup zone, carrying Olinski, and fighting off the Chinese at the same time. We could force our way through, but they'd track us down and wipe us out before we went five hundred meters." Riley kicked the tree Mitchell was leaning against. "Damn! We've got to come up with a plan."

Mitchell agreed. "Let's bring everyone together and talk it over."

18

"Offer the enemy a bait to lure him."
Sun Tzu: *The Art of War*

Changbai Mountains, China
Saturday, 10 June, 0930 Zulu
Saturday, 10 June, 5:30 P.M. Local

Thirty minutes of brainstorming had turned up no feasible plan.
Riley kept silent, but he knew what the plan had to be. He'd
known all along. Mitchell must also see that they had only one
choice. Riley had desperately hoped someone else could come
up with a less drastic course of action. No one had.

Riley was getting ready to speak when Mitchell beat him
to it. "All right. Enough. It's time to face reality. We can't
run from these guys. Not only can we not outdistance them
carrying Olinski—and I don't want to hear any more bullshit
from you about getting left behind," the captain warned
Olinski, "but also there's no point in going west. For all we
know there's another search line coming up the mountains on
that side. There must be people at the crash site. West is out.

"North and south are out, too. The search line extends as
far as we can see in both directions. We'd never be able to
do an end run around the flank. For all we know it extends
fifty kilometers each way. That leaves us with the original
problem. We have to either head east or hide in place. We're
fooling ourselves if we think we can do either.

"The bottom line is that we have to make the Chinese
change their tactics. There's only one way I can think of to
do that. Set up a diversion."

Mitchell let the significance of what he had just said sink
in for a few seconds.

Olinski was the first to react. "I volunteer, sir. If you all could get me up to the high ground over there to the north, I could use the SAW and get their attention."

Mitchell had expected this and shook his head. "No. If the people doing the diversion are going to have any chance at surviving, they've got to be able to run. I'm not sending any-body on a suicide mission."

Riley raised his hand for attention. Everyone fell silent. "Here's what I propose. Two men, healthy men, take an SVD sniper rifle and the SAW machine gun. They go up in higher ground along that finger there to the north. Just after dark the one with the SVD starts taking out the Chinese along the search line. I'm sure they won't be practicing strict discipline. Hell, they'll probably have fires going all along the line. We shoot enough of them, and keep it up, until they have to react.

"The rest of the team hides. The best place will probably be down near the stream over there. Hopefully, once the shooting starts, the Chinese will break their line and move past those team members who are hiding, missing you in the dark. Once the Chinese go by, our guys head on down to the pickup zone. I'm pretty sure you'll be able to do it in the con-fusion. If you make any accidental contact, you can use the silenced submachine gun to take care of it.

"The two guys in the hills keep the Chinese's attention as long as they can, then try to make it down to the pickup zone or, if that isn't possible, try to escape into the hills. Two healthy guys might have a chance where the whole group of us wouldn't. We coordinate a pickup zone back in the mountains for those two. If the rest of the team gets out tonight, you get base to run another exfiltration for those two on another night."

Riley stopped and looked at the captain. They both knew they had to go with this plan. It was the only way. It was feasible—all except the last part, Riley thought. There's no way those two men would survive. But at least they'd go out fight-ing.

The detachment commander stood up. "I agree, unless any-one can come up with a better suggestion." Mitchell looked each team member in the eye. No one said anything. "I'll de-cide who does what. Dave, come with me."

Riley and Mitchell walked about twenty meters away from the team and sat down on two rocks.

Riley preempted the captain. "Listen, Mitch. I know you're going to volunteer yourself to do this. Deep inside you know that's bullshit, for the same reasons you gave Olinski. We've got only four healthy men—me, Hoffman, Chong, and Comsky. It's got to be two of us. One of the two has got to be a trained sniper. That's between Comsky and me. We need to leave Comsky with the main party because he's the medic. That means I'm the one with the sniper rifle."

Mitchell didn't protest. He hated the decision. But it was the right decision.

Riley continued. "Then it's between Hoffman and Chong for the SAW. Chong's qualified on the SAW and it's his weapon. I'd also prefer having Chong with me. If anybody can navigate our way through the mountains at night and keep us from getting tracked down, it's him. I'll leave Hoffman with you for another reason. If the exfil bird doesn't come tonight—and you and I both know it's a long shot—he's your best bet for figuring out something when you get to the coast, whether it be hot wiring a boat or rerigging a radio. You're going to need him."

Mitchell let out a deep breath and closed his eyes for a second. "You're right, as always, Dave. It's going to be you and Tom. I'll give him the news."

46th Army Headquarters, Yanji, China
Saturday, 10 June, 1000 Zulu
Saturday, 10 June, 6:00 P.M. Local

Yanji was a mining and industrial city with a population of one hundred thousand. Tugur was running the search operation from the regional army headquarters in the center of town. The six Z-9 attack helicopters of the 3d Aviation Regiment were crouched in the fields surrounding the headquarters along with eight S-70 transportation helicopters.

Tugur had taken the time to interrogate the hunters and miners who had been picked up in the sweep. Checks had confirmed their identities, but despite that, the local commander had been too frightened of the wrath of General Yang to release them. Unfortunately, that was the extent of his initiative. He had not thought to ask the prisoners if they had seen anything unusual. Tugur made up for this deficiency in his interrogation. They all replied in the negative, except for one disgruntled old miner who complained that someone had stolen the battery from his truck the previous night.

Tugur was interested in the report of the stolen battery. Who would go all the way up to the mountains to steal a battery from a truck? And if the terrorists had done it, why steal the battery and not the truck? Tugur puzzled over this but could not come up with an answer. He put it aside in the activity of coordinating the sweep's halt for the night. Still the detail gnawed away in the back of his mind. Something about the battery was important; he could feel it.

Changbai Mountains, China
Saturday, 10 June, 1100 Zulu
Saturday, 10 June, 7:00 P.M. Local
From the tall tree Riley watched the olive-green tide reach high water for the day only a kilometer and a half away. He observed the soldiers' preparations for the evening. Like soldiers anywhere, they were gathering wood for fires to take away the night's chill. Riley noted the lack of defensive preparations. The trucks, with their heavy machine guns mounted over the cabs, were not tactically placed in positions with good fields of fire. Instead, they were haphazardly parked in the places most convenient for the company commanders.

The line had made it almost a kilometer past the pickup zone—only a fraction of an inch on the map in Riley's pocket but a significant distance on the ground. Riley continued to study the terrain as the sun went down. He and Chong would move out to the sniper position on the ridgeline as soon as it got dark. Satisfied that he had seen all he wanted to, Riley climbed down.

The rest of the team was waiting for him at the base of the tree. They'd spent this time building a small terrain model, using dirt, sticks, and small rocks. The men gathered around the scale model as Riley made his report, pointing out the places he was talking about.

"The sweep line's made it along a front basically from here, to here, to here. About a klick and a half from here and a little under a klick in front of the pickup zone, if you draw a straight line from our location to the PZ. They don't seem concerned about making contact. Looks like there'll be a bunch of guards standing around fires all along the line. The fires are about thirty meters apart. I still don't think you could sneak through. The off-duty people are bedding down for the night all around, wherever they feel like it. The vegetation isn't thick enough here to cover you."

Mitchell nodded his head in agreement as Riley continued. "The plan we decided on still stands. Tom and I will go up to this position here on the ridge. We'll leave at twenty thirty, after it's fully dark and they've had a chance to settle in down there. We'll take two of the remaining sets of PVS-5 night-vision goggles. The rest of you will move down here, to this stream that runs into the river. Hide as best you can in the thick vegetation along the bank. At zero zero thirty local I'll start picking off people along the guard line. It's about two thousand meters from where I'll be shooting to the nearest Chinese, so they're going to have to move forward to engage me. Once they get inside a thousand meters, Tom will open up with the SAW. We'll keep engaging them until they get to within five hundred meters, at which time we'll head on up into the mountains."

Riley turned to Mitchell, and the captain began to brief them on the rest of the plan. "After Dave and Tom engage, we wait. In the confusion, we try to find the best time to move through the Chinese line along the stream bank. They might even move everyone out and pass us by. At worst case, they're going to have to thin their line to go after these two. Either way, we go through. I'll be in the lead with my silenced MP5 and wearing the last set of PVS-5s. Hoffman and Comsky will carry Olinski. C.J., you bring up the rear. Hoffman and Comsky will use the silenced .22s if they have to shoot. C.J., you take Olinski's shotgun.

"We've got an hour and a half from when Dave starts shooting to make it to the pickup zone. We'll wait there until 0500. If no aircraft comes by that time, they most likely aren't going to be coming. We use the remaining two hours of darkness to move downslope and find a hiding place. The next night we'll continue on to the border. Any questions?"

C.J. raised his hand. "What about the markings on the pickup zone? And frequency? The aircraft is going to have a hell of a time finding that place—if it comes at all. Also, there still might be shooting going on. We probably ought to be up on the radio to assure them that we're really there."

Mitchell agreed. "We've got four infrared chem lights left; we can use those for pickup zone marking. We've also got infrared strobes on all our vests. Olinski will have the PRC68. We think it still works after Hoffman put it back together. If Ski sees or hears anything resembling a friendly helicopter, he's going to start calling on the agreed-upon frequency. Anybody else?"

Hoffman stirred and looked at Riley. "Top, they don't need to get within five hundred meters to engage you. They can start engaging you from the search line using the 12.7-millimeter machine guns on the trucks. They've got the range to reach out there."

Riley had figured his junior engineer would make that observation. He hoped no one would ask too many questions about the diversion team's role. Most particularly he hoped no one would ask questions regarding their survivability. "I've thought of that," Riley answered. "Those machine guns have the range but they're not going to be able to find us until they get close. I've got a couple of tricks I'll use to hide my muzzle flashes. The Chinese are going to have to move. Once we start popping their people off, they'll be so mad they'll be hard to hold back. I just hope enough of them come forward to allow you all to slip through without making contact."

Camp Page, ChunChon, Korea
Saturday, 10 June, 1229 Zulu
Saturday, 10 June, 9:29 P.M. Local

"Camp Page tower, this is army helicopter 579. Request permission to depart airfield on a heading of eight zero degrees. Over."

"Roger army helicopter 579. You are cleared for taxiway and departure. Over."

Jean Long released the brakes on the Blackhawk as Lassiter increased throttle. The aircraft rolled on its three wheels out to the main runway that ran the length of Camp Page. They turned and faced to the east.

Jean tenderly lifted the collective and slipped the cyclic forward, and the heavily laden helicopter pushed away from the clutches of the earth. A two-foot gap appeared beneath the wheels. Getting the feel of the unusual center of gravity caused by the internal fuel bladders, Jean hovered there for ten seconds. She glanced over at Lassiter, who smiled, shrugged, and nodded. Increasing power and lift, she quickly gained altitude and flew off toward the high mountains that encircled ChunChon to the east.

Yongsan Army Base, Seoul, Korea
Saturday, 10 June, 1230 Zulu
Saturday, 10 June, 9:30 P.M. Local
Hossey was laboriously working his way around the Pentagon via phone extensions. No one he had talked to on the night duty staff had any knowledge of a live mission run in this part of the world. It was almost as if there had not been any authorization for this action.

Hossey looked at his military phone book in frustration. He opened it one more time and started from the front, looking for any number that might connect him with someone who knew what was going on.

Changbai Mountains, China
Saturday, 10 June, 1230 Zulu
Saturday, 10 June, 8:30 P.M. Local
Team 3 was splitting again, and this time it appeared to be permanent. Dave Riley could tell that Mitchell was very unhappy about the situation. Chong was standing at the edge of the little grouping, saying good-bye to the rest of the team. Riley stood next to the captain.

"Take care, Mitch, and get these guys out."

Mitchell nodded. It was hard for him to speak. He felt completely helpless. This wasn't the way it was supposed to be. Nothing in his training had ever prepared him to order two of his men to go on a one-way mission. Not only that, but Dave Riley was his best friend. He didn't know what to say, but he tried anyway. "If there was any other way, Dave. I just can't come up with anything."

Riley put his arm over his friend's shoulder. "I know that. Hell, we both came up with the same plan. You just get those guys out and it'll all be worthwhile. You've got to hang in there and drive on."

Mitchell nodded. He didn't trust himself to say any more. The two men embraced briefly. Riley picked up his SVD and walked over to the rest of the team. Not much was said. There was nothing noble or heroic about the scene. Just a pervading sense of sadness tainted with desperation—the same atmosphere that has been present before battle since the beginning of time. Heroism and nobility seemed to come from others talking about events after they were over. Now, as they faced the spectre of death, none of the participants wanted to play their roles. Reasons for being here, and for doing what they did, didn't seem to add up anymore.

Riley smiled and, as he walked out of the camp with Chong, softly called out over his shoulder, "See you all back in Korea."

Sokch'o Air Traffic Control, East Coast, South Korea
Saturday, 10 June, 1306 Zulu
Saturday, 10 June, 10:06 P.M. Local
Sokch'o was the northernmost sizable South Korean city on the east coast. As such, the air and sea routes around it were guarded vigilantly. The entire coastline from the nearby demilitarized zone, south one hundred kilometers, was entirely fenced in to prevent infiltrators from swimming in. The airspace was tightly managed out of Sokch'o airfield.

On the radar screens at Sokch'o, Flight 579 suddenly disappeared. The Korean operator had been watching the flight with growing concern. According to the flight plan he had called up on his computer, 579 was on a training flight from ChunChon to Sokch'o and back. The flight had crossed the shoreline only one minute previously. The controller had expected it to turn any second and head back west. Now it was gone. He keyed his mike. Speaking with great difficulty in English, he broadcast: "United States Army helicopter Five Seven Nine. United States Army helicopter Five Seven Nine. This is Sokch'o Control. You have gone below allowable altitude. Acknowledge. Return to altitude. Over."

He waited a minute, then transmitted again. Still no reply. After five minutes, with no sign of 579 reappearing or replying, the operator reported to his supervisor. Ten minutes later, still with no response, a downed aircraft report was broadcast and search aircraft were alerted.

On board 579 Colin Lassiter had the aircraft skimming the wave tops as the Korean shoreline disappeared behind them. Jean Long was slouched back in her seat, trying to rest. In the cargo compartment, Hooker and Trapp had finished unpacking the duffel bag they'd brought aboard. Now they worked in the cramped space between the four bulging fuel bladders, stowing the weapons Hooker had brought from Yongsan and preparing for other contingencies.

They tied a 120-foot nylon rope to each of two large O-rings bolted to the top center of the cargo compartment. After making sure that both ropes were securely attached, they coiled each one separately in a weighted canvas bag. This was done carefully, to ensure that each rope would deploy without snags if the bag was thrown out the door of the helicopter. The weighted bag would pull the rope to the end of its 120-foot length.

The two men then carefully unbolted the frame for the two forward internal tanks and replaced all the bolts with wraps of 550 cord, the same line used for suspension lines on parachutes. This would allow the two forward tanks to be quickly cut free and removed, when empty, to make space for the team.

With the coastline out of sight, Lassiter gently eased the helicopter around to a heading of 42 degrees—right up the middle of the Sea of Japan.

US-SOCOM Headquarters, MacDill Air Force Base, Florida
Saturday, 10 June, 1320 Zulu
Saturday, 10 June, 8:20 A.M. Local

Colonel Moore didn't like coming in to work on a Saturday, but having been gone the whole past week participating in the exercise up at Fort Meade, his in box was overflowing. He wanted to get a jump on the paperwork before Monday.

Moore was halfway through his first cup of coffee, and a quarter of the way through the contents of his in box, when he came across the duty log from the previous night. It was in his box because it was Moore's responsibility to brief his boss, the G-3, on Monday morning on everything that had happened over the weekend.

Moore slammed his mug down on the desk as he turned the page and read the notation about the strange phone call from a Colonel Hossey in Korea.

"What the hell," he muttered as he punched in the home phone number for the major who had been on duty then. He waited and then heard the line picked up on the other end.

A sleepy voice answered. "Major Mills."

"Mills, this is Colonel Moore. What is this notation in your duty log about a phone call from a Colonel Hossey in Korea?"

There was a brief pause. "Oh, yeah, sir. Some nutcake called and said that he was the commander of DET-K and that he had some men on the ground in China who needed to be exfiltrated. He said it was part of some mission he was running for us."

Moore's mind raced as he considered this. "Did he say what kind of mission?"

"No, sir. He did say that he had lost his commo with an SFOB we had set up at Fort Meade, so I figured this guy was one of those people you spent the week with up there at Meade, trying to test our security or something."

"What did you tell this guy?"

"I didn't tell him anything, sir. I hung up on him. He tried calling back a few times and I hung up on him every time. It was an unsecure line and I figured it was some sort of test."

"All right." Moore hung up the phone. Maybe it was just a further test by the Strams people. The thing that bugged him, though, was that Colonel Hossey *was* the DET-K commander. And the phone call had come just after they shut down the simulation. In the simulation the team had exfiltrated successfully. Moore rubbed his eyes. This whole thing was very strange. He looked at the clocks on the wall. It was 2:30 in the morning over in Korea. Probably couldn't get ahold of Hossey right now. He decided to make some calls first thing Monday morning, though, and check this out.

Korea
Saturday, 10 June, 1330 Zulu
Saturday, 10 June, 10:30 P.M. Local
The disappearance of army aircraft 579 quickly gained notoriety. Sokch'o Control contacted Camp Page Control with the report. Camp Page Control alerted the battalion commander of the 309th Helicopter Battalion. When the battalion commander found out that no one had authorized the flight, and also that live Stinger missiles were on board, he quickly notified his higher headquarters at the 17th Aviation Brigade in Seoul.

Following standard procedures, a nationwide alert was put out for the missing helicopter. All U.S. and Korean agencies were informed. A search was mounted off the coast in the vicinity of Sokch'o to look for helicopter wreckage. It didn't occur to anyone that the helicopter had not crashed.

Changbai Mountains, China
Saturday, 10 June, 1345 Zulu
Saturday, 10 June, 9:45 P.M. Local
Mitchell led his men carefully through the dark. It was only seven hundred meters south to the streambed, but they were moving very slowly.

The night was clear. The moon would be rising in another two hours. Until then, they had only the starlight to guide them. Mitchell was wearing the only set of night-vision goggles; the rest of the team stumbled along in the dark. Only four hundred meters to the east, they could see the fires of the Chinese picket line.

Mitchell tried to force all thoughts out of his mind, except for those needed to make this move. He didn't want to think about the two men heading up the mountain. He didn't want to think about the slim chance that a helicopter would make it to the pickup zone tonight. He didn't want to think about what he would do when the helicopter didn't show. In spite of his efforts, these thoughts swirled around in his mind.

He was walking slowly, to allow those behind him to keep up. Hoffman and Comsky carried the stretcher, watching each step to avoid dropping Olinski. Hoffman, at the lead end of the stretcher, was only two feet behind the captain, following two small pieces of luminous tape sewn into the back of the

captain's black watch cap. Comsky held onto the trail edge of
the stretcher and shuffled his feet along the ground to avoid
tripping. C.J. brought up the tail, staying in contact by continuously reaching out and touching Comsky's back.

After only a hundred meters, Mitchell realized that he was
going to have to help carry Olinski. The man's weight was
too much for Hoffman. Mitchell grabbed the lead end of the
right stick with his left hand. His right arm was still tied
against his side to prevent the sutures from pulling out, and
his MP5 hung on its sling on his chest. The indomitable
Comsky handled the tail end of the stretcher by himself.

Mitchell led the way through the undergrowth. They were going downhill slightly, as the terrain sloped into the streambed.
After forty minutes, they reached the edge of the thicker undergrowth along the bank. Mitchell cautiously guided them downstream. He wanted to get as close to the picket line as they
could before the action started. Slowly he moved them another
two hundred meters closer. He halted the team in an area of especially thick underbrush. Carefully, trying not to make any
loud noises, they crawled under the bushes and sat down in a
tight circle to wait. It was 10:45 P.M. Another hour and forty-
five minutes until the shooting started.

**US-SOCOM Headquarters, MacDill Air Force Base,
Florida
Saturday, 10 June, 1552 Zulu
Saturday, 10 June, 10:52 A.M. Local**

That phone call the previous night was bugging Moore. It
was a loose end, and he didn't like loose ends. If the Strams
people were still playing their game, he wanted to know
about it. They had more important things to worry about here
than some stupid simulation.

Moore grabbed the file for the Dragon Sim-13 exercise from
his safe and flipped through it until he found the administrative
phone numbers for the Tunnel. He scanned the list until he spotted the office number for the man who had outbriefed them yesterday. Moore wasn't sure if anybody would be at work on a
Saturday, but he wanted to try and clear up this thing. Moore
punched in the number on his secure STU III phone. He waited

as it buzzed on the other end. On the seventh buzz he was just
about to hang up when it was picked up.

Fort Meade, Maryland
Saturday, 10 June, 1553 Zulu
Saturday, 10 June, 10:53 A.M. Local

Wilson had barely heard the ringing of the secure phone on
his desk. He was in Meng's office, where the two were going
over the Medusa program. Wondering who could be calling
on a Saturday, he jogged out and picked up the phone. "Doctor Wilson here."

"Doctor, this is Colonel Moore. Could you please go secure?"

I hope he isn't calling about the damn after-action report,
Wilson thought as he turned the key that made the phone secure for classified conversations. "Yes, sir. What can I do for
you?"

The voice at the other end sounded hesitant. "This is kind
of strange, but I'd like to know whether you all are still running something with Dragon Sim-13."

"What do you mean, Colonel, running something? We shut
down yesterday right after you all left."

"Well, my duty officer got a strange phone call last night
from someone claiming to be the commander of DET-K, saying something about having troops on the ground in China
that he had to get exfiltrated. I was wondering if it might
have been someone from your Tunnel, checking up on us after the fact, so to speak."

Wilson frowned. "No, sir. No one from here called as far
as I know. Like I said, we shut down yesterday morning. Did
you call Colonel Hossey in Korea to see if he really was the
one calling?"

"It's after midnight over there, and I doubt that anyone will
be at the DET-K compound. I'd have to contact the Eighth
Army duty officer to get ahold of Hossey. I really didn't want
to go through all that hassle if someone was just pulling a
prank. I am worried, though, because whoever was calling obviously had some classified information about the exercise."

"Well, I can't help you on this end."

"Thanks anyway. I'll try tracking down my people. Maybe it was one of them. Out here."

Wilson put the phone down slowly. It *was* odd. He looked down Tunnel 2 at the door to Meng's office. It had been a strange morning ever since he had shown up, three hours ago. Meng had been acting very weird, even for him. As the two of them worked on the Medusa program, Meng had seemed to be trying to pass on to Wilson as much information about the program as he could—almost as if Meng felt he wasn't going to be around much longer.

Something occurred to Wilson. He looked down his phone number list taped to the top of the desk and punched in a four-digit number on the secure internal NSA phone. The phone was picked up on the first ring.

"Imagery. Sandra."

"Sandra, this is Ron Wilson from the Tunnel."

"Yeah, Ron. What's up?"

"Could you check on something for me?"

"Sure. What do you need?"

"My boss, Doctor Meng, had some pretty interesting imagery of a crash site that we were going to use. I was wondering if you could give me an idea of where and when that imagery was taken. Doctor Meng said something about you all pulling it from your files yesterday."

"Wait a minute. Let me check the log." The minutes stretched into two. Finally Sandra was back. "If you're talking about some photos we faxed down to you and over to Korea early yesterday morning, I've got it here. Let's see, it was 0614 Zulu on the ninth, and that was hot off the computer down link. Real-time stuff. I don't know why Meng thought it was coming out of the files. He asked for it specifically by location."

Wilson looked toward Meng's door. "Could you tell me what area that imagery was covering?"

"Let's see. Yeah. It's in China. Northeast. Manchuria. Real close to where the Chinese, Russian, and North Korean borders come together."

Wilson felt as though he'd been punched in the stomach.

"Hello? Ron, you there?"

"Yeah. Thanks, Sandra." Wilson slowly lowered the phone.

It couldn't be, but he knew it was. He switched over to his STU III.

US-SOCOM Headquarters, MacDill Air Force Base, Florida
Saturday, 10 June, 1556 Zulu
Saturday, 10 June, 10:56 A.M. Local
"Colonel Moore."

"Sir, this is Doctor Wilson. Go secure, please."

Moore still had his key turned. "I'm secure. What's up?"

"I suggest you try to get ahold of Colonel Hossey as soon as you can."

Moore frowned. "Why? What's going on?"

"I'm not exactly sure, sir. I need to do some checking on this end. But there's something strange going on reference Dragon Sim-13. I'll get back to you as soon as I know more, but I think you need to talk to Hossey. That might really have been him on the phone."

Moore rolled his eyes. What the hell were they trying to pull up there at Meade? "All right. I'll try and get through. Let me know what's going on as soon as you can."

Moore slammed down the phone. He looked under his clear blotter at the organizational chart for US-SOCOM units, and decided to try the DET-K headquarters first on the off chance that someone might be there. He punched in the overseas access, then the DET-K commander's number.

A busy signal. The frown lines on his face deepened. He sat there and began punching in the number every thirty seconds.

Sea of Japan
Saturday, 10 June, 1606 Zulu
Sunday, 11 June, 1:06 A.M. Local
Jean Long looked at the fuel gauges. The Blackhawk's thirsty turbines had sucked dry the third internal fuel bladder ten minutes ago. They were presently working off the fourth, and last, 285-gallon bladder. When that one was empty, they'd be left with the 362 gallons in the aircraft's regular fuel tank. What all that meant was that they had less than 430 kilometers of fuel left. They were presently located 50 meters above the Sea of Japan, 120 kilometers due south of Vladivostok. They had just

enough fuel to make it safely back to Korea. They did not have enough fuel to make it the almost 300 kilometers to the exfiltration pickup zone and back. It was decision time.

Jean glanced at the digital clock on the instrument panel. She checked the Doppler. They were in the right vicinity. She looked at Colin Lassiter, who was presently at the controls. "It's time to go up."

"Roger that, ma'am." Colin pulled in collective, and 579, six thousand pounds lighter with the three empty bladders, shot up into the dark night sky. In another minute they'd know if the plan Trapp had come up with was going to work. As Lassiter brought them level at fifteen hundred feet, Jean reset the FM radio to a setting of 40.50. She turned the radio to its lowest power setting.

Jean placed her left foot over the floor mike button. She hesitated for a second, glancing over her left shoulder at Trapp and Hooker huddled among the fuel bladders in the back. Hooker grinned wildly and gave her an enthusiastic thumbs-up. Trapp keyed the intercom on the headset he was wearing. "Time to do it. We're already in enough trouble. Doing this will only add another twenty years in Leavenworth to the five hundred they're going to sentence us to."

Jean laughed. "Hell, we're already way past the point of no return. Here goes." She clicked down the transmit button with her foot. "Attention any listening station. This is U.S. Army helicopter 375. I have an electrical fire on board and am declaring an inflight emergency. Any station picking up this broadcast please acknowledge. I say again. This is U.S. Army helicopter 375. . . ." She released the mike key.

The message went out, bouncing over the wave tops and dying out in a twenty-five-kilometer radius from the helicopter.

Yongsan Army Base, Seoul, Korea
Saturday, 10 June, 1608 Zulu
Sunday, 11 June, 1:08 A.M. Local
Hossey had been searching deeper into his phone book, looking for someone who would believe him. All he had gotten so far were a few promises from people that they would check on things Monday morning. In reality, it didn't even matter at this point. The course of action was already committed.

He hung up after his latest futile attempt and leaned back in his chair. Almost immediately the phone rang.

"Hossey here."

"This is Colonel Moore from US-SOCOM. Go secure."

Hossey turned his key. Maybe finally he would get some action. "I'm secure."

"What the hell is going on, Colonel?"

Hossey wasn't sure where to begin, but he tried.

Changbai Mountains, China
Saturday, 10 June, 1610 Zulu
Sunday, 11 June, 12:10 A.M. Local

Riley shivered. It was more than the cold. In twenty minutes the killing would begin. He and Chong were positioned almost eighteen hundred meters away from the Chinese picket line. They weren't in the best position, but it would do. They were about two hundred meters higher than the picket line trace, crouched among jumbled rocks and stunted pines along the first crest of the ridge that marked the northern side of the draw. More than three thousand meters to the southeast of their position, the other members of Team 3 would be waiting along the streambed.

Riley looked through the scope on the SVD. The rifle and scope were rated effective out to only twelve hundred-meters, but Riley felt confident that at this range he could hit some of the soldiers along the picket line. He counted fifteen of them silhouetted against the fires. There was no wind to correct for. The two-hundred-meter drop required some adjustment, but Riley had done enough long-range firing to be able to account for that.

Thirty meters to Riley's left, Chong was hidden, with the SAW propped between two rocks. He would hold his fire until the Chinese started moving forward and got within a thousand meters. Both men could use their night-vision goggles to aim their weapons. It was awkward, but would allow them to fire more accurately, particularly once the fires were put out and the Chinese started advancing.

Riley glanced at his watch again. Another fifteen minutes. He put down the rifle and tried to relax.

Sea of Japan
Saturday, 10 June, 1610 Zulu
Sunday, 11 June, 1:10 A.M. Local

"Army helicopter 375, this is the USS *Rathburne*. We have you on radar at approximately ten miles, on a heading of two one zero degrees. We are prepared to render assistance. Over."

"Roger, USS *Rathburne*. We are turning on a heading of three zero degrees and heading your location. We have the fire under control. Do you have a helipad? Over."

"Roger, army helicopter 375. We have a landing pad. It will be cleared for your arrival. We are turning our landing lights on now and will track you in on radar. Over."

Lieutenant Peppers was the officer of the watch aboard the *Rathburne* when the distress call came in. What an army helicopter was doing in the middle of the Sea of Japan, he had no idea. With a female on board, yet. They hadn't even had the helicopter on radar until it suddenly rose onto the screen ten miles off their starboard bow. The *Rathburne* was an hour and ten minutes into its route south to rejoin the rest of the battle group off the coast of Korea. They hadn't been warned of any helicopters in the area.

Peppers, a 1984 Naval Academy graduate, had acted promptly. He'd grabbed the microphone for the ship's FM radio and offered the use of the helipad. Once that was acknowledged, he sent a crewman to wake up the captain. He ordered the helipad prepared for an emergency landing. On the radar screen, he watched the glowing dot rapidly drawing near. It took the captain of the ship, Commander Lemester, two minutes to make it to the bridge. By then the helicopter was only thirty seconds out.

Peppers quickly briefed Lemester as they watched the searchlight of the army helicopter appear in the night sky. On the fantail helipad an emergency crew waited with fire extinguishers. The helicopter slowly settled down and landed. The crewmen ran forward.

Not only was there no sign of fire but, as the first crewman reached the opening doors to the cargo compartment, he was greeted by the muzzle of an AK-47 automatic rifle, wielded by an extremely short man. On the opposite side, another man

carrying an AK-47 disembarked. The petty officer in charge of
the emergency crew didn't know what to make of the situation.
The two groups stared at each other as the whine of the helicopter died down and the blades slowed to a halt.

Commander Lemester emerged from the hatch leading to
the fantail and came upon this extraordinary scene—two men
holding rifles on his crewmen. He stared in amazement for a
few seconds, then bulled his way forward. "What the hell do
you think you're doing?"

The larger of the two men walked over to him. Lemester's
eyes grew wider as he recognized Trapp. Not again.

Fort Meade, Maryland
Saturday, 10 June, 1614 Zulu
Saturday, 10 June, 11:14 A.M. Local
Wilson had spent the last fifteen minutes digging through the
master computer. Every time he felt he was coming close to
an answer, he'd run into a locked file that only Meng could
open. Wilson decided it was time to stop fooling around. He
left his terminal and went to Meng's office. The old Chinese
man was still working on the Medusa program. "Who was on
the phone? What took you so long?"

Wilson didn't say a word and waited until Meng glanced
up. He looked his boss in the eye. "I was just talking to Colonel Moore down at US-SOCOM. He wanted to know what
was going on with Dragon Sim-13. Apparently it didn't end
the way the simulation showed. I just went through the master computer files. What's in the file locked under your personal code?"

Wilson watched in surprise as Meng slumped into his chair
and put his head in his hands. "Look for yourself," he muttered. "The code word is 'Goddess.' "

Sea of Japan
Saturday, 10 June, 1615 Zulu
Sunday, 11 June, 1:15 A.M. Local
It wasn't even a standoff. With millions of dollars of sophisticated weaponry on board, the *Rathburne* was not prepared
to deal with two men holding automatic rifles on the ship's
captain. There was a ten-man contingent of marines on board

and, within five minutes of the helicopter landing, they had ringed the helipad. By then it was too late.

Trapp pressed the muzzle of the AK-47, taken from Hooker's personal gun collection, against Lemester's throat. He repeated the demands. "I'm going to tell you this only one more time. We want this helicopter fueled *now*. If you don't, or if those jarheads try anything stupid, two things are going to happen. First off, I'm going to blow your head clean off. Then my friend—who, by the way, isn't all together upstairs—is going to release the dead-man's switch he's holding. That box, if he releases pressure on the switch, can radiodetonate a twenty-pound satchel of C-4 inside the helicopter. The C-4, combined with the fuel the helicopter does have on board, will really mess up the rear end of your ship. All we want is a little fuel. It isn't worth a lot of people dying over."

Lemester stared at the small man sitting in the back of the helicopter. The man waved crazily and smiled at the naval officer. He held a small box in his right hand. Lemester didn't know what the box was but he had to assume it was a detonating device. Lemester had no idea what was going on. There was no way he'd jeopardize the safety of his ship. The man could have his fuel. There would be other ways to deal with this.

Lemester yelled to Peppers. "Send two men out here to refuel this helicopter."

Peppers briefly considered disobeying. He didn't like the idea of giving in to the demands of these terrorists. They'd obviously taken the crew of the helicopter hostage. Still, he had been trained to do as ordered. Also, he couldn't come up with a better plan. He detailed two men to bring the fuel hose forward.

Five minutes later they were done. 579 was ready to go. Long gave Trapp the thumbs-up. Trapp let out a sigh. The first part was done. Now came phase two. As Long started up the helicopter, Hooker climbed out of the back cradling a satchel in his arms. With his AK-47 slung over his back, he walked over to the coiled fuel hoses and placed the satchel down. Then he walked over to join Trapp on the edge of the helipad. The helicopter lifted off and flew into the night sky.

Trapp could tell that the ship's captain was totally bewildered. The navy people had undoubtedly assumed that he and Hooker were two terrorists holding the aircrew hostage, but now it was apparent that they were all working together. Trapp knew that the ship's captain was trying to figure out why the two of them were staying on board.

Trapp smiled at the captain. "That satchel my friend placed over your JP4 fuel tanks has the C-4 in it. He still has the detonator in his hand. We'll stay that way for a while, until the helicopter is definitely out of range of your surface-to-air missiles and beyond reach of any air force help you might call. So why don't we all sit down and get comfortable."

Lemester's shoulders slumped in defeat as Trapp motioned for him to sit down on the edge of the helipad.

US-SOCOM Headquarters, MacDill Air Force Base, Florida
Saturday, 10 June, 1621 Zulu
Saturday, 10 June, 11:21 A.M. Local

Moore didn't waste any time on preambles. "What have you people done?"

On the other end, Wilson tried to explain as best he could. "Doctor Meng continued running the operation when he cut off your communications with the FOB after the briefback. Meng simulated being the SFOB and gave the authorization code words for the mission to go."

"For God's sake, why?" Moore yelled into the phone. He looked at the clock and cut into Wilson's sputterings. "I don't have time for this. I've got a helicopter inbound for China that I have to do something about." Moore hung up and started leafing through his phone book.

He didn't know Meng's motives or how he had manipulated all of them, but the conclusion was inescapable. The mission had really been accomplished, and now Hossey had talked somebody into flying back into the operational area. Things were getting out of hand. It was time for damage control.

19

"When he concentrates, prepare against him;
where he is strong, avoid him."
Sun Tzu: *The Art of War*

**Changbai Mountains, China
Saturday, 10 June, 1630 Zulu
Sunday, 11 June, 12:30 A.M. Local**

Riley smoothly pulled back on the trigger and the bark of the
rifle echoed across the draw. A Chinese soldier, warming
himself at a fire, was slammed back as the 7.62mm round
tore a fatal path through his chest. Without conscious thought,
Riley did as he'd been trained. He arced the muzzle of the
weapon to his second target, standing at the next fire. The
man had heard the first shot but didn't know what it meant.
He never would, as Riley's round hit him in the center of the
chest and he tumbled in a heap.

Riley fired all ten rounds in the magazine. Seven hits for
ten shots. Four of them appeared fatal. He reloaded a fresh
magazine and decided to wait a few minutes to allow the Chinese to react. He didn't think his muzzle flash had been spotted because there had been no return fire. He'd let the flash
be seen during the next magazine. The whole purpose of the
diversion was to draw out the Chinese. Hiding his location
wouldn't do that.

In the Chinese lines, confusion reigned. The immediate reaction of the soldiers on guard was to put the fires out and
get under cover. Those who had been sleeping were awakened and hastily joined their comrades. No one shot back because no one knew what, or where, to shoot.

The local regimental commander received fragmented reports
from his battalion commanders. The 3d Battalion had two men
shot, both fatally. The 2d Battalion had five shot, two fatally.
The shots were apparently coming from the high ground to the

north and west. The regimental commander was at a loss. He had never been trained to act on his own initiative. He relayed his report to division, with a request for orders on how to respond. Meanwhile, he belatedly ordered the battalion commanders to awaken all their men and get them under cover.

The battalion commanders shook their heads in amazement at the regimental commander's uninspired orders. Still they were content to stay where they were. No one was anxious to move out against an unseen threat.

Just in front of the Chinese lines, Mitchell heard the shots and watched as the fires went out. The members of Team 3 could hear shouting from the Chinese positions. Mitchell peered through his night-vision goggles, trying to determine what was going on. It looked as though everyone was getting under cover, with no sign of the forces moving forward. He decided he'd give them some more time to get organized and react. He waited ten minutes, and then the shooting started again.

USS *Rathburne*, Sea of Japan
Saturday, 10 June, 1634 Zulu
Sunday, 11 June, 1:34 A.M. Local
Helicopter 579 had left almost twenty minutes ago. Trapp checked his watch one last time. It was out of their hands now. He was seated next to the captain of the *Rathburne* on the edge of the helipad. Hooker was on the other side of the captain, still holding the detonator in his hand.

Trapp lowered his AK-47 and bowed slightly at Lemester. "I guess they're far enough away. You can go back to running your ship now."

Lemester glared at the man with barely restrained anger. "What about the bomb over there? I want the detonator."

Hooker laughed. "You mean this? Here." He threw it at Lemester, who anxiously fumbled it before making the catch. "That's the remote control to my TV set back in Korea. I don't think I'll be needing it anymore. The satchel is my dirty laundry from the past week. I'd appreciate it if your ship's laundry could take care of it."

Lemester failed to see the humor in the situation. He yelled for his marines to come forward. "Throw these two in the brig."

Lemester turned to Peppers. "Did you radio in this situation to headquarters?"

Peppers shook his head. "No, sir. You ordered me to do nothing that would jeopardize the ship."

Lemester swore. Sometimes these Annapolis graduates took things too literally. "Lieutenant, how the hell do you think these idiots would have known if you had made a radio call? The air force could have scrambled some jets from Korea or Japan and intercepted the helicopter. It's probably too late now."

Lemester shook his head. "Of course I told you to do nothing. They could hear everything I said. I expected you to use some initiative. You idiot! Get out of my way." The captain climbed up to the radio room.

Changbai Mountains, China
Saturday, 10 June, 1640 Zulu
Sunday, 11 June, 12:40 A.M. Local

Riley peered through the night-vision goggles, which were pressed up against the four-power scope. He could barely make out some men gathered around a truck, looking as though they were arguing about something. Probably officers, Riley guessed. He aimed at them and fired five rounds in rapid succession. This time his muzzle flash was spotted. Another truck, farther to the south, opened fire with its heavy machine gun, and the green arc of tracers drew a line from the truck to a point just south of Riley's position. Five other trucks quickly joined in. Riley slid back under cover as random rounds flew overhead.

The regimental commander heard the machine gun fire in response. Still no word from division. He didn't know what to do. His 3d Battalion commander called back in with a report of two more men wounded and a tentative location of the firer—along the ridgeline on the north side of the draw, about two kilometers to the west. The regimental commander was amazed. That was a long way for such accuracy.

Finally division responded. "Move out and subdue firer. Attempt to capture, if at all possible. Reinforcements on the way."

The regimental commander relayed the orders and ordered his 3d Battalion, the northernmost one, forward; his 2d and

1st Battalions were to stretch out to keep the picket line intact. He contacted the commander of the regiment to his right flank and informed him of the plan.

12:46 A.M. Local
The 3d Battalion commander was less than enthused when he received his orders to move out. The machine-gun firing had died out and there was no return fire. Maybe they'd hit whoever was shooting. The 3d Battalion commander doubted that. He relayed his orders to his company leaders, and slowly they got their units on line. The other two battalions blundered about in the dark, trying to stretch their lines to cover the breach that would be caused by the departure of 3d Battalion.

After the heavy machine-gun fire died out, Riley crawled back up to the crest of the ridge and peered over it toward the Chinese lines. He could make out some movement. He slid a round into the chamber from a fresh magazine and waited.

Eighth Army Headquarters, Yongsan, Seoul, Korea
Saturday, 10 June, 1649 Zulu
Sunday, 11 June, 1:49 A.M. Local
Major Thomas did not look forward to the upcoming briefing. General Parker, commander of the Eighth Army, Korea, had ordered the duty officer to keep him informed if any word came in on the missing helicopter from the 17th Aviation Regiment. Two minutes ago the general had walked over from his quarters across the street, ready for the latest update. A downed aircraft was a command-one priority in Korea.

Parker ran his hands through his mussed-up gray hair and unzipped the sweatshirt he had thrown on. "All right, Thomas. What's the latest?"

"Yes, sir. First off, you need to know that we just got word that the helicopter was sighted."

"Great. Is the crew all right? Where did it go down?"

"We don't know where it's at right now. It landed on the USS *Rathburne* more than two hours ago in the Sea of Japan." Thomas could see the confusion on the face of his boss.

"Whoa! What was it doing out there?"

"Sir, I just called Colonel Hossey down at DET-K and

asked him to drive on up here. He's called a couple of times and he says he has some information on the helicopter."

Parker shook his head. That was even further out in left field. "What does DET-K have to do with this?"

"I'm not sure, sir."

Parker frowned. "All right. I assume the bird is still on the ship."

"No, sir. We don't know where it's at."

"What do you mean you don't know where it's at? They took it into custody, didn't they?"

Thomas shook his head. "The helicopter landed with some men with weapons who said they had a bomb on board. Took the captain of the ship hostage and demanded that he refuel the aircraft. He did so and the helicopter took off again. They left two people on board the ship with the bomb and they threatened to detonate it if the navy tried to call or shoot down the aircraft. The ship has the two in custody now. One of the two gunmen is the DET-K sergeant major."

Parker rolled his eyes. "Where is the helicopter going now?"

"I don't know, sir."

"Is there any more?"

"Yes, sir. We've got the identity of the crew of the helicopter. There is a Captain Jean Long as one of the pilots. The other pilot is a warrant officer named Colin Lassiter.

"We also got some more information on the configuration of the bird. It had four internal fuel tanks mounted, which give it the range, with the refuel from the *Rathburne*, to fly a hell of a long way. Also, it had two live Stinger missiles mounted on it."

Parker looked at the map on the wall of the operations office. Where could that helicopter be flying? He grabbed the secure phone and punched in the number for the 6th Air Force in Japan.

"This is General Parker, Commander Eighth Army. I need some jets in the air and an AWACS. Vicinity . . . ," he put his hand over the receiver and looked at Thomas. "What's the grid for the *Rathburne*?"

Thomas gave it to him and Parker relayed it. "I want the commander on the AWACS to contact me as soon as he's airborne. We've got a helicopter on the loose up there and we need to lasso it."

Changbai Mountains, China
Saturday, 10 June, 1649 Zulu
Sunday, 11 June, 12:49 A.M. Local
Mitchell could see and hear movement in the Chinese lines, but even with the night-vision goggles he couldn't tell what was happening. For all he knew, the Chinese might be moving the whole skirmish line forward. He knew they had spotted Riley's position when the machine guns mounted on top of the trucks began returning fire. It was already 12:50. He'd give it another twenty-five minutes, then they'd start moving forward.

Eighth Army Headquarters, Yongsan, Seoul, Korea
Saturday, 10 June, 1655 Zulu
Sunday, 11 June, 1:55 A.M. Local
Parker glared as Colonel Hossey walked in. "What is going on, Colonel? I've got your sergeant major in the brig on a navy ship and a helicopter flying somewhere around the Sea of Japan with a lot of fuel on board. Where is that bird going and why?"

Hossey sighed. He'd been trying to tell his story all day and now finally someone wanted to know. "Sir, I've got men who were on a classified mission in China trapped there. I had to get them out tonight and using that helicopter was the only way."

Parker's eyes grew wide. "That helicopter is on the way to *China*?" The general looked at the map. "Jesus Christ, man. It's going to have to go over either North Korea or Russia to go in from the Sea of Japan. What did . . . ." Parker paused as the duty officer indicated the phone.

"Sir, it's General Gunston, 6th Air Force commander on the STU III."

Parker grabbed the phone. "Parker here."

"This is Jim Gunston, Stu. What is going on? My duty officer has scrambled some jets and he also has an AWACS going up in response to your request. I just finished contacting my chain of command at the Pentagon, but no one on duty there knows anything about this."

Parker glanced briefly at Hossey. "I'm not too sure either. All I know is that I've got a helicopter inbound toward China from the Sea of Japan on an unsanctioned mission. We need to stop it."

There was a pause and then Gunston came back on. "I've got four F-16s from Misawa flying toward the position you gave, to try and intercept. I've also got an AWACS going up—it should be on line in about fifteen minutes. I don't think they'll be able to intercept the helicopter, though. It's got too much of a lead. Also, I'm kind of leery of putting all this into action so near Soviet and North Korean airspace. It's going to spook them."

Parker insisted. "We need to give our best shot at interception. I'm trying to find out right now what's going on. Let me know as soon as you learn anything." He hung up and faced Hossey again. "Start from the beginning."

Changbai Mountains, China
Saturday, 10 June, 1710 Zulu
Sunday, 11 June, 1:10 A.M. Local
It took the commander fifteen minutes to get his 3d Battalion on line, ready to move. The 1st and 2d Battalions were still not organized. The regimental commander decided not to wait. He gave the order for 3d Battalion to move out; stretched in a line, the four hundred men covered a nine-hundred meter front as they marched forward. They left a gap of almost a kilometer and a half behind them. Men from 1st and 2d Battalions scrambled to fill the gap, in turn opening holes in their own fronts.

At the army headquarters in Yanji, Colonel Tugur was finally awakened with the news. He quickly reviewed the reports and cursed as he read that the regimental commander had ordered his men forward. It was too late to stop them. Quickly he ordered more reinforcements into the area. He wasn't sure what was happening, but it could be a diversion—a fact that the regimental commander had apparently overlooked. Tugur also ordered all the helicopters to be prepared to take off. He relayed the information to General

Yang up in Shenyang. Tugur knew that the responsibility for what happened tonight would be on his shoulders.

Riley could pick out the beginnings of a line moving toward his position. He decided to let the soldiers get close enough for Chong to join in the fun. Chong was still positioned about thirty meters to Riley's left, hidden securely behind some boulders. Riley gave a brief whistle and Chong whistled in response. He was ready. Riley put his weapon down and stretched his shoulders and arms. He took several deep breaths and leaned back against a rock. He had several minutes before he had to start killing again.

Mitchell pulled on Hoffman's arm, indicating that they were going to move out. The captain wanted to get closer to the Chinese lines. Hoffman reached over Olinski and grabbed Comsky, who in turn alerted C.J. They hefted up the stretcher, and the centipede of humans moved slowly out of the bushes where they had been hiding.

They walked for ten minutes, gaining fifty meters. Mitchell halted them and peered ahead through his goggles, trying to see what was ahead. He couldn't detect any movement or guards. He tapped Hoffman again and they started moving. Suddenly the crack of the SVD, closely followed by the burst of the SAW, sounded to the north.

1:25 A.M. Local

Riley fired his first round carefully. Now that the moving skirmish line was only a thousand meters away, he could hit with a higher degree of accuracy. He ignored his feelings. The men out there would kill him if they could. It was kill or be killed. His first round was a head shot and took out a platoon or squad leader giving orders.

Riley fired the rest of the magazine quickly, shifting from target to target. In twenty-five seconds all ten rounds had been fired and all had hit. After Riley's first shot, Chong had joined in and the red tracers from the SAW had weaved their destructive path along the advancing line. Heavy machine guns from the trucks, still in their support position, and medium machine guns from the dismounted unit roared a reply.

Lacking night-vision equipment, the Chinese gunners could fire only in the general vicinity of the muzzle flashes and the point of origin of the red tracers.

Mitchell could see the firing off to their left rear. Apparently some Chinese troops had moved forward. Mitchell could only hope that the line in front of him was thin enough to pass through. Only another hundred meters to where the picket line had originally been. Still no sign of anyone ahead. Mitchell tugged on the stretcher and they moved forward cautiously.

Tugur read the latest report with a bit of puzzlement. A machine gun joining in the rifle fire? So there were at least two people up there. Maybe this wasn't a diversion. Maybe the terrorists had seen that they were trapped and preferred to die fighting rather than be hunted down.

Colonel Tugur ordered the first pair of Haitun Z-9 helicopters into the air. There wasn't much the helicopters could do in the dark, but Tugur wanted them up there, just in case. He would rotate his six gunships, keeping two in the air for the rest of the night if need be.

1:30 A.M. Local

The nearest troops were only five hundred meters away. Time to be moving on, Riley thought. He crawled over to Chong. "How you doing?"

Chong looked like an alien with the bulky goggles on. "Not bad, Top. I've fired only two magazines, so I've got four left. Those heavy machine guns are getting the range on us, though. Had a couple of rounds hit damn close last time."

Riley agreed, the Chinese were getting the range. Riley briefly considered not firing again, but he decided they had to. He couldn't be sure that the other men on Team 3 had made it through yet. They had to play the game until the end. "I'll fire five rounds fast and you give them one long five-second burst. Then we're out of here."

Chong nodded in agreement. They set up their weapons side by side on the outcropping. Riley scanned the line and picked a target who seemed to be giving orders. "Ready?"

"Yep."

Riley fired his five rounds in less than three seconds, shifting rapidly from target to target even as the Chinese soldiers dove for cover. Chong fired one long burst. The two pulled in their weapons and slid down the loose rock, putting the outcropping between them and the enemy. It was just in time—the return fire was extremely accurate, and incoming rounds cracked by overhead.

"Let's go!" Riley led the way as they scrambled to the north, keeping the outcropping between them and the Chinese for as long as they could. After a hundred meters they had to climb up and were exposed to the enemy. If the Chinese had had any night-vision gear, Riley and Chong would have been spotted immediately as they clambered up the inclined rock wall. As it was, they were invisible in the dark, even as the skirmish line moved forward and swept over the position they had occupied.

Mitchell heard the brief burst of fire from Riley and Chong's position as he approached the area where he estimated the Chinese picket line had been. The shortness of the burst of fire told Mitchell that those were probably the last rounds Riley and Chong would fire in the diversion. The two were probably running by now. Still, they had held their position for almost an hour—far longer than expected. The Chinese response had been slow and uncoordinated.

The remaining members of Team 3 stepped forward slowly and cautiously, moving through the trees lining the riverbank. Mitchell was sweeping from left to right and back with the night-vision goggles. Off to his left he could barely discern a truck about seventy meters to the north. Between the truck and the stream he could see nothing else. They passed the remains of one of the picket-line fires.

They shuffled along slowly, the lead three struggling with the stretcher, C.J. following with his one good hand holding onto the back of Comsky's vest and Olinski's shotgun slung over his back. Mitchell was beginning to feel optimistic about their chances of making it through, when a voice close to his left front called out in Chinese.

20

"Invincibility depends on one's self; the enemy's vulnerability on him."
Sun Tzu: *The Art of War*

Changbai Mountains, China
Saturday, 10 June, 1730 Zulu
Sunday, 11 June, 1:30 A.M. Local

Mitchell froze at the sound of the Chinese soldier's voice. He looked to his left front and through his goggles could clearly see a soldier step out of the dark shadows of the trees. Mitchell wasn't sure how well the soldier could see them. With a type 56 automatic rifle the man gestured for them to stop, then called out. Mitchell debated whether to drop the stretcher and fire his MP5 as the soldier came closer. He decided against it. He didn't think he could fire faster than the Chinese soldier. Mitchell hoped C.J. didn't use the shotgun or else they'd have the whole world down on them in a few seconds.

Mitchell could tell that the soldier was confused, but he could also see that the man had his finger on the trigger. The Chinese soldier came up next to Mitchell and peered at him strangely. Mitchell knew that with his goggles on he was an unusual sight. Mitchell waited. The second the soldier turned his attention elsewhere, he would fire. He figured he had a fifty-fifty chance of killing the man before he got off a shot.

Mitchell was thinking through this plan when the sound of three quick puffs startled him. The Chinese soldier collapsed. Mitchell turned to see Olinski propped up on one elbow on the stretcher, holding his silenced High Standard .22.

The team leader quickly broke out of his frozen stance. "Comsky and Dan. Let's put down the stretcher and throw the body in those bushes."

When they were done, Mitchell quickly gestured for the

rest of the team to follow, and they moved out. He led them another three hundred meters past the skirmish line and then halted the small party. They crouched down in the dark. Mitchell knelt next to Olinski and whispered, "Good shooting."

"Thanks, sir."

Mitchell wiped the beads of sweat from his forehead. That had been close. Too close. If it weren't for all the confusion and thinning of lines caused by the diversion, they'd never have gotten away with it. He wondered how long they would have before the body was discovered.

He allowed Hoffman and Comsky five minutes of rest, then they moved out again. Another twelve hundred meters and they should be at the pickup zone.

AWACS Surveillance Plane, Sea of Japan
Saturday, 10 June, 1732 Zulu
Sunday, 11 June, 2:32 A.M. Local

Colonel Pete Ehrlich was the commander of the airborne warning and control system (AWACS) plane that General Parker had ordered into the air. As the modified Boeing 707-320B leveled off at thirty-five thousand feet, Ehrlich ordered the thirty-foot dome radar dish, riding on top of the fuselage, to be activated. The advantage the AWACS had over ground-based radars was its ability to look down. The radar signals emitted at altitude were not blocked by the terrain or curvature of the earth. Ehrlich and his crew had an accurate radar picture almost two hundred miles in diameter as the rotodome completed a revolution every ten seconds.

Quickly they began the process of identifying and coding out all known images. Civilian aircraft liners were blanked off the screen. Military training flights were also blanked out. In a short while they had a manageable screen. Only a few spots of activity were left—the four F-16s flying the intercept and search mission, a lot of helicopter activity just south of Yanji in China, and a lone blip inching toward the coast of North Korea, still over international waters.

The radar operator pointed. "That's our boy right there. It's not transmitting any identification transponder code, and it's flying right on top of the waves. Airspeed's right for a Blackhawk."

Ehrlich picked up the headset to call General Parker.

Changbai Mountains, China
Saturday, 10 June, 1735 Zulu
Sunday, 11 June, 1:35 A.M. Local

Riley and Chong continued to climb. Another kilometer north, and three hundred feet in altitude, would get them over the northern side of the draw. Then they'd see if the picket line was intact to the east. If it wasn't, they'd turn that way and head for the border. If it was, they would have to turn west and head farther up into the mountains.

Behind them they could hear the Chinese overrunning the position they had occupied. A sharp crack resounded through the night air, followed by sudden firing. Riley smiled grimly to himself. The grenade he had left behind, attached to a trip wire, had been triggered. The Chinese were responding by shooting wildly into the dark. With a little luck they might shoot each other. At the very least it would slow them down a little.

Riley looked to the east and could see the glow of the moon starting to rise over the horizon. In another fifteen minutes, visibility would improve. That would reduce the large advantage the night-vision goggles gave him and Chong. They would have to start using the terrain for concealment, not just the darkness of the night. Riley also knew that more troops were going to be pouring into the area. He and Chong had to get as far as they could while night lasted. Even as they picked up the pace, they heard the sound of helicopter blades beating the air to the south and getting closer.

Riley took a quick glance over his shoulder and saw the bright searchlights of two helicopters probing the darkness near the site he and Chong had occupied only twenty minutes ago. Whoever was in charge of the search apparently felt that it was worthwhile to fly the helicopters at night and expose them to possible small-arms fire in the attempt to find them. On the ground Riley could also see the headlights of numerous trucks, bringing in more soldiers.

* * *

Colonel Tugur listened to the confused reports coming in from the regimental commander in charge at the shooting site. The position the firers had occupied had been overrun, and no trace of the shooters, other than expended cartridges and a booby trap, had been found. Tugur ordered the two Z-9s to move in with their searchlights to aid in the hunt.

Tugur was angry with the regimental commander. The man had ruptured the cordon they had so carefully designed to capture the terrorists. In his haste to attack, the man had opened up gaps. Tugur didn't think that whoever had been shooting could have outflanked the attacking force and escaped. They had to be moving farther into the mountains. Still, there was the slight possibility they might escape. He ordered even more reinforcements into the area.

He instructed the other four gunship helicopters to start up. He also ordered four S-70 helicopters to fly reinforcements above and to the west of the terrorists' likely location. Each aircraft could carry ten men. Tugur planned to emplace a number of squads higher up in the mountains and have them work down, catching the terrorists between them and the picket line.

Eighth Army Headquarters, Yongsan, Seoul, Korea
Saturday, 10 June, 1740 Zulu
Sunday, 11 June, 2:40 A.M. Local

General Parker had listened as calmly as he could to Hossey's story. The fact that the Special Forces colonel couldn't explain the reasons behind the mission, nor could he shed any light on why this Colonel Moore at US-SOCOM was now saying the mission should not have gone, made the whole thing more ludicrous than it already was. The story of a Chinese computer scientist at Fort Meade instigating all this was the icing on the fruitcake.

The ring of the STU III phone cut through Parker's thinking. He indicated that Major Thomas should answer. "Put it on the speaker."

Parker waited as Thomas turned on the voice box. "Parker here."

"This is Jim Gunston."

"What have you got, Jim?"

"The AWACS has picked up an aircraft making its way toward the North Korean coast. It's moving at about a hundred and thirty knots and down in the waves. We're pretty sure that it's the Blackhawk. Also we're picking up a lot of Chinese helicopter activity in the Changbai Mountains, south of Yanji. That's really unusual, because the Chinese very rarely fly their helicopters at night."

"Can you intercept the Blackhawk?"

There were a few seconds of silence on the other end. "No. The F-16s can't intercept in time. Also, there's another problem. That helicopter is flying just outside the twelve-mile limit from the coast in international airspace. It's way down in the wave tops and hasn't been picked up on radar yet. If we send some F-16s in there after it, we're definitely going to alert the Soviet and North Korean radar."

Parker considered this. "What about Wildcard? Can it make it in time?"

There was another pause. "It definitely wouldn't make it in time to stop them. The bird is only about ten minutes out from crossing the coast and only about fifty minutes out from where all this Chinese helicopter activity is. We've got to figure that's where the bird is heading. It would take Wildcard more than an hour to make it there. Plus, it would take us at least ten minutes to get it airborne."

Parker thought about the implications. "Launch Wildcard. I want it to be very clear that Wildcard is not to violate Soviet or Korean airspace. But I want it to get as close as it can to the Blackhawk. We need to keep our options open."

Again, a pause on the other end. Then Gunston's troubled voice came over the line. "Wildcard is only over here for classified test flights. It's not meant to be operational yet."

"I know that, Stu. I've seen the test results. It's already done more in practice than we're asking it to do now. I don't want it to violate sovereign airspace. Just hang off the coast until we figure out what's going on."

"All right. No harm in that. I'll alert them and get them airborne."

Changbai Mountains, China
Saturday, 10 June, 1745 Zulu
Sunday, 11 June, 1:45 A.M. Local

After fifteen minutes of creeping in the dark, wary of another encounter with Chinese soldiers, Mitchell finally arrived at the intersection of the unimproved dirt road and river, which was the guide point for the pickup zone. He shot a 320-degree azimuth and led the rest of Team 3 off through the woods. The pickup zone was about four hundred meters away. The moon had risen and even those without goggles could see relatively well. Mitchell would have preferred no moonlight.

They could all hear the sound of vehicles moving in the dark. Even as they left the dirt road behind, they could see the glow of headlights on it as reinforcements poured into the area.

Sea of Japan
Saturday, 10 June, 1745 Zulu
Sunday, 11 June, 2:45 A.M. Local

While Lassiter flew, Jean Long did some final navigational calculations. They were headed on the right azimuth for landfall just south of Najin and should reach the shoreline in another five minutes. Then it would be twenty to thirty minutes to the pickup zone.

Already one of the internal tanks was dry and they were well into the second one. They would be working on the third when they landed at the pickup zone. That ought to leave enough room to get the survivors on board and also make the helicopter light enough to lift off with the additional weight.

During the hours of low-level flight above the wave tops, Jean had tried not to think about what they might find when they got to the PZ. Colonel Hossey had told her that the message said one man was dead and three wounded. Worrying about her husband would drain energy she needed to fly and navigate, so she had resolutely refused to allow her thoughts to dwell on the possibility that Mitch might be one of the casualties.

Jean scanned the instrument panel, then keyed her intercom to talk to Lassiter. "How do you arm these Stingers?"

Her copilot gave the answer she expected. "I don't know. I've never flown with them before. I imagine that switch down there on the lower right arms them. I know this button here on the cyclic fires them."

Jean had never flown with Stingers either. She hoped Lassiter's guess was right. With a little luck they wouldn't need the missiles.

Changbai Mountains, China
Saturday, 10 June, 1750 Zulu
Sunday, 11 June, 1:50 A.M. Local

Mitchell scanned the small open field with the night-vision goggles. Aided by the light of the moon, the field appeared as it would in daytime. Its size was adequate for landing a helicopter. Several small trees would have to be cut down, however.

He turned to the other members of Team 3 who were crouched in the tree line on the southeastern corner of the field. "Hoffman and Comsky will help me take down those trees. C.J., you stay here with Olinski. Ski, turn on the FM and start monitoring it."

The three men moved out into the field. Using their survival knives, they began hacking down the small trees that would have impeded the landing of the helicopter they all hoped was on the way. C.J. watched as the men worked. He could hear the rumble of vehicles going by only four hundred meters to the east on the unimproved road. It was obvious that the Chinese were bringing more units into the area. He could also hear and see the two helicopters off to the northwest searching the ridgeline.

Riley and Chong had made it over the crest of the northern ridgeline. They paused briefly to rest while Riley checked the terrain to the east. As far as he could see were the headlights of numerous vehicles moving to the north and south. Making it to the coast was out. He turned and looked up the ridgeline to the peaks of the Changbai Mountain Range. This was not the direction he wanted to head, but it seemed to be their only choice.

He gestured to Chong, and the two resumed their scramble

up the ridgeline. The two Z-9s were still flying only a kilometer to their south, quartering the ground in a grid pattern. They would be overhead in less than fifteen minutes. Riley wasn't afraid of being seen by the helicopters as long as it was dark. Avoiding the searchlight would not be difficult. Tomorrow morning would be a different story. Riley was not optimistic about their chances of seeing another sunset.

Their chances further diminished as two new S-70 helicopters, with searchlights on, flew by to the south, higher into the mountains. The two aircraft carefully set down about two kilometers to the west. They landed about eight hundred meters apart, then took off, heading back toward the coast. Riley had little doubt about what was happening. Someone in the Chinese headquarters was getting smarter. Their last option was being taken from them. They had nowhere to go.

Riley turned to Chong. "They're putting troops in ahead of us, up there, with those helicopters."

Chong wearily rested the butt of his SAW machine gun on the ground. "What now, Top?"

"We keep heading into the mountains. That bird can carry only ten troops on board. The net's thinner that way. We have a better chance of fighting our way through by going up." Riley looked up into the darkness. "They're only about two klicks away, so we'll find out soon enough. I'm tired of running."

2:00 A.M. Local

The pickup zone was clear. Mitchell sat with his back against a tree at the edge of the small clearing. The other members of Team 3 were crowded close around. They were all exhausted. Mitchell hated to think of what would happen if the helicopter didn't come and he had to get everyone moving again to find a hiding place before dawn.

Mitchell couldn't remember the last time he'd had a good night's sleep. Ever since the phone call to Jean's quarters had started him on this mission, he'd been running down on energy and sleep. No matter what the danger or situation, the body needed rest. Adrenaline could keep you going only so far. They were all cold, hungry, and tired. While they were moving, the physical exertion and fear kept the cold away.

Now that they had stopped Mitchell could feel the night's chill penetrating his bones. He shivered briefly, the movement initiating pain in his cut that was beneficial in a perverse way—the pain kept him awake. He thought briefly of his wife in Korea, imagining her safe and asleep in her bunk. He wondered if he'd ever spend another night with her.

He tore his attention back to the present. There hadn't been any firing up in the mountains for quite a while. Mitchell wasn't sure if that was good or bad. He assumed that Riley and Chong were still running. The overflights by the S-70s indicated that the Chinese were probably airlifting troops into the mountains, which was bad news for the two men on the diversion team. Mitchell tried to accept that situation—they'd taken a chance on running the diversion. If an exfiltration helicopter didn't come tonight, he wasn't sure any of them would make it out. The Chinese now knew that there were people alive. Even though they were through the picket line, there would still be extensive troop operations throughout the area. The guard Olinski had killed would point the search back toward the border once the body was discovered. .

Comsky was checking Olinski's and C.J.'s injuries in the dark, doing what little he could for them. Olinski was doing fairly well. Both breaks appeared to be clean. He was alert and monitoring the FM radio. C.J. was in worse shape now. The fall and subsequent movement had further aggravated the shattered arm. The man had lapsed into a sleep that was closer to unconsciousness. It was going to be very difficult to get him moving again. Mitchell knew he would have to, though. They couldn't carry another man.

Mitchell held his strobe light in his left hand. He checked to make sure that the infrared cover was firmly on. He was prepared to run out into the field and turn it on the second they had an indication that a helicopter was inbound. The IR cover on the strobe would prevent it from being seen by the Chinese helicopters. Only someone wearing night-vision goggles would be able to see the bright flash.

2:04 A.M. Local
The lift birds continued to fly by every eight minutes on either side. The two gunship Z-9s had flown by three minutes

ago. Riley and Chong had easily hidden from the helicopters' searchlights. Now they were moving cautiously through the dark. Somewhere ahead enemy soldiers were working their way down toward them. The terrain along the ridgeline was broken and jagged, with a few stunted trees growing amid the jumble of rocks that crowned the long finger of high ground heading into the mountains.

Riley and Chong moved from boulder to boulder. In the bright moonlight they both removed their night-vision goggles and hung them around their necks. Getting into a moving firefight with goggles on was not a good idea—the muzzle flashes from weapons at the closer ranges would temporarily blank them out. The illumination provided by the moon would be more than adequate. Riley held his SVD at his waist, slowly panning the muzzle from left to right as he scanned the terrain ahead. His M79 grenade launcher was ready at his side. Chong followed closely behind and to his right, leaving himself an open field of fire for his SAW. Both had unsnapped the covers on the holsters of their 9mm pistols. They were as ready as they could be.

21

"When the strike of a hawk breaks the body
of its prey, it is because of timing."
Sun Tzu: *The Art of War*

Airspace, North Korea
Saturday, 10 June, 1810 Zulu
Sunday, 11 June, 3:10 A.M. Local

Both pilots were awake and alert despite being tired. They'd
been in the air almost six hours. The two had been switching
off every thirty minutes, with one flying under goggles and
the other resting. It had been an exhausting regimen. Now the
two pilots would have to be at their peak. Jean and Colin
both had their goggles on as they wound their way through
the foothills of the Changbai Range.

Lassiter concentrated on reading the map and ensuring that
they were on the correct heading, while Long kept watch
ahead, flying the terrain. In two minutes they crested the first
ridgeline.

"That was the border," Lassiter called out. "We're over
China now."

Anxiety churned in their stomachs as Long slowed the helicopter to eighty knots and started flying west, only twenty-
five feet above the treetops. They knew the risks they were
running now. Not only the Chinese but the terrain could be
their enemy: a power line strung across in front of them, a radio tower, a microwave relay station, a tall hill coming up
suddenly out of the dark. Any such obstacle could spell disaster.

Long headed west ten kilometers and then turned to the
northwest, searching the ground for the small river that was
to be their guideline. Lassiter continued to call out the instrument readings to her. They had agreed that she would fly the
leg in. He would fly the leg out.

Long concentrated on flying. For the whole flight she had not allowed thoughts of what they would find on the pickup zone interfere with her performance, and she wouldn't now.

There was a quick intake of breath through the intercom. "Jesus, Colin. Take a look ahead."

Lassiter looked up from the instruments and scanned the night sky. It was obvious what the captain was referring to. He counted four aircraft in the sky ahead, higher in the mountains. Helicopters with their searchlights on.

"We're in for fun and games now."

Long took another view. "But it's also a good sign, in a way. It means the Chinese are looking for somebody too. It means there are people alive."

Changbai Mountains, China
Saturday, 10 June, 1812 Zulu
Sunday, 11 June, 2:12 A.M. Local
At Yanji the radar operator in the mobile unit again counted the number of blips on his screen. It still wasn't right. One had entered his screen at the eastern edge, almost looking as though it had come out of North Korea, and was now intermittently appearing and disappearing. The radar image did not have an identifier code.

Junior Lieutenant Baibang called on the radio for the second time, asking the helicopter to identify itself. Again no answer. It was also flying too low to the ground. Supporting the 3d Aviation Regiment on numerous training missions, Baibang had never seen a regimental helicopter fly that low during the daytime, never mind at night. Baibang picked up the radiophone to army headquarters.

It wasn't hard for Mitchell to stay awake, despite his exhaustion. Shivering saw to that. The Chinese air activity was continuing. He wasn't sure he would be able to tell if an American aircraft was inbound until it just about landed. He looked over at Olinski to make sure that he was still monitoring the radio. Olinski had the little plug from the FM radio in his ear and was holding it in place with his good hand. He saw the captain's glance and gave him a negative shake of the head. Mitchell quickly scanned the others in the party.

Comsky was peering into the dark woods, pulling security. Hoffman was scanning the pickup zone. C.J. appeared to be unconscious.

Mitchell checked the glowing hands on his watch: 2:14 local. He was tempted to pick up and start moving now. Even if a helicopter was inbound, they wouldn't be foolish enough to come in with all the air activity. They hadn't thought of this when they'd made the diversion plan. Now it was too late. An inbound helicopter was sure to be spotted.

2:16 A.M. Local

Tugur's presence had finally made things start functioning in the division forward headquarters. The report of the unidentified helicopter reached him only four minutes after it was called in. It was another piece of the puzzle falling into place. Things were beginning to make sense. The firing had probably been a diversion.

Tugur immediately called General Yang at Shenyang and quickly updated him. "We've got an unidentified helicopter inbound. It's only about ten minutes out from where the troops are fighting. I've already diverted all the Z-9s to try and intercept. We need some air force jets down here just in case."

Yang concurred. "I'll call the airfield here and get them moving. You must stop that helicopter. Force it down if you can. If not, shoot it down. I'll get back to you. Out here."

The AWACS's large rotodome continued to track 579 as it flew through the Changbai foothills. Colonel Ehrlich watched as the helicopter wove its way through the terrain. It was about ten minutes' flying time from all the Chinese activity. Whoever was flying that thing sure had balls—it was flying right into a hornets' nest.

One hundred and twenty miles to the west of the coast, Ehrlich also had the four F-16s out of Misawa circling. And somewhere out there, screaming toward the coast at more than a thousand miles an hour, was Wildcard. Ehrlich was in radio communication with the aircraft if he needed to talk to them, but radio silence was the standard operating procedure for Wildcard. Its orders were to take up a position twenty

miles off the North Korean coast near Najin and be prepared
for further instructions. Ehrlich didn't know what was going
on, but things were going to get hot real soon.

Chong discerned the enemy soldiers first. He gripped Riley
on the arm and pointed. Riley stopped and squinted into the
darkness. There were ten of them, seven hundred meters
away and heading downslope. The Chinese were spread out,
weapons at the ready, with twenty meters between each man.
Riley looked around quickly. About a hundred meters ahead
of them was a small knoll of boulders rising slightly above
the rest of the ground. He pointed it out to Chong. "We'll
make our stand there."

2:19 A.M. Local
Junior Lieutenant Baibang started guiding the Z-9s toward
the inbound helicopter. He had two Z-9s coming down from
the mountains out of the north. He gave them an intercept
path directly toward the intruder. Three others were lifting off
out of Yanji. The sixth Z-9 from the 3d Aviation Regiment
was unable to fly because of maintenance problems. Baibang
gave two of the three out of Yanji an intercept vector straight
down the river. The third he gave an easterly approach, just
in case the unidentified aircraft turned and ran for the border.

The inbound intruder was flying at about eighty knots. The
Z-9s could easily beat that in a flat run at altitude. Baibang
glanced at the clock. The two out of the mountains should intercept in eight minutes if all factors stayed the same.

Even as he finished giving instructions, a new voice came
over his radio. "Yanji Control, this is Tiger Flight leader. We
are four J-7s just lifted off and heading your way. Request approach and intercept information. Over."

"We've got four fast movers lifting off out of Shenyang,
sir."

Ehrlich swore. "This thing's getting out of control. They
must have picked up the Blackhawk on local radar." He
turned and looked across the cabin to the bank of equipment
and the operators sitting in front of it. "Do you have any
emitters down there?"

A young air force technician turned from the screens toward the colonel. "Yes, sir. I've got a dual emitter located in Yanji—820 megahertz 280 pulse, and 890 megahertz 650 pulse. From the signal wavelength, I'd say it's close to a P-15 Flatface early-warning radar. A little off. Probably a Chinese copy."

Ehrlich turned back to his side of the plane. "How long till the fast movers are in the area near the Blackhawk?"

The analyst next to the radar operator quickly calculated. "Twelve minutes, sir."

"All right. Relay the data to Wildcard and the F-16s. Bring the F-16s in to fifty miles off the coast. How long until Wildcard is on station?"

"Twenty-five minutes."

"Get me General Gunston on the line."

2:20 A.M. Local

"Start calling, Colin."

Lassiter keyed the FM radio with his right foot. He read from the note attached to his knee pad. "Duncer, Drager, Dirtie, Dwinki, Doinke, Dopple, this is exfiltration helicopter. Over." He waited a second and then repeated the message, again using the mission code names of all the members of Team 3 left behind.

Mitchell saw Olinski start abruptly. "What have you got?" he hissed.

Olinski shook his head as he strained to listen. Then he nodded vigorously. He grabbed the small radio and pressed the send button. "Exfiltration helicopter, this is Dopple. I say again, this is Dopple. We are awaiting your arrival at agreed-upon location. It will be marked with infrared strobe. I say again, infrared strobe. What is your ETA? Over."

"Roger, Dopple. We are five minutes out. Mark pickup zone in three, and stay on the net. We're going to need to load fast. Over."

"Roger, exfil aircraft. What type of aircraft are you? Over."

"Blackhawk. We'll land facing east. Over."

"Roger, facing east. We'll be ready. We've got five pax. One on stretcher. Over."

"Roger, five pax, one of which is on a stretcher. Listen up—we've got internal tanks on board. The front two are empty now and held in place with 550 cord. You're going to need to cut the 550 cord and dump the two tanks as soon as we land. We've got only the two pilots on board and can't help. Over."

"Roger. Cut out two front internal tanks. We'll be ready. Over."

"ETA five minutes. Over."

Olinski turned to the other members of Team 3, all of whom had been listening to his end of the conversation. "We've got a Blackhawk five minutes out. Sir, you need to mark the pickup zone in three minutes. Comsky and Hoffman, get ready to bring me out. When we get to the bird we need to cut out the front two internal fuel tanks and throw them off. They're held in with 550 cord."

Mitchell pulled out his strobe. Fatigue and the cold were forgotten. He turned to Comsky. "Get C.J. awake. I'm going out into the field to mark the PZ." Mitchell started moving out as Comsky shook the pilot. C.J. painfully became conscious.

"Let's go, man. Our ride's coming. There's a bird inbound."

Riley and Chong settled in among the boulders on the crest of the small knoll and watched the Chinese squad approach in the moonlight. They were only two hundred meters away now, moving slowly toward them. Riley whispered to Chong. "Another fifty meters and we start firing. You work our right to left. I'll start our left to right."

Chong checked his machine gun and ensured that he had a round in the chamber and that the hundred-round drum magazine was seated properly. Riley laid out two more ten-round magazines for his SVD next to his left hand, where he held the stock of the rifle, for quicker reloading. He unhooked his M79 grenade launcher from his vest and removed the fléchette round, replacing it with a 40mm high-explosive round. He put the launcher down next to him. They were ready.

Eighth Army Headquarters, Yongsan, Seoul, Korea
Saturday, 10 June, 1823 Zulu
Sunday, 11 June, 3:23 A.M. Local

"This is General Gunston. I'm going to patch you in to Colonel Ehrlich, who's monitoring the situation from the AWACS. It will save time, rather than having everything relayed through me. I'll monitor on this end. He's got some news. Hold on a second." There were some beeps and clicks and then Gunston was back on. "Go ahead, Pete. General Parker is on the line."

"Yes, sir. Things are getting hairy over there. We've got the Blackhawk only a couple of minutes out from the area of all the activity. It's obviously been spotted, since we've got five Chinese helicopters vectoring in on it—two heading straight for it, two straight in from the north, and one moving to the east. They're about four minutes out from intercept and are being guided by a local radar. We've also got four fast movers scrambled out of Shenyang. They're nine minutes out."

Parker cut in. "What about our forces?"

"I've ordered the F-16s to move in to fifty miles offshore. Wildcard will be twenty miles off the North Korean coast in twenty-two minutes."

Parker considered the situation. "What do you think, General Gunston?"

"Sir, that helicopter is never going to make it out. Those Chinese helicopters vectoring in are probably armed. The Blackhawk doesn't have a chance against five of them, especially if they're being guided in. Even if it escapes them somehow, it still has the fast movers to contend with. It might dodge the jets for a while by getting low into the terrain and outmaneuvering them."

Ehrlich came back over the net. "Sir, we're running out of time. I'm also starting to get some radar signals from the North Koreans. I think all the Chinese air activity has spooked them. I'm patched in to both Wildcard and the F-16s. What do you want me to do?"

Parker closed his eyes. Whatever his decision was, the consequences would be severe.

Changbai Mountains, China
Saturday, 10 June, 1823 Zulu
Sunday, 11 June, 2:23 A.M. Local

Mitchell turned on the strobe. His eyes squinting, he scanned the skies. Out of the wood line, Comsky and Hoffman carried Olinski, who was still on the radio with the helicopter. They could hear the inbound bird now, off to the east.

Jean Long was guiding along the river. Ahead, through the goggles she could see the lighter line of the unimproved road snaking across the ground. Not far now. She slowed down further, to fifty knots.

Lieutenant Wei felt the adrenaline race through his veins. He had never felt like this before. He was piloting the lead Z-9, following the azimuth given by Yanji Control. He couldn't see much by the light of the moon. According to Yanji they were only three minutes away from the intruder, who was slowing down. Wei pressed his send button and called the second aircraft. "We'll make one pass to see what's happening and spot the intruder. Then we'll turn around to the left and do a gun run. Guide off me."

2:25 A.M. Local

Riley took a deep breath, then let it out. "Are you ready?"
"Roger that, Top."
"On my round."
"Roger that."
Riley took another deep breath and held it. He pulled back on the trigger and the SVD spoke. Immediately he started sighting in on the second target as the roar of Chong's SAW rent the night.

Mitchell swung his head and listened. He could hear the helicopter close by now, but he thought he heard more firing up on the ridgeline. He heard it again. The burst of a SAW. It could mean only one thing. Riley and Chong were still alive, and they were fighting. Mitchell looked at Olinski, who lay on the ground next to him. Olinski was still monitoring the radio and hadn't heard the firing. Hoffman and Comsky were leading C.J. to the center of the field to join up with them. As the helicopter closed in, the roar of the bird covered up any sound of firing from the hills.

Long and Lassiter spotted the strobe at the same time. It flashed brightly on and off in their goggles.

"Roger, PZ. We've got your location. Turn off the light so we can land. Over."

A second later the light was out. Jean slowed the helicopter to a hover over the open field. She could see the men clustered below as she swung the aircraft about and faced to the east. She concentrated on bringing the helicopter down next to the small party on the ground.

Lassiter's voice came over the intercom. "We've got company heading this way. I count two helicopters coming in from the northwest. About two minutes out."

2:26 A.M. Local

Mitchell closed his eyes as the four powerful blades of the Blackhawk threw loose grass and debris through the air. The helicopter settled on its wheels only eight feet from where they crouched. Immediately Mitchell, Comsky, and Hoffman ran forward. They leapt on and began hacking at the 550 cord holding the two front internal fuel tanks. They freed the right one and shoved it out the door. Comsky jumped out and ran over to C.J. He picked up the injured pilot and thrust him into the helicopter, as Mitchell and Hoffman shoved the other forward tank out the left door. Mitchell grabbed C.J. and sat him down as Hoffman and Comsky ran back, hoisted the stretcher, and carried Olinski on board. The whole operation had taken only forty seconds. Mitchell turned and gave the pilot the thumbs-up.

With their goggles and helmets on, the pilots were unidentifiable to the men in the back. As Lassiter lifted off 579, Jean Long unbuckled her harness and turned around in her seat. She closed her eyes briefly in thanks as she saw her husband right behind Lassiter's seat. She threw a headset to him.

Mitchell caught the headset and put it on as the bird lifted over the trees on the eastern edge of the pickup zone. He keyed the intercom. "We've got two more men farther up along that finger to the northwest."

"We've got company!" Lassiter yelled through the set as he accelerated the helicopter and jerked it hard to the left. Those in the back were tumbled on top of each other. C.J. screamed with pain as he landed again on his shattered arm. Two helicopters roared by out of the northwest and started to circle.

"The next one will be a gun run," Jean yelled. "They're circling to the east to come back. Turn north and dive into the riverbed."

In less than a second Mitchell took all this in: His wife was on board. They were being attacked by Chinese helicopters. And up there on the ridge, he could see the red and green tracers of Riley and Chong's firefight.

Riley had hit his first two targets before the rest could find cover. The sudden silence was deafening.

"How many did you get, Tom?"

"I'm pretty sure I got two. How about you?"

"Two. That leaves us six. We've got about five minutes before they get reinforced."

There was a burst of fire from up ahead and green tracers flew by to their right. Another burst. "Shit! We'll never make it running." Riley looked at Chong. "What do you say, wild man?"

Chong had made his peace in the dark of the previous night. He was ready. "This is as good a place as any. I'd rather take a stand here than get chased down by helicopters come dawn."

"OK then. This is it. I'll see if I can take out these six ahead. You might as well cover to the east. That's where our next visitors will come from."

2:27 A.M. Local

The lead Z-9 strained as it banked in a steep left-hand turn. Wei had only a brief glance at the aircraft as they flew by. An American UH-60 Blackhawk. This was going to be a real challenge.

Wei calculated in his mind as he completed the turn and

gave chase. From what he had seen of the S-70s the transport battalion had, the Blackhawk held a great edge over his helicopter in terms of maneuverability and speed. The Americans also held a big edge at night.

Wei grinned. He had two aces up his sleeve, however. The first was that he was armed and the American wasn't. The Blackhawk was just a transport helicopter. The second was that there were five Z-9s and only one Blackhawk. He watched with grudging admiration as the American helicopter dove for the riverbed and fled north only a few feet above the water.

Lassiter had 579 down very low, skimming just above the surface of the river. Although he was down lower than the enemy could go, he was forced to go much slower than the other helicopters at altitude. As he took a left-hand bend in the river he glanced back. The running lights of the lead enemy helicopter were only eight hundred meters behind. In the moonlight he tried to make out what type of aircraft was chasing them. The only one he knew that had a built-in tail rotor was some sort of Aerospatiale. Maybe an SA-365 model Dolphin.

Junior Lieutenant Baibang was trying to keep up with the chase. The intruder had disappeared from his screen—probably down too low for him to track. He could see the two center Z-9s turning to the north in apparent chase. He ordered the Z-9 to the east to stay in a holding pattern. The two to the north he ordered into blocking positions along the river, which the intruder seemed to be following. The intruder would reach the blocking force in about forty seconds.

2:28 A.M. Local

Wei watched as the dark silhouette of the Blackhawk disappeared around a westerly turn in the river. Since he was flying well above tree level at three hundred feet, Wei decided to cut the corner of the bend and try to make up some of the distance between the two aircraft. He knew there was a blocking force only a kilometer ahead, but he wanted to get as close as possible before they brought down the intruder.

He flew over the elbow of land and looked down into the
river.

The American was gone! Wei started slowing down as he
looked around. Where did they go? The second Z-9 shot past
him as the pilot of that bird belatedly tried making the adjustment. Wei banked right and caught movement out of the corner of his right eye. He turned his head just as the American
rose out of the riverbed. Wei sighed to himself with relief.
The UH-60 must have flared to a halt and let him fly by. The
American was probably going to double back toward the border. He might have made it, too, if I hadn't slowed down in
time, Wei thought.

Enough of this playing around. Wei started banking hard
right as he ordered his copilot to prepare to fire the miniguns.
The Z-9 was only halfway through the turn when Wei saw a
flash of light on the side of the Blackhawk.

"Again!" Lassiter yelled as the closest Z-9 exploded into a
ball of flame. Jean Long punched the firing button and the
second Stinger leapt from the side of the helicopter. The trailing Z-9 was about nine hundred meters to the west and had
started a long, sweeping turn to come back. The supersonic
Stinger raced it down in a second and a half. The heat-
seeking missile flew straight up the right exhaust of the Z-9
and the helicopter blossomed into flames.

Mitchell keyed the intercom in his headset. "Head northwest. Straight toward that ridgeline."

Lassiter accelerated. Northwest was as good as any other
direction. If those helicopters had reported in, the Chinese
would know that he had followed the river. It wouldn't be
smart to do that again.

Riley stared to the east at the ball of fire that had been ignited in the sky. Then there was a second one. "What the hell
is going on?"

A burst of automatic fire up ahead caused him to turn his
attention back to matters closer at hand. Hidden behind a
rock, he fired the M79, blooping another high explosive in
the direction of the surviving Chinese.

2:29 A.M. Local

Baibang didn't know what to make of it. The two Z-9s in pursuit had disappeared from his screen. He couldn't raise them on the radio. He called the two hovering just above the riverbed to the north—no, they hadn't seen anything.

Baibang was puzzled. The intruder should have reached the blocking force thirty seconds ago. And where did the two in pursuit go? He ordered the two in the blocking position to move south along the river. Then he called the J-7s to give them final vectors. He gave the jets a course that would put them to the east of the last sighting of the intruder. No matter what happened, the intruder eventually was going to have to head for the coast.

"Goddamn!"

Colonel Ehrlich swiveled his head to look at the radar operator. "What's the matter?"

"Did you say that Blackhawk was armed, sir?"

"Yeah. They had Stingers on board. Why?"

"Then you can splash two Chinese helicopters."

2:30 A.M. Local

"There. Ahead and to the left. Did you see those green and red tracers?" Mitchell was leaning forward, pointing between the two pilots. "The red is our people."

"Who's up there, Mitch?" Jean asked as Lassiter swooped in toward the firefight.

"Dave Riley and Tom Chong."

Riley heard the rotor blades coming toward them. He arced another high-explosive round toward the Chinese, then looked south, while Chong continued to cover their front. At first Riley didn't see anything. He was expecting to see the searchlights of a Z-9 coming at them. He quickly pulled up his goggles and turned them on.

Riley blinked. A Blackhawk. He pulled up his SVD and took aim at the cockpit. The goddamn Chinese were trying to land troops right on top of them! He started to squeeze the trigger when something occurred to him. Every other helicopter they'd seen tonight had searchlights on—this one didn't.

Riley remembered Olinski's words in the briefback about the Chinese pilots—that they didn't fly blacked out because they didn't have night-vision goggles. Riley figured they had nothing left to lose. He'd take a chance.

2:31 A.M. Local

There it was. The intruder was back on his screen briefly. Off to the north. Baibang called the two Z-9s and redirected them to the new location. He called the inbound J-7s.

"Tiger Flight leader, this is Yanji Control. I have you with an ETA of one minute. Change heading to three three zero zero mils. The intruder is heading north from last reported location. Over."

"Roger, Yanji Control. Activating our tracking radar now. We should pick up something soon. Decreasing altitude to one thousand meters."

"Get your harness buckled, Tom!" Riley yelled out. Chong turned in surprise. "We've got a Blackhawk inbound." Riley turned on his infrared strobe and held it up.

On board 579, Comsky slid open the left door while Hoffman slid open the right. Each man held a 120-foot nylon rope in a deployment bag. Lassiter flared the Blackhawk to a halt eighty feet above the ground by the IR strobe. The two bags were thrown out and hurtled to the ground.

"I've got this one," Chong yelled as he ran forward. He pulled the deployment bag off the rope and hooked the end loop through the two snap links in the shoulders of his vest. Twenty feet away Riley did the same. The two ran together and linked arms.

No shots had yet been fired by the Chinese soldiers. They probably assumed that the helicopter was one of their own, but Riley knew they'd soon wake up and take action.

"We've got them!" Mitchell yelled as he peered off the deck of the cargo compartment. Lassiter snatched in collective and quickly pulled the helicopter over onto an easterly heading.

Riley and Chong felt their vests tighten around them as the rope became taut. Their feet came off the ground and they were savagely swung out to the west by centrifugal force.

Riley gasped for breath as he and Chong held onto each other, momentarily forgetting where they were. A line of green tracers stitching the night air quickly reminded them.

As he straightened out the Blackhawk, Lassiter keyed his intercom. "Two more helicopters coming out of the east."

"Find someplace to land. We've got to get them in." Mitchell watched tracers make a pattern around Riley and Chong and pass by the helicopter.

"We can't. There's no time. Pull them in!" Lassiter responded.

Mitchell was astonished. "How the hell are we going to pull them in? I've got only two healthy bodies back here!"

Long turned to Lassiter. "I'll take the controls. Go back and help them."

Lassiter unbuckled and climbed over the seat, back to where Hoffman and Comsky were struggling with the left rope, pulling it up inch by inch.

Chong felt his rope jerk. He looked up and saw someone hanging over the edge of the deck, signaling him to separate from Riley. He tapped Riley and pointed up. Riley let go.

Long glanced to her right and saw the Chinese helicopters closing rapidly. She was flying at only seventy knots with the two men dangling below. She also had to stay 150 feet above ground level to keep from slamming the men into the earth. She looked around, trying to think of something to do.

2:32 A.M. Local

Baibang was running out of airspace. He now had the intruder on his screen heading east. Two Z-9s were closing rapidly on it from the east. He ordered the third Z-9 to also start an intercept vector to the north. As he finished giving that order, his radio crackled again.

"This is Tiger Flight leader. I've got the intruder on tracking radar. Preparing to fire."

"Those fast movers are on top of our bird. We need to do something now."

The young operator who had been tracking the action looked up at Colonel Ehrlich. "I can do something, sir. Give me a few seconds."

* * *

At an altitude of a thousand meters, the J-7's tracking radar easily picked up 579. The lead pilot armed a pair of missiles—Chinese copies of the Russian AA-2 Atoll. His hand paused over the guidance switch. The AA-2 missile under his left wing was guided by a built-in infrared heat seeker. The one under the right wing was guided by radar homing using the plane's radar.

The pilot chose the left missile. Since his target was so slow moving, he'd pass by too quickly to keep his tracking radar on it. He got on the radio and ordered his wingman to do the same.

Only one thing to do, Jean Long decided. She banked left, straight toward the onrushing helicopters. By doing this, she reduced both the amount of time they would have to fire and the Blackhawk's silhouette.

2:33 A.M. Local
The pilot of the lead J-7 yelled over his radio, "Fire." Two Atoll missiles leapt forward, one from each aircraft.

The 579 was moving at 70 knots, the two Z-9s at 125 knots. The Blackhawk closed the five-hundred-meter gap between them in three seconds. The Z-9 pilots had not anticipated this maneuver and were able to fire only a quick, poorly aimed burst from their miniguns before the Blackhawk shot past them. The Z-9 pilots stared in amazement at the two men suspended below the aircraft.

The Atolls made up their electronic minds immediately after leaving the wings of the J-7s. They went for the hottest targets available.

"Jesus Christ!" Chong closed his eyes as the two helicopters approached and roared by. He was dangling only ten feet from the edge of the deck. The night sky lit up and the force of the two explosions buffeted his body and the Blackhawk.

2:39 A.M. Local
"Tiger Flight leader. This is Yanji Control. You just shot down two of ours! The intruder is still moving southeast."

The Tiger Flight leader swore. So much for infrared. This

was his first time in combat and his first time firing live missiles. He wouldn't make that mistake again. He didn't have a
choice now anyway. As the J-7s completed a sweeping turn
and started their second run, Tiger Flight leader called his
wingman. "Fire your second missile on radar guidance.
Launch five kilometers out and slow to just above stall speed
to keep your radar tracking."

His wingman acknowledged.

Ehrlich stared over the operator's shoulder at the image of
the J-7s closing again on the 579. He didn't know what had
just happened, but there were two fewer Chinese helicopters
and 579 was still flying. He didn't think the Blackhawk could
survive another encounter with the fast movers. "Whatever
you're doing, we need it now," he said to the radar operator.

"Just another second, sir." She was furiously working her
computer keyboard.

"Now!" Tiger Flight leader ordered.

His wingman's thumb closed on the firing switch in con-
cert with his. Two more Atoll missiles were launched.

2:40 A.M. Local
Chong was pulled into the cargo compartment. Staring out,
they could all see the burst of flame and the twin streaks of
light, as two missiles came screaming toward them.

The AWACS radar operator punched the "Enter" button on
her keyboard. "That should do it."

Mitchell and the rest of the men in the cargo compartment
watched mesmerized as the two missiles closed rapidly. Then,
suddenly, they both veered off. One flew almost straight up
into the night sky. The other turned down and impacted with
a roar into the ground. Chong turned to help the others begin
pulling in Riley. He noticed, for the first time, that the right
side of his uniform was covered with blood.

2:41 A.M. Local

The Tiger Flight leader stared at his tracking screen in confusion. The clear image had dissolved into meaningless clutter.

"Yanji, this is Tiger Flight leader. We're switching to guns. Give us a vector back to the target. All our tracking radars are down. Over."

The flight leader reached over to his console and flipped the arming switch for the 30mm cannons mounted in the wing roots on either side of the plane. The other pilots did the same. Firing fifteen hundred rounds a minute, the cannons would make short work of the intruder.

"Roger, Tiger Flight leader. I'm going to loop you around to the west so you can come at the intruder from the rear. Turn right to heading one eight five zero mils."

Baibang grabbed his other handset. "Wolfpack Three, this is Yanji Control. Over."

The remaining Z-9 came on the net. "This is Wolfpack Three. Over."

"Wolfpack Three. Turn on a heading of zero eight zero zero mils. The J-7s are going to do a gun run. I want you to head for where the intruder would cross the border, just in case. Over."

"Roger. Heading of zero eight zero zero mils."

2:42 A.M. Local

With Chong's help they had Riley halfway up. Chong could feel no pain or discomfort. Nor could he see any sign of a wound other than his blood-soaked uniform.

Jean knew they were running out of time. The border was five minutes away and the coast was twenty minutes farther. The fast movers were zero for two, but sooner or later they'd get their act together. She didn't have any tricks left. As soon as they got the last guy in, she'd drop down and try to out-maneuver them.

"Maintain one eight five zero mils. Over."
The Tiger Flight leader acknowledged Yanji Control.

"Jam the ground radar in Yanji, too," Ehrlich ordered.

2:43 A.M. Local

They pulled in Riley, and Chong now knew where the blood had come from. "Jesus Christ. Look at him!" Chong grabbed Comsky and pointed. Riley's uniform was completely soaked with blood. As Chong unsnapped the team sergeant from his harness, Comsky immediately began searching for the wound.

It wasn't hard to find. Riley must have been hit just after they were picked up. Two rounds had punched small, neat holes in his lower right stomach. The trajectory of the rounds had carried them through his body and out his upper right back. The exit wounds were a mess of torn flesh and bone. Pulling bandages out of the aircraft's first-aid kit, Comsky worked desperately to stop the flow of blood.

Jean Long had 579 back down in the trees. The two jets flew by just above their stall speed at two hundred knots. She couldn't understand why they appeared to be searching for her visually. Why didn't they just use their radars?

The Tiger Flight leader wanted to slam his instrument panel in frustration. Without his on-board radar, and now without Yanji Control, he was almost blind. Somewhere below, the intruder was running. The border was approaching rapidly. The Tiger Flight leader looked down. If he didn't turn now, he'd cross into North Korean airspace. He keyed his radio. "Break off."

2:43 A.M. Local (China Time Zone)

The radar operator sighed. "Sir, the Chinese jets have broken off."

For the first time, Ehrlich felt that the Blackhawk had a chance.

3:48 A.M. Local (Korea-Japan Time Zone)

Lassiter was back in the front seat. Jean Long gratefully relinquished the controls to him. Eighteen to nineteen minutes to the coast. The Chinese jets had broken off at the border.

In the back, Comsky had stopped the flow of blood from Riley's wounds. Comsky leaned over and spoke right in Mitchell's ear to be heard above the turbine engines and blades. "He's not going to make it if we don't get him to a hospital ASAP. One of those rounds, maybe both, went through his right lung. He's lost a lot of blood."

Mitchell looked at Riley. He was lying on his right side; Hoffman was holding bandages over the wounds, and putting pressure on the sucking chest wound to help close it off. Mitchell didn't know what to do. So close. They'd made it too far to lose someone now.

3:58 A.M. Local

Ehrlich anxiously gripped the edges of his chair as he watched the blip representing 579 crawl toward the coast. Not much farther to go. The radar operator turned and looked at him.

"Sir, we've got two North Korean MiG-21s moving in at Mach 1.5 from the southwest. Direct for 579."

"Goddamn!" Ehrlich cursed. The Blackhawk might still stay low enough to avoid the MiGs, but once it hit the coast there'd be no place to hide. The MiGs would have a turkey shoot—Ehrlich had no doubt that the North Koreans *would* shoot.

He looked over at the female technician who had jammed the radar of the Chinese jets. "Can you jam the MiGs and North Korean ground radar?"

The woman shook her head doubtfully. "I've got to find the frequencies first. The North Koreans are acting smarter than the Chinese. They're using their radar only in bursts."

4:06 A.M. Local

The coast was one minute ahead. Lassiter and Long scanned the night sky.

"There, at four o'clock." Lassiter looked where Long indicated. He could see the running lights of two jets flying along the coast at about three thousand feet. "Once we cross the beach and hit the water, they're going to be on us."

Long shrugged. "You got any better ideas?"

"No."

"Then let's do it."

4:07 A.M. Local

The North Korean flight leader turned on his tracking radar. The blip representing the intruder appeared on the screen. Noting the location he quickly turned off the radar to prevent possible jamming. He didn't know who or what the intruder was, but his orders were to shoot it down. He looked out his left window and spotted it. An American-made helicopter!

"There's the intruder. Follow me." The flight leader banked his aircraft and started a run in toward the helicopter flitting across the wave tops. His eyes narrowed in anticipation as he placed his thumb over the trigger for his twin-barrel 23mm cannon. Another fifteen seconds and the helicopter would be history.

"Here they come." Lassiter started evasive maneuvers, turning and banking erratically.

The North Korean flight leader looked through his gun sight. The helicopter was bobbing in the cross hairs. Still, between the two of them, they ought to be able to get in some rounds. It would take only a few of the 23mm slugs to destroy the fragile helicopter.

He edged his finger over the trigger. Just another second. Suddenly a screeching tone sounded in his headset and a light on his console flashed red.

"Missile lock-on!" the flight leader screamed. He violently threw his MiG into evasive maneuvers. His wingman followed suit. The leader turned on his radar and stared at it. Where had the lock-on come from? There was nothing on his screen except the helicopter. It couldn't have come from there. The warning meant that an enemy fighter had locked *its* targeting radar on his aircraft.

The tone went off. He turned his aircraft back toward the helicopter. Suddenly the screeching tone sounded again. As he broke away, the flight leader saw the silhouette of an aircraft shadowing him and his wingman. He'd never seen anything like it before—it looked like something from outer space. The aircraft didn't appear to have a fuselage, just a short, squat flying wing.

Realizing he had to deal with this unknown threat first, the flight leader kicked in his afterburners and gained altitude in an attempt to loop back behind his pursuer. He still had nothing but the helicopter on his screen. As he rolled out, the target lock-on sounded again. Trying to break the lock-on, he caught another glimpse of the strange aircraft following tightly behind. There were two of them now.

The tone fell silent. Realization seeped through the North Korean pilot's brain. If the strange aircraft had wanted to shoot him down, it could have done so by now. Three lock-ons were more than enough. They were giving him a message: Stay away from the helicopter.

Even if he managed to get behind the enemy planes, the lack of a radar image would put him at a severe disadvantage. The pilot was caught between his sense of duty and his sense of self-preservation.

Then he had a new thought. Whatever was shadowing him had never been seen before by a North Korean pilot. He would be the first to report it. Perhaps that would help assuage his superiors. Having rationalized himself out of an untenable situation, the flight leader broke and ran for home, calling for his wingman to follow.

4:08 A.M. Local

"Where the hell did they go?" Jean Long was twisted in her seat, peering to the rear. She couldn't see the MiGs. The sky was clear.

"I don't know. And I don't care." Lassiter wasn't going to argue with their good fortune.

4:10 A.M. Local

Comsky finished checking Riley again. He'd given him a syringe of morphine. The medic reported back to Mitchell. "He's going into shock and is aspirating blood. I think his left lung may have been nicked too. If we don't get him to a hospital with suction soon to clear his lungs, he's going to drown in his own blood."

Mitchell acknowledged the information and keyed his headset. "Jean, Dave was wounded when we were picking him up. He's got a sucking chest wound. Comsky says if we don't get him to a hospital soon, he'll be dead."

"We're a little more than five hours out of Korea. That's the closest possibility. We refueled off the *Rathburne* coming in, and it's about three hours to the south. We can try that. I'm not even sure we're home free from the North Koreans yet. They can still catch us with their jets. I don't know why those two MiGs broke off, but there may be more on the way."

Lassiter broke in. "I don't think we have to worry about MiGs anymore. Take a look up at 2 o'clock." Long turned and looked where Lassiter was pointing. The moon shone off the wings of two F-16s passing by in escort.

22

"And therefore the victories won by a master
of war gain him neither reputation for
wisdom nor merit for value."
Sun Tzu: *The Art of War*

Eighth Army Headquarters, Yongsan, Seoul, Korea
Saturday, 10 June, 1915 Zulu
Sunday, 11 June, 4:15 A.M. Local

General Parker was emotionally exhausted. Listening in to
Ehrlich on the AWACS for the past half hour had been nerve-
racking. Against all odds, things appeared to have worked
out. 579 was clear of the coast. Wildcard had scared off the
MiGs. The F-16s were now on station escorting the helicopter
back. Parker keyed his mike. "Colonel Ehrlich. What's the
status of Wildcard?"

"I've got it located just off the coast, sir, in case the MiGs
decide to give it another try. I know we've got the F-16s on
station now, but I don't want to let anybody close to that helicopter. Wildcard worked better than we expected. Apparently
even the tracking radar on the Korean MiGs couldn't pick it
up. I'll keep Wildcard there for another twenty minutes and
then send them home."

Parker was relieved. The first operational mission flown by
the Stealth fighter had proven a success. The two Stealth fighters
had been stationed in northern Japan the last three months conducting classified training flights near Russian airspace, testing
the aircraft's capabilities against the radar array on the Soviets'
east coast. The performance during this crisis had proven the
plane's capabilities and worth. Of course, it had also disclosed
the aircraft's operational existence to the North Koreans, but
Parker felt that was a price worth paying. The Stealth fighter's
existence would have come out in the next few months anyway.

Parker keyed the mike again. "Do you have any communications with the helicopter?"

"We haven't tried yet, sir. It doesn't have secure capability."

"Can you talk to it if you need to?"

"Yes, sir. We can broadcast on the guard net, and that will override whatever frequency they're on now."

"Get them on the radio and then patch me in," Parker ordered.

"Yes, sir. Wait one."

Parker heard Ehrlich make the call.

"Army helicopter 579. Army helicopter 579. This is Tango Station. Over."

There was a long pause, then a woman's voice came over the air. "Umm . . . Tango Station, this is 579. Over."

"579, this is Tango Station on an unsecure link. We're the people who have been looking after you the past half hour. We also control your escort. I have someone in your chain of command who wants to talk to you. Over."

"Roger, we're standing by. Over."

Ehrlich keyed in Parker. "Go ahead, sir. Your transmissions will be relayed through us to 579. Just key your mike when you're ready to talk to them. Let me know when you want me to shut them out. Over."

Parker keyed his mike. "579, this is . . ." he hesitated and looked at Major Thomas. "What's our call sign?"

"Papa Sierra Twelve, sir."

Parker thumbed the mike. "579, this is Papa Sierra Twelve. What is the status of the personnel you picked up? Over."

"Papa Sierra Twelve, this is 579. We've got four wounded, one critically. The medic says that if we don't soon get him to a hospital equipped with suction he won't make it. The others are all stable. Over."

Parker paused and looked at Thomas and Hossey. "Any ideas?"

Thomas shook his head. "There's nothing closer than here as far as hospitals go."

"They could land on the *Rathburne* again," Hossey suggested.

Parker contacted 579 again. "This is Papa Sierra Twelve.

The only place we have that is closer than coming here is the same place you refueled. Over."

"This is 579. We understand. Heading for that location now. Could you check to see if that location has the facilities to handle our patient? Over."

USS *Rathburne*, Sea of Japan
Saturday, 10 June, 1920 Zulu
Sunday, 11 June, 4:20 A.M. Local

Commander Lemester couldn't believe it. "Say again. Over."

The speaker on the bridge crackled. "I say again. Reverse course and assume a heading of three-five-four degrees at maximum speed. You have an inbound helicopter with wounded on board. Over."

Lemester rubbed his forehead. He had a hell of a headache. The caller had identified himself with the classified call sign of the commander of the U.S. Eighth Army in Korea. Lemester wasn't sure if the commander of Eighth Army could order him around, not being in the direct chain of command of the *Rathburne*. On the other hand, that fellow was a four-star general. What the hell, Lemester decided. They were getting pretty good at picking up mysterious helicopters. One more wouldn't make much difference.

"Roger. We're coming about. Over."

"Do you have medical facilities to handle . . . ," there was a pause, "a pneumothorax? Over."

"Wait one. Over." Lemester grabbed his intership phone and dialed the dispensary. "Doc, can you handle a pneumothorax?"

"Not really, sir. I don't have the right equipment. I could probably stabilize it."

Lemester keyed his mike. "That's a negative. Over."

Airspace, Sea of Japan
Saturday, 10 June, 1925 Zulu
Sunday, 11 June, 4:25 A.M. Local

Riley was conscious now. At least his eyes were open. His overall situation was deteriorating. Comsky had redone the bandages and tried to fashion a valve to allow air to get out, but it wasn't working well. Riley's skin was turning blue and the veins in his neck were distended. Mitchell watched as Comsky forced his finger into the bullet hole to release some of the air that was building up between the outside of the lung and the chest cavity, desperately trying to prevent the lung from collapsing.

Jean gave them an estimated time of arrival at the *Rathburne* of 6:30 A.M. Another two hours.

The team's successful mission and exfiltration was now overshadowed. Mitchell shook his head. He wasn't sure what they had accomplished, and he certainly wasn't sure that the price they were paying was worth it. Blood was a valuable currency.

They'd gone this far and now everyone had run out of ideas. He gripped Riley's hand. "Come on. Don't quit now."

In the front, Jean Long had taken the controls from Lassiter. They were down at a hundred feet and she had the throttle wide open.

"579, this is Tango Station. Over."

Lassiter keyed the mike. "Tango Station, this is 579. Over."

"Your present destination doesn't have the facilities to handle your most serious casualty. Over."

Lassiter looked at Jean. "What now?"

Eighth Army Headquarters, Yongsan, Seoul, Korea
Saturday, 10 June, 1926 Zulu
Sunday, 11 June, 4:26 A.M. Local
General Parker looked around the room. "Any bright ideas?"

Major Thomas was already dialing the phone. "Yes, sir. Tell the helicopter to keep on heading for the *Rathburne*. If I remember rightly we ought to be able to work something out."

Airspace, Sea of Japan
Saturday, 10 June, 1927 Zulu
Sunday, 11 June, 4:27 A.M. Local
"579, this is Papa Sierra Twelve. Continue on course for refuel point. We've come up with an alternate plan. Over."

Jean Long looked distrustfully at the radio. She called over the intercom to her husband. "What do you think, Mitch?"

"Go for it. We don't have much choice."

Jean keyed the mike. "This is 579. Roger. Over."

6:14 A.M. Local
Jean Long expertly flared the Blackhawk over the fantail of the *Rathburne*. She settled the bird down and slowed the engine to idle. Everyone sat still. In the dawn's dim light she

could see some of the crew of the frigate staring at them from the edge of the large helipad. The chronometer on the instrument panel said 0614.

Two figures approached the helicopter. Mitchell slid open the right door and Sergeant Major Hooker and Chief Trapp climbed into the crowded back.

"Who was hit?" Trapp asked anxiously. Mitchell pointed at the body that Comsky was preparing for the move. The medic was tightening down the bandages, especially the ones across the chest. "A lot of people would have given up by now," Comsky whispered. Still, they knew that willpower could do only so much.

Trapp shook his head. What a screwed-up mission. Dave Riley dying would be a hell of a way to end it. Trapp looked out the open door as another helicopter roared in from the west with all its lights on and settled down twenty feet away from 579. Its side doors slid open and two men carrying a stretcher raced over. Comsky opened the door closest to the other aircraft and waved the men in. As he rapidly helped them strap Riley to the stretcher, he yelled in one of the men's ears, giving him Riley's status. As soon as they got him tied in, Comsky leapt out and helped them carry Riley to the other aircraft. He got in with the stretcher. Both aircraft lifted off and headed to the southwest.

Inside the other helicopter, Comsky stared in amazement as the medics got to work. He'd heard about the new UH-60 aerial medevac helicopters but had never seen one. The aircraft had more equipment than many emergency rooms. Already the onboard medics had rigged suction into Riley's lungs and had an IV going, trying to replace some of the lost blood. It was going to be touch and go, but Riley's odds had improved dramatically.

Osan Air Force Base, Korea
Saturday, 10 June, 2330 Zulu
Sunday, 11 June, 8:30 A.M. Local
The medevac helicopter landed at the helipad of the base hospital. 579 was directed to land outside a hangar on the main airstrip. Jean Long protested that 579 should land at the hospital also, since she had other wounded on board. The request

was denied. The airfield tower promised there would be ambulances waiting at the hangar.

As she hovered above the tarmac and brought the aircraft down slowly, the helicopter was surrounded by air force police cars with their lights flashing. The helicopter came to rest and she shut down the throttle. The doors to the hangar swung open and a ground guide gestured for her to roll in. As soon as the aircraft cleared the doors, they were shut.

When the blades halted, Mitchell opened the cargo door and stepped out. Two men in three-piece suits were waiting for him. Mitchell sighed. The spooks were here to take over. The one in apparent charge stepped forward. "I understand you've got some more wounded on board."

"Yeah, that's right. Three."

"The ambulances are right outside. I'll have them bring in the stretchers." The man gestured to his partner. "The rest of your people need to stay on board for a few minutes."

The unidentified man looked at Mitchell. "We need to keep things under wraps. I can't tell you all that has gone on, but suffice it to say that things are pretty screwed up. It's my job to do as much damage control as possible."

Mitchell didn't care. He walked away from the man and went around to the right side of the helicopter. He gave his wife a big hug and kiss as she stepped out of her door.

Fort Meade, Maryland
Sunday, 11 June, 0130 Zulu
Saturday, 10 June, 8:30 P.M. Local

Wilson watched with sadness as the men in the suits escorted Meng out of the Tunnel. He shifted his attention as the man who had led the party into the Tunnel more than an hour ago stopped in front of him. "I don't need to tell you, but everything that has happened with Dragon Sim-13 is highly classified. You will discuss this with no one."

If you didn't need to tell me, then why did you? Wilson thought sardonically. But he dared not say it. These men were scary. "Right. Not a word."

As the door shut behind Meng, Wilson thought about how little he had known about the man other than his brilliance at programming. Before the men came to take him away, Meng

had revealed to Wilson the reasons he had sent the go code
words. Wilson sympathized with Meng, although it didn't appear that all that effort and blood had achieved anything.

US-SOCOM Headquarters, MacDill Air Force Base, Florida
Sunday, 11 June, 0200 Zulu
Saturday, 10 June, 9:00 P.M. Local
Colonel Moore was ordered not to brief even his own commander on the events of the past twelve hours. He hated the
smug spook who relayed that information. This was an event
that was going to be swept under the rug.

As Moore drove home, he wondered idly whether the team
had really blown the pipeline.

Osan Air Force Base, Korea
Sunday, 11 June, 2300 Zulu
Monday, 12 June, 8:00 A.M. Local
Team 3 was intact again. O'Shaugnesy, C.J., Olinski, and
Riley were in the same ward of the hospital. The rest of the
team was gathered around the beds. Even the presence of
the spooks outside the ward door couldn't put a damper on
the feelings inside.

Mitchell's side had been rebandaged, and he now stood
at the foot of Riley's bed with the other ambulatory members
of Team 3. His wife was close by his side, her hand wrapped
around his. Through the windows to their left, a new sun was
rising over the mountains of South Korea. They'd been standing in the same positions for forty-five minutes.

Finally, their wait was over. Dave Riley blearily opened his
eyes. His entire chest and stomach hurt like hell. He saw
Mitchell and his wife and the other team members and managed a bleak smile. He painfully tried to whisper something.

Mitchell came forward and put his ear next to Riley's lips.

Riley tried again. "I told you I'd see you in Korea."

POSTSCRIPT

> "Therefore it is said that one may know
> how to win, but cannot necessarily
> do so."
> Sun Tzu: *The Art of War*

Hills of West Virginia
Tuesday, 19 December, 2300 Zulu
Tuesday, 19 December, 6:00 P.M. Local

The newspaper was filled with news of the American invasion of Panama. The old man had no time for that. His interest was drawn to a smaller article.

Meng rubbed his old scar as he read. Members of Congress were reacting with outrage to a report that the president had sent a high-level diplomatic mission to China only a few weeks after the Tiananmen Square massacre. The trip by Mr. Eagleburger and Mr. Scowcroft had violated the president's own ban on such liaisons, the paper reported. Additionally, the secretary of state had just told reporters that a trip made last week was the first high-level contact the administration had had with the government in China. The media did not like being lied to.

Meng shook his head. He knew why that first trip had occurred so soon after the massacre, but he would never be able to tell anyone. The Americans still used his knowledge, but now he was well guarded and had no access to anything of a critical nature.

His stomach twisted in disgust as he continued reading the article. The administration also had just announced negotiation of a $300 million sale of three satellites to China. The president was determined to maintain commercial relations with the People's Republic of China.

The almighty dollar ruled. Meng wondered what would

happen when the dam finally broke in China. How would the present American course of action look then?

Meng knelt on his praying mat and said a prayer to the souls of the men, American and Chinese, who had died because of his manipulations. He had done what he could and failed. It made all those deaths seem much less worthy.